APRILYNNE PIKE

Random House 🏠 New York

Text copyright © 2018 by Aprilynne Pike
Jacket art copyright © 2018 by Emi Haze
Interior powder art © by Shutterstock/artjazz
Map adapted from Jacques-François Blondel's *Architecture Française,* vol. 4 (1756)

Visit us on the Web! GetUnderlined.com

Educators and librarians, for a variety of teaching tools,
visit us at RHTeachersLibrarians.com

Library of Congress Cataloging-in-Publication Data
Names: Pike, Aprilynne, author.
Title: Shatter / Aprilynne Pike.
Description: First edition. | New York : Random House, [2018] | Series: [Glitter ; 2] | Summary: "After being forced to marry the evil King, Dani must use her power as Queen to stop selling Glitter for good and escape with Saber, the boy she loves"— Provided by publisher.
Identifiers: LCCN 2017006072 | ISBN 978-1-101-93374-9 (hardcover) | ISBN 978-1-101-93377-0 (ebook)
Subjects: | CYAC: Kings, queens, rulers, etc.—Fiction. | Courts and courtiers—Fiction. | Drug dealers—Fiction. | Adventure and adventurers—Fiction. | Versailles (France)— 18th century—Fiction. | Science fiction.
Classification: LCC PZ7.P6257 Sh 2018 | DDC [Fic]—dc23

Printed in the United States of America
10 9 8 7 6 5 4 3 2 1
First Edition

Random House Children's Books supports the
First Amendment and celebrates the right to read.

FOR KENNY,
YOU KNOW WHY.

1. Hall of Mirrors

THE QUEEN'S APARTMENTS

2. Peace Drawing Room
3. Queen's Bedchamber
4. *Salon des Nobles*
5. Antechamber of the *Grand Couvert*
6. Guard Room
7. *Escalier de la Reine*
8. Loggia
9. *Salle du Sacre* (Coronation Room)

THE KING'S APARTMENTS

10. Guard Room
11. First Antechamber
12. Second Antechamber
13. King's Public Bedchamber
14. Council Chamber

THE KING'S PRIVATE APARTMENTS

15. King's Private Bedchamber
16. Clock Room
17. *Antichambre des Chiens*
18. Dining Room
19. King's Private Office
20. *Arrière Cabinet*
21. *Cabinet de la Vaisselle d'Or*
22. Bathchamber
23. Louis XVI's Library
24. New Dining Room
25. Buffet Room
26. Louis XVI's Games Room

THE STATE APARTMENTS

27. Drawing Room of Plenty
28. *Salon de Vénus*
29. *Salon de Diane*
30. *Salon de Mars*
31. *Salon de Mercure*
32. *Salon d'Apollon*
33. War Drawing Room
34. Hercules Drawing Room

THE QUEEN'S PRIVATE CABINETS

a. The Duchesse de Bourgogne's Cabinet
b. *Cabinet de la Méridienne*
c. Library
d. Bathchamber
e. Private Office

MADAME DE MAINTENON'S APARTMENTS

f. Second Antechamber
g. First Antechamber
h. Bedchamber

THE KING'S PRIVATE CABINETS

i. King's Private Bath
j. Gilded Cabinet

THE COURTYARDS

A. Queen's Courtyard
B. Monseigneur's Courtyard
C. *Cour de Marbre* (Marble Courtyard)
D. *Cour Royale* (Royal Courtyard)
E. *Cour des Cerfs* (Courtyard of the Stags)
F. The King's Private Courtyard
G. *Cour des Princes* (Princes' Courtyard)
H. Chapel Courtyard

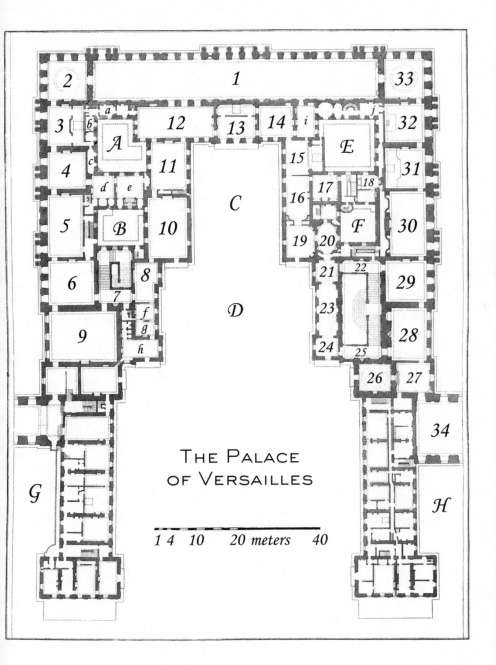

THE PALACE
OF VERSAILLES

1 4   10   20 meters   40

INTERLUDE

I MARCH DOWN the aisle, my face shrouded beneath a veil of *tulle,* and if my eyes are empty or haunted, no one can possibly tell. I'm slow and ponderous in my lavish Baroque wedding gown but feel naked and vulnerable without Saber at my shoulder. Even the white corset reinforcing my posture seems insufficient to keep my innards in place; my heart is climbing my throat, and my stomach has become an aching pit.

I pause as the twinkling constellation of camera flashes momentarily blinds me. I shouldn't be here. I blink against the purple afterimage, waking the Lens in my right eye; the calendar it superimposes on my slowly returning vision shows an urgent notification, set weeks ago by Angela Grayson. My mother's digital ghost is reminding me not to miss my own wedding. A push from beyond the grave.

Just one more thing to do. I take three steps forward and hand off my bouquet to a waiting attendant. A last-minute substitution when the one I'd selected died.

His Majesty glances over his shoulder and looks almost surprised to see me. Perhaps he should; he's given me ample reason to develop cold feet. Atop the murder that launched this sordid affair, he's imprisoned the man I love, and holds my ailing father hostage. I'd have left them both behind had things gone according to plan. What choice did I have? I couldn't marry the King.

I *still* can't marry the King.

But Reginald betrayed me. *Cheated* me. Took my money and agreed to spirit me away—but only when he has no more use for me. The anger that manages to cut through my despair is short-lived, but it propels me another step toward the altar. Another step toward the throne.

There are other ways out, of course. There have always been other ways out. But I refuse to retreat to the impoverished fringes of civilization. I refuse to trade one kind of misery for another. And having come within a breath of losing him forever, I refuse to leave Saber behind.

I can only help him if I stay. I can only stay if I become Queen. And I only become Queen if I continue down this aisle.

I never wanted to be Queen. But I was too desperate. I chose badly, and Molli died for it. She can't have died for nothing. This is my penance. This is the price I have to pay. I will sift through the shattered wreckage of my dreams in search of something sufficiently sharp to cut my way free. And this time, I *will* take Saber with me, though hell should bar the way.

PART ONE

THE PRICE OF LOYALTY

ONE

TWO DAYS LATER

"YOU SUMMONED ME, MY LORD?"

Summoned was the actual word used. Summoned to his private office. Hardly the typical language of newlyweds. My shiny-new husband waves a hand dismissively. "Yes, yes. The meeting will be called in ten minutes," Justin Wyndham says, not looking at me. He's shuffling papers, shoving some in folders and others in drawers.

The bastard is nervous; this is his twitch. I store that tidbit away reflexively.

"All nobles with any voting power whatsoever will be given one hour to find their way to the grand theater so no one can claim they were denied entry due to seating capacity."

I stand silently.

The King notices nothing. "Your father is being cleaned and dressed at the clinic as we speak. You should head over; I imagine you'll want some time to prepare him."

"For what, Your Highness?" My voice is flat, but I can't seem to manage anything else since my marriage.

His eyes sparkle with fury, and he lets a stack of paper fall to the desk with an audible smack. "For the vote, Danica. The god-forsaken vote that saves us both."

Oh yes. We're on the cusp of the entire reason my mother was able to blackmail Justin into marrying me. Dead mother. Ironic, that. "Hmm," I say softly, stepping up and running one finger lightly over a paperweight. "Odd. I don't feel very saved."

Justin's fingers rise to crumple his cravat, and he barely catches himself in time to keep from ruining the fabric. His fingers flex, and a sheen of sweat glistens on his forehead. I've never seen him so disconcerted. Even that can't evoke a spark of pleasure. "Don't make me threaten you again, Danica. I'm so weary of it."

"That makes two of us," I say dryly. "I don't need your threats—I want your promise instead."

"What?" he growls between clenched teeth.

"Saber. I want him back." Saying it shows him my weakness, but I don't care. Not about the vote or these games or who's more powerful. I just want Saber back.

Justin rolls his eyes and turns away, peering into the mirror behind his desk and adjusting a bit of hair. "No."

"You're not really in a position to bargain, my lord." And although it's true, I don't feel any satisfaction in the words.

He spins and slams his hands down on his desk. "You will *not* traipse around with that commoner in front of the court. It's sheer mockery."

"It won't matter if you're not the King."

The words are smoke in the air between us. His fingers tremble, but he doesn't speak.

I shrug. I should be pressing my advantage, but I'm a breath away from utter surrender. "I've sold my soul—feel free to threaten my life, my body, I don't care. I don't even resent that you'll win. You give me the one thing I want, and I'll give you the one thing *you* want."

He stares at me, his breath short, and I watch one bead of perspiration trail down the side of his face before he snorts in disgust and turns from me to dab it away with a handkerchief. He knows I'm different now. I'm broken. Utterly. I wonder if he thinks he did that.

"I have nothing left to lose," I say, monotone. "Nothing in the world except for him. Not truly. Perhaps you think that makes me vulnerable. But in truth it makes me desperate and reckless. I'll do whatever is necessary for Saber, and I won't hesitate to hurt anyone who gets in my way." I wave a hand languidly in the air. "You, the entire kingdom, I don't care. Give him back to me, or this evening Sonoman-Versailles will crown a new King."

He stares into my eyes—looking, perhaps, for the downside. But I'm not bargaining for good value anymore. I want Saber, and to hell with the rest. After a long moment, Justin nods. "The moment the votes are cast, I'll authorize his release."

"Charges dropped?" I have to pin this spouse of mine down on every detail. Every loophole.

"Consider them expunged."

Even better. "I expect him to be waiting in my rooms."

"Did you want a bow tied around his neck?"

"Don't be disgusting; he's not a *thing*," I snap, a lightning bolt of anger searing through my emotional fog. Because to one man, that's exactly what Saber is: a possession to be bought and sold. "I do think a visit to my father is in order," I say, pulling a pair of gloves from my *pannier* pockets and wiggling my fingers into them. "Now that you and I have come to an agreement. Oh," I add, turning to look at him over my shoulder, "you'll want to release Lord Aaron from his rooms as well."

"You think you can convince him to vote in my favor?" the King says with a sneer.

I laugh, a breathy, pathetic sound, even to my own ears. "Hardly. But consider this a favor from your new Queen—you won't want anyone to suspect that you specifically prevented Lord Aaron from attending the vote."

His Majesty regards me silently, brow furrowed.

"Trust me," I say wryly. Then much more loudly, "Mateus! Open the damned door."

I sweep out as soon as the gap is wide enough to accommodate my *panniers,* forcing the reedy man to stumble backward. With my chin high and my corset far too tight, I walk down the hallways without looking left or right, even as courtiers try to catch my attention. A red dot flashes in the corner of my eye as a verbal ripple travels through the crowd. I know what the message is without reading it.

The meeting announcement. The not-so-secret meeting at which the shareholders of Sonoma Inc. will elect—or, perhaps, reelect—a chief executive officer of the company and King of the pseudo-state of Sonoman-Versailles. A rebellion six months in the making to unseat the man I married two days ago. The very threat Justin married me to fend off, by activating voting shares assigned only to a sitting Queen.

Me.

It's time. I feel ill.

The cries for my attention grow loud—building like rumbling thunder—but I ignore everyone, and none dare to bodily interfere. I am the Queen. By the time I reach the *Orangerie*, heading toward the medical center at the former *Hameau*, I'm half convinced I'm going to have to make use of the bushes to empty my stomach.

I never actually thought I'd be here. The great voting meeting, two days after I gained control of the Queen's shares, which the King needs to stay in power. I've spoken to almost no one since Reginald brought me back to the palace. My father has been under medical supervision, Lord Aaron confined to quarters, Saber imprisoned, and my mother and Molli dead. I close my eyes as the eviscerating pain of that reminder rolls through me. I let it; I deserve it.

Reginald said he wouldn't allow Saber to die in prison, but I've learned what Reginald's word is worth. How long does Saber even have? I don't know how he can tell when that awful chip in his head starts to count down.

Maybe he can't. When I briefly saw him three days ago, it had seemed insensitive to inquire too closely about the details of his captivity. What I do know is that if Saber has overestimated Reginald's power to set him free, and that countdown reaches zero, the hardware implanted in Saber's head will destroy his brain.

Of course, keeping Saber alive is merely a temporary accomplishment as long as we're both under the control of the egomaniac holding the reins. I pause at that thought. Which one do I mean? Who has more control over us: Justin or Reginald? It's difficult to tell these days.

In spite of the deal I just struck with His Highness, tendrils of misgiving take root in my mind. Duke Tremain is confident he's garnered enough votes to succeed in his plans to replace the King with his son-in-law, Sir Spencer. I know it'll be close. If Sir Spencer became King, even as the duke's puppet, he would be able to release Saber. Surely. He could even bill it as a consolation prize to the former Queen, thrown down after only two days. He'd be a better ally than Justin in every possible way.

Better for the kingdom? I don't know. But as far as I'm concerned, the kingdom can burn.

For the first time since I was dumped on the steps of the palace on the morning of my wedding, my eyes burn with the threat of tears. I haven't let myself cry—I've hardly let myself *feel*—for fear that I won't be able to stop. As if on cue, a call flickers to life in the periphery of my Lens. I take it the moment I see who it's from.

"Danica, Dani, where are you?"

"Lord Aaron!" I stop walking, and when the tears flow down my cheeks, it's from relief and joy rather than frustration. Still, I swipe at them hastily, cursing myself for losing control, not because something bad happened, but because I'd stopped expecting anything good.

"They've just released me. No explanation. I blame you."

"Perhaps," I confess with a hiccup and laugh that make me sound on the verge of hysteria. Maybe I am.

"Where are you? Your Queenly credentials must have kicked in—you're completely off my grid."

"On my way to the medical center to see my father." Panic is a hurricane within my belly. "Can you meet me? I could use your . . . advice."

"I confess myself surprised you're not surrounded by petitioners. I've gotten fifty coms since opening this call."

"Don't think they aren't trying. I left the palace without speaking to anyone. I'm at the west end of the *Orangerie.* Are you on your way?"

"Have you ever seen me jog?"

A mental picture of Lord Aaron running about with his brocade coattails flying and his coiffure all askew makes another bubble of laughter rise in my throat. "Of course not."

"You're about to," he replies, noticeably breathless.

I turn toward the palace and wait, scanning the various possible exits. Less than half a minute later, my humorous imagining becomes reality before my eyes. I hadn't even considered his heels, which make his already-stiff gait even more awkward.

"You look ridiculous," I observe as he takes several deep breaths before touching his damp cheeks to each of mine, *faire la bise.*

"Only for you, darling. I can't believe His Highness let me out."

"You were right; it was me." Saying so feels more like making a confession than claiming credit. "I told him it was in his best interest not to appear to have kept you specifically from the vote."

Lord Aaron's panting stops completely. "Did he ask why?"

"I think he was afraid to lose my momentary good graces," I say seriously. "I would never spill your secrets."

"You helped him."

"I helped *you*."

Lord Aaron nods, as both statements are entirely true.

"What do I do?" I whisper.

"I don't know."

"You're Sir Spencer's love—how can you not know?"

"It's hard for him to talk about. You think *you*'re closely monitored?" Lord Aaron shakes his head. "He doesn't want it."

"He'd be a good King."

"Indeed. If only we were actually voting for a King. Well, if we vote for Justin Wyndham, we will be voting for a King. But a vote for Sir Spencer is merely a vote for a pawn of the duke."

"I made a deal with Justin," I confess after several long, tense moments. "The Queen's shares for Saber's release."

Lord Aaron's response is a cross between a snort and a sad laugh. "I wish I could join you. How can I vote against Spencer? And yet a vote for the takeover is a vote to destroy even the tiniest possibility of a future with him."

"But why? I know it could be a long wait, but divorce—"

"No. Above all, a CEO must curry favor. An ex-wife with the power and votes Lady Julianna will inherit? It would be the end of his career for certain. Look how many power couples stay together despite hating each other."

"If it's something Sir Spencer doesn't want, why does that matter?" What I don't add, but am certain Lord Aaron hears, is that I know a thing or four about unwanted thrones.

"I've thought about it for days, Danica—weeks—and I'm still unsure what the right answer is. How am I supposed to advise you?"

"Ultimately you'll vote for Sir Spencer, though, won't you?"

"I will always support Spence, Danica. Always. I just don't know what that means in this case. Win or lose, he ends this day with an enormous target on his back."

TWO

MY FATHER IS still shirtless when I arrive at his room, but his hair is brushed and pulled back into a queue, his breeches and stockings freshly laundered. A nurse is dusting him with talc, using a broad, short-bristled brush.

"Ah, you're here," she says. She helps him into a loose linen shirt, and my throat constricts at the sight of the father I once knew, making an appearance for the first time in over a year. His eyes are clearer than I can recall since the night Sierra Jamison died, with the hands of the man who's now my husband around her throat. Mere weeks ago I turned down a tempting compromise from His Murderous Majesty, in part because I was afraid my father wouldn't survive cold-turkey withdrawal from the high doses of Glitter he'd been using. Part of me resents that, with the help of the medical staff, he's actually done rather well. Another part is simply grateful I've caused the death of only one of my parents.

The nurse turns my father's care over to a liveried dressing-bot, who helps him into his *gilet* and formal frock coat as the older woman gestures me to the side of the room. "I don't like releasing him, even for this brief time," she says sternly.

"But—"

"I understand the necessity. Your Highness," she adds as an afterthought. "I'm simply asking you to keep a close watch on him. I could send one of my assistants to escort him if you wish."

I'm already shaking my head. "I need him to appear healthy and hale. The next few hours are of grave importance, even for you."

The woman purses her lips but nods. The staff of the medical center are rarely natives of Sonoman-Versailles, but their livelihood is as much at stake as any Louie's. "I'll have to depend on you to assist him personally, then."

"I wasn't raised to be a pampered, helpless Queen," I say softly.

She cracks a smile, clears her throat and turns her attention to her tablet, swiping through information on his eChart. "He's been going back and forth between sweats and chills, thus the talc; trying to prepare him for anything."

I spare a glance at my father, almost regal in his velvet coat as the bot nimbly ties his cravat. It's truly a transformation. But I see what she's saying—it's a delicate veneer.

"We think he's through the worst of it. But only in the last twenty-four hours or so. He—" She hesitates, then plunges on. "He responds remarkably well to small doses of morphine."

She lets her sentence hang and peers closely at me. Sweat builds up under my arms as I hold a pose of patient, ignorant expectation. "And?" I prompt once the silence grows excruciating.

"My lady—Your Highness," she corrects. "There's nothing on our charts, but has your father been seeing a Parisian doctor, perhaps? Is there any chance he's been receiving prescription pain relievers?"

I blink, letting my heavily coated eyelashes sweep as far up and down as possible in a show of innocence. *"Pardonnez?"*

"Pain relievers: oxycodone, hydrocodone?"

I mask my guilt with an expression of utter befuddlement, even though I know the main ingredient in Glitter is from the opioid family.

"It's just that we found traces of adhesive on both arms when he was admitted."

"Ah, the nicotine patches," I say, as though finally understanding. "He had to stop smoking when we moved into the palace—about four years ago. He tries to keep them out of sight. I assumed he got them from the clinic, but if he was going into Paris—"

"I had the same thought. But his blood work doesn't support it."

I scrunch my face up in confusion as my heart starts to race. "I don't understand."

"No nicotine in his blood. Just traces of opiates and atropine. It would help a lot if we could get a better idea where those came from."

"Traces—" I cut myself off by biting the tip of my tongue so hard I flinch. With the massive doses my father was using, there should have been far more than traces. But then, I hardly know what sort of processing goes into the production of Glitter, or how the body metabolizes it. Perhaps this is normal. Part of the drug's success, even.

I keep my silence behind a mask of daughterly concern.

Whether she interprets my silence as ignorance or callousness, the nurse moves on. "Whatever caused this massive reaction has had an effect on his neural pathways. We seem to be looking at irreversible mental impairment."

"Mental impair—"

"Brain damage."

I can't hide my horror, but I suspect it appears to be a normal reaction. The kind of reaction any concerned family member would have to the news that an "illness" has damaged a loved one's brain. Not the guilty conscience of a drug dealer who's been told that she helped her father fry his mind. "But he looks so clear," I rasp, the distress in my voice for once unfeigned.

"He is. And were he a twelve-year-old boy, we'd be overjoyed."

I physically draw back at that.

"He walks, talks, cares for himself, processes information. But compared to his annual evaluations, we see a steep decline."

I swallow hard and draw myself up, trying to regain control of this situation. My father. My bright, smart father, who was my only parent to encourage my love of math and tech. "You said it *seems* to be irreversible?"

"Well, it's always hard to say for certain—"

"At the moment you can only speculate, yes?"

"Informed speculation is—"

"So, as far as you're concerned, my father is much improved and well on his way to a potentially full recovery." I stand tall, towering over her by several centimeters, and stare down with every ounce of Queenly grace I can scrape together.

She stammers a few incomprehensible syllables and her cheeks flush red, until she looks up into my eyes to reply. Then the color seeps away, leaving her white-faced, her mouth hanging open a crack.

"I will appreciate your *official* pronouncement to that effect," I say slowly and quietly.

The woman's mouth gets tight again, and I can see the indecision in her eyes.

"It's not a lie," I say softly, cajoling. "You said it yourself— difficult to predict for certain."

"It is," she says grudgingly.

"Excellent." I walk over and lay a finger on the cravat the bot has tied neatly about my father's neck. "This truly is a lovely facility. The Queen holds a place on its board of advisers. I look forward to sharing my enthusiasm for your work at the next budget meeting."

The look on her face says the veiled threat has been understood.

After repeated and varied warnings, my father and I are finally seen off at the front doors of the clinic. My father carries a carved walking stick that could be mistaken as simply decorative, and his other arm is clasped tightly on my arm.

One recommendation was particularly helpful—that he not stress his eyes or brain by wearing his Lens. A ready-made excuse for failing to receive the coms doubtless pouring in to pester him about today's vote.

"Father, how are you feeling?" I ask once we're out of earshot.

"It's . . . it's hard to say. I—I would like to feel better, Dani. You know what would make me feel better."

"Father—"

"Please. You pay the man; you must know how to reach him. You have to—"

"Father!" I face him, grasping both of his shoulders and wondering momentarily when he got so *short*—but he's merely slouching. "If you want any hope of feeling better ever again, you've got to get through this vote, then finish out your hospital stay. There's nothing I can do while you're in there."

He swallows hard. "But after?" he asks hopefully.

"One thing at a time," I say, rage and regret simmering like acid within me. If I have anything to say about it, he'll never see a speck of Glitter again in his life.

"Who should I vote for?" he asks, and there's confusion in his tone. I'm not sure he comprehends what's happening—how close the kingdom is to a complete overhaul. He might not even be able to name the candidates. I don't dare ask; the votes of mentally incompetent shareholders are moot until a proxy is appointed, and there's no time for that.

"No one," I say, more sharply than he deserves, then struggle to put my emotions in check. "You'll sign in to your account and hand your tablet to me. I'll vote for us both."

We walk for nearly a minute before he speaks up again. "Who will you vote for?"

I hesitate, and my ribs throb where my stays dig in. "I haven't decided."

We enter the palace and there's a line outside the theater, but my father and I go around the crowd and into the royal box. I don't know if I'm relieved or disappointed to find the box empty. Is it better to know where your enemy is, or avoid them entirely?

The first and only time I attended another meeting like this one, my father had just inherited voting shares from his stepbrother and brought me along. He wanted me to see how our kingdom was run. At the time, I'd been far more interested in the technology than the politics—Amalgamated, the company responsible for creating the palace's mainframe, M.A.R.I.E., and the household bots that replaced human servants many years ago, was also contracted to oversee our electronic voting system. As a budding programmer, I peppered the technicians with questions about their encryption devices. Sometimes they even answered me.

They're here today in their dark jumpsuits emblazoned with the Amalgamated logo, so drab among the *coiffed* Sonoman crowd. Even as they distribute slates to shareholders, they might as well be invisible. Like the technology hidden throughout the palace—ubiquitous and mostly unseen—the technicians are intended to be overlooked. Intended to be forgotten.

My father submits to the Amalgamated slate's biometric scans and hands me his tablet computer. Literally hands me control of his shares. Those, combined with the voting shares on my own device, make me one of the most powerful people in the room. I feel nothing of the sort.

As the techs finish their work and head for the exits, the door on the far side of the stage opens and Justin enters, trailed by several highly placed members of the board, including Duke Tremain. Amid a buzz of whispers, the audience rise to their feet. Justin doesn't so much as glance my way, but my throat tightens and I feel oddly threatened.

We take our seats and the meeting begins.

The opening speeches are predictably dull. Profit and loss, quarterly projections, asset depreciation. The sorts of things we mostly leave to accountants, really. From my vantage point above most of the audience, I see several courtiers playing flash games instead of listening. If I weren't feeling so nauseated, I might be doing the same.

Duchess Wakefield, our chief officer of operations and the person conducting the meeting, comes to the agenda item we're all waiting for. "Duke Raven Tremain, to speak in support of proposal forty-two, the removal of Justin Wyndham as chief executive officer and King of Sonoman-Versailles."

There are a few gasps from the crowd, and I'm shocked that *anyone* didn't know. I slide a glance over to Lord Aaron, sitting with friends in a neighboring box, pretending to be half asleep, with his normal devil-may-care affectation. In another box across the way is Lady Mei, and when she catches my glance, she waves and tips her head toward the stage with wide eyes. I shrug in response, as though it couldn't matter less.

The King sits on the stage, one arm draped languidly over the back of the empty chair beside him, a knowing half-smile on his face. The nervousness evident only an hour ago in his private office has vanished. Even Duke Tremain seems a touch ruffled by His Majesty's nonchalance as he stands at the podium and passionately lays out his case for deposing Justin Wyndham and replacing him with the Honorable Sir Spencer Harrisford.

The speech is over before I fully appreciate that it's begun. I suspect that the duke is suffering from an abundance of confidence—in his mind he can't comprehend who would vote for this veritable child over him. Or, at least, for another child guided by his heavy-handed counsel. After Duke Tremain concludes, Sir Spencer doesn't rise to speak. He remains seated beside the wife he doesn't love, barely moving a muscle. The message is clear—the board will be voting in a puppet.

The King rises and makes a show of rebuttoning his velvet jacket. When he raises his chin to face the audience, he doesn't even look threatened. I haven't the slightest idea what he intends as his response. An emotional plea for the name of Wyndham? A scalding rebuttal pointing out the obvious trickery in Duke Tremain's plan?

But he does neither.

Instead, a chart appears on the screen just above him. It's labeled PHARMACEUTICAL DIVISION, and my father, even in his diminished mental state, lets out a whistle of appreciation.

Seven hundred percent growth over the next three years, declares the text beneath the graph.

Another chart appears over our monarch, this one titled ROBOTICS DIVISION and separated into Sonoman profits and Amalgamated derivatives.

Three hundred and fifty percent growth in the next five years, the words beneath the chart declare.

Murmurs are rising from the audience, and Duke Tremain looks as though he's being force-fed lemon juice.

A third chart, labeled simply LABOR.

Sixty-five percent overhead reduction in the next five years.

Once more the screen changes, and it's not a chart this time, simply the words OVERALL INDIVIDUAL SHAREHOLDER PROFIT.

"Two hundred and ninety-nine percent," the King says. Slowly. Clearly. His words reverberate around the silenced auditorium.

Then he bows low and returns to his seat.

His kingdom for six words.

It's brilliant, truly. Acting as though Duke Tremain's proposal were so inconsequential it's not even deserving of his attention—as though this new plan were what he'd intended the meeting to be about all along. The unspoken implication being that the plan will roll forward only if he remains in his position. It's a gamble, but he's laid out some serious bait. Not to mention intrigue.

The exits are sealed, M.A.R.I.E. disabled. The time for consultation is over. For the first time in months, I wish my corset were looser.

This is the moment my mother promised to the King months ago—that I would use the Queen's shares, and my father would use our family's shares, to support Justin. But there's no one—no blackmail—to enforce my decision anymore. If I support the King, I'll retain the power I gained by becoming the Queen. If I support the King, Saber will be waiting for me when I return to my rooms.

Assuming Justin keeps his word.

I touch first my own screen and then my father's, casting every single one of our combined votes. Then I close my eyes and try to decide what the hell I'm going to do next.

THREE

THE CELEBRATION CONTINUES until the rosy hours of dawn, but finally I'm allowed to retire to my rooms. My rooms by right, as I'm still the Queen of Sonoman-Versailles.

I don't know how it happened; I voted for Sir Spencer.

It seems Fate has an incredibly perverse sense of humor.

On his own merits, the King changed enough minds to succeed not only without me, but in spite of me. I couldn't do it. I couldn't vote to further inflict Justin Wyndham upon this kingdom. Lord knows I've hurt the people in this palace enough in the last few months.

He won anyway.

Amalgamated is paid well to keep the voting process private and secure, so there should be no chance of Justin discovering my duplicity. But I'm suspicious of *should*s.

He can never know. He might actually kill me. Or worse.

So far, he doesn't know a thing. Indeed, at the "spontaneous" *fête* that followed the announcement, His Majesty grabbed me around the waist, spun me off my feet, and planted a hard kiss on my mouth, before laughing with a gaiety I'm not sure I've *ever* seen from him.

But I gambled with Saber's life and it's killing me. I'm terrified of what I'm going to find—or not find—on the other side of these doors. I touch the intricate detailing on the faux-wooden panels, and my fingers tremble, my throat so dry I can scarcely choke out the command that gains me entrance.

At first I think the room is empty—but no. There, in my bed. A large lump.

I stagger forward as a sob builds up in my chest and tears stream down my cheeks; I reach out a hand. I almost can't bear to wake him. He's likely been waiting for hours, and he can't have slept well while imprisoned. I clamp my hand over my mouth to quiet the tide of emotion I've been holding back all day, but it's not enough, and soon his green eyes are fluttering open. Saber snaps to attention at the sight of me, sitting up and pulling me to him, my skirts heavy across his lap. He's whispering soothing words in his native tongue, and his lips pepper my face, but I'm sobbing too hard for him to even attempt to kiss my mouth.

The fear I didn't dare to acknowledge finally rises to the top— that he'd been dead since the morning of my wedding. That his chip had triggered and no one—at the King's order, of course— had bothered to tell me. That his body was just lying there, abandoned and cold on the tile floor of the bare prison cell.

My chest finally stops its spasms, and when Saber's hands start unfastening bits of my clothing, it's not to assuage any hunger more complex than a need to be *close*. My *panniers,* the stiff overdress and petticoats, my heavy jeweled shoes: all barriers. He just wants to hold me.

He reaches for my corset strings, and I suck in a loud breath.

"Danica," he says, and my heart shatters all over again when it comes out as a mild rebuke.

"It was a hard day," I whisper. My stays are too tight. Have been from the first moment I managed a brief respite from my wedding party to summon a dressing-bot. I wait for Saber to lecture, loathing the thought, but I should have had more confidence in him. He simply loosens the ribbons, then ties them again. My head spins, but I don't faint.

When the rest of my finery lies in a pile on the floor, he tucks us both under the comforter, our bodies snugly spooning. I give a tiny thought to the possibility that security is watching us, but how could it matter now? I'm married, documents signed, and the King has been affirmed CEO. Certainly a tryst on my part could threaten nothing of the King's.

Saber whispers close to my ear, "Tell me you didn't come back to Versailles for me."

Of course. He doesn't know what Reginald did. The agony of that betrayal hits me again, and tears leak down my face. I pretend for everyone else; I can't do it for him. Not when I don't have to. He seems to understand and holds me tighter, one arm wrapping around my stomach. "Reginald brought me back," I finally whisper. "He told me he never specified *when* he'd take me away. And he wasn't ready yet."

Saber mutters what I'm quite sure must be a string of Mongolian curses. "This is so like him," he finally says. "I should have—it doesn't matter. As usual, it's over and he won." He hesitates, his fingers tracing details in the lace on the cap sleeve of my shift. "You're married?"

My innards freeze and I clench my fingers over my wedding ring, as if the gesture could hide what I've done. "Yes."

"And Queen?"

I groan and bury my face in his neck.

"Did he . . . ?" He stops. "Did—"

"No." I cut him off with a harsh whisper. The last time I confronted the King before Saber was imprisoned, he'd threatened to take me by force. But he didn't—not even after we were wed.

Saber pulls back, staring into my eyes, perhaps disbelieving. "Why not?" he finally asks.

But I don't have an answer. "He came to my room after the reception." I squeeze my eyes shut, remembering the terror. "I was so scared. All the high nobles escorted us in here—courtly tradition and all. They cheered and toasted and, well, let's just say it's a good thing they no longer undress the bride and groom and tuck them right into bed. I might have been sick."

A low chuckle from Saber shakes me from the vivid recollection, enough to unclench my knuckles and try to massage feeling back into my fingers. "Then what?" he asks.

I shrug. "He opened the champagne that was waiting here, poured me a glass, drank the rest right from the bottle, and went to sleep."

I don't tell him about the quarter hour during which the King removed one piece of his clothing, took a swig, removed more clothing, and repeated the process until I wanted to scream from the tension that seemed to scrape the skin from my bones. In the end, he'd been wearing a slouching set of breeches, looking almost exactly as I'd found him the night he stood over Sierra

Jamison's body. Complete with his long, silken hair pulled back at his nape, his chest bare, and the hollow just below his hipbones peeping out from the waist of his breeches; too beautiful to be such a villain.

And as I had on that night six months earlier, I cowered.

He'd turned and looked at me in my corner, then strode over. I stood, still fully dressed, the glass filled with champagne gripped between my fingers as I wondered how best to use it as a weapon. With one arm braced on the walls on either side of me, he'd leaned in, his body so close I could feel the heat radiating off him. "I want you," he'd whispered, and I closed my eyes, knowing I was about to be raped. "And I could take you tonight." He trailed a finger down my cheek. "But that doesn't please me. When you give yourself to me, it will be because you choose to."

And then he withdrew, so fast that by the time I opened my eyes, there was nothing in front of me to focus on. He threw the empty bottle into the fireplace, where it shattered into a million pieces, before stalking to my bed, tossing back the coverlet, and sliding beneath it.

"He didn't say anything to you?" Saber asked, pulling me back to the present.

"No," I lie.

"And you haven't brought it up?"

"If a man said he was going to shoot you tomorrow, and then he didn't, would you remind him?"

Saber loops an arm across my chest and pulls me even tighter against him. "No, I suppose not. So . . . what now?"

I shake my head. "I don't know." I turn to him, our faces near enough to share the air we breathe. I whisper so quietly even M.A.R.I.E. can't possibly make out my words. "I didn't think I would be here for the wedding. I expected to be able to escape, but . . ." I tilt my neck so my brow touches Saber's chest. "It's not just the palace I didn't escape from. I can't stop thinking about what I've done. I keep turning down the hall to Molli's apartment and remembering all over again that she's not there. She haunts me now. Maybe forever."

Saber strokes my hair silently. An open condemnation might have hurt less. He knows I never meant to harm my friend, but he also knows—as surely as I do—that Molli is dead because of me. Every single day I relive the moment the King unknowingly handed Molli the Glitter after it slipped through my trembling fingers. She was dead within hours, drowned in thirty centimeters of bathwater.

Embers of slow-burning anger creep into my chest and I welcome them. They're easier to manage than self-hatred. It's his fault too—the King's. Not for that moment with Molli, precisely, but for being the unbending, selfish, power-hungry creature that has driven me to the choices I've made. "He's a monster," I whisper.

"Which one?" Saber says wryly.

"Both," I grumble, realizing that Reginald continues to be a greater threat to Saber than the King. "I feel like I'm stuck in quicksand. The more I thrash and kick, the deeper I sink. Somehow, I'm in worse trouble than before, and I don't know how to begin getting out of it." My chin trembles, and I force myself to smile, running my fingers through Saber's sleek, straight hair. "But I'm glad I have you. You make everything better."

"I'm not sure that's saying much, under the circumstances," he says with a grin.

I roll my eyes, but his levity chases away a touch of my despair.

He swallows hard and avoids my eyes when he whispers, "What are we going to do about the Glitter?"

I let several seconds pass as I remember his declaration when I said I hated Glitter.

You don't hate it enough.

"Must we?" I whisper. "For one night can we forget about it?"

His jaw tightens but then relaxes. "One night."

I don't dare wait even that long for my next worry. "Saber, your chip—"

"—is fine," he interrupts firmly. "It's been years since Reginald gave me anything less than the two-week maximum, and he's not the sort of man to lose his property by accident. If he decides it's time for me to die, I'll die." I try to protest his macabre declaration, but he puts a silencing finger on my lips. "I've been dealing with this for years, so you let *me* deal with it. You have enough to worry about."

My laugh is drenched in bitterness. "More than you? I don't think so."

He lets my comment pass while the room continues to brighten with early rays of sunrise. I haven't felt tired until now. I spent two days hiding in an emotional fog, followed by the *mascarade* of celebration after the vote, then the exquisite joy of finding Saber in my bedchamber. After that roller coaster I feel weary, wrung out, and beaten.

"Is it weird?" Saber asks as I struggle to keep my eyes open. "Being married?"

There's an edge in his voice. He hates it, but he can't bring himself to blame me. "Weird?" I take a breath to stall, and consider. "It's certainly . . . surreal. I was there at the wedding; I was in the dress and I said the words and signed the contracts. But the whole time it was as though it were happening to someone else. Like I was watching through someone else's eyes. I hate him," I add in a fierce whisper. "It feels impossible to be married to someone you hate."

"Pretend you're not, then," Saber says simply.

I run my hand through his hair again. How can such a simple gesture be so endlessly satisfying? "When Reginald brought me back I was devastated, but part of me was just glad to be in the same building as you."

Saber looks at me, his eyes deep pools of something sad that I can't quite understand. "I'm not worth it, Danica. I adore you. I think I love you. But you have to understand that there's no future with someone . . . someone like me. Certainly not a future worth everything you've done."

My tongue itches to argue. To deny his condemnation. To promise that I'll find a way to free him. But that step is, I think, distant at best. I don't agree, don't even nod, but I pull him close and sigh when he lays his cheek against my chest, and for the first time in days, my body relaxes. His breathing slows and I enjoy the feel of his limbs molding against mine—though as he falls asleep, his every twitch and jerk gives me a mild flutter of panic, stoic assurances notwithstanding. Only by placing my ear to his chest, where I can hear each beat of his heart, am I able to banish his perpetual death sentence into the corner of my mind.

My own eyelids are heavy, but I have trouble making my brain slow. My husband is still the King and I have Saber back.

Step one is complete. But there's no time for celebration.

Step two: figure out step three.

FOUR

MY FIRST *LEVER* as Queen. I suppose it ought to feel momentous, but since the King has had me doing this particular chore for months, it feels almost comfortingly normal. Lady Mei powders my shoulders with gardenia-scented talc, and I try not to sneeze. "The duke has been raging about, trying to find out who voted for the King because he was certain he had it in the bag," she whispers. "People lie in public, but when it comes to actually voting, they let their real selves show."

I swallow hard—she's only telling me this because she assumes I voted for my husband. Everyone does. They all thought the King would lose. But if I voted for Tremain, that means there are even more people than he suspects who turned coat. There must be; numbers don't lie.

"Tremain is blaming the young shareholders," Lady Mei continues, using a fan to hide her mouth from the eyes—and lip-reading Lens apps—of our audience, then handing it to me. "'Fickle,' he says. Several of us think some votes changed your way because we like your Glitter."

My face registers shock before I remember to mask it. "You think so?"

"Of course. Easier to buy Glitter from the Queen." She smirks, and I'm clearly supposed to appreciate the news that my illegal dealings continue to have unexpected and far-reaching consequences.

The crowd of tourists jostles and applauds as the *lever* concludes and we exit the bedchamber, into my back rooms. Before I can open my mouth, the ladies are pulling paper euros from their *pannier* pockets and stacking them on my dresser. Between this and the half million from before my wedding, I'm pushing my first new million all over again. I stare at that stack of money and I hate it. Hate it with a red-hot fury that threatens to spill out of my tight control.

Until I have a thought. Perhaps there is yet some purpose for it.

I'm startled from my brainstorm by Lady Mei jabbing her elbow into my side. "Something sparkly, perhaps?" Oh yes. Their payment. I've saved exactly enough Glitter to give each lady a canister for her service in my *lever,* but I have nothing else. And several hundred thousand euros' worth of orders.

I don't know what to do. Reginald promised more, but I don't know how much, and I certainly couldn't say when it will arrive. All I can hope is that Reginald loves money and hates Sonoman-Versailles enough to keep supplying me. To keep his word. Because I've certainly discovered that honor doesn't compel him.

After letting my ladies out the small back entrance from my private rooms, I nearly bowl headlong into Saber—holding an enormous white box with a silver bow.

"It was waiting beside the rail in your bedchamber when the tourists exited," Saber says darkly. "I don't know how he managed. That man has tricks I can't begin to understand."

My mouth goes dry. For over twenty-four hours we've avoided even mentioning Glitter. We don't want to fight. But here it is, in Saber's very hands, and we can postpone it no longer.

Saber sets the box on the floor, and I crouch beside it and lift the lid to find the entire thing crammed full of canisters of Glitter, in more than the three colors I'd been mixing. Evidently, Reginald thinks the Sonoman ladies should have their choice of varied hues of drug-laced eye shadow, in addition to the foundation, lip gloss, and rouge. The thought of rouge makes my stomach lurch, remembering the glint of Glitter on Molli's face. I place a hand over my stomach and breathe deeply; every thought of Molli feels like a knife to the stomach. I keep expecting the knife's edge to dull, but it doesn't.

"What do I do?" I ask.

Saber stands there, peering steadily at me. "Quit?" he says dryly. "Just say no?"

"It's more complex than that and you know it."

"But is it really?"

"Yes!" This whole damnable situation is even worse than when I made the original decision. Thanks to Reginald's perfidy, I'm exactly where I would have been had I done nothing at all, minus one dear friend and one scheming mother. Plus one criminal nemesis and a clawing court of addicts.

And plus one Saber. That part I find difficult to resent.

"I don't know," Saber finally says. He kicks the box, not hard enough to do damage, but the inventory clatters loudly within. "Reginald doesn't care about people or their lives or their families—he just wants to make money. But I know you. You do care." He lifts an eyebrow. "At least you used to."

"I do!" I hurry to say. "But . . ." What can I say? I'm not sure there's ever going to be a good enough reason for Saber.

He meets my eyes for a moment, then looks away.

"Even if I wanted to continue selling long-term, which I don't," I add for Saber's benefit, but perhaps also to hear the words come out of my own mouth, "I can't. My business model isn't sustainable," I say. "It was never supposed to *be* sustainable. The whole operation is held together with resin and twine. Eventually customers are going to run out of jewelry, and the CFO will have to hike the credit exchange rate and . . . and—" I breathe deeply, pressing the back of my hand to my mouth. "The nurse at the clinic told me my father's brain has been damaged."

Saber stands straight, away from the wall. "Does she know about the patches?"

I shake my head. "She noted the residue, but I said they were nicotine patches." I close my eyes and give voice to my greatest fear. "Is that going to happen more, or . . . ?"

This time when I turn my face up to Saber, he's glaring at the wall over my shoulder, looking both angry and guilty. "It's probably more related to dosage," he says softly, and I remember that most of my father's drug habit was foisted on him not by me but by Saber. Against Saber's will, but by him nonetheless. I wish I hadn't said anything. "There were times when I wasn't convinced he'd be *alive* when I got here for a delivery."

It's odd to remember that Saber had a life before me, but he was involved with my father for almost two months before we met.

"I don't blame you," I say genially. "I don't blame you for anything Reginald ever makes you do."

"Doesn't make it feel any better when I'm doing it," he says tightly, and I clamp my mouth shut. He sighs. "Sorry, that's not the point. You have to decide what to do with this." He nudges the box with his foot.

"We," I correct.

"You," he sends right back. "In the end, I'm still Reginald's man."

He's right. He can't be caught discouraging me. He tried as best he could, in the beginning, and I mistook his warnings for contempt. Fleetingly I wonder what sort of punishment he might have faced, had I actually backed out then.

My feet start to lose feeling from the way I'm crouching, so I flop backward onto the ground, legs sticking straight out in front of me in possibly the least graceful pose I've adopted in years. Saber cuts off a bark of a laugh, and I smile up at him despite the feeling that my stays are cutting me in two.

"I'm tired," I protest. Then add, "I didn't get much sleep last night."

"No, no you didn't," he murmurs.

But the box won't be ignored, though staring at it silently yields no answers. "When I started, I was so afraid that Justin would kill me. And I was angry," I say, looking up as Saber joins me on the floor, sitting cross-legged. "I was so sure of what I'd seen. I wanted him to pay."

"You *were* so sure? The woman he strangled? Have you changed your mind?"

My shoulders slump and I shake my head in confusion. "I don't know. He's told me multiple times that it was an accident and, to be honest, it kind of grosses me out to even think about it. But I *did* surprise him when I dropped that platter."

Saber lets me sit in silence, contemplating this. Contemplating just how guilty I truly am, perhaps.

"Regardless, the danger is different now. I can't imagine myself safe from Justin," I add darkly. "But by making me his Queen, he's made me far more difficult to simply *remove*. I'm not even certain he realizes it. Before, I justified everything I did because I was afraid for my life, or the lives of other possible victims. Now?" I flutter my hand at the box. "Now I'm damned if I continue and damned if I quit." Reginald's words from so very long ago echo through my head: *If you* truly *think your pathetic life is worth five million euros . . .* I don't know what price tag I'd put on my life, but I've already cost Molli everything.

She can't have died for nothing.

"Would it be so awful to stop? You could look at this entirely differently. That your confirmed role as Queen means you can't dabble in this sort of stuff anymore." Saber looks at me, and his eyes are filled with desperation, begging me to make the right choice this time. "You don't need the money anymore."

"I can't simply stop," I say bleakly, the truth jarring straight down my spine. "Going on a little longer feels somehow less awful than having done everything for nothing."

"That's rationalization and you know it."

"If I stop all at once, my customers will go into withdrawal and it'll be obvious what's been happening," I argue. "I can claim to have been duped by my supplier, but I'm not confident in the outcome."

"And what would they do? Dethrone you?"

I remain silent. There would be social consequences, certainly. But I can't tell Saber the real reason I can't stop yet: if I quit selling Glitter, Reginald will take Saber back.

A little longer. That's all I need.

"Come on, Dani," he whispers. "Be better than this."

I curl up, resting my arms and head on my popped-up knees. "I used to think I was a decent person. I'm not sure I am anymore. No, don't," I rush to say before Saber can protest. Before I can find out *if* he was going to protest. "I thought that because I was doing this for good reasons, I could do it without becoming . . . tainted. But I have. It's like blackest ink, and you can't touch it without getting stained. At this point, I'm mostly afraid of how much worse it will get before I can finally be through."

Saber says nothing, just reaches over to run his fingers along my neck, massaging gently.

"So I . . . keep going," I say, and his fingers tense on my neck. "But I try to limit my damage. I don't take new customers, and I start to spread the word that I've reached maximum production capacity. When it's gone, it's gone."

"You'll be stampeded every time you get a delivery if you say that. Just a warning." Saber's tone is sharp, and frustration pours from him like waves.

I hang my head. "I don't know what else to do. If I can't stop, at least I can keep it from growing. Maybe it'll help some of the users cut back," I add in a mumble, not really trying to disguise my wishful thinking.

"Maybe."

"And I can sell less and less product each week. Force people to use it more sparingly. I don't know that there's a better way."

Saber nods, acceptance rather than agreement. "Let's be off, then," he says, offering both hands to pull me up. "It is your day to be seen."

"It's funny," I say, looking down at the white box. "I got into this mess to take control of a fate that was galloping off without me. Now I'm less in charge than ever."

Saber reaches an arm around my shoulders and squeezes me as he places a kiss on my brow. "I know. But let's be honest; it's not funny at all."

FIVE

SABER FOLLOWS DOCILELY behind me, playing his role to
the hilt as I wander up and down the hallways of the palace, to
the accompaniment of murmurs and even a few calls of "Your
Majesty!" The tourists, of course, not the residents. I'm no longer
permitted to escape the palace on Wednesdays, not really. I can
take a stroll outside, but I may no longer flee far into the gardens
for hours at a time to escape the gawking of our visitors. I am to
be gawked at. And this first Wednesday, *everyone* wants to see me.

Everywhere I go, people drop into low bows and curtsies. I
barely catch sight of someone's face before it turns toward the
floor. No one talks to me, no comforting smiles. I'm lonely. How
wrong that feels when I'm surrounded by dozens of people at any
given moment. Saber's presence helps, but I can't even touch him
lest I betray our relationship.

Lady Mei joins me and links our arms as I'm traversing
through the public *salons,* and a smile curls on my lips. I'm more
glad of her company than I expected.

"I heard you have new Glitter—is it true?" she asks, and my
smile melts away. Of course. "I have mine from this morning, but
Kata sent me for some for her. I paid Lady Sesay already."

"Certainly," I say distractedly, blinking away the sudden sting of tears as I hand her some eye shadow. "Look, new colors," I add, then want to clamp my hand over my mouth. I'm trying to breed less excitement over the makeup, not more.

"Oooh, I love this," Lady Mei says, glancing down before slipping the canister into a pocket. "Can I get one of these for my payment next week?"

"Certainly," I say with a tight smile. Lady Mei squeezes my hand before spinning off to join her cousin.

Lord Aaron sidles up beside me and places my hand atop his arm, saying nothing—he's a dark cloud of moodiness by my side, but I find my fingers squeezing his arm anyway. Dark cloud, yes. But he's *my* dark cloud.

"How's your friend?" I whisper, darting a glance back at Saber, still trailing behind me.

Since the failed *coup* there's a tense awkwardness between the major players in each faction, and Lord Aaron is caught in the middle. I haven't heard from him, but whether that's a matter of melancholy or politics, I can't yet guess. Sir Spencer usually joins the younger crowd for games in one of the *salons* where he and Lord Aaron can make secret puppy eyes at each other, but I haven't seen him all day. I suppose the only thing worse than being the puppet leader of a hostile corporate takeover is being the puppet leader of a failed corporate takeover.

Lord Aaron's smile wavers for only a moment, but I catch it. "Afraid," he says bluntly. "Your lord husband hasn't rained down any consequences yet, but you know he will."

"I can speak to the King," I offer, even though the thought of going to the King and pleading for his enemy fills me with aching trepidation.

"I'll pass along the offer," Lord Aaron says in a whisper. He hesitates. "Until then, perhaps it's best you know that Lady Cyn is decked out in a rather garish display of finery and is making sure her supposedly private conversations are being overheard by every tourist in the Hall of Mirrors."

I close my eyes and take a slow count of five before whispering, "She means nothing—her power disappeared the moment His Royal Husbandness said *I do*."

"You truly think that?"

I turn, facing him. "I think that because it's true."

Lord Aaron isn't known for being hedgy, so when he hesitates, I give him a pointed look and fist one hand on my hip until he relents. "If it were anyone other than her, and if His Majesty were actually treating you like the Queen, it wouldn't matter. But neither of those is the case."

My hand falls from my hip, and I don't catch my dropped jaw for several seconds. "What do you mean, he isn't treating me like the Queen? I've been doing the *lever* since before we were wed! If this is about—" I break off and draw him closer, strolling over to an empty alcove. "If this is about the fact that we haven't consummated our marriage, I hardly think that applies, and moreover—"

"That's not what it's about at all, Dani. Lud, what a turncoat you must think me to be."

I squeeze his arm. "Not in the least, hence my surprise."

His feathers resettle, and I try to get my own to do the same. I have few enough allies these days; I can't afford to jump down the throats of the ones who remain. "Who is the most famous royal member of the court of Versailles *ever*?" he asks.

"Marie-Antoinette, I imagine."

"Precisely. The *Queen*. And why, pray tell? Why not the King, who built this place to begin with?"

"Because they chopped off her head?"

"Untrue." He hesitates. "Not the head-chopping part, but I completely disagree that it's the reason she's so famous. Try again."

I think about my answer as my eyes sweep along the line of rooms, keeping an eye on Saber as he's summoned from group to group, to hand out Glitter. "She was beautiful. And scandalous."

"And she didn't hide it. Never did anyone try to take her place. Why? Because it was impossible. She shone at every moment—she personally made certain of that. No one could have looked into a crowded room and not known which lady was the Queen." He pauses until I give him my full attention. "If Jeanne Poisson had been around one generation later and had gone for Marie's husband instead of her father-in-law, no one in history would have even heard of the infamous Madame de Pompadour. Why? Because no one—not even that famous mistress—could compete with Marie-Antoinette."

I know my face is pale, even though I'm quite certain frightening me wasn't the intention of Lord Aaron's rousing speech.

"Lady Cyn wants to be the Madame de Pompadour of your court. You can step down and let her, or you can be Marie-Antoinette."

"I don't want to be here at all," I say in a small voice.

Lord Aaron narrows his eyes, far more seriously than I'm accustomed to. "There was a time when I didn't want to be here either. But despite all our efforts, here we *both* are. We have to watch out for each other and for ourselves."

I look down at the carpet, despising the truth.

"You've had a setback; I'll not deny it. If you're still looking for a graceful exit from the Palace of Versailles—and it sounds like you are—I can promise you'll never get one without power in court. If you lose that power before it's even truly yours, you'll never get it back. That's what will happen if you let Lady Cyn eclipse you, especially in these honeymoon days of your reign."

It's all too easy to hate Lady Cyn for everything she's done in her efforts to outshine me over the years. When I had no power to speak of. I hate the idea of her succeeding at anything, much less beating me. But she's been playing a completely different game all along—she, the game of court intrigue, of hierarchy and influence, and I, the game of commerce and misdirection. I admit, I'd thought myself rid of her. But something else he said catches my attention. "My reign?"

"Your *reign*," he repeats. "Through all the drama, I think you've forgotten that you're not simply an unhappy seventeen-year-old newlywed. You're the joint ruler of a small, fabulously wealthy country. You *are* the Queen, Danica."

It's splendidly obvious, of course, but Lord Aaron is correct—I haven't thought of it in quite that way.

"You have rights. You have privileges." He pauses, then rushes on. "At the very least you're owed the use of the crown jewels.

And you should be wearing some every time you step out of your *boudoir*."

I very nearly fall off my heels. "Crown jewels? Lord Aaron, what in the world is Lady Cyn discussing?"

He sighs dramatically. "She's trotted herself out decked in likely every piece of jewelry His Highness has ever gifted her, and is acting as though they were presented to her only in the last few days. I happen to know the bracelet she's wearing was given at her coming out as a generic royal gift. I remember seeing one like it in your own collection."

I refuse to let aggravation at him show on my face, but I do raise one eyebrow. "Is this all truly about Lady Cyn out-*sparkling* me?"

"You've been so focused on amassing euros that you've forgotten the most important currency in Versailles isn't euros. And it isn't Sonoman credits, either."

"It's the favor of the King," I say, hating the way his argument is starting to gel.

"His, or the proxy favor of those who have it. And if she's the lady who has the King's favor, then who doesn't?"

Ice runs through my veins. "Me."

"Does history even *remember* Jane Shore, Madame du Barry, Elizabeth Blount, Louise de La Vallière? No. The only mistresses anyone remembers are the ones who became Queen." He pauses. "Or the ones to whom a timid Queen yielded her power."

"I don't care about being remembered. I don't *want* to be remembered."

He's already shaking his head. "Don't cede your power—"

"I don't care about power!" I snap in a rigid whisper.

"I know you're angry with the King, but Danica, what's the last thing Lady Cyn did to you, purely from spite?"

The blood drains from my face. "She told the King that Saber was carrying drugs." Getting Saber back softened my memory. I can't afford to be soft anymore.

"And the fallout from that? He could have died, Dani. And what if they'd found them on *you*? It would have blown everything. In fact, Lady Cyn's single word in the King's ear could have destroyed your entire escape before Reginald had a chance to do it himself, and thrown *you* in jail instead of Saber."

My heart races as I connect more dots. If Saber hadn't been imprisoned, Lord Aaron would have hacked Saber's and my way out of the palace instead of getting me into the prison. Ultimately, if Lady Cyn hadn't tattled on Saber, he and I would have escaped the night before the wedding.

In the end, Reginald still betrayed me, but without that variable, Lady Cyn could have single-handedly toppled everything I'd worked for.

"Unintended consequences, perhaps," Lord Aaron continues when I say nothing. "But imagine what she could do if she were *trying* to truly ruin you instead of just get the King back. Now imagine she has the power of the court behind her."

"It would be a disaster," I whisper.

"Besides," Lord Aaron says with a grin, "isn't there some part of you that wants a little revenge for years of bullying?"

Not caving to his humor, I sigh and lean against a pillar. "I'm too young for this."

"Marie-Antoinette was only fourteen when she wed. Queen Victoria of England was your age."

I roll my eyes up to meet his. "I wasn't being literal. Can't I whine without critique?"

"Only if you're going to do something about it."

Unfortunately, if Lord Aaron is right about the end result, he's also right about how Lady Cyn is trying to get there. It feels wrong that such a serious discussion comes back to jewelry, but thus is the absurdity of my life. "What am I supposed to do? Walk up to my husband and demand crown jewels?"

"Sounds pretty girl-power to me."

"I was kidding."

"You shouldn't be."

I blink at him a few times, inadvertently waking my Lens.

Lord Aaron, seeing the microfilament light up, smiles. "Lens him. Do it now, while you're feeling brave."

"Am I feeling brave?" I ask under my breath. But he hears me. *"Mais bien sûr!"*

"You can't just Lens the King," I grumble.

"I can't. I wager *you* can."

I give him a sidelong glance.

"This is precisely what I'm talking about, Dani. Have you even looked at your new privileges? I bet you can just walk through doorways even I can't hack. You can't expect power to fall in your lap, darling. You have to take it."

I stare hard at him, but before my Lens can go back to sleep I whisper, "Justin Wyndham. Location." To my surprise, rather than returning a headline denying access, a palace map overlays my vision and a blinking red dot informs me that His Highness is strolling in the *Cour de Marbre.*

"Oh," I say, the surprise catching me too off-guard to formulate an appropriate response. "Well."

"You're owed far more than he's giving you," Lord Aaron says. "Take it."

SIX

AFTER ASKING SABER to stay out of sight—and getting a glower in return—I slip into the courtyard, where I'm almost bowled over by a wall of noise. I should have known the King would be speaking to the press. He has to do that, sometimes, especially on Wednesdays. I suppose I ought to, as well.

Maybe.

Lord Aaron is right—I have no idea how to be Queen, and leveraging queenly power in my favor seems the wisest course. I've got to be a quick study.

I suck in a breath and touch the hard busk at the front of my corset before striding across the marble squares of the courtyard toward my new husband. I approach Justin from behind and take perverse pleasure in the small start of surprise he gives when I slip my arm onto his.

"Ah," he says, covering beautifully. "My lovely bride. Ladies, gentlemen, I think this is my sign to bid you *adieu*." A few of the reporters groan and others continue shouting questions, but His Highness waves and bows deeply—I drop naturally into a curtsy at his side—and we slowly saunter back toward the palace.

"Thank you for that," he says, his voice a little hoarse. He snaps at a liveried young man in the corner, summoning him to his side. "They're relentless today. Word's out about the attempted *coup*, and though the press has all the business acumen of a *croque-monsieur*, even they can understand how the reactivation of the Queen's shares shifted the outcome. The *recent* reactivation, of course, being their angle. Refreshment," he orders, and his voice isn't at all loud, but commanding. The young man rushes off, making little bowing motions as he hurries away.

My husband walks with purpose. Not that we're rushing— he's the epitome of regal procession, and even with my training by Giovanni, his innate presence eclipses mine. Makes me feel like the commoner I was born. He's the only one who can. Not even Lady Cyn can pierce the armor my posture and poise give me. This, *this* is what Lord Aaron means. The King wears his power like a heavy fur cloak. Sometimes, along with an actual fur cloak.

I covet that power, only realizing it at this moment. A Queen with power wouldn't be backed into a corner in her own bedchamber. A Queen with power wouldn't find her heart racing at the thought of speaking to her joint ruler. A Queen with power wouldn't glance down every hallway in fear of what she might find.

And a Queen with power might—just might—find a way to escape in one piece.

I bite my tongue, using the jolt of pain to straighten my spine and gather my courage. "I sought you out for a reason, my lord."

"I expected nothing less," he replies dryly.

"I want my jewels."

"Surely you didn't leave them in your parents' household?"

I glower at him. "The *crown* jewels. I should be wearing them."

The King regards me coolly, and just as I feel like quaking under his scrutiny, the young man returns, bringing us both a glass of . . . something. I don't even care what it is—I care that it's in a shining gold goblet, a symbol of power and respect that I get to share in. The King takes his without so much as glancing at the man, much less offering his thanks. As much as it grates on my sense of good manners, I follow suit.

"What are you about, Danica?" the King asks once we're moving again.

"My rights," I say, trying to remember all of Lord Aaron's arguments. "I'm the Queen now, and no one looking over a crowded room would be able to tell. That's unacceptable."

"You think a few jewels will change that? Or did you want to wear the coronation crown every day? Perhaps carry around the ruby scepter?"

"The jewels will be a start," I say, ignoring his jab. "I also want access to the Queen's gowns and *accoutrements.*"

He stops sharply at that. "You want to wear my dead mother's clothing?"

"I want access to the Queen's wardrobe." I don't let any flicker of emotion cross my face. "You yourself have complained about my gowns on several occasions. Your mother's blue gown from her twentieth-anniversary ball—that one is legendary. And the silver embroidered one your grandmother is known for having worn to the kingdom's bicentennial gala. I need to be seen in such things."

"Those gowns belong to my family," he says through clenched teeth.

"I'm your family now."

For once, I've left the King speechless, and I relish the victory. I turn and begin walking—in that same processional style Justin has been using—and this time it's he who has to catch up.

"Why are you harping about this now? We've been married for almost a week already."

"We had other concerns—like keeping you on the throne. That done, it's time to move forward."

He drops his voice to a low hiss. "I'm still dealing with the PR fallout of an attempted *coup,* while every scandal feed in the country runs stories about corruption and child brides, and you're seriously lobbying for fancy clothing and jewelry?"

"You wanted a wife, you wanted a Queen, you got one. But I'm afraid, my lord, that the drawback is that now you have a wife and a Queen."

"Inconveniences I apparently failed to foresee," he grumbles.

"It'll be far more difficult for you to continually deny me my rightful place than to simply get your toad Mateus to draw up a comprehensive list of Queenly privileges that I can peruse at my leisure." I pause and then charge ahead with the one thing I *really* want. "And do be sure to put a private office on that list."

"*Pardonnez?*" the King retorts, actually raising his voice this time and drawing the attention of a handful of tourists and courtiers.

"As of"—I pause and make a show of counting on my fingers—

"four days ago, I'm a voting shareholder. So I'd like to know where my private, unmonitored office space is. I presume I have one, as it is a guarantee to every voting shareholder." In the wake of my mother's death, His Majesty revoked the unmonitored privacy once afforded to select courtiers' offices within the residential wings of the palace—claiming it was for everyone's safety—but there are numerous alternatives.

He leans nonchalantly on his walking stick. "I'm not convinced you do."

"Surely your mother had an unmonitored office," I say dryly.

"I'm quite certain my parents *shared* the office that is currently mine," he says softly; even without an audience, he seems ever at pains to make me look petty. I struggle to say something intelligent before His Highness, but he beats me to it. "Perhaps that's not a long-term solution that will work for us."

He holds out his empty glass, not even glancing in its direction before releasing it, simply assuming there will be someone waiting to catch it—I don't hear a clang, so apparently he was right.

"But, my love, I'm afraid I've nothing else to offer at the moment." A smile hovers at the corner of his mouth. "A recent change of policy has created something of a shortage in suitable workspace."

Damn. "You're giving me free run of your office, then?" I hedge.

"Anytime you need to discuss sensitive voting issues *with me*, you may intrude upon my privacy. But only then," he adds in a sharp voice. "I'll work on assigning you an unmonitored space of your own. Perhaps as a birthday present?"

I stare at him silently, knowing he truly could grant me unmonitored space in a moment. "I'll look forward to unwrapping it," I say, my voice very calm, almost friendly.

"Very good," he says, leaning over and kissing my hand as though he weren't a completely pompous ass. "Now," he says, straightening, "shall we see to your fripperies?"

LORD AARON WAS absolutely right—the monarchy owns millions upon millions of euros' worth of jewels, some historic, some more recently acquired. But when the King escorts me to the vaults in the basement of the palace, past flesh-and-blood security guards in ballistic vests and even a brief peek at an armory stocked with guns in dizzying array, I walk into a living lesson on the words *worthy of a Queen*. I really shouldn't be so surprised. If there's one thing I've discovered about the Palace of Versailles in the last six months, it's that all the important stuff is in the basement.

"It's not too much?" I ask skeptically as I study my appearance in the mirror. I've never worn such large jewels and find it difficult to be certain of the line between tastefully extravagant and gaudy, so I lean on Lady Mei to help me make them work.

She is, of course, tickled at the honor.

"It's *almost* too much," Lady Mei says, her eyes sparkling in the mirror from just behind my shoulder. "That's what *perfect* means. Now, spin."

With a laugh, I rise from my dressing table stool and make a face at Lady Mei before turning about. I'm in one of my newest gowns, accessorized with a capelet from the Queen's wardrobe. It's cloth of gold—literally, linen interwoven with precious metal. I'd read of such things, but never truly understood. I'm not sure it would be *possible* to understand without actually seeing it, feeling it, wearing it. And it's as heavy as one might imagine.

My hair is piled atop my head and striped with ropes of pearls dotted with rubies as big as my thumb. A necklace and matching earrings, inset with rubies and diamonds, complement my gown, and for once I don't resent the shimmering, eight-carat diamond wedding ring that has graced the left hand of every Queen of Sonoman-Versailles for three generations.

Four, now.

"Ugh," Lady Mei says, but when I turn to her, she's leaning close to study her own reflection.

"What?"

"I look downright plain compared to you. I decided not to wear my ruby necklace, and now I have regrets." She straightens and narrows her eyes at the mirror, as though it were purposely diminishing her. "I'm going to go fix that." Without another word, she blows me a kiss, flutters her fingers in a wave, and makes her exit.

Saber walks in grumbling, messing with the cravat he still hasn't quite learned how to tie correctly.

"Do you surrender?" I ask with one eyebrow raised.

"Please?" he says. Normally he suffers through having a bot tie it, but on Wednesdays, he's stuck with me. I can't pull off a Mathematical, but I do a decent Napoléon. At the very least, I'm better at it than him.

"Come here," I say, with mock-fussiness. He stands in front of me, his hands resting at my waist, and gazes at me with such heat my fingers tremble as I wrap the silk about his neck. "Stop that."

"Stop what?"

"Looking at me like that."

"I don't know any other way."

I can't stop the exceptionally sappy smile his words provoke. I must blush as well, because Saber chuckles as I finish his knot.

"Dressing this way is starting to feel normal, God forbid."

"You look quite dapper," I quip, in a snooty voice. "And me?" I spin, letting the heavy skirts of my dress flare and tossing out my arms with a flourish.

But he doesn't reply.

"Saber?" I ask, nerves shooting through me when he remains silent.

I glance over my shoulder in panic, but his eyes are soft. Almost sad. He steps closer and touches the underside of my chin with one finger. "You look like a Queen."

SEVEN

I'M BRILLIANT AS the sun walking into the Hall of Mirrors, on the King's arm. Privileges come with duties attached, and I can play the role as well as any actor, complete with elaborate, expensive costume.

Lady Mei's taste must be on; all the furtive glances I get reflect approval.

I'm expected to open the dancing with His Majesty—and I do so with a patently false beaming smile—but he forces me through only a single set. When I leave his side I seek out Saber, who's near the ladies' retiring rooms, subtly palming money and passing around containers of Glitter.

Seeing him at work sours my mood and I realize I've been preening. I remind myself that I need to play the game without acquiring a taste for it—but also that playing the game means keeping a close eye on the King. A glance is all it takes to confirm what I could have guessed. The moment my back was turned, he sought out the company of Lady Cyn, whose appearance now—even in all her finery—pales in comparison to mine. Her family is wealthy, and I know the King bestows expensive gifts on her, but there's simply nothing and no one in the palace who can compete with four generations of opulence.

Lord Aaron was right—I have to claim my place or she'll take it from me.

I'm trying to figure out what to do next when I realize I already hold the best weapon for my opening *salvo*. I stop Mademoiselle Janelle Olivier, one of my *lever* staff, with a soft hand on her shoulder as she's leaving with a handful of canisters to disperse.

"Janelle, if you could mention it to the others," I say under my breath. "No more Glitter for Lady Cyn. Nor," I add, making my soft voice sharp, "for anyone caught sharing with her. Understood?" I meet her eyes in a hard stare.

The lady gasps as though that were the harshest punishment I could possibly mete out. Forget Lord Aaron's lecture on power; this is personal. This is for years of trapping me in corners or stepping on my train to make me stumble. I give Janelle a haughty, Queenly look, and she gulps and says, "I'll spread the word, Your Majesty."

I watch her scurry from group to group and smile as she gives wide berth to some of the circles gathered at the edge of the dance floor. Even though the message is meant to eventually get to Lady Cyn, Janelle would be foolish to go right up to Cyn's people and lay down the threat. Word will travel quickly enough, with no immediate repercussions for any given messenger. Lady Cyn will know only that the original edict came from me.

Moreover, Janelle has just given me a visual update on the state of the court—and how divided it is. There are groups of *hers,* and groups of *mine*. If I had more social sway, Janelle wouldn't bother to so assiduously avoid Cyn's groups. I may be the Queen, but so far it's my people who stand in fear of her people.

I glance over at Lord Aaron, but he's not watching me. I hate how often he's right, though it makes me grateful that he's in my camp. I'm fighting battles on three fronts, not two, and I almost failed to notice. Justin and Reginald may be my Scylla and Charybdis, but the war for influence over the court is also a war I have to win. And I can, if I'm smart. And ruthless.

So what's a Queen to do if she wants to win a war? Why, she must gather her generals, of course.

"I WANT A private dinner," I announce to the King, barging into his office and slamming the door behind me.

"With me? I'm flattered," he says without even glancing up from his tablet.

"Hardly. Is this room *ever* monitored?"

"Never. M.A.R.I.E. hears me, but never records. Like in all private offices."

I ignore that jab. "Then you listen to me. I am the Queen and I deserve to have my own damned rooms unmonitored when I want to have an actual conversation with a handful of friends." By the end of my little speech I'm leaning over with both hands slapped flat on the desk, my face mere inches from his.

He clears his throat and rolls his chair backward to create space between us. "Do I have to attend?"

"I said friends."

His jaw tightens, but that's all the reaction he gives me. "Who?" he finally asks.

"Lord Aaron, Lady Mei Zhào"—I hesitate—"and Sir Spencer Harrisford."

"Not a chance."

"Afraid we'll stage another *coup*?"

He clamps his mouth shut, glaring daggers at me.

"Sir Spencer didn't want it. You ought to know that. He didn't want a single thing that was done to him when he came here two years ago."

"Right," the King drawls.

"Just because *you'd* do anything to keep your throne, you imagine everyone must covet it."

"Most people do," he says casually, studying his fingernails.

I slide a hip onto the royal desk and pull myself up to sit atop a stack of papers, never mind the King's dismayed looks. "Sir Spencer is a rather unfortunate blend of you and me. On the one hand, forced into a marriage he didn't want, used as a puppet by a grasping schemer." I point to myself. "All this made easier by the fact that he was still quite shocked by the sudden death of both his parents." I tilt my wrist, pointing at the King. "I understand he was quite . . . biddable in his grief."

It's a gamble. Justin's parents are not only his Achilles' heel, but also a potential trigger for his volatile temper. I don't know which way the dice will fall tonight. When I told Lord Aaron I'd speak to the King on Sir Spencer's behalf, I'm not certain this is what he intended. Nonetheless, empathy can be a sharper weapon than hate and I'm not picky about what goes into my arsenal.

"What the hell does this have to do with your dinner party?" the King bursts out in exasperation.

Diversionary tactics it is. "I want a dining room and I want it unmonitored! I'd like to assure my guests that for one evening they needn't worry about politics and scrutiny and you—yes, *you*—and I can't do that if I know M.A.R.I.E. is taking notes."

He lets out a low growl and tugs at his cravat, unraveling the knot. He's going to have to get a dressing-bot in here before he can be seen in public again, and I love that I've riled him.

"For someone who fought every attempt to make her Queen, your defeated sulking was incredibly short-lived," he says, his voice edged like broken glass. "Suddenly it's jewels, gowns, special security privileges that have *conspiracy* scribbled all over them— you've done nothing but make demands for *days*!"

"You made the bargain, Justin. You kept your throne by giving the other one to me. I kept my end of the deal." The lie slides off my tongue like butter. "Now is hardly the time to complain about the price."

"*I was coerced!*" he yells, slamming one hand against the top of his desk. "And so were you, but only one of us seems to regret it." He sniffs and straightens, getting ahold of his temper. "Besides, believe it or not, I prefer to keep my word, once given. I also prefer to deal with people who associate with me *willingly*. You'll recall I offered you a way out."

"I also recall that you rescinded it by the time I said yes." He's being surprisingly candid, all things considered. Finding myself unaccosted in spite of being alone with the King makes me bold. "After that, can you really blame my mother for any of this?"

Justin pauses, considering. He considers for rather a long time. In a gesture that sets the hair at the back of my neck on end, he rises, rolls his shoulders back, and shrugs out of his formal evening jacket, laying it over the arm of his chair. He steps around the desk to face me, the picture of easy sexuality in his linen shirt and deep maroon waistcoat, his dark brown curls soft and shiny at his shoulders.

Perhaps I'm to be accosted after all? I take comfort in the fact that I have a clear path to the door.

"Fine," he says silkily. "Have your dinner. And the next night, you have dinner with me. Alone."

"Why?" I blurt.

He raises one hand and runs his knuckles down the side of my face. I don't let myself flinch. "Because I want to know you better. You *are* my wife, after all. Maybe we don't have to hate each other so much."

"You're not going to wrap your hands around my throat and demand it?" I say flatly. "Back me into a corner and declare you can take me against my will anytime you desire?"

"I told you from the beginning: if you wouldn't fight me so hard, I wouldn't have to guide you so roughly." He looks quite amused with himself.

I hide my disgust at his predatory logic. "Deal."

He seems surprised that I've acceded so easily. Should I have negotiated harder?

No, that sort of thinking is what led me to turn him down when he first offered to send me, along with Saber and my father both, away from all this. I won't be stupid twice. If you're getting what you want, and believe you can spare the cost, say yes.

"How will I know?"

"Know?"

"That the room is unmonitored. That you've kept your word. And don't you dare tell me I'll have to trust you. We both know I don't, and that I have good reason."

The look he gives me is . . . inscrutable. When he speaks, it's not to me, but to the mechanical mind that maintains the palace and the lifestyle of its inhabitants.

"M.A.R.I.E., access profile, Danica Wyndham, executive override four seven alpha tango. Display surface facility monitoring isometrics."

I don't jump when my Lens activates without my request, but it's a close thing. The palace's familiar floor plan is superimposed on my vision, as if I'd just asked for someone's location.

Justin continues. "Set facility monitoring privileges to level seven, read-only."

The palace map, ordinarily outlined in white, takes on a green cast—except for a handful of rooms I recognize as nonresidential workspace, mostly belonging to executive officers. These are outlined in red.

"What you're seeing is monitoring status: green is on, red is off. Simple. *Quis custodiet ipsos custodes?* Now you do."

I stare blankly.

"*Juvenal?* No? Never mind. The point is, you have your assurances. It will display on a tablet as easily as your Lens via M.A.R.I.E.'s app. Show your guests. Have your dinner. Remember my price."

He said "read-only." So I'll have no way to adjust the monitoring—only to check it. But just knowing it's there, having access to the data, is an important step toward manipulating it. A flurry of delight swirls in my chest for an instant, but I'm suddenly beset by the worry that I'm being conned.

That skepticism must show on my face, because Justin holds out his hands in protest. "You sat right here and listened to me do it. Unless you think I was able to code that response between the time you made your request and now . . . ?"

I raise an eyebrow at him and he curses under his breath.

"You used to be so much easier to deal with."

"I used to be a lot stupider."

"I liked you stupider."

"I bet you did."

"Is there no winning with you? Do you want me to go back to denying you every pleasure, every freedom?" He presses close, invading my personal space, his chest pressed hard against mine, his face a breath away. "I told you I could make your life a living hell and I *haven't*. Don't I get any credit for that?"

I turn my head so he's breathing onto my neck instead of my cheek. "Credit for decent human behavior? What sort of trick pony do you think you are?"

"The facility monitor program works," he says, leaving me and pulling his jacket back on. "Trust me. Root around in it on your own; get your friend Lord Aaron to look at it; go to the head of the godforsaken security department, for all I care. But that's the last time you get to question my work without consequences. And you won't like those consequences."

He strides toward the door, pauses halfway there.

In a breathy whisper he adds, "Or maybe you will."

EIGHT

I SEND GUARDS for Sir Spencer. Overkill, perhaps, but it's not beyond the realm of possibility that my lord husband might attempt to assassinate his political rival. I don't flatter myself that I could stop him if that were truly his aim, but I would prefer it not be while said rival is *en route* to my party.

Still, I worry until the doors open to reveal the liveried guards with Sir Spencer a few paces in front of them, looking pale and wan, but unharmed.

"Your Majesty," he says, bowing low, not meeting my eyes.

"Sir Spencer." I gesture to a spot at the cozy table, elegantly set but only just big enough for four. He edges past me awkwardly, a stranger in a strange space. I've been hearing about Sir Spencer for ages, watched him carefully at assemblies and *soirées,* but we've spoken scarcely a dozen words to each other in all that time. How can someone I scarcely know feel oddly like a brother?

Lady Mei pops in moments later with her usual bubbly chatter. She's not Molli—she will never be Molli—but her company has its own appeal. I abandon my Queenly *façade* and pull her close for a hug. A little *Ooh!* escapes her mouth as I apparently shock her into both silence and stillness. But in a moment she softens and squeezes me back. It makes me feel momentarily human.

Lord Aaron slips in as I'm frantically blinking away a mist of tears. I smile and kiss his cheeks, then point him to the table while I seal the doors.

Just the four of us. No Saber tonight. I can't plot against Reginald and allow Saber to know any details. He didn't like being excluded, but in the end there simply wasn't anything he could do about it.

"Please help yourself," I say, gesturing to the small feast laid out on the *buffet*. I retrieve my tablet and open it to the facility monitoring schematic.

The Queen's Rooms are outlined in red.

I chafe at the few minutes that pass as everyone fills plates, wishing I'd thought to have them arrive a few minutes early. I was promised one hour of privacy, and everything that needs saying must be said during that time.

"All right," I say the instant the four of us are back in our seats. I'll let them eat while I talk; nerves have killed my appetite. I reach into my *pannier* pocket and pull out three contact holders and lay them on the table. "Lenses out."

Sir Spencer and Lord Aaron don't hesitate, but Lady Mei looks at me strangely.

"Please?" I add, but my tone is fairly terse.

She studies me for several more seconds, and I hope she's not going to continue to be reluctant, but finally she takes one of the holders and removes her Lens.

"I have just under an hour during which M.A.R.I.E. is not monitoring this room, and we're about to commence a battle on multiple fronts. By the time we leave, I need a plan. So I don't have time to be gracious and kind—I barely have time to be civil. Lady Mei," I say, turning to her, "you're here because I need your help. But you're late to the party, so to speak, because you can't keep your mouth shut."

That very mouth falls open in shock for several seconds before Lady Mei regains her composure and closes it with a sharp snap.

"You know it's true," I add with an eyebrow raised. She answers only with a deep flush of her cheeks. "But I think I can induce you to do so. I'm going to tell you three things that no one outside this room knows, and if a single one of them gets out—the barest hint that even sounds like any of these things—believe that I will use my new position to ruin you."

Her eyes are so wide I'm a little afraid she's going into shock. "You're blackmailing me into being your *confidante*?"

"Yes," I say without shame.

"What about them?" she asks, flinging her arms out at Lord Aaron and Sir Spencer.

"They've proven themselves already."

Lord Aaron smacks Sir Spencer's back when he chokes.

But tonight isn't about their secrets; it's about mine. "We're about to play a high-stakes version of the age-old game Two Truths and a Lie. One: six months ago, Lord Aaron and I broke into your house and stole your family's Madame de Pompadour sapphires. We put them back," I add at her audible gasp. "Two: the King and I despise each other, as, against my will, my mother blackmailed him into marrying me for the support of my father's shares in Monday's attempted *coup*. And three: Lady Cyn found out she was carrying the King's child the day before our wedding and begged him to call it off. She's so angry at me because the King—obviously—refused."

Lady Mei's eyes are so wide I briefly wonder if they could actually fall out of their sockets. I've thrown her into the middle of our pool of deception and the bottom is very, very deep. She's stopped eating, perhaps has gone a little pale, but seems otherwise hale. Which is excellent, as I don't have time to coddle her.

"The test has begun. Two of the things I just told you are absolutely true. One of them is utterly false. All of them are the best possible gossip. The two truths could possibly get out on their own—unlikely, but possible. But you let the wrong one slip, and I'll know it was you," I say quietly.

"You don't trust me," Lady Mei says.

"Would you in my place?" When she says nothing I add, more gently, "I *want* to trust you. That's the only reason you're here." I take a deep breath. "And I am going to trust you—all of you— with one very, very big secret, starting this very night. This," I continue, laying a canister of Glitter in the middle of the table, "is why you're here tonight."

"Your makeup?" Lady Mei asks, clearly not following. I sympathize; I've practically whiplashed her with information tonight.

"Exactly. This is what I was asked to sell, by a man who claimed he could give me a new life and identity outside Versailles. Unfortunately, I later discovered that it's laced with an addictive recreational drug so new that no one has even heard of it. And instead of helping me flee before the wedding, he left me here and insisted I continue to sell his product."

Neither complete lie nor truth—I've been keeping it in reserve, my grand alibi. *I didn't know the makeup was drugged! I'm as much a victim as anyone!* After all, as far as anyone—including Lord Aaron—knows, I wear it too.

"You knew all this?" Lady Mei asks, her eyes darting to Lord Aaron and Sir Spencer for the barest moment before returning to the sparkling Glitter in the middle of the table.

I watch the men carefully. Lord Aaron caught on to Glitter's nature more or less independently, and used it to his advantage. He has to know I was aware of that nature early on, since I deliberately withheld it from him, but it's not something we've discussed in detail. I asked him not to ask, and he didn't; I suppose true friends never do. But Sir Spencer? I've made a lot of assumptions about how much he knows—how much Lord Aaron has been confiding in him. Fortunately, my suppositions are confirmed when the two exchange a glance and then both nod.

"But how ... who did ... ?" I see the moment it registers on Lady Mei's face. "Molli," she says softly. "You told Molli and not me."

I refuse to look away from her accusation.

Lady Mei laughs weakly. "I do have a weakness for gossip," she murmurs into her glass before taking a large swallow.

"Not anymore, I hope."

"I don't have much of a choice."

"No, but I'd like to believe that now that you know how serious this is, you'd have chosen to join us anyway."

She gives me a coy, one-shouldered shrug, but I can see her eyes sparkling.

Good.

"Now, my three enemies: the King, Lady Cyn, and Reginald."

"Reginald?" Lady Mei asks.

I hesitate. But I need another friend. Another young lady of the court. "Reginald is the man who agreed to give me a new identity and a new life. He's not from Versailles. He's a Parisian, a crime boss of some sort. I should have realized he would deal badly with me, but I was desperate."

"Desperate . . . to not be the Queen of Versailles." There is no criticism in Lady Mei's question—only a deep confusion. She eyes Lord Aaron. "Am I the only conspirator among us who actually likes it here? Oh, don't give me that look," she chides as his carefully plucked eyebrows creep toward his hairline. "I'm carefree, not stupid, and I love my friends, though you brood and conspire to abandon me. And sell me tainted *maquillage*," she adds, turning back to me. "Though it is very fine makeup, and surely no worse than sneaking a cigarette *avec mes amies*. Don't let it trouble you."

It's hard not to goggle at how smoothly Lady Mei trivializes my betrayal. I'd like to believe that my story was simply that persuasive. I can't help but suspect it's actually her addiction to Glitter at work. Either way—I'm on a schedule.

"I'm more troubled that he's trapped me," I say, tapping a finger on the Glitter canister still sitting in the center of the table. "If I stop selling Glitter, he'll rat us all out to INTERPOL. It could potentially trigger the collapse of the entire kingdom. But with your help, I think we can arrange Reginald's downfall, without destroying Versailles. Lord Aaron, I need a tracking device, and I'm too closely watched to do it myself."

"One M.A.R.I.E. can't detect?" he asks, and I hear wariness in his voice.

"Easier—it just needs to be small enough to avoid human notice."

Lord Aaron grins. "Hardly worthy of my skills."

"The smaller, the better."

"Consider it done. Why?"

I spread my hands on the tabletop. "At the moment, I have no advantage over Reginald whatsoever. If I can ferret out where the Glitter is coming from, perhaps I can cut Reginald out of the equation." It's a delicate claim—I can't forget that I'm technically talking to addicts who might resist a plan to destroy Glitter at the source.

"Your . . . secretary, he doesn't know where it comes from?" Lord Aaron asks.

I shake my head emphatically. "He needs to be involved as little as possible. I fear that even an errant whisper of our doings could endanger his life. And no, I will not share that secret tonight," I say, raising a finger and pointing at Lady Mei, whose mouth is already open and forming the question. *Or ever,* I add to myself.

Lord Aaron understands and nods grimly. Ever the activist; Saber's slavery must vex him no end, and I love him for that.

"A GPS tracker, then?" Lord Aaron asks, breaking the awkward silence.

"Indeed," I reply, returning to the business at hand. I must get better at hiding my weakness. "Within the week, if you could."

Lord Aaron considers, and then nods.

I touch my napkin to my lips. "That's step one with Reginald. On to Lady Cyn. She has no idea how great a threat she actually is to my endeavors, but her inadvertent interference is a complication that must be done away with. This is where you come in, Lady Mei. For the next week or so, you're proving yourself. Proving your ability to keep a secret. But while you're at it, I want intel on Lady Cyn. I can access her public schedule, but I want to know when and where she meets with the King."

Lady Mei blushes and averts her gaze, but I don't stop.

"You must be subtle." I lean forward. "I want to know who her friends are these days, and I need to know their every indiscretion."

Lady Mei's eyes widen and she looks back and forth between Lord Aaron and Sir Spencer, universally known as two of the friendliest gentlemen at court, clearly expecting some protest at my viciousness.

At their silence, she turns wide eyes back to me. "I feel as though I hardly know you," she says with wonder.

I lay a hand on her knee and try for a comforting smile. "I picked you because I adore you," I say gently. "Don't forget that. I'm testing you, it's true, but I wouldn't bother if you hadn't been my loyal friend for years. I need you. I need another lady in my corner, and you're incredibly resourceful."

The smile Lady Mei sends back is tight, but genuine.

"And the King?" Lord Aaron says, bringing us back on track.

I suck in a breath and hold it. "I'm still working on that," I say reluctantly, hating that I have nothing to use against him. Yet. "I fear him. Now that the confidence vote is passed, he seems inclined to grant me favors, but only when cajoled and always accompanied with unseemly threats. Sir Spencer, I've spoken to His Majesty on your behalf—let him know that you never wanted his throne. Perhaps you can eventually find your way back into his good graces. But he's understandably angry with your father-in-law, and he's looking to punish someone. At the moment, I simply ask you to keep your eyes and ears open."

"I'm not in my father-in-law's good graces at the moment either," Sir Spencer says. "But I'll do what I can."

"I appreciate it. If you, any of you, need to communicate something with me that needs to stay out of M.A.R.I.E.'s monitoring queue, com me with a question about the gardens. We can arrange a meeting. I'm now privy to which rooms in the palace are or are not being monitored at any given moment, so—" I pause when a gasp escapes from Lady Mei's mouth.

We all turn to her, and she presses her linen napkin to her lips. "Do excuse me," she says. "Continue."

I hide a grin—she's grown accustomed to the water in this cesspool rather quickly, I think.

"I'll ask the question our lovely friend doesn't seem to be able to find words for," Lord Aaron says coolly. "How in the world did you gain access to such information?"

"A deal with the devil, Lord Aaron. The way I acquire most

things these days." He rolls his eyes and I continue. "So with careful planning we should be able to avoid most eavesdropping."

Silent nods all around—my coconspirators are turning pensive—time to seal the pact.

I remove three canisters from my *panniers.* "The three of you know what this is now. I cannot proceed further without giving you the choice that has been robbed from everyone else." I swallow hard, guilt tightening my throat. "You are my inner circle—you may have as much or as little Glitter as you choose, *gratis.* I give you that choice in reparation for the damage I've already done to you. All three of you. I strongly recommend you cut down, beginning now, but any smoker can tell you that cold turkey is a bitch."

The silence is heavy around the table. But three hands reach forward, and I can only hope that sound minds made that decision, not chemical-driven need.

NINE

ONCE THE GREEN outline returns to my rooms on the monitoring display, I bring out the dessert and liqueurs. We eat and drink for another half hour to keep up appearances, but it's clear that no one's feeling especially jovial. Lady Mei, for certain, will need a few days to process the situation into which she's been inducted. But the mood is basically cheerful when we part ways at the doorway of the temporary dining room.

"Did you have fun?" Saber asks when I walk into my bedroom, already pulling off my long gloves.

"Fun? Hardly."

"Sorry to have missed it," he says softly, though his arms are crossed over his chest and I know he resents being left out. Understands, but resents. I lay my head against his cheek and feel his warm skin to assure myself that he's alive. The other night I realized my fingers were pressed to his wrist, checking for a heartbeat. Reginald's betrayal boils my blood, but part of me can't help but be grateful. I thought I could leave Saber behind and look back on him fondly from my new life. I understand now that I'd have slowly withered on the inside without him; knowing he was alive, and the situation I'd left him in.

"If you don't know anything, I won't have to ask you to lie," I whisper into his ear.

Saber pulls back and looks at me, and I can read the questions in his eyes, but I can't answer them. Not right now. He sighs and flops backward onto the huge bed. "You make my life complicated."

"But exciting, right?"

He closes his eyes and shakes his head, but when he opens them again, his expression is serious. "Excitement isn't something my life has ever lacked."

My smile wilts.

"Oh, don't," Saber says. "I didn't mean to spoil the mood."

I climb up onto the bed beside him, and my skirts pouf into a taffeta arc. "I was trying to be sensitive by not having you there."

Saber reaches under the edge of my skirts and grabs one of my ankles. "Because you were talking about Glitter, or because you were talking about me?"

I pause. I'd thought it was obvious. He and I talk about Glitter all the time. Perhaps it's more accurate to say he and I *fight* about Glitter all the time. "You. Sort of. Mostly Reginald," I tack on. As though that makes it better.

Saber doesn't look at me. He focuses on the ribbons of my dance slippers instead—picking at the knot and then unwinding the ribbons from around my ankle. "It wouldn't be hard for me to die, you know."

"What?" I feel the blood drain from my face and I don't understand his macabre subject change.

"You think it's so awful being a slave, but it wouldn't be hard for me to just die. Forget traditional suicide—I could catch a bus out of town on the last day of my countdown and be dead before I got to Dijon."

I clutch his hand at that, but my throat is too tight to make words.

"All I'm saying is that you seem to think that my life is worse than death, but all signs point to me preferring to live. Maybe you should take that into consideration."

I duck my head, tears swimming in my eyes. "How do you do it?" I whisper, my voice quavering. "I think of Reginald . . . of him *owning* you, and it hurts." I touch my fingers to my sternum, where even now, my chest aches.

Saber is calm, cool, as he runs his hands up my calves, past my knees, to where my silk garters are tied. "I learned a secret a long time ago. When I was maybe ten." He looks up and meets my eyes. "I'm never going to be free in my body."

I open my mouth, but he talks over me.

"*Never.* The tech is too good." He leans forward, those green eyes fierce and fiery. "But I'm free here." He points at his temple. "As long as I hate every wrong thing he makes me do—as long as I refuse to surrender the morals and standards my parents gave me—I'm still my own man." He shrugs and looks away, as though embarrassed to have revealed so much. "That's why I fight you so hard. I can't accept what you do. I can't justify it. If I do, I'm letting go of the only freedom I can still call mine."

Guilt is a blanket smothering me and I gasp for air.

"You want to rescue me?" Saber asks.

I nod.

"Then stop selling Glitter," he whispers.

My mouth drops and I don't have any idea what I would have said next, because a pounding on the door makes me jump and let out a quiet shriek. Recovering, I let loose a string of French curses under my breath that makes Saber snort. Since I didn't wear it to my dinner, I still don't have my Lens in, so I have to decide whether to answer the door without being able to silently check with M.A.R.I.E. who's on the other side. While I'm deciding, a second rap sounds, sharper than the first, and the unmistakable voice of everyone's favorite monarch bellows out, "Wife?"

"How did this become my life?" I groan quietly.

"Should *I* answer it?" Saber asks with a mischievous grin.

"I'll do it. I'm trying to get on his not-quite-as-bad side."

"Does he have one of those?"

"I'm doing my best to find out." I scoot awkwardly off the bed and pad across the room. I open the door and stand there with an expression of extreme tolerance generally reserved for tantrum-throwing toddlers. "Yes, my lord?"

"Duke and Duchess Sells are hosting an informal *soirée*."

"*Soirée?* It's almost midnight!"

The King continues as though I'd said nothing. "Much of the high nobility will be in attendance. The Queen should be as well."

"And you had no notice of this?" I ask, not bothering to hide my skepticism.

"I did. But I forgot I had a wife. A Queen. You're a bit new; I think it's understandable. It's important—come on." He at least does me the courtesy of offering his arm, not grabbing me and dragging me off. I wonder if I can consider that a victory.

"I—" I stop and heave a sigh. I raise the edge of my skirts to show one foot bare, the other clad only in its stocking.

His Highness' gaze instantly slides over to Saber, standing straight and tall, peering almost sleepily right back at the King. "Put them back on," he says after a pause. "I'll wait."

Turning, I call over my shoulder, "Close the door. I'll be out in a few minutes."

"You're my *wife*," he says, with a definite growl in the last word. "I hardly think a flash of your ankles is going to shock me."

"It might," I answer, retrieving my shoes and one stocking from atop the bedspread. "You've never seen them before."

He taps his finger against his lips and considers that. "I feel certain they must have been on display at your first *lever*, and yet it's not your *ankles* I recall you flashing."

I grind my teeth, wishing I were close enough to slap him, and have to concentrate on the laces of my shoe to keep from retorting.

"Are you ready now?" he asks, oh-so-innocently, when I flip my skirt back down over all but the very tips of my slippers a few seconds later. "You should put on some of those jewels you were so desperate to claim."

"I thought you said it was informal."

"I should have said *impromptu*. You'll learn in time: nothing is actually informal when you're royalty."

"Fine." I walk over to my vanity table and open the wooden box that holds the jewels I selected for earlier today, and pop in my Lens for good measure. Once I'm sparkling with diamonds and emeralds, I turn and wordlessly gesture at my person for my husband's approval. Chafes, that.

"You'll do," he says gruffly, and holds out an arm.

But—in a fit of *pique*, heedless of my own warnings—instead of walking to the King, I approach Saber, who bows slightly and offers an arm of his own.

"Your secretary need not attend," the King snaps.

"No? But he's ever so useful," I purr, petting his bicep.

"Not this time." The King's voice is a deep, throaty sound that cuts like a blade.

I turn and simply glare.

"I don't think you understand, *Your Highness,*" he says witheringly. "We're going to the home of a member of the highest nobility. I suspect this gathering will be held in the duke's private, unmonitored office. You and I should be there, and *no one else.*"

My breath catches and my heart rate surely doubles. This is no party; I'm being brought in on a secret meeting of the King and his allies. Because I'm the Queen.

"Shall we?" the King asks, and when I lay my hand on his arm he sweeps me from the room, off to the den of some of the best-dressed lions in the world.

DUCHESS SELLS OPENS the door for us personally, and when I shake her hand I palm her a canister of Glitter, feeling even guiltier than before. She points us toward her husband's private office—unmonitored, according to the map I discreetly summon to my Lens. In direct contradiction of the King's recent pronouncement concerning residential offices. Laws don't matter when the monarch is your bosom bud, apparently.

I keep my face impassive and my hand clasped on Justin's arm as I take in the attendees. It appears most people are already here—presumably because we were a little late, seeing as how the King forgot he had a Queen. I'm surrounded by *la crème de la crème* of the Sonoman-Versailles court: the Dukes and Duchesses Sells, Florentine, Wakefield, and Darzi, along with the Marquis and Countess Voroman-Wills and the Marquis and Countess Garcia, and the Countesses Poe. No one here with less than a three percent stake in Sonoma Inc. Myself included.

After a few minutes of talking, drinking, and loading plates with decadent desserts, Duke Sells taps a spoon against his glass. He nods at his wife, who locks the door. Justin seats me prettily on one of the two chairs clearly situated to indicate the front of the room, then kisses my hand with a courtly flourish.

He doesn't sit.

"My lords, ladies, you all know why we're here," he says, addressing the small group. "How do we punish them?"

My heart thuds so hard in my chest I'm almost surprised no one else hears it. I feel ill.

And surprisingly envious. My own secret dinner pales by comparison.

"Tremain must be forced to sell his voting shares," Duchess Darzi says. "He can't be allowed to try again."

"We can look into that," His Highness says, nodding. He turns to murmur something to a youngish lady in the corner—the daughter of Marquis and Countess Voroman-Wills, I think. She's taking notes on an actual piece of paper. Sneaky.

"Is eviction off the table?" Countess Garcia asks.

"Of course," His Majesty says dryly. "It's difficult to torture a man *in absentia*. What else?"

Some make suggestions touching on inheritance and positions within the company. Others focus on social ostracism and general shunning. But their petty, almost trifling proposals don't satisfy His Majesty.

"What of the boy?" Duke Darzi asks.

My attention snaps into sharp focus. Sir Spencer. If Sir Spencer finds himself disgraced and miserable, Lord Aaron will no doubt spirit him away via his Foundation people. And himself as well. Then where will I be? I have to do something. But Sir Spencer is so inextricably linked with the sinking ship that is the Tremain family.

An idea stirs within me, and I wonder if I've just stumbled on a solution to everything. As the conversation buzzes around me, I examine it from all angles. Try to find the flaws.

"Husband," I say when the conversation has a momentary lapse. The King turns, giving me a sharp look of warning that only I see. I've never referred to him as such in public before. "What if we used Sir Spencer to humiliate the duke?"

The King studies me for a long moment, clearly not trusting me, wondering if it's he who's about to be humiliated. "How so?" he finally asks.

I force myself to think twice, speak once. This is the only chance I'm going to get. "Suppose you privately offer Sir Spencer a hasty divorce from Lady Julianna on the condition that he immediately begin flaunting the long-term affair he's been having under the duke's nose." I count off on my fingers: "Legally separate the master from his *protégé*, deprive him of control over the substantial voting stock Sir Spencer inherited from his parents, destroy the familial legacy the duke expected from his daughter, and make him look like an ignorant fool, all in one go."

The entire room is silent for so long I feel sweat start to break out at the small of my back, trickling down under my corset.

"This is brilliant," Countess Ardetta Poe says breathily. "Is it true?"

I don't dare twitch a single muscle in my face. "The affair? Indeed. The two are desperate to be together openly."

"But will the young upstart agree to it?" Duke Wakefield asks.

I smirk. "I feel entirely confident that he will. Puppet or not, he never wanted to play this role. I daresay he'll jump at an escape. Especially"—I pause before taking my biggest risk—"if it could spare him from some of the other consequences I'm certain he's expecting."

There's a bit of grumbling at that, but they're all so anxious to rain down embarrassment on the Tremains that they come to terms easily enough.

"Diabolical," Countess Maria Poe says to me with a saucy grin, saluting me with her glass. I incline my head in acknowledgment and force a calm smile. Is this how it begins? The heady satisfaction of pulling someone down?

"This," the King says, lifting the tips of my fingers near his lips, "is why I married her. As brilliant as she is beautiful, and as devious as both combined."

My stomach churns as I fix the smile on my face. I've just made my first big move on this chessboard of court politics.

TEN

THE BEST TECHNOLOGY is invisible. That's the first rule taught in Sonoman-Versailles' Assisted Coding for Semiautonomous Mechanical Systems, my favorite advanced programming class—back when I had time for such things. Flashy, cutting-edge tech is naturally impressive, but on the surface, the Palace of Versailles is a marvel of *eighteenth-century* aesthetics. From the very beginning, with King Kevin, the overarching question of the Palace of Versailles was, can the benefits of technology be realized without sacrificing *décor*?

The answer, developed with the help of Sonoma's frequent corporate partner, Amalgamated, was the "three Cs"—compression, communication, camouflage. Following the first C, some devices shrank until they were essentially invisible, like the Lens that can show me anything I might see on other screens. But compressing technology has physical limitations; for example, a Lens can't broadcast or receive sound. It's possible to supplement the Lens with transceivers—devices that serve both as speakers and microphones—but in Versailles, it's also common to just rely on the palace's existing audio systems. Or run a lip-reading app.

This is partly down to the limits of miniaturization. I visited

M.A.R.I.E.'s server bank once: rows upon rows of obsidian obelisks that function as the brains of the palace, kept cool and sterile in the basement levels. The Mainframe for Autonomous Robotic Intelligence *Enhancement* includes that *E* for a reason. Through the miracle of wireless communication—our second *C*—it makes our devices "smarter" than they could ever be on their own. Everything, from the bots that help me dress to the doors through which I walk, is monitored and adjusted by large, bulky pieces of tech, which just happen to be somewhere else.

Of course, the bots and keypads and tiny actuators that operate doors and windows *can't* be somewhere else—that would defeat the purpose. In comes the third *C*, camouflage: LED displays that *mascarade* as paintings and microphones concealed in *objets d'art* are essentially unnoticeable. Earrings and necklaces mask transceivers for use outside the palace; even personal tablets can be wrapped in cases giving them the appearance of leather-bound books.

"As a result of the three Cs, it's easy to forget the technology is there at all. But that's one thing we absolutely *cannot* allow ourselves to—am I boring you?" I ask when Saber interrupts my monologue with an exaggerated yawn.

"No, no," he says with a grin. "Talk about what you like; the sound of your voice is enough for me. I just don't want you to think you have to explain every tiny thing." He shrugs. "If you say we need to walk through the orchard, I believe you, and I'm happy to walk through the orchard."

I suppose it *was* a far longer answer than he expected when he asked why I took off my earrings. Still, Saber's casual lack of interest in the monitoring technology that's always at the top of my list of worries is baffling. Not for the first time I wonder if I've been oversold on the virtues of security in Sonoman-Versailles; Reginald seemed to have little enough difficulty spiriting me away, after all. Not to mention delivering boxes of drugged cosmetics and resetting Saber's countdown. I still don't understand how he does it.

On the other hand, who's to say how much worse things would be now if I hadn't maintained vigilance against surveillance in the past?

So—the orchard it is, for the long walk I promised him last night.

"After last night I want to be as honest as I can with you, Saber," I say as we stroll along the wooded paths. "I'm going to destroy him."

"The King?" he whispers.

"No. Well, him too. But those plans are sketchy and don't affect you much. I mean Reginald."

Saber stops in his tracks and I have to pause and turn around. "Don't do it," he says. "You don't understand. If he catches the slightest wind of the idea that you're after him, he'll make you wish he'd just killed you. It's . . . that simple."

I raise my chin. "It used to be that simple. Now I'm the Queen."

"That won't stop him. You've seen him ignore your palace security with impunity. People, Glitter, it doesn't matter—he can get it in and he can take it out. What makes you think a new title gives you better protection?"

He's not wrong, but I can't let it deter me. I can only let it make me more vigilant. "This is why I don't want you to know anything. To protect *you*."

"I don't need protection."

"You will if he suspects you're in on it."

Saber doesn't answer because he knows I'm right. It's at moments like this that his utter lack of freedom feels so large it pushes everything else out. "I told you what you could do to help me," he says so quietly his words are barely audible.

"And I told you that I need more time," I say, citing the only response I was able to give him when I returned, exhausted, from the meeting with the high nobility. "Look at it this way," I add. "Ultimately, the goal is to break up the Glitter ring that Reginald runs. Isn't that a noble cause?"

His sardonic look tells me he's not buying it, but I forge ahead anyway.

"It would help if I knew more about Glitter," I say, changing the subject as I take his arm and start our slow stroll again. "Where does it come from? How is it made?"

Saber sighs.

"Come on. I could have asked you months ago—what would you have said, if you weren't trying to protect me now?"

"That just *asking* those questions is liable to get us both killed, or worse," he grumbles.

I don't know what to say to that.

We walk in silence for several minutes and I've decided he's not going to answer, when he says, "It was stolen. Some research scientist working on the next big painkiller got greedy—saw the potential for street pharm. Wanted to make some money without waiting for regulatory red tape, so he hooked up with Reginald."

"Where is he now?" I whisper. But I think I already know the answer.

"Dead. Once the product was completed and Reginald found a way to get the ingredients without his help, the guy became a liability instead of an asset. He was removed," Saber says, as simply as though commenting on the weather.

I swallow hard, but I have to ask. "Did Reginald make you do it?"

"The scientist? Of course he did."

The air squeezes from my lungs but I try to hide it. I don't want Saber to think it's disgust. It isn't. Not for him, anyway.

"So without the scientist, who makes the Glitter?" I choke out.

Saber ducks under a branch and turns to lift it for me. "He scoops up clueless grad students from the Sorbonne. They never really understand what they're a part of. From what little I know, it's not complicated work. The plants are the most important part."

"What sort of plants?"

Saber shakes his head. "No idea. They come from some lab—and before you ask, I don't know where that is either. My part in the business comes further down the line." He smiles wryly, but the expression is brittle. "You can imagine I don't care to pry."

"Yes, I can," I reply softly. But he's given me a place to start. "Thank you," I whisper.

Saber sighs his exasperation and starts walking again without replying. I can feel the disapproval rolling off him, but I appreciate that he's doing what he can—and letting me make the choice.

We stroll up the steps and into the medical center—our secondary objective—arm in arm, before he lets me go and resumes his usual place behind me. I spot the nurse who last spoke with me about my father and approach without bothering to look at anyone else.

"How is he?"

She looks up, startled, and gives a respectful nod of her head rather than a proper curtsy. I let it pass. "Your father? Let's see." She swipes a few times on her tablet, presumably looking up his chart. "Ah. He's sleeping at the moment."

"I meant long-term," I clarify, suppressing my annoyance. "Is he ready to be released?"

"Well," she says, drawing out the vowel, "his vitals have stabilized. We've been discussing a transition to in-home care, at least for a few weeks—"

"Excellent. Nurse Kozlov, yes?" I say, reading the embroidery on her scrub top. "How much vacation time have you accrued?"

"Oh no," she says, holding her hands out in front of her. "I am *not* using my vacation time to go live in that palace and babysit your father. No offense," she adds in a near-mumble.

"Absolutely none taken," I assure her. "Perhaps *vacation* is the wrong word. Can the clinic spare you for a few weeks of off-site work in Languedoc-Roussillon? I hear it's lovely this time of year."

"Languedoc-Roussillon?"

That's not a *no*. "There is a retirement community there, owned and run by Sonoman-Versailles. A vacancy has been set aside for my father, as soon as you decide he's ready. I'd like for you to accompany him and help him settle in. I would, of course, make sure it's well worth your time." I proffer a thick envelope, and when she peeks in at the brick of ten thousand euros she starts to look panicked, so I add, "You would, of course, receive your usual salary, plus incidentals. This is merely a gift of personal appreciation."

"I—I'm not sure that's legal," she whispers, but the way her fingers clutch at the envelope, I can see that I simply need to soothe her conscience.

I laugh lightly—musically. "Perhaps not in France, but don't forget, Ms. Kozlov, we're in *my* country."

A smile tips up one side of her mouth and her fingers tighten around the bait. I have her. "I'll talk to my supervisor," she says. "And see what we can arrange."

"Have her com me directly if she has any questions. Saber," I say with my most winsome smile, drawing him into the conversation—if nothing else, to abolish the air of secrecy that a large envelope of money always exudes. "Make a note to prioritize coms from Nurse Kozlov and her supervisor . . . ?"

"Dr. Wells," the nurse pipes up.

"Wells," I repeat, beaming. "Do let me know when arrangements can be made, and I'll connect you directly to the palace's *concierge*."

"I—" She moves as if to return the envelope, but I make a clicking sound with my tongue and wave it away.

"No, no. I have full confidence in your capabilities. You'll make it happen."

"Yes, ma'am. Your Highness. Oh, did you want to see your father?"

"I don't think so," I say, tugging on my gloves and hoping the relief doesn't show in my eyes. "Let him sleep. He has a considerable journey to make soon."

We're down the steps and nearly a minute on our way before Saber breaks the silence. "That was neatly done."

"I rather think it was," I say, enjoying the truth of it. "I confess I'm absurdly relieved that he'll be out of the King's immediate grasp. But I feel a bit guilty as well, because it takes the consequences of my own actions out of my immediate sight."

"My actions," Saber counters.

"No," I say, turning to him. "I never, ever, fault you for *his* orders. Ever."

Saber makes a face like he wants to argue, but we've had this discussion too many times for him to think it will go anywhere.

The wind blows at my curls and I swat them away, wishing all my problems were so easily dismissed. "I'm like a child who thinks she can hide by covering her eyes," I say with a strangled laugh. "If I can't see what Glitter can do, perhaps it won't actually do anything."

"We both tell ourselves what we have to in order to live with ourselves. At least we have that in common."

I squeeze his arm and point toward a fountain on the far side of the green—extending our walk without appearing entirely aimless. When we finally arrive back at the palace, the gossips are buzzing because Sir Spencer and the King have been closeted in His Highness' private office for hours.

I choose to take my tea in the *Arrière Cabinet,* the space just outside the door to the King's office. There, I'm guaranteed to be the first to see Sir Spencer emerge, assuming he ever does. Saber joins me for a light lunch, then moves to hover just behind my shoulder, playing his role as secretary to perfection. I com Lady Mei to attend me under the pretense of needing a partner for a game of *piquet,* but I warn Lord Aaron to stay out of sight for the time being.

As I blink my messages away, I wish it were Molli who was joining me instead of Lady Mei. Or perhaps I wish it were the two of them. Or that I had appreciated both friendships more while it was even possible. I flutter my lashes and shove a small sandwich into my mouth to keep my eyes from watering.

A few minutes later Lady Mei slides into a seat across from me and holds her tongue as I deal cards onto the tiny tea table. As we play—our voices masked by the swish and slap of cards—she whispers, "Lady Cynthea is still seen most frequently with Lady Giselle Maass, though you stole Lady Nuala a few months ago."

I let a smile hover at the corner of my mouth. "Lady Nuala is not a trifle to be *stolen,*" I say with a mock-loftiness that Lady Mei will appreciate. "I simply showed her Lady Cyn's true colors and let her make her own choice." I lift a cup of tea to my lips and sip silently. "She chose wisely."

Lady Mei raises an eyebrow. "She's also been much in company with Lady Annaleigh Garcia and Lady Breya Voroman-Wills. She's drawn them even closer since Lady Nuala jumped ship."

I freeze. *Breya.* That was her name. The daughter who was taking notes at the "party" last night. Who saw me announce my brilliant, brutal plan—and bore witness to how impressed the highest nobility was. There could definitely be something to use in the young lady. I don't share that tidbit with Lady Mei just yet.

And the other: Lady Annaleigh Garcia. The daughter of the Marquis and Countess Garcia. Those two were also at the meeting last night. Lady Cyn is surrounding herself with daughters of the nobility who support the King.

I think she may discover that she's armed herself with a double-edged sword.

"Just . . . young *ladies*?" I ask.

Lady Mei flutters her fingers. "Casual friendships with lords and gents. Only a fool would flaunt the fact that she's the King's mistress and then allow other men into her more intimate circles. Though it would be lovely if she were, Lady Cyn is no fool."

"Unfortunately not," I agree ruefully as Lady Mei takes my trick.

We're on the second hand when the office door opens and Sir Spencer emerges. Before the door shuts fully, I catch a glimpse of His Highness, still sitting at his desk, scribbling on his tablet with a feathered stylus.

Sir Spencer is pale, his already light complexion drained of color, but as his eyes meet mine, I catch something in them I haven't seen in months. A year. Maybe ever.

Hope.

I let myself smile just enough for him to see it, and he gives me a wan smile in return before blanking his expression and striding resolutely away.

The King took the bait.

I glance up at Lady Mei and wink, then lay a high trump and take her best pointer. At this moment I feel unbeatable.

ELEVEN

I DON'T KNOW what to expect from my private dinner with the King. Saber was . . . *irritated* isn't quite the right word, but his agitation began fraying on my nerves as I prepared, and I finally had to send him off to his room.

This also gave me a chance to ask the dressing-bots to tighten my corset. I need to be utterly in control of myself this evening, and my boning holds me up—holds me together when I can't do it alone. Saber doesn't understand; I'm not sure he *can*. Even now, as I glide down the lightly populated hallways, I revel in the pressure circumscribing my midriff.

By the time I walk into the King's lavish private dining room, drenched in jewels and wearing one of my finest gowns—satin battle armor, truly—the entire palace is alive with rumors and speculations. After Sir Spencer emerged from the King's office but spoke to no one, I sent Lady Mei to listen to all the suppositions and report back. I can't help but feel a sense of pride that not a single one comes anywhere close to what I know to be the truth.

The King has his back to me when I enter, and when the doors clang shut behind me, he speaks without turning.

"Interesting developments today."

"I imagine so," I reply.

"As part of our negotiations I, of course, had to ask Sir Spencer who it was he'd been seeing." He pivots and walks toward me, a glass in each hand and eerie warmth in his eyes. "You told me the morning of the vote that I wouldn't want anyone to think I specifically prohibited Lord Aaron from attending. I hardly had the mental space to consider your comment at the time, and decided it would be best that no one in the court thought I was prohibiting *anyone* from attending the vote. So I ordered him released."

He hands me one of the glasses and I take it, but I say nothing, nor do I take a sip. I only stare.

He smirks. "You helped me. Nothing stays secret forever, and if their affair had come to light soon enough, and Lord Aaron had still been under house arrest, I could very well have been suspected of defrauding the shareholders. A new vote would have been called for." He pauses and drinks, his expression growing serious. "With a cloud of suspicion hanging over me, a second vote would likely have gone the other way. Why did you do it?"

"I wanted Lord Aaron released."

But he's already shaking his head. "There were easier ways. You thought that particular strategy through. Why?"

I gesture airily with my glass. "You're trying to find a hidden agenda where there was none, Justin. With the information you learned today, you couldn't think he voted in your favor. Perhaps I was working against you."

"Not if you were considering the long term. And I get the feeling you're considering everything in the long term these days."

Damn Reginald! If not for him, *long term* wouldn't be anything I associated with Sonoman-Versailles, much less its illustrious ruler. But I wave my gloved fingers dismissively. "You want me to admit that I knew it was in your best interest? Fine. That doesn't mean it was altruistic of me. If you had the choice of being married to the King or married to a disgraced, thrown-down ex-King, which would you have chosen?"

He laughs at that. "You really are your mother's daughter," he says, tipping his glass to *ting* against mine.

"Take it back," I hiss, before I can think better of it.

He pauses, frozen with his glass halfway to his mouth. "Oh, that's right," he says, returning to himself. "Even death doesn't bring forgiveness to that woman."

"How was your meeting with Sir Spencer?" I walk over to the long, formal table that is the central feature of the large room and stand beside the place clearly designated for me. The one *not* at the head of the table. A bot wheels forward to pull out my chair and scoots it firmly beneath me as I sit.

The King hesitates, and I can tell he's deciding whether or not to push the previous subject; I'm grateful when he decides to let it pass. "You stopped by Lord Aaron's apartments last night."

A jolt of terror makes my eyelids flutter. I hate every reminder that he spies on me. "I thought a friendly warning was in order," I say. No need to add that Lord Aaron was asleep and didn't answer his door.

"Understandable, I suppose. Watching out for your friends." There's a steely edge in his tone. "Your friendship with Sir Spencer must be quite close."

Ah—that's his game. If I'm friendly with Sir Spencer, he

imagines I might have played some hidden role in the Tremain conspiracy; that perhaps my placement now is that of ace in the hole. Strangely enough, I decide honesty is the best policy, just this once.

"I scarcely know Sir Spencer, actually. It's Lord Aaron who's my intimate friend. Has been for years, which you'd know if you'd been paying any attention to court instead of chasing tail. Like everyone else, I heard whispers about the duke's agenda when the wedding between Lady Julianna and Sir Spencer took place, but you might recall that I was as surprised as you when the date of the vote was set."

He studies me for a long time. "Truly?"

"I have no motivation to lie about this." Not anymore.

"Not one that I see, but I'm discovering a whole different side of you. I like it, by the way." He grins and drops into his chair, looking relaxed and pleased with himself. I don't know this easy, friendly Justin, and he makes me nervous.

"How long had you been planning the divorce?"

I don't go for honesty this time. "I did inform you that I was inviting both gentlemen to my dinner last night," I say, reaching for my glass.

"I thought so."

No reason to correct him.

"Brilliant, though. Sir Spencer was *very* pleased." The King lifts his glass and turns it in his fingers, studying it as though looking for a flaw. "Unless he's the finest actor I've ever known, he *really* hates that family."

"Can you blame him? They took advantage of him at his most vulnerable moment to further their own selfish goals." I glare very meaningfully at the King, but he pops a piece of fruit into his mouth, utterly oblivious.

"The divorce will be made by executive order—being supreme head of the government has many perks—and by the time it's announced, it'll already be final."

"When will that be?"

"Two days. Takes forty-eight hours for the divorce to take effect, and I initiated procedures at my meeting with the upstart. I'm planning a palace-wide brunch, scheduled to begin half an hour after everything's official." He grins and rubs his hands in excitement, then turns to me seriously. "On the hush until then. I have several surprises to unveil."

"Such as?"

He fairly beams at me. "You'll have to wait and see. Oh, one that I won't announce publicly, but perhaps you'll find this interesting: I've also annulled the prenuptial agreement and will return all assets to their original owners. Sir Spencer reclaims his full inheritance, and Lady Julianna gets nothing at all, since she hasn't yet inherited from her father. I can't stop her father from giving her *his* shares in the future, but now she'll have no way to gain control of both families' votes. Back when the match was proposed I argued it was foolish to put so many shares in one basket, so to speak, but it was a losing battle. Not this time," he says with a grin. "Can't stop two legal, consenting adults from getting married, but so long as one wants out, I can push a divorce through."

"So equitable of you." I can't help but find a good deal of justice in that, since the duke made the match solely for the voting shares that came with Sir Spencer's inheritance.

"Well, Sir Spencer took a bit of convincing in that arena. He's . . . kindhearted. A difficult virtue. It's what made him so easy for Duke Tremain to manipulate in the first place. I hope your friend Lord Aaron has more of a spine than his appearance would suggest. That boy's going to need protecting."

I sputter and cough on my drink. "Boy? Sir Spencer's a year older than *you*. And as for Lord Aaron's appearance, you, of all people, have no room to—"

"Calm yourself, pussycat," His Highness says, and I grip my napkin to keep from tossing the contents of my glass in his face. "I get a little"—he pauses and then smirks—"swaggery when I'm feeling victorious. I meant nothing by it."

I give my attention to my plate until the awkwardness is so stifling I feel as though it might suffocate me. "My lord?"

He jerks to attention, as though he was completely comfortable in the tense silence, and I hate him all the more for it. "Yes, love?"

I squirm at his endearment but save that battle for another day. "You asked for my presence this evening before you knew anything of Sir Spencer's dissatisfaction. What is the point of this dinner?"

He looks at the formal spread before us, what appears to be genuine bafflement on his face. "Were you not hungry?"

I glare.

He regards me with the barest hint of amusement.

"You traded this dinner for a *favor*," I say, emphasizing heavily. "If there's anything I've learned about you since we became betrothed, it's that you're too good a businessman to ever give anything without getting something in return. So, *Justin*"—I practically spit his name—"what is it you're after?"

He smiles and it's disconcerting how much it lights up his eyes. This isn't a cold, public smile, but one that suffuses his entire face. It's a handsome smile, and the frightening fact is that I *notice* it's a handsome smile.

"I wanted time in your company. Is that so hard to believe?" He holds up a hand, stopping my protest. "Six months ago, yes. Even a week ago, perhaps. But last night I saw that *something* come out to play, and it was ruthless and brutal. It was *very* attractive."

I bat my eyes innocently. "Attractive? Surely you can't have tired of Lady Cyn already? Last I saw her, she was still breathing."

He rolls his eyes. "Plainly *neither* of us is in a position to lecture the other on fidelity, and while discretion is not always your strong suit, I think you understand that."

Baiting aside, he's right. There's plenty of mutual cheating going on, and double standards never made anyone more likable.

"Here's what I think you *don't* understand, Danica. I know what I am. I'm not a kind person. I certainly wouldn't categorize myself as a good person, though I'm not nearly as bad as you'd like to believe. Or perhaps simply not the *type* of bad that you'd like to believe. I'm selfish, stubborn, ambitious, and utterly ruthless when it comes to getting what I want. And I see no reason to let someone else's version of morality govern my life."

I listen with a prickle traveling up my spine as he outlines his vices and calls them virtues.

"Last night," the King says, leaning forward with his chin propped on his elbows, "I saw a young Queen who was also all of those things." He reaches out and clasps my fingers before I can pull away. He brushes his lips across the skin, once, twice, then stays there, murmuring words while his mouth tickles my hand. "I find myself wanting to get to know that Queen."

"Again, you set this dinner *before* last night's meeting," I say, hoping he can't feel my fingers trembling as he turns my hand over, caressing my palm.

He laughs, relinquishing my hand. "There, you see? Stubborn, just as I said. I'd intended to spend this evening laying out what you would and would not do for the next several months as I roll out the projects I unveiled at the vote. I intended to put the fear of God into you, make you aware of your position and role in *my* court, and threaten you if necessary." He rises to refill his glass, then turns and leans a hip casually against the sideboard, grinning seductively. "But I'm beginning to think I'd like to see where you take things on your own for a while. Perhaps we can be a team."

"We are not a *team*," I retort. "And we never will be."

"You say that, but your actions tell a different tale. If you think strengthening my rule while profaning my name makes us *not a team,* I'm not inclined to disabuse you." The King comes back to the table, taking slow steps that remind me of a tiger stalking prey. "You go right on thinking you have standards and morals and a conscience to keep you on that straight and narrow. But truly,

Danica, you're lying. Not just to me, not just to everyone in this court. You're lying to yourself."

"You're wrong," I say weakly, the choices I've made since that night in the hallway assaulting my conscience from every possible angle.

"Am I? You're still somewhat new to ruling a kingdom, so consider this tidbit a favor in kind from your new husband: *uneasy lies the head that wears a crown*. We're a newly married King and Queen, freshly confirmed by popular vote. Everyone will be scrutinizing us. We're headed into the refiner's fire, and all that's false will be burned away. When that happens, when you can no longer hide from yourself, who will be right? You, or me?"

I leave without eating dessert.

TWELVE

"I HAVE TO SEE HIM, SABER. FACE TO FACE."

I'm standing in my silken nightgown, my whole body shaking, not with fear, but with anger. A new box filled with Glitter sits at my feet, delivered sometime after I went to sleep and before I padded into my dressing room to pick my clothing for the day. I almost fell over it.

Saber groans his frustration, still trying to chase the sleep from his eyes after having woken to my shouts and surely thinking I was in danger. I should feel bad but I'm too furious at Reginald. "I didn't see who brought it," Saber says. "I don't even know if he brought it personally, and I would be willing to bet he didn't."

"But you know how to contact him, and don't even try to deny it. There's no way your countdown always ends on a Wednesday, so I know he's not just sneaking in with the crowds. He's *somewhere* and he and I need to talk."

Saber tosses a balled-up glove at the wall in an uncharacteristic fit of *pique*. "I don't like it when you talk to him. I don't like you anywhere near him. He stabbed you in the back once already—I would think you'd prefer to not have him around."

"Well, certainly I don't *prefer* it," I mutter. "I'd prefer he was rotting in a jail cell somewhere, or possibly floating facedown in the Seine. But since I'm forced to work with him at present, I need a consultation." I finger a new pot of Glitter gloss before tossing it back in the box with a clatter. "I ran out of product yesterday, except for the six canisters I always set aside for my *lever* staff. So I *am* due for a refill, but I don't want him to start bringing higher quantities. I have to explain that to him. Firmly. Plus, I need to know what I owe him."

"Owe him?"

"He hasn't collected payment for product in two weeks, and I do *not* want to be in debt to that man. Besides," I grumble, "I must know up front what kind of price hike he's going to insist upon for fully assembled product instead of raw materials. The longer we go without an agreement on price, the more clout he has to rip me off."

"Does that part even matter anymore?"

"It matters because Reginald is the kind of person you can't say yes to any more often than absolutely necessary, or he'll assume the answer is *always* yes. And there are a great number of things I cannot say yes to. Besides," I add, pointing at a chest in the far corner, "I'm running out of space to hide the money. With bots cleaning these rooms every day, and the Royal Asshole still denying me an unmonitored office, there aren't very many places I can stash it. Paying Reginald would help."

What I don't say is that Lord Aaron slipped me a tiny tracker yesterday—hardly more than a silver sticker the size of a pea, designed to withstand every countermeasure Lord Aaron could think of. I knew he'd come through for me. But so far I've only been *receiving* deliveries. By slipping the tracker in with Reginald's payment, I can begin gathering information.

But I can't tell Saber that part.

"He is poison, Danica. He kills everything he comes in contact with and you want me to bring him to you."

"Bringing me to him would also be acceptable," I say with a grin, trying to lighten the mood, but my attempt fails dramatically and I wish I hadn't even tried. "I owe him money, Saber. A *lot* of money. Seeing him one time, face to face, can't possibly be worse than being in his debt."

Saber seems to deflate, his shoulders bending inward. "You have a point," he says wearily, fingers fluttering at the ribbon atop the box. "I'll do what I can."

"Thank you," I say, my shoulders finally relaxing. Enough that one strap of my nightgown slips right off.

A low purr rumbles in Saber's throat and he reaches out to stroke my bare shoulder. "Can't we stay in today?"

His lips touch that sensitive spot where shoulder meets neck and I close my eyes and hum my approval. "I wish," I say with a groan. "But I can't relax, much less enjoy myself, with this box full of . . . cosmetics . . . sitting here."

"You torture me."

"You like it."

"True." He straightens and pulls the strap back onto my shoulder. "Oh, what a waste. Can you handle the first hour without me? They're going to swarm you."

"You think so?"

"Oh yes. When you weren't at last night's *soirée*, they swarmed *me*, and I had nothing to give them." More softly, he adds, "Ever seen an addict up close when they're denied their fix? That reckless light in their eyes?"

I remember a few weeks ago when my father miscounted his patches and ran out early. Knowing it won't be quite the same with the courtiers does little to lighten my heart. Saber's right; it won't be pretty.

"I can handle it," I say, as much to myself as to Saber. "Let's fill my *panniers* completely. Maybe between the two of us we can get rid of it all today and won't have to worry about it again until next week."

"Dispensing the product is only part of *worrying about it*," Saber says. "You're going to have to deal with it on some level every single day from here on out. But yes, being able to simply say 'it's all gone' keeps you from having to make decisions about who gets the last canisters."

It takes almost half an hour to dress, and because Saber is watching, I can't ask my bots to pull my laces quite as tight as I'd prefer, but considering how much weight in Glitter I'll be hauling, perhaps that's for the best.

By the time the lined cages beneath my skirts are stuffed to capacity, I'm so loaded down with Glitter that my pelvis feels quite compressed. I hope Saber's right that most of it will be taken off my hands—hips—quickly. This weight, this pressing, doesn't feel anything like my corset. It doesn't make me feel safe and held tight; it only makes me heavy and weak.

Before I leave my rooms I pause and run my fingers up Saber's arm. "Please," I say gently. "Find him. I need this. I need to talk to him."

"I don't like it." He leans forward and kisses me. A whisper-soft meeting of lips that makes me want more. "I'll do as you ask, but I want my objection noted. I'll join you as soon as I can."

"But—"

"Later," he says with a laugh. "Go."

I push out my bottom lip melodramatically, but take a deep breath and head out of my bedchamber. I'm not three steps from the double doors before I'm besieged by a gaggle of young ladies, all waving money so obviously I feel my temper start to rise.

"Ladies," I command. "Decorum, if you please!"

They fall silent and subdued, gathering around me in a nervous semicircle. "Good morning, ladies," I prompt, inclining my head graciously.

A few gasps sound as they realize how rude they've been. "Your Highness" echoes around the circle, and they each fall into a low bow, spreading their silken skirts out on the floor around them like pastel flowers.

"*Merci.* We must never, ever forget that in the palace there is always someone watching you," I intone very quietly. "Judging."

The ladies look crestfallen and several murmur quiet apologies before a rough line forms.

"I need two, please," says a young lady whose parents were in attendance at the secret meeting—Mireille, I think.

"One only," I say firmly, and then raise my voice and look around the group. "My supplier has reached the limits of his production capabilities. Until such time as he can expand his operation, we shall have to do a bit of rationing among ourselves. I know we're all capable of such civility."

Concern shows in their eyes.

"I always use two," Lady Mireille protests.

I purse my lips and think quickly. "At the assembly tonight I will happily sell a second canister to anyone who wants one, assuming I have any left. But we must allow everyone to receive a first canister."

Lady Mireille scowls but pays for her single pot, no doubt already planning to ambush me the moment I walk into the Hall of Mirrors tonight.

The next young lady, a Mademoiselle Simone, tries a new ploy. "One for me and one for my sister, Belinda," she says. And I hear her suck in a breath and hold it.

I raise an eyebrow and, to her credit, she doesn't so much as blink.

But I'm not stupid. "Mademoiselle Belinda will have to come retrieve her cosmetics herself. I can nearly always be found in some public place, so that should pose no problem at all."

Simone's face is a mask of forced control and for a moment I think she's going to tear up. I did that. There are no right answers in my life anymore.

She maintains her composure and drops a graceful curtsy, then continues on her way.

Word spreads like wildfire, and by the time Saber finds me an hour later, my hips are thanking me for having unloaded nearly the entire batch of Glitter. Saber must have come by way of my rooms, because his messenger bag is round and taut, and I quickly fill him in on the rules I've established. "You'll have to be firm—they've already displayed quite a propensity for trickery," I mutter.

"Ah well," he says. "I was waylaid by a Mademoiselle Simone and Lady Mireille on the way here. They both seemed like they were trying to get away with something, but I couldn't justify telling them no."

I laugh, even though it's not funny at all. "Second pot for both of them, then, little swindlers." I turn and give him a half-grin. "Looks like you're going to have to stay close to me to make sure that doesn't happen again."

"What a shame," Saber replies, his voice low and husky.

I hate to derail that line of thinking, but I need to know. "What did he say?"

As expected, Saber's expression goes flat. "This afternoon. He'll meet you in the *Orangerie*. He says he can disguise himself as a gardener and you can talk briefly."

"I can't give him money out there."

"He said to put the payment in last week's Glitter box and he'll have his man swap them out."

"He wants three weeks' worth of payment next week?" I grumble. Unless I can think of some way to plant the tracker on Reginald himself, it'll be as much as another week before I can just slip it in with a payment.

"I thought maybe you could use the same boxes to transport the profits you have now to Lord Aaron's private office," Saber says. "Seems at least as good a hiding place as any."

"Since Giovanni's no longer available to me," I say, though

that is by my choice rather than his. Reginald knows I hid my profits with my dance master previously; I can't justify dragging him back into this cesspool. Though after all that, poor Giovanni must have been shocked and appalled to see me show up in the news coverage of my high-profile wedding.

Lord Aaron appears in the doorway to the Hall of Mirrors— looking for me, judging by how he jerks his chin up and weaves his way through the crowd.

"Ah, speak of the devil," I say with a wave.

"Have you seen Sir Spencer today?" he asks when he reaches us.

"Haven't you?"

Lord Aaron shakes his head. "I caught him briefly yesterday and he said he couldn't talk to me. Not yet. I—"

"Don't worry," I say, putting my hand on his arm and lowering my voice. "Everything went well. The King is planning a grand reveal. Tomorrow, he says."

"What—"

I raise one hand to cut him off there. I can see that Lord Aaron will find no peace unless I tell him. "I tried to catch you at your rooms the other night, but you were already abed. I can give you the basics now," I murmur. "Kindly remember that if they get out, it's my head."

Lord Aaron merely rolls his eyes; he needs no words to say *I'll add it to the pile.*

"He's offered Sir Spencer a divorce," I breathe softly, close to his ear.

I've caught Lord Aaron off-guard and he struggles to regain composure. "Truly?"

"I suggested it. The King thought it was a marvelous idea—a way to strike back at the duke." I chuckle low in my throat. "You should have seen him. He was ecstatic."

"An ecstatic Justin Wyndham? Well, that shouldn't make anyone nervous in the least," Lord Aaron says cynically.

"Try not to worry," I say. "He's going to annul the prenup entirely, restoring Sir Spencer's full inheritance."

A crease of concentration splits Lord Aaron's brow. "He must truly hate Tremain."

I shrug, glancing over at Saber—who's giving us a bit of breathing room by dealing with my grabby customers himself. "I never thought to empathize with His Loftiness, but . . . wouldn't you?"

Lord Aaron doesn't answer and I'm concerned that I'm not getting quite the reaction I'd anticipated.

"At least try not to worry *too* much," I amend, turning toward the pressing crowd. "Everything will be out tomorrow." Lord Aaron drifts silently near my elbow for a few minutes, but at some point I look up from a conversation and see only his velvet-clad back, disappearing down the hallway that leads to the Tremain apartments.

THIRTEEN

SAVE FOR THE handful of canisters I've held back for my *lever* ladies and my friends, the entire box of Glitter is gone before I can head toward my meeting with Reginald that afternoon. Between the "preorders" and the honeymoon that never actually happened, this is the first time a single—albeit large—box of Glitter will have to last people for an entire week.

And it's already gone.

I'm both relieved and horrified.

Saber and I wander the perimeter of the *Orangerie* for about ten minutes before he raises his handkerchief to his mouth and coughs gently while pointing out Reginald. Having always seen Reginald in intimidating street wear, I wouldn't have known him in dark gray coveralls and a sun hat, his shaggy hair pulled back and secured with an elastic band. He's even found an old-fashioned pair of gold-rimmed glasses with an early-model Lens projector perched atop the frames. He looks rather adorably bumbling with a pair of clippers in his hand and grass stains on his knees.

How very bizarre.

Unfortunately, his costume affords few places I can plant the tiny tracker and not have it simply discarded with his clothing at the earliest opportunity. I'm going to have to think of something else, and quickly.

I edge close to the tree he's haphazardly lopping small branches from and turn my profile. "Reginald." I don't bother masking my hostility. I have to act precisely the way he'd expect me to. Make him feel like he truly knows me and can predict what I'll do.

"There you are, Your Majesty. I don't much like being summoned."

"I don't much like being cheated."

"I didn't cheat." I hear the smile in his tone and I curl my toes in my slippers to make myself stand still. "I simply interpreted the rules a little differently than you did."

"I didn't come here to argue." Arguing with Reginald is like running around in circles, hunting for a finish line.

"Then why are we here?"

"What do I owe you?" I say flatly.

"Owe me?"

"Don't be obtuse. For the Glitter."

"Well, now. I've been doing a lot of your work, haven't I? And haven't asked for anything in return."

"That's not a number."

"Saber here said you need more."

"He most certainly did not. He knows that's not at all what I want."

"Ah, so Saber works for you now, does he?"

"I think we both know who he'd choose to work for, if he had any say in the matter."

"But he doesn't." Reginald chuckles and the sound makes the hairs stand up on the back of my neck.

I glance up at Saber and there's a clear warning in his expression.

"Girl, if I asked Saber to break your legs for me, he'd do it. And you know why? Because he knows it'd be better for you if he did it than if he refused and I did it myself." Reginald takes a big bite out of the tree with his clippers and the cracking sound makes me jump. "Do you know how often I've sent him to rough up a client? To break fingers, or legs, or necks? To put families out on the streets? Don't depend on Saber too much without remembering what he is."

I keep my gaze fixed on Saber through that entire awful speech, and he wilts before my eyes. It's subtle, but I see it. A tiny droop in his shoulders, a tightening around his mouth, the shine dulling in his eyes. Reginald isn't lying. Saber was right when he told me I had no idea what the meaning of *no choice* was.

"We're not here to talk about Saber. We're here to talk about payment," I say when I find my voice. My corset feels as though it's strangling me even though it's two centimeters looser than yesterday.

"Million a week."

"Please," I scoff. "I used to pay you a hundred thousand."

"For raw. This is all prepped and hand-delivered besides."

"You're destroying my margin. With such low profits I might as well be selling *actual makeup*."

"What do you care? You've already paid me for your new identity. By the time I have it ready for you, you'll have more than enough to live comfortably and anonymously to the end of your days."

"I'll give you half a million. For one box, once a week."

He shrugs, almost uninterested, which only makes me angrier. "This isn't a negotiation. You'll give me one million, packed in one of your pretty boxes, every week, and I'll swap it out for the Glitter."

I hate him. "Reginald—"

"You'll see. You'll have no trouble meeting the price. Surely a girl raised in a corporatocracy understands the concept of supply and demand."

I clamp my mouth shut.

"I see we're agreed. That means three million in that box next week or I'll order Saber to take it out of your hide."

Saber's steady gaze keeps me frozen in place.

"Are we done here?"

"No, we're not done here," I say through gritted teeth. "I'm already completely out of places to hide my money. If you don't take at least the first million today, I can't sell any Glitter this week. It's as simple as that."

"Fine, fine," he says with a shake of his head. "Such a helpless Queen you are! I'll send someone for it this evening. But don't say I never did you any favors."

At that moment the inevitable occurs. One of my faithful customers sees me and bustles over to buy a canister of drug-laced cosmetics. I try to fob him off quickly, but it takes several minutes to convince him that I truly am out—I'm neither lying nor withholding it as some sort of personal grudge.

By the time I turn back to Reginald, the *Orangerie* holds nothing but trees. One of them so mangled the actual gardeners might not be able to save it.

I can empathize.

IT'S NEARLY TWO in the morning before the court disperses and Saber and I get some time together, shut away alone in my bedchamber. The topic of my afternoon meeting with Reginald hangs like a specter in the room, but I don't want to give the bastard another single moment of my day. Instead, I help Saber shrug out of his dress jacket and linen shirt, sit him down in front of me on the plush carpet, and begin rubbing his shoulders.

He groans in appreciation as I work on knots and sore spots, and I revel in the simple enjoyment of doing something for him. There's so little I can truly give him. His clothing is all a disguise, and provided by the palace, and any gift I might try to purchase for him would be tainted by my Glitter profits.

But this I can give him: my time, my attention, the affection I so often have to withhold when the court can see us.

"Being Queen takes up more of my time than I expected," I say. "It seems odd to say that I miss you when we're in each other's physical company so frequently, but I do."

He reaches for my leg where it sits just beside his hip, and circles my ankle with his fingers. "I know."

The silence settles around us, unbroken except for the little grunts from Saber as I find tender muscles. Even though it's a comfortable silence, I'm driven to make the most of our time, so

I search for a topic that isn't touchy in some way. I don't want any more friction tonight.

And I come up with . . . nothing.

I can't stop the giggle that escapes my lips.

"What?" Saber asks, craning his neck to look at me.

"I thought this would be a great time for some nice, easy conversation—*sans* drama—so I was trying to come up with a topic. And there isn't one. Everything's sensitive for us."

Saber grins, catching on. "Can't talk about your childhood."

"Or yours."

"Both our families are off-limits."

"And our jobs."

He's laughing openly now. "Please let's not talk about our jobs."

"We can't discuss plans for the future."

"Are you kidding? We probably shouldn't even talk about our plans for tomorrow." He wraps both arms around me and pulls me down to the floor, my head on his shoulder as we both snicker.

"Has there ever been a couple quite so badly matched as us?" I ask.

"Surely somewhere. Oh, I've got it, the little mermaid. They were pretty doomed from the start."

"Romeo and Juliet?"

"Please," Saber scoffs. "They just made bad life choices."

"Lord Aaron and Sir Spencer," I say, sobering.

"Getting closer, but even their situation is about to get better."

I nod, knowing he'll feel it, even if he can't see it. "It's the right thing to do, isn't it? The divorce?"

"I think . . . ," Saber says, and then pauses and begins again. "I think that considering the muddle they started in, it's as good a choice as you could possibly have made."

"Even though it breaks up the Tremain family?"

"They roped him in by trickery anyway, didn't they?"

"They took advantage of his grief."

"Close enough. In a way it . . . it frees Sir Spencer."

I smile when Saber uses the word *free*. Even if he can't apply it to himself yet, at least he's thinking about it. I roll to my stomach and prop my chin on my hand with a sigh. "I represent everything you hate. Why in the world do you like me?"

"*Love* you," he says sternly.

I can't hide my smile at his words. "Love me," I correct in a whisper.

He holds my eyes for a long time, and I'm not convinced he's going to answer me. Or he's going to slough off the question and say something humorous. But he surprises me. "You look at obstacles and you see an opponent. Something to be fought and defeated. It never occurs to you that you can't overcome . . . anything, really." He lifts his hand to my face, running his knuckles down my cheek. "I wish I were more like that."

I duck my head as my face flushes, but Saber grins and pushes himself half up from the floor. "And I love this," he says, kissing the tip of my nose. "And this." His lips move to my cheek. "And this." My breathing quickens when his lips brush the sensitive skin at the side of my neck. He touches the edge of my chemise, just barely sitting on my shoulder, and with a flick of his fingers, he pushes it off to slide a few centimeters down my arm.

Lifting a hand to his chin, I raise his head to mine and kiss him softly, my tongue caressing his bottom lip before pulling back to meet his eyes. "I love you too," I whisper.

He kisses me hard and holds me tight against his chest as though I might disappear. He always does this—holds me like this is all temporary, like I'm going to fade away at any moment. But with so many changes lurking on the horizon, I understand his desperation. Feel it myself.

"Tomorrow everything will change," I say.

Saber's lips brush my bared shoulder. "Not everything."

FOURTEEN

ONLY IN THE Palace of Versailles is a public breakfast scheduled for one in the afternoon, and still people complain about the early hour. For this momentous occasion I'm dressed in an elaborate silver gown with split velvet skirts, originally made for Justin's grandmother. It's a slimmer, flounce-laden design from the early 1600s, but I'm not carrying Glitter today, so I don't need my secret pockets.

I'm ready early, of course, and soon have nothing to do but fret. My coms to Lord Aaron go unanswered—though Lady Mei is quick to respond with the excuse that no one is talking. Should I have given her a hint? So far she's done well—I haven't heard even one convoluted version of any of the secrets I'm testing her with. Not even the pregnancy lie, which was the juiciest morsel I could come up with. If she makes it through today, I'm going to start trusting her.

I crave her company. The companionship of another lady, especially one who loves frivolity as Lady Mei does, keeps me from sinking into despair. Her light playfulness is something I've never possessed—especially lately. She revels in the games and intrigues that make me feel ill. I know it's because the consequences aren't nearly so dire for her, but that spark of light helps to keep me afloat.

Finally it seems like the appropriate time to head to the Hall of Mirrors, where the breakfast is being held. I squeeze Saber's hand before I open the doors to my bedchamber and we have to play aloof acquaintances again.

The relief I feel when I see the King standing at the head of the room, conversing with the Duke and Duchess Sells, is peculiar. Uncomfortable, like an ill-fitted glove. I nod to Saber to follow me as I cut through a handful of courtiers and come to stand by Justin's side.

"It's amazing," the King whispers to me out of the side of his mouth. "No one suspects a thing. Look over there."

He gives a small nod, and I see Duke Tremain standing beside his wife and Lady Julianna, garbed in her typical bright colors, which I find garish and she clearly adores. Lady Julianna is one of the few younger ladies of the court whom I've never really had much social contact with, and I find myself realizing I know almost nothing about her except that she's Sir Spencer's wife. Is that sad? Or simply loyalty to Lord Aaron? I'm no longer sure.

The Tremains stand stiffly, well clear of the circle around His Highness, holding themselves aloof even among their supporters. Their postures proclaim that they're mindful of their power and influence, but also acutely aware of their social downfall— and their lack of favor with the King. Lady Julianna is clinging to Sir Spencer's arm; he looks uncomfortable, but no more so than usual.

"The players are all here; the show's about to begin," the King says, his voice quaking with excitement. I've never considered him particularly *mature,* but in this moment he's downright boyish.

I catch sight of Lord Aaron, trying to appear nonchalant beside Lady Mei, who meets my eyes as though sensing my attention. She flashes me a quick smile and then looks away, perhaps thinking she shouldn't be acknowledging me. She's new to the secrets game, but she's trying.

The King nods an acknowledgment to Saber, standing just beyond my shoulder, then flicks his head to the side, dismissing him. I'm too frozen in fear and apprehension to watch how Saber reacts, but I feel the heat of his body vanish from my side, leaving me unreasonably cold.

His Highness takes my hand and leads me up to a dais, then parades me to the center. I feel every bit the trophy wife he's made me out to be.

By my own insistence, I remind myself. *My own choice. My penance.*

A hush falls over the crowd, and the King passes me in front of him with an impressive hand-switch-and-pull move that turns me just enough to bell my skirt. I have a hazy memory of seeing his father doing exactly the same thing with the late Queen on television and, mirroring the memory, I dip into a deep curtsy for the crowd. The King follows with his own bow a moment later. It occurs to me that if this young man I've somehow ended up married to weren't a narcissistic, murdering, power-hungry monster, he might make a decent husband. Instead, he's merely an accomplished ringmaster. The thought puts me in an odd melancholy.

We settle into our chairs, which, though not precisely thrones, are more ornate than the other seats on the dais. The crowd in the hall follows our lead. At the same time, a few people wend their way toward our table, including Lord Aaron, and, yes, after a long moment, Sir Spencer—disentangling himself from his wife, who looks after him in confusion. The six meet at the foot of the steps almost together and head up single file, ladies first. The crowd quiets, realizing something is happening, then begins to buzz again as the guests pair off: Duke and Duchess, Marquis and Countess . . . and Sir Spencer and Lord Aaron.

The King gives Sir Spencer a long, meaningful look, and I see him melt a bit beneath Justin's gaze. By the time a plate is placed in front of me, my stomach is churning so violently there's no way I can eat a thing. But I push my food around and take sips of water, hoping I'm fooling someone.

The King eats with gusto, as though nothing important were happening at all. When I start twisting my napkin in my lap, where no one but he can see it, he reaches over and lays his hand atop mine, stilling me. "A few more minutes," he says in a soft voice that's surely meant to calm.

I recall Lord Aaron's words about what would make Justin Wyndham ecstatic, and wish I'd given them more credence. He's practically rubbing his hands together in glee. The divorce isn't the only plan he mentioned at our dinner—just the one he was willing to tell me about.

Finally, when I'm nearly ready to toss my entire plate on the floor just to make *something* happen, the King rises and taps his glass with his spoon. "My lords and ladies," he says once the crowd settles into silence. "It's been quite an eventful few weeks, hasn't it? My royal wedding." He pauses and turns to me, bowing solemnly. I try to smile, but my face feels broken. "A shareholder revolt." At that he raises his glass to the Tremain family.

The audience titters nervously. I feel my own face flush at his brazen address of the still-tender subject, but when my eyes dart to the clearly enraged Duke Tremain, I see that he's glaring not at the King but at Sir Spencer. He clearly understands that Sir Spencer has abandoned them, though he can't yet puzzle out why.

"And, of course, my own victorious reemergence," the King continues. Applause starts up somewhere but, uncharacteristically, the King doesn't pause to preen, speaking over it instead. "With so many grand events, changes are inevitable, and I wanted to bring a few to your awareness."

He assumes a commanding, straight-backed posture that makes me wonder whether there was a Giovanni-esque teacher in his past. "This is the twenty-second century, and though we embrace the trappings of the Baroque, we're not savages. Marriage should be more than a blending of fortunes for the furthering of one's political ambitions. Inspired by the bliss of my own recent marriage, I find myself unable to tolerate the idea of a loyal subject trapped by circumstance in a marriage of despair."

Now it's my turn to try to halt a red flush working its way up my neck. I'm certain everyone in this room is aware that Lady Cyn has spent the last two weeks swanning about, making sure the court knows she remains the King's *paramour* despite his wedding vows. Damnably, His Majesty is right—I'm in no position to lecture on fidelity—but to raise the issue so publicly, at such a gathering, is *humiliating*. I force myself to continue gazing at my supposedly adoring husband.

"Therefore, as King of Sonoman-Versailles and at his personal request, I hereby dissolve the marriage between the Honorable Sir Spencer Harrisford and Lady Julianna Tremain and annul the marital contract, effective thirty minutes ago."

A chorus of gasps erupts from the crowd, and Duke Tremain rises from his seat with a shout. But two of His Highness' burliest guards are already there to place heavy hands on the duke's shoulders, returning him roughly to his seat.

Sir Spencer's eyes shine with a light I've never seen before—and it helps me understand Lord Aaron's attraction, and how terribly tortured he was in his marriage. He must have doubted, until the moment the decree was made, that the King would keep his word. He turns to Lord Aaron and they smile at each other.

Then a shadow clouds Sir Spencer's countenance—the briefest flicker of darkness. He scoots his seat closer to Lord Aaron's, lays an arm over the back of his chair, and leans forward and kisses his temple.

The audience explodes into shrieks and whispers, and I feel sick inside. Even though I know how strongly these two feel toward each other, how desperate they must be to stop hiding, *that* gesture was staged. It was for His Highness' purposes, and I can't help but resent that this moment between them will always be a little bit tainted.

"Furthermore," the King says, his voice echoing loudly

through concealed speakers, drowning out the crowd, "tyrants cannot be permitted to stand, so by royal decree, Duke and Duchess Tremain are hereby stripped of their titles and Sir Spencer Harrisford is ennobled as Duke Spencer Harrisford."

At that the din in the hall grows so overwhelming I have to fight the urge to clap my hands over my ears.

Still the King continues, nearly shouting into the microphone. "Along with the title, Duke Harrisford—excuse me, Duke Spencer, you're no longer married," he clarifies with a polite bow of his head, twisting the proverbial knife into the Tremains. "Duke Spencer inherits the symbolic duchy in the form of the Tremains' twelve-room suite in the south wing. Those of you who wish to offer condolences may call on the Tremains at the former home of my own dear wife's parents, the Graysons."

I fancy I can *feel* a thousand sets of eyes turn my way, though my own remain fixed on a point just over His Highness' right shoulder. The King's decrees are incredibly harsh, but one risks these kinds of consequences when one attempts to overthrow a government, don't they? Even in an enlightened corporatocracy. But the humiliation being heaped on the Tremains is ... unfathomable. My own contribution to their punishment is almost trifling by comparison.

I wait for the guilt.

It doesn't come.

I smile instead.

The King raises both hands into the air, and though the hall certainly doesn't return to the silence of the beginning of his speech, his next words are at least audible. "As a show of goodwill, the new Duke Spencer has agreed to offer half his voting shares for private sale."

Goodwill? I seriously doubt that. It was Sir Spencer's *punishment*.

The combined expressions of outrage, disbelief, and confusion form an overwhelming cacophony as the court sheds decorum entirely. Voting shares in Sonoma are almost impossible to purchase, ever. But the King's announcement is little more than thumbing his nose at his detractors; the CEO of Sonoma Inc. has right of first refusal, meaning, simply, that Justin will buy up all the Harrisford shares himself and will henceforth, essentially, be untouchable.

The Tremain faction, the only genuine threat the Wyndham dynasty has ever faced, is finished. The rebellion is over, and Justin is the undeniable victor.

The King lowers his arms and turns to me, holding out his hand for mine. Overwhelmed, I simply do as I'm expected, and the King sweeps me away, down from the dais, ignoring the crowd's many shouted questions. Guards bar anyone from following us—a measure rarely taken within the palace, where we're accustomed to royalty walking among us—and with a strange suddenness, we're alone in His Highness' office.

The King is walking tall, jauntily, and I realize that this is the true Justin Wyndham. Smart, charismatic, brilliant, yes. But ruthless and cutthroat in a way no nineteen-year-old should be.

"You loved that," I say softly.

"Of course I loved it."

"You destroyed Tremain's life."

"He tried to destroy mine."

"You used my home. You didn't even ask."

He scoffs at that. "I don't have to ask; I'm the King! Besides," he adds offhandedly, "you don't live there anymore, and neither does your father."

"He's in the hospital!" I snap. Even though I don't intend for him to stay there long.

"Your father departed for Languedoc-Roussillon this morning," the King says, waving away my concern. "I assumed you knew; was that not your signature I saw on the travel requisition?"

I blink. My father is . . . gone. I wasn't even there to see him off. Did he put up a fuss about that? Was he even sufficiently lucid to understand what was happening? The revelation threatens to derail me—but of course, that's why the King mentioned it when he did.

I refuse to give him the upper hand.

"You dragged me into it. You *implicated* me!" My words are angry. I think I should actually *be* angry. Why am I not?

"I *credited* you. It was your idea! And it was excellent," he adds, as though I could want that praise. "I was thinking corporate. I wanted to render him powerless, to tear down his life's work the way he tried to tear down mine—tried to tear down my parents' legacy. But you? You came up with something better."

He looks down at me and it's only then that I realize he's still holding my hand; he's been holding it since he helped me rise from my seat on the dais. I want to snatch it back, but now he's gripping it in earnest, lifting it to his lips to place a long, slow kiss on it.

"You know we could make a true partnership of this, don't you? We're so young—we could be a power couple that rules for *decades*, Danica. We would live in the history books for ages."

I'm shaking my head almost spasmodically and backing away, tugging on my hand until he releases it.

"I'm not asking you to be lovelorn. You needn't even leave your 'secretary' behind. We all need entertainment, *bien sûr*. But we're a *match*, Danica, a real match. We could be amazing."

"I'm not like that," I manage to whisper.

His Highness steps toward me, a wide smile on his face, and leans close to my ear. "Then why are your eyes shining like a child in a sweetshop?"

My mouth clatters shut. Are they? My hands rise to my cheeks and they're hot. Not with anger. Nor even with illness. I am *thrilled*.

I love this.

FIFTEEN

THE FRENETIC PALACE buzz is like nothing I've ever seen. In some ways it's worse than the morning of the big vote. Then, there was mystery and hope and fear and the unknown; now, we're witness to a great downfall and we must all cast ourselves in the role of cowardly onlooker or taunting bully.

I don't know where I fit. No, I'm *afraid* of where I fit.

"M.A.R.I.E. wouldn't even open their doors. There were trunks and boxes stacked—neatly, mind you—all along the hallway," Lady Mei says. She and Lady Nuala, along with Tamae and Lady Ebele from my *lever* staff, are gathered around me in a corner of the *salons*. "Duke Tremain—well, not the duke anymore—was the picture of stoicism. But the mother sobbed and sobbed and yelled a bit, and near the end started to throw things. And Mademoiselle Julianna was said to have shouted the most dreadful things at her parents."

The ladies around me gasp, and I stare at them, feeling like I've forgotten the proper way to respond. "Such a shame," Lady Nuala says. "None of this was her fault." And I suppose she's right. I've always thought of Lady Julianna as simply part of the greater mass that is the Tremain family, but was she really? Was she as much a puppet as Sir—no, *Duke*—Spencer? How many of these young ladies are completely at the mercy of their parents' choices?

Wasn't I at that very mercy mere months ago?

"But what a way to react," Lady Ebele says, a hand on her hip and her chin held high. "A person is defined by how they act not in times of prosperity, but in times of challenge. Lady Julianna is simply showing her true colors."

A murmur of halfhearted approval meets her words, and I realize that no one wants to say the wrong thing, even if they might disagree. Moreover, their eyes keep darting to *me* to see what reaction I will have. I am the person in power; my reaction will be the "right" one. But I simply turn my eyes to the rest of the room. There's a luncheon assembled, but few dare depart their cluster of friends—except perhaps to flit to another cluster to trade old gossip for new before flitting back again. Who needs food when we can glut ourselves on the carrion of our peers' disgrace?

I should feel bad. I should regret my part in Lady Julianna's downfall. But I find that I don't. I don't know how involved she was in the scheme to trap Duke Spencer into marriage, but at the very least, she was complicit. It's a *kind* of guilt. One I know too well.

But since I can't face blaming myself for the same crime, I instead lash out at Lady Julianna. "She had it coming," I mutter, cementing her social downfall.

The circle buzzes again, each girl having been given permission to indulge in her pettiness. "Eventually they got all their belongings settled, but you're well aware of the size of that place," Lady Ebele continues, demurring to me with respect as she insults my former home. "And only the two bedrooms. Lady Julianna—

just Mademoiselle Julianna now—will go from titled, independent, married woman to sharing a bedroom with her little sister." The look on her face marks this news the greatest tragedy of all.

Unable to stand there and marinate in the pool of *schadenfreude* I just created, I grab hold of Lady Mei's arm and pull her along with me, making my way down the length of the *salons*. I don't excuse my abrupt exit; I'm the Queen.

Saber trails silently behind us and, for once, I find myself avoiding his eyes. We haven't had a chance to discuss anything that has happened in the last two hours, and I truly don't want to know what he thinks of me at this moment. I think of our intimate conversation last night and feel as though I've betrayed him somehow.

As we pass through the Mercury Drawing Room, I spot Sir Spencer and Lord Aaron standing together, not touching more than a shoulder bump now and again as they converse, but clearly a couple nonetheless. I sense that their joviality is a bit forced, but it doesn't bother me as much as it did this morning. Everyone pays a price, and this is theirs—a dramatization of affection in the public eye for the freedom of love behind closed doors.

At our approach they drop into bows, the courtiers around them following suit. Lord Aaron was *so* right—everything is different now that I look like the Queen. More importantly, now that the King is treating me like the Queen. I was by his side on that dais this morning—to say nothing of my appearance before the highest of the nobility in the secret meeting where this whole *charade* was begun. Honestly, I'm even starting to feel like a Queen.

And wondering how far that power can carry my own schemes.

I can feel Lady Mei trembling at the social honor of being the Queen's closest *confidante* this evening, paraded about before the high nobility. At my left elbow. She often is. She's proving herself, day by day. And I'll ask more of her. Perhaps the time will come when I'll ask more than she wants to give. I wonder what she will say.

"Your Highness," Lord Aaron says. "I was hoping to see you. Might we have a word?"

"Of course," I say formally, and the courtiers surrounding us hang on my every word. "Duke Spencer, if you'll keep this one out of trouble?"

"A challenge indeed," Duke Spencer says playfully. The crowd titters as I hand Lady Mei off to Duke Spencer, who, in turn, passes Lord Aaron to me.

I wave off a few hangers-on as he leads me very purposefully into the King's Clock Cabinet. It's a small chamber, open to the public during daytime hours, but only one door is available without special credentials; it's about as private as we're going to get. Once we pass into the room, Saber takes up a position in the open doorway, glaring at anyone who tries to enter. An unwritten royal privilege.

"How are things? With Sir—Duke Spencer?" I ask.

A wry chuckle rolls out of Lord Aaron as he leans a hip against the table, and his entire face lightens. "They're good. It's . . . amazing to not hide. I can't deny that it feels like a dream come true."

"But?" I prompt when he falls silent.

"I wasn't in that meeting between your husband and my love," he says, staring straight ahead. "I don't know what the King said, much less what he implied, but I get the impression that Spence feels very much indebted to the King. And that the King wants very much for him to feel that way."

I nod soberly. "An unspecified debt is always a source of unease."

"I'm trying not to think about it too hard. I've grown quite good at not letting myself think about the future and making the most of the now." A gentle smile lifts the corners of his mouth. "It's much better when the now is good, though. Much, much better."

"Will you stay with him in his new quarters, then?" I ask, our heads still close together. *Will you stay?* is the question I truly want to ask, but don't dare.

He nods. "For now. Even though it's been his home for two years, he's ill at ease in that large apartment, all by himself. I don't blame him. My bachelor lodgings are rather cramped by comparison, but I always know exactly who's in my house." He scoffs. "Did you know the Tremain apartments are equipped with seventeen bots?"

A stab of guilt over Molli and her family's single bot jabs at my heart. I swallow my emotions and try to stay cheerful. "Seventeen bots?" I say with a forced grin. "Only five people lived in that entire household."

"It's a large place. I'd never been invited before, naturally." He shakes his head. "It must have been such a close thing the day of the vote. I can only imagine the influence that kind of money could buy, and you know I'm no pauper. Added to the political sway of their name, the mind boggles. Old family, here since the beginning." He squeezes my hand. "If Tremain had won, none of this could have happened."

I think about whom I voted for, and guilt simmers in my stomach. I thought of Saber, not the new duke, and perhaps I also thought about revenge on the King. I hate wondering if I was willing to throw away my friend's happiness in the name of revenge.

But I didn't. I was thinking of Saber. Of a new King who would certainly order his release. I *was*.

I lean closer to Lord Aaron and say, too quietly for Saber to hear from his station guarding the door, "I was able to place your device yesterday."

"Reginald came to pick up payment?"

"It took some badgering, but yes. I'd like to send one device with each payment, get an idea how his money flows through Paris. It would be nice to attach one to the man himself, but—"

"But you're not suicidal, I take it?"

I smile. "Can you make more?"

"Now that they're designed, fabbing them is easy enough. The big question will be how much they use the catacombs. The tracker won't work underground. I've programmed it to hide from bug scanners, but that means it might stay quiet for long periods of time. The power cell should keep it going for a week, ten days maybe. If the first one has checked in at all, I'll let you know. But I have to go back to my private office computer for that—I didn't want it routing through anywhere obvious."

"Speaking of offices, Lord Aaron, where is yours?"

"Business wing. Like most everyone's. Why?"

"I have some things I'd like to store somewhere . . . safe . . . for a few weeks. With your permission, of course."

"Freely granted. I'll show you how the tracker works, too, if you like."

"Why, Lord Aaron," I say wryly. "I can't remember the last time you offered to show me your code."

"Alas, we've all been too frequently indisposed of late," he laments dramatically, and for a moment I remember the feeling of being newly arrived to the palace, fourteen years old and brimming with curiosity, anxious to learn M.A.R.I.E.'s secrets from an impeccably garbed, younger Lord Aaron, who so readily extended me a friendly hand. Once he found out I was good, we used to exchange long lines of code, improving it each time it passed hands.

Simpler times. For all of us.

We stroll out of the King's Clock Cabinet and must, inevitably, deal with the present and its inhabitants once more. I don't realize that Lady Cabral has approached our little cluster until I hear her arguing with Saber just behind me.

"Is there a problem?" I ask, turning in annoyance.

The woman straightens, thrusting her hand into the folds of her skirt. After flashing Saber a nasty look—which only makes me want to snub her entirely—she approaches, drops a quick curtsy, and holds out her hand for mine. I feel her tuck quite a large stack of bills into my palm and she says, with a touch of mania, "I just want to make sure I'm first. I'm paying double to guarantee I get a canister next week before they run out. I didn't get one yesterday."

I'm stunned, and I know the surprise shows on my face before I get a chance to wipe it away. Reginald told me I'd have no trouble making the million I now owe him for each batch. He knew this would happen, and I suppose some part of me knew it too.

"I merely want a guarantee," she pleads.

"Saber," I say, straightening, "make a note, please. Lady Cabral is first on our list."

Saber glares at me for one beat too long for true subservience, then nods and pulls out his tablet and stylus.

"Maybe don't tell too many of your friends," I whisper, giving Lady Cabral a naughty smile. "We can't be putting *everyone* first, can we?" I've guaranteed that everyone will know by the end of the night. She drops a very low bow, better suited to a formal ceremony than a clandestine drug deal, and rushes off.

"I'm not sure that was your best move, Your Highness," Saber says, the three of us standing in a triangle as Lady Cabral fairly sprints away, glancing back twice before disappearing around a corner.

"No, it's perfect. Not everyone can afford the extra, or perhaps will only be able to pay it occasionally. It'll help everyone cut down."

"I think you underestimate the pull," Saber says. "Reginald is hoping you'll sell more Glitter, not get a higher price on the same quantity."

"He . . . told you this?"

Saber shakes his head. "I know how he thinks. He'd rather have more clients hooked. Better for him."

Well, if anyone would know how Reginald thinks, it would be Saber. "You may be right. But I've got to do *something* to meet Reginald's new price. Plus, I still owe six canisters to my *lever* staff, and I've promised three particular little bandits their own share, should they desire," I say with a grin, knocking Lord Aaron's shoulder with mine. But humor fails to escape the gravity of circumstance. "If they pay double they can get on a priority list. Limit the names to, say, half our usual shipment? If I have to double the price again in a few weeks, then so be it."

Lord Aaron whistles under his breath and Saber raises both eyebrows. "And if you have to double it in a few *days*?"

I swallow hard and try to consider whether that could actually happen. My response comes out in a whisper.

"Then so be it."

SIXTEEN

"A WEDDING GIFT? CAN I SEE?"

My arms go weak at my husband's voice—even though he sounds entirely friendly. *Too* friendly? It's hard to know where caution ends and paranoia begins. I tighten my grip on the white box. Saber has a similar one, wrapped in fancy paper and tied with an ornate bow, and both are full of hastily stacked euros. The money is concealed beneath fluffy bath towels, but it's a shallow precaution—toiletries don't exactly make the cut on gifts fit for a queen. I take the quickest of breaths, then turn to face Justin with a placid smile.

Which almost flips to a scowl. He's got Lady Cyn on his arm, and she's sporting an amethyst necklace so shiny it can only be new. I can't say for sure whether Justin gave it to her or she purchased it for herself to keep up the illusion, but I want to rip it off her skinny neck.

His Highness steps closer and reaches for the lid, but I spin, keeping the top of the box away from his prying fingers as my heart pounds in my ears. "Tosh, it's not a wedding gift: it's for me. It's almost my birthday, as you well know. Lord Aaron has offered to store the early arrivals for me."

"You do hate to wait for anything," he says with a laugh, but his tone is sufficiently cool to betray suspicion.

"I'd hoped to have my own private space to store them," I say, "but I was assured that office space is at a premium just now."

"So the facilities people tell me," the King says, taking the bait—at least for the moment. But he gives me a sharp glare, and where my tone was playful, his is inflected with warning. He must see more in my expression than I intended to let slip. "Such a heavy load for you, my love, and a long walk. Allow me." He reaches out, and though Lady Cyn makes a gallant effort to hang on to his arm, she eventually has to admit defeat and let her hands fall to her sides.

"Oh, I couldn't possibly," I say, evading his grasp. "This one is my favorite."

He peers at the box skeptically. "How do you know? It's wrapped."

I rub one cheek against the edge of the satin ribbon that flows over the side of the box. "Yes—but it has the *prettiest* packaging, and that's enough for me. Surely you understand?"

The King seems amused by the subtle slight—and more, perhaps, by Lady Cyn's apparent obliviousness. "If you're certain?"

"I am."

He nods and watches as I get my little train moving back down the hallway. Lady Cyn nudges her way back to my husband's side and casts me a triumphant smirk that I pretend not to see.

"You're a fool if you think he bought that," Saber whispers once we're out of the King's sight.

"He didn't," I reply. "But all I truly needed was to get away.

From both of them," I add acerbically. I wish I'd had time to do—
to say—something else. Something to remind my husband of his
own repeated insistence that, *publicly* at least, we must be per-
ceived as a happy couple. A happy *monogamous* couple. But the
risk was too high; I had to retreat. This time.

Duke Spencer meets us at the entrance to Lord Aaron's small-
ish office at the far end of the business wing, and even as we
exchange pleasantries, I find myself shifting from foot to foot im-
patiently. Once we're inside and unburdened of our parcels, Lord
Aaron dismisses the bot and closes the door. I collapse against
the wall and blot my brow with a handkerchief, wishing I could
reach the drips sliding down my back and into my bruisingly tight
corset.

"That was supposed to be much easier."

"Was it not?" Duke Spencer asks, a worried glance at Lord
Aaron.

"Ran right into the King," he answers.

Duke Spencer says nothing but visibly pales, and for the thou-
sandth time, I wish I knew what passed between him and Justin
on that day in the King's office.

"His Highness has displayed an alarming determination to
get his hands on pretty things," I say, removing the tops of the
boxes to check that everything is as it should be. When I lift the
bath towels, Duke Spencer gasps.

I straighten in alarm but turn to find he's staring at the money.

"I've never seen so much cash in my life," he says, and shame-
fully I remember when I was so innocent. This amount of cash is
never assembled for legal, aboveboard dealings. Even though I'm

sure he's made purchases far larger than what can be bought for paltry millions, digital currency is less personal, somehow. Less visceral. "How much is in there?" he asks.

"About two million," I say, angry when my voice cracks. Shame and guilt gnaw at my ribs, though I thought I'd grown numb to regret. I don't say a word about the other two million Saber and I carefully counted out and left in the largest box in my dressing room to cover Reginald's next payment. This is only my *profit*.

"Two million. And you've been bringing out similar amounts for several weeks?"

I nod, not wanting him to get too caught up in the web of lies that is my Glitter trade. He's already in deeper than I'd prefer, and has incurred costs at which I can only guess.

He lets out a soft whistle and shakes his head. "What is this doing to the exchange rates?"

I should have expected such a calculating response from the son of two international business executives. If memory serves, they headed the American agricultural offices until their untimely death—a dark mirror of the tragedy that made Justin a King before he reached adulthood. "How honest do you want me to be?" I ask softly. *How embroiled in this do you want to become?*

Duke Spencer pauses to consider and I'm again impressed by this somber, thoughtful person who's such a contrast to my bright, emotional friend. Opposites attract, I suppose. I'm enjoying finally getting a chance to know him, but he reminds me so much of Molli's gentle nature that I fear I'll accidentally taint and destroy him, too.

"In this case?" he says, almost brusquely. "Completely."

I take a deep breath, then stall by reaffixing lids to boxes. "The exchange rate took a beating initially. We drew too much money out too fast. When Duchess Darzi mentioned Duke Florentine's concern, I encouraged people to pawn their jewels, so most of the cash is coming in from Paris at this point."

"Ah," the duke says, running one hand through his golden hair. "That's what stabilized the exchange rate. At least until everyone starts trying to replace their jewels."

"Which they might not do," I hurriedly say. "I've always encouraged the courtiers to sell old and unwanted things." But my cheeks are heating and Duke Spencer gives me a look of skepticism I richly deserve.

"Good thing no one in Sonoman-Versailles is accustomed to buying themselves more than they strictly need," he says blandly.

I swallow hard and turn away.

"So the kingdom will feel the fiscal results of your little business for years to come?"

"It was only supposed to be five," I mumble.

"Five?"

"Million," Lord Aaron answers for me. "Five million to get out before the wedding."

"Ah—that was this Reginald fellow's price," Duke Spencer says, piecing together what I revealed at our dinner.

"Indeed," I whisper, knowing my voice will shake if I attempt a higher volume. Saber steps up behind me, snaking one arm across my chest, hand cupping my shoulder, pulling me securely against him.

"So what now?" Duke Spencer asks. There's power in his voice.

He's learning more than he expected about how far into the muck I've dug myself. Of course he wants to know what my plan is.

Except that I don't truly have one. Not a clear one, anyway. I shake my head. "I still want to get away."

"Seems easy enough. You're nearly eighteen. Aaron has introduced me to some really fantastic people from the Foundation for Social Reintegration—"

"*Easy* is the wrong word," I cut in, not particularly wanting to have a conversation about Lord Aaron's favorite philanthropy. The Foundation does good work, helping former Sonoma employees who are also citizens of Sonoman-Versailles—and thus have salaries tied up in the credit system—transition to noncorporate living arrangements. But the fact remains that their inability to take me away six months ago because of my age is the reason I had to turn to Reginald in the first place. It doesn't make me love them. "Over the past few months I've accrued some . . . debts . . . that must be paid before I can leave."

"Debts?"

"Metaphorically, I mean. People I have to rescue. A few I need to destroy." I feel Saber shift behind me, and I know I'm going to get an earful later, but in front of Lord Aaron and Duke Spencer he'll hold his tongue.

"And the money will help you?"

"Doesn't money help everything?" I ask wryly.

"Point." Duke Spencer pauses and then reaches for Lord Aaron's hand, twining their fingers. "Well, I—we—owe you a great debt, Your Highness—"

"Please don't call me that. Not here."

He's silent for a moment, and I like how Lord Aaron also remains quiet, letting Duke Spencer speak for himself. How often did I see either Lady Julianna or the former Duke Tremain speak right over the top of him? "All right. Danica, then?"

"Please," I whisper.

"Danica, we are in your debt. In settling your obligations as you see them, be assured that you have our loyalty and assistance. For as long as we can give it."

I don't bother to hide my surprise. "You intend to leave as well?"

"The court hasn't been kind to me," Duke Spencer says tightly. "This is the first good thing that's happened since my parents died, and still there are invisible strings attached."

"Indeed," I reply, angry on his behalf.

"And you know Spencer was the only thing keeping me here to begin with," Lord Aaron adds.

"But it'll take some time to disentangle our interests," Duke Spencer continues, "so please don't feel hurried on our behalf. I don't know what kind of timeline you're working on, but we're certainly open to delaying our departure if it means we can be of service to you."

"Thank you," I whisper. I take a long shuddering breath and turn to Saber. "Could you go downstairs to the kitchens and fetch me a bottle of Pellegrino? Please? I'm feeling . . . unsettled."

"I'll help," Duke Spencer says, stepping forward. But Lord Aaron's hand stays him.

"I assume I shouldn't hurry," Saber says ruefully, rolling a glare my way. He doesn't wait for a response—simply strides out the door, swinging it closed behind him.

"He's the one you're determined to rescue?" Duke Spencer asks. "Ah—just a guess," he adds when my eyes go straight to Lord Aaron. I really must learn to stop underestimating people's shrewdness.

"You're not wrong. But I didn't send him away to discuss that. I—as the Queen, I'm privy to His Highness' calendar. In ten days, he'll leave for just over a week. I'd like to use that time to travel into Paris to chase any leads we've gotten from the trackers."

"Assuming there are any," Lord Aaron says, digging a battered old tablet out of his desk. "Not a lot of hits so far."

"Optimism, Lord Aaron, please." I look to Duke Spencer. "If the three of us go with Lady Mei, everyone will assume it's a pleasure outing."

"And your man?" Duke Spencer asks, eyes going to where Saber exited.

"Saber must be involved in these affairs as little as possible." A long silence follows as Duke Spencer waits for me to expound. Lord Aaron and I have a conversation of hard looks. Duke Spencer has already puzzled most of it out, but Saber's secrets aren't mine to tell, and I know what he'd say if I sought his permission. I won't betray him.

"Where is the King going?" Lord Aaron asks, thankfully changing the subject.

"That, I don't know."

Lord Aaron raises his eyebrows.

"You think that's odd?" I ask.

"Yes! The King's travel plans are announced in general terms, for security reasons, but they're almost always announced—it's a publicity thing." He consults a newer, more official-looking tablet than the one associated with tracking Reginald. "But this is definitely not on the public calendar. If he's taking an unannounced trip, odds are good it's something to do with those plans he flaunted at the shareholder meeting."

"Do you imagine I can do something with that?" I ask.

"Find out where he's going and I might have a better answer for you. It could be a first step. Last we spoke, you had no idea how you were going to move against the King. Has that changed?"

"No," I whisper. "But maybe this can lead to . . . I don't know, to *something.*" I glance at the elegant grandfather clock standing in one corner of Lord Aaron's office. "I've got to prepare for dinner," I say ruefully, rising to collect my small reticule from Lord Aaron's desktop. "I'll be in touch. Until then, remember, we're cheerful, idiotic courtiers, enjoying Duke Spencer's new promotion, and the new freedom you both have, with not a care in the world or a thought in our heads. The last thing we could possibly be getting into is espionage."

SEVENTEEN

"YOU'RE NOT GOING to give up on this, are you?" Saber asks as we enter my bedchamber.

"No," I say, setting my reticule down on my dressing table and allowing a dressing-bot to relieve me of my heavier adornments— including an overskirt made entirely of silver netting. It's almost as heavy as a *pannier* full of Glitter; I'll have to put it back on for the formal dinner tonight, but for the moment it's a relief to have it off.

Saber sheds his own *accoutrements* with no assistance: his trusty leather messenger bag, the cravat he hates, embroidered livery jacket, and white gloves. They fall into a heap on the floor, and he no longer complains when a second bot hurries over to tidy up. How strange it must be for him—someone who grew up a slave in a criminal street organization—to live for months among such finery.

He crosses his arms over his chest and studies me. "Are you doing this for me?"

"What?"

"You've paid Reginald. You could simply stop selling Glitter and sit back and wait for him to decide he's ready to take you away. I've asked you to do just that. But you won't. You're still selling."

"I—" But he cuts off my justifications.

"You're trying to track down the source of Glitter. You're trying to *take down* Reginald—a seasoned crime boss. Don't deny it; I'm not an idiot." He turns and looks hard at me. "Are you doing it for me?"

I sputter for a moment before drawing in a breath and forcing myself to be calm. "Of course I'm doing it for you. How can you expect me not to?"

"I didn't ask you to," he snaps back.

"I didn't need to be asked." Tendrils of anger curl up my spine, and I feel hot and then cold.

"You're hurting people, Danica. And you're doing it in my name. How do you think that makes me feel?"

"*Loved,* maybe?"

His chin falls and I know I've said the wrong thing. I'm just not sure why. "I don't want you to do this for me. You're not just hurting the people out there," he says, gesturing toward the doors. "You're hurting yourself. You're making choices that will leave you changed, and I don't want you to destroy yourself to save me."

"You want me to put myself ahead of you?"

He clamps his mouth closed.

I shake my head, lifting my chin. "No. I reject that sort of thinking. You don't get to tell me I can't sacrifice anything I damn well please for you. You don't get to make that choice."

"Then what choice *do* I get to make?"

My chin starts to tremble, and I grind my teeth to get it to stop. "Whether or not you'll still love me when I'm done."

He sighs, long and noisy, and steps forward to wrap his arms around me. I'm too tall to fit fully beneath his chin, but there's a nice, soft hollow at the crook of his neck that cradles my cheek perfectly. "Of course I will. But . . . you can't win against him. And not just him—this is so much bigger than Reginald. You've got to know that."

"Of course there's someone above Reginald," I say with irritation, hating how unwilling he is to do anything to save himself. "And above him, and above him. But I have to do something about him, Saber. Just because a whole problem is bigger than one person can solve doesn't mean they should give up on the part that they *can* solve."

He doesn't respond for a long time, and when at last he speaks, it's scarcely above a whisper. "Then let's make a deal."

"A deal?"

"I worry about you. I worry about this." He puts his hands around my waist, but I'm unsure what he's talking about. "If you succeed, if you get away, there's no other culture in the world that still wears these. And even here, no one wears their corset the way you do."

I turn away from him and my face flushes hotly as I realize what he's talking about. "You don't understand," I mumble.

"I *do*," Saber says, pressing his face into my line of sight, giving me no choice but to look at him. "I know you think you need this. That it helps you cope with everything in your life. But, Danica, you can't walk twenty meters on your own without it. It doesn't make you strong—it makes you *weak*."

"You do *not* understand," I say, voice unsteady.

"Danica, your muscles cannot physically support you without the help of your corset. You can't deny that."

And I can't. But hearing it spoken aloud stings like a slap.

"I won't stand in your way. If Reginald asks what you've been doing, I'll lie, consequences be damned. But in return, you let me help you get stronger. When the time comes that you're ready to walk away from this hell, I want you to do so on your own."

My body is trembling, and the full import of his concern hits me when I realize that all I want in this moment is to pull my laces tighter—to rebel against him by letting the ache of my polyethylene boning soothe my anxiety. "There's nothing you can do," I whisper.

"There is. Exercises, every day, to build up your muscles. Loosening your corset a little bit each morning."

I step around the delicate gilded chair that always sits at my dressing table, needing to put some kind of barrier between the two of us. "That's ridiculous," I say, my tone lofty.

"Every. Day."

"I don't need anything like that."

"Yes, you do," Saber says. "And I'll help you." He gives himself a self-deprecating glance. "Honestly, I could stand some exercise myself. Your pampered life is making me soft." He pats his flat belly, where I've skimmed my fingers down a veritable washboard of abdominal muscles on many occasions. If he's put on an ounce, I don't know where.

But his humor can't reach the panic fluttering in my chest like a caged bird. "You think I don't know how to do crunches?"

"Of course you know. You're smart. Smarter than me, for sure. But everyone can use a little push now and then." He steps closer, and when he takes my hands I know he can feel how cold they've grown—how hard they're shaking. "Sometimes, brilliance isn't being able to solve every problem by yourself—it's recognizing when you can't. Let me help. Because you're right, it's more than doing some crunches. I want to free you from your need for this. Wouldn't you rather be free?"

"Wouldn't you?" I shoot back in challenge, and feel vaguely satisfied when he licks his lips and draws a deep breath.

"Yes. And even *wanting* it terrifies me. I've spent *years* smothering that want, because there's nothing worse than wanting something you know you will never, under *any* conceivable circumstances, ever have again." His hands shake as they clench around mine. "That's why it's a fair deal. I'll help you take one step toward freeing me if you let me help you do the same. We'll be terrified together."

I think of the awful things Reginald said in the *Orangerie* and know that my attachment to my corsets is nothing, *nothing* compared to the practiced stoicism that keeps Saber sane. But knowing doesn't make the first step any easier. I can't say it—I can't say *yes*—but Saber sees the acquiescence in my eyes, the tiny dip of my chin that is all the sign I can give. He comes around behind me and begins unfastening the delicate hooks up the back of my gown. "Now?" I choke out.

"I should have started weeks ago," he murmurs, letting his warm breath touch my earlobe. "I let myself get distracted."

It's different than other times he's undressed me, because I know what's coming next—and it's not soft kisses and warm caresses. But he soothes me with every step, like a skittish horse being bridled for the first time. My gown ripples to the luxurious carpet, and he unties the satin ribbons at the back of my corset, murmuring in Mongolian the whole time. It's his best trick. I can't understand a single word, but hearing him whisper in his native tongue—in the language he spoke when he was free—makes me remember that he once *was* free. That if I succeed, one day he'll be free again.

I close my eyes and focus on his words, trying to ignore the feeling of the laces letting go until they're loose enough to unfasten the hooks on the busk. He pulls the whole contraption away, and I reach for the back of the spindly chair for support.

"No," he whispers. "Stay standing."

"I might faint."

"I'll catch you."

A wave of dizziness washes over me and my knees threaten to buckle, but I force them straight and open my eyes, focusing on one spot across the room the way I do in dances when we spin. It takes a good minute, but finally the dizziness seeps away. "Now what?"

Saber leads me to the synthetic wood floor outside the railing and lays down two towels. He spends some time talking me through crunches, rockers, bends, twists—showing me more ways to work different parts of my abdomen than I ever imagined existed, with long breaks between each attempt. He demonstrates, I follow as best I can, and soon we're both sweating. Saber pulls his shirt over his head so I can see the muscles he's working flex and ripple beneath his skin.

Soft, *mon œil*.

When I so much as attempt planks, however, the dizziness returns with a vengeance. I lie on my stomach, cheek resting against the cool flooring, my abdomen a useless pile of jelly. And I'm all too aware I didn't actually do very much.

Back before I started lacing, I used to run and climb and play like most people my age—like all children everywhere, I assume. Why did I stop? Saber is right—as he so often is. I'm too weak to be able to physically cope without my corset, and that's no way to embark on a new life. But what if I've started too late?

Saber is lying on his back beside me, not touching me, not even breathing heavily, even though he worked much harder than I did.

"When the time comes," he says softly, "I need you to go."

"Go?"

"With Reginald. When he's ready. I need you to promise me." He rolls over and runs a finger up my arm. "I'll do my very best to have you ready. Physically, I mean. You won't be winning a body-building contest anytime soon," he says with a grin, and I groan from the floor, where I've barely moved for the last five minutes. "But when you walk away, I want you to do so completely under your own strength. Okay?"

I nod with my eyes closed, not only because I'm exhausted but because I don't want to see in his eyes that he's fully accepted that he won't be coming with me. He assumes, when all is said and done, that Reginald will make good on his promise to give me a new life somewhere, and Saber will go back to being . . . what he's been.

I don't press the issue. My infinitesimal nod was only an acknowledgment that I want to be able to walk away on my own.

I didn't give my promise that I'll leave him behind.

EIGHTEEN

"YOU'RE CERTAIN?" I ask, bending over Lord Aaron's desk to peer at his tablet.

"Nothing's certain with two data points, but it's a start. The first payment that you were able to place about ten days ago was on the move for a while. It stopped at these *maisonettes* for several days, then cycled through *La Défense* before losing power—probably someone spent it there, and it was working its way through merchants' tills. The second one from two days ago went to the same *maisonettes,* but now—"

"—it's over a hundred kilometers into the countryside," I say, my eyes scanning the data scrolling across the screen. "But that could be, what, one of Reginald's men sending money home to his aging mother?"

"Only if his aging mother runs a company for mad punsters. Look." Lord Aaron pulls up satellite imagery showing a midsized farming operation. The facility and surrounding acreage is tagged *Pharmaison SARL.*

"Saber said Glitter was grown in a lab by pharmaceutical researchers." My heart is pounding in my ears. "That can't be a coincidence. We found the source of Glitter."

"That's one possibility," Lord Aaron says slowly.

I resist the urge to say something impatient. The King's departure this morning started a blaring countdown in my head, and I'm anxious to make use of the time we have. For the next week, there's no one in Versailles who outranks me. I'm not a corporate officer—I have no particular say in the company's day-to-day operation—but what would I do with control of the largest agribusiness in the world, anyway? Ship some extra corn to Australia, for kicks? No, what I have is the ability to move freely and make any inquiries that might occur to me, with no one to answer to until His Majesty returns. It's not a blank check, exactly, but it's more freedom than I've had in months.

After forcing myself to take several deep breaths, I ask, as calmly as I can manage, "What other possibilities do you have in mind?"

Lord Aaron looks up at me. "Worst case? Reginald found the trackers and is hoping to murder you somewhere picturesque."

"YOU'RE SURE ABOUT this?" Lord Aaron asks for the third time as we saunter down the front steps of the palace, waving back at those watching through the windows of the Hall of Mirrors. Two bots are following us, bearing ribbon-bedecked picnic hampers. As we're going out on a clandestine mission, it seemed only appropriate to draw as much attention to ourselves as possible.

"I'm *fêting* a newly minted young duke with his well-heeled suitor and a marquis's daughter, heiress to one of Sonoma's oldest legacies," I say through a broad smile as I acknowledge Tamae and Lady Nuala waving sulkily at us from the balcony of the Hall of Mirrors. "It's the sort of thing bored, obscenely wealthy adolescents do all the time, or so I'm assured."

As I announced this morning, an hour after the King's helicopter took off, we're taking a day trip to the countryside, just the four of us. Which certainly didn't make the other hundred people who seem to think I'm their bosom friend very happy. Thus the sad faces on the balcony.

"You don't think anyone suspects?" Lord Aaron presses.

"After the last two days I suspect no one in the palace remembers we know how to read, much less pull off a secret expedition."

"True. My head is killing me and I blame you."

We've even spent some time establishing our cover, indulging in enough mindless decadence over the last few days that no one in court could have missed it. As *charades* go, vapid hedonism has its charms. Though late nights weary one quickly—*soirées* lasting to dawn, limping back to my bedchamber for a few stolen moments with Saber—the courtiers seem to be gulping it down like expensive champagne. Rather at the rate they literally gulp down said champagne. We apparently did such a thorough job of it that when the King left, he went so far as to warn me not to turn into a regular bacchanalian while he was gone.

His words were light, even a bit leering; likely he suspects our ruse. Still, he left on schedule, and I doubt there was anything he could do except, perhaps, tell that weasel Mateus to keep a close eye on us. Which he certainly can't do if we leave in a fancy SUV.

"But it's Paris," Lord Aaron continues as the doors close and the car rolls away from the palace. "I can't help but feel we're vastly overdressed." He looks around at our very typical dress: gowns and jackets with breeches.

"Baroque attire is its own disguise."

"As the only person in this vehicle who has actually lived out in the real world, I feel obligated to point out that it's also exceptionally memorable," Duke Spencer says, climbing into the sumptuously upholstered self-driving SUV beside Lord Aaron. "More than you may realize."

"But you're also in the best position to know what this so-called real world thinks of us," Lady Mei points out. "They think we're crazy."

Duke Spencer stifles a snort and doesn't have to agree.

"Either they'll see us as empty-headed Louies, and we'll tell them we're lost," she says, adjusting her voluminous satin skirts, "or they'll think we're investors and give us a tour."

"Or file a complaint with the WTO for prying into their trade secrets," Duke Spencer says, almost gloomily. "Or attack us in a fit of patriotic zeal. Sonoma may own half the farmland in France, but that hardly makes them anxious to sell us more."

"What would you have me do?" I ask, spreading my gloved hands before me. "Call ahead?"

"No," Duke Spencer replies, "no, of course not. I'm sorry. I'm ... out of my element, as you might imagine. There are so many worst-case scenarios, I can't seem to keep track of which is *actually* the worst."

"Welcome to my world," I say wryly, eliciting laughter from Lord Aaron and Lady Mei. Soon enough, Duke Spencer joins in. I muster a smile—in truth, my own concerns are at least as serious as those expressed by the duke. I've programmed the car to reverse course at a moment's notice, but I can't *not* follow up on this possible insight into Reginald's operation. Each day that I fail to make progress toward a solution is a new opportunity for everything to come crashing down on my head.

Soon Lord Aaron's cheek finds Duke Spencer's shoulder, and even Lady Mei is quiet as the SUV eats up the kilometers. The silence that settles around us is comfortable, welcome. An emotional oasis.

Though what I could really use is a physical oasis. I hurt in places I'd forgotten I had. I used to get sore arms and shoulders during my more intense lessons with Giovanni, but nothing like whatever Saber's doing to me. When he presented the idea, I figured he'd have me do a million sit-ups and crunches, but he's doing something entirely different, where I'm constantly lifting various body parts and holding them in the air. The result is that I'm sore from neck to knees every single day. He told me the aches would ease up in time, but so far they haven't lightened so much as a feather.

The gradual loosening of my daily corset has begun as well— one centimeter every other day. Saber lobbied for one a day, but I'm already concerned about the speed. It took me over half a year to lace down as far as I have, and it was imperative I make him understand that he can't undo it all in two weeks. Even if my body could handle it—and I have serious doubts—my mind could not.

I still fight the impulse to run back to my room and have my bots cinch my ribbons every time I see Lady Cyn, or when my husband is in a particularly foul mood, or when my customers behave erratically—which seems to be happening more and more often of late. There are moments when I have to drag Saber into an empty room and make him wrap his arms around my waist and squeeze me as tightly as he can until I can regain control of the panic that's always waiting to slip through my fingers.

"Whatever else we see today," Lord Aaron says, staring out at the sunny green fields north of Paris, "I do love a trip out into the countryside."

"I've never been," I say.

"Truly?" Lord Aaron asks, raising his head from Duke Spencer's shoulder.

I shrug. "I've never been farther from the palace than Paris. I was born in the city of Versailles, and my father was very dedicated to his job. My father's brother was a company man of the nobility, and my mother was an only child, so there was no one to visit elsewhere. And face it—we Sonomans make rather dreadful tourists."

Everyone laughs at that. We certainly stick out among the rest of the world with our elaborate dress and formal mannerisms. Some of the courtiers, often the younger ones, are obsessed with the cultures of the outside world and spend hours researching them on the feeds, watching videos of everyday life outside our little country, but I was always satisfied with what we had. I don't know anything else, and even now I'm not sure what I'll do when I finally break away.

When. Not *if.*

The Nav screen shows that we're getting close, and I nudge

Lord Aaron. We all prepare ourselves to pretend we're doing nothing but attending a lavish picnic in a random field.

"Is this right?" I ask as we turn down a dusty but well-paved road lined with surprisingly tall security fencing that completely obscures our view of the fields. "I confess I don't get out much, but I'd have thought maybe barbed wire, or even just chain link. Isn't this overkill?"

"You're thinking like a Sonoman," Lord Aaron says. "In agribusiness, there's not much point putting up expensive walls. You'll never miss an ear of corn. This is a *biotech* firm we're approaching, judging by their name and what little I found on the feeds. A single plant could potentially be worth hundreds. More on the black market."

Our SUV crunches onto a gravel road that ends at a small guard shack outside an impressive-looking gate—features I'm unprepared to address, as they were apparently erected after the most recent satellite survey.

"What now?" Lady Mei asks, the same panic I'm trying not to show raw and bare in her voice.

"We—ask for directions," I say shakily. "Blame the Nav computer."

The SUV stops at the gate automatically, and a uniformed man emerges from the shack. I try not to notice that he's wearing a gun at his hip. With a shaking finger I push the button to lower the window closest to me and don a bright smile.

"Ma'am," the guard says, touching the brim of his hat. His vest boasts no name tag or corporate logo.

"I—"

"Oh, excuse me," he interrupts, and then, incomprehensibly, bends into a stiff bow. "Your Highness. I didn't recognize you." He rises, and I study him with eyes that I hope aren't wide with shock. "Were we expecting you today?" He consults a clipboard, and when he lifts a few pages, my whole body freezes as I catch sight of the familiar stylized Demeter insignia of Sonoma Inc. at the top of the first paper.

Why are we at a farm seemingly owned—or at least run—by *Sonoma*?

"You should have received notice," I bluff shamelessly. "But these things have been known to fall through the cracks."

He laughs as though I've told an exceptionally funny joke, and I force my smile to stay glued to my face. "They sure do." His accent is neither Sonoman, like mine, nor French, like Reginald's. After a moment I realize it's American, like Duke Spencer's. "Is His Majesty here with you?"

"He's on an extended trip, actually. But he suggested I might enjoy touring all the Parisian facilities, now that I'm Queen." I look up through my eyelashes flirtatiously. "This one's next on my list."

"Of course. If you'll pull through to the main building, I'll find out who we have available to show you around." He hesitates. "Unless you're here for a surprise inspection."

Trying to falsify *that* seems like overkill to me. And would almost certainly result in some sort of paper trail.

"Perish the thought. We're just out for some fresh air and maybe a picnic."

"I'll let Owens know, then," the guard says with a smile, and the heavy gate opens on a little gravel lot where half a dozen other cars are parked, one with the Sonoma logo on the side.

"I don't understand what just happened," Duke Spencer whispers once the window is closed. He sounds a little shell-shocked.

"Nor do I," I reply, a little dazed myself.

"This is a Sonoma facility. I'm not the only one who saw the logo, am I?" Lady Mei asks.

"Something rotten in Denmark," Lord Aaron says dryly.

We all tumble out of the SUV and stretch our legs. I'm glad I eschewed my usual formality for a lightweight frock—supposedly modeled after the costumes Marie-Antoinette once wore to the fake farm we Sonomans converted into a medical center. I thought the design was charming when I ordered it on a whim, but I never thought I'd be doing anything like *this*. Traipsing about an *actual farm*?

The woman who comes out to greet us isn't exactly dressed in a business suit, but she looks more official than the guard, and her polo shirt has the Sonoma insignia embroidered on it.

"Welcome, Your Highness," she says, inclining her head to me. It's odd—while my husband is this woman's boss of bosses, technically she's not a citizen of Sonoma, so I'm nothing to her but a figurehead who happens to also be a shareholder. I'm struck again by how much more power Justin has than I do by simple virtue of being the CEO as well as king. His influence is international. Mine is practically superficial. I need every edge I can get, and I have a feeling today's little field trip is going to lend me quite an edge indeed.

If I can only figure it out.

Greetings are exchanged, and we follow the woman toward a remarkably modern-looking building—like the gate, new enough to be missing from satellite photos of the area. She comments on the rich soil, the crop rotation, the weather over the past few months—all the sorts of maddeningly mundane things one might expect to hear on a tour of a semi-remote company farm, and none of the things I really want to know.

"Are those bots out there?" Lord Aaron asks, pointing at something glinting in the field.

"Oh, you must not be aware," the woman says pleasantly. "This is the proving ground for the new Amalgamated bots as well as our *papaveris atropa* cultivation. The crops are completely cared for by bots. Why revolutionize one area of commerce when you can revolutionize two?" she adds with a laugh. Lord Aaron and Duke Spencer chuckle along politely; Lady Mei remains quiet as a church mouse.

"Amalgamated—" Lord Aaron sounds very serious as he asks more questions about the bots, but I stopped listening the moment Dr. Owens said *papaveris atropa*. Those words have already changed my life; I would never forget them, though I heard them spoken only once, months ago, by a man with a heavy French accent. I can't say anything to the others at the moment, but now I understand.

This is Glitter.

NINETEEN

SABER SAID THERE was a pharmaceutical company involved. A company Reginald's original scientist stole the plants from. I knew all that. The idea that the company might be Sonoma never crossed my mind. Sonoma is first and foremost an agricultural concern, partnered with Amalgamated in the robotics industry. I didn't even know we *had* a pharmaceuticals division until the King put up that graph at the shareholder meeting.

A prescription drug like this—something as powerful as Glitter, but clean and legal—is revolutionary. This is going to be Justin's legacy as King. This must be the project he was talking about, the one that kept him on the throne. And it's somehow tied up with Amalgamated as well. The bots minding the fields—that's where they come from. A partnership, and an immensely profitable one. What did he say at the meeting? Seven hundred percent profit growth? Either Justin is more modest than I could possibly have guessed, or he has woefully underestimated the value of what he has.

But Reginald is stealing it. Sabotaging the King. And I'm helping him. If Justin ever finds out . . . there's no telling what he'll do.

I've been in over my head this whole time.

Duke Spencer seems to sense my dismay and offers an arm. I take it numbly, feeling as though my brain has choked on this barrage of revelations and now refuses to process anything until I've made it to the far side of a good, long panic attack.

Lady Mei—the only one of us who seems to be keeping her head—bids a smiling goodbye to the farm staff and even waves out the window as our SUV pulls away.

"Well," she says mildly after we've driven in silence for a few minutes, "you three have been gathering storm clouds since we set foot on that property. You saw something there that I didn't. Any chance I'm to be let in on the story this time?"

"I can't believe this is happening," I say.

"It's a disaster," Lord Aaron agrees, hands spread out in front of him.

And I've put my friends right in the middle of it. I close my eyes and lean back against my seat. *Again.* "It's worse than I ever imagined," I say softly.

"I know. They're going to roll them out in France—and soon, from the look of things. We'll put half the globe out of work."

I narrow my eyes and peer at him. "Lord Aaron, I don't think we're talking about the same thing."

"The *bots,* Danica, surely you saw—I was talking to Dr. Owens about them the whole time."

I blink. "No, we're definitely not talking about the same thing." But I say it softly, and he doesn't seem to have even heard the words.

"They're an adaptable model," he continues, alive with a desperate mania I haven't seen in him for a while. "With manual dexterity enhanced by years of testing in the palace. *Our* palace! It's always been Amalgamated's end game, of course, but I thought we had more *time*. Ten thousand jobs will vanish overnight. And that's only the first day! There's no way the Foundation can absorb so many—"

"Foundation? What Foundation?" asks Lady Mei, blessedly cutting off his rampage before I can snap that I'm far more invested in freeing the man I love than a bunch of workers I don't know—workers who have choices and get paid for their work and aren't *owned* by someone else. I should care—I know I should—but I'm having trouble seeing beyond myself at this moment.

"The Foundation for Social Reintegration," Duke Spencer says, quietly, one hand rubbing Lord Aaron's back, trying to calm him.

"The—those activists who are always hanging about, making a nuisance of themselves? Oh!" Her eyes widen and she points at Lord Aaron. "They vandalized the orchards last year. You know they ruined my favorite blue early-Baroque dinner gown? They threw paint—"

"Apologies. I shall order you another," Lord Aaron says crisply, "as I'm among their chief financiers."

Lady Mei's eyes grow wide, and for once she has nothing to say.

"The Foundation does have a number of anticorporate, anti-GMO members who like to make a ruckus," Duke Spencer explains, "but the main reason they exist is to help Sonoma employees who get paid in Sonoman-Versailles credits."

"Why would we need help?" She bristles.

"*You* don't. Most of the residents of the palace don't. But those who wish to quit—or who get fired—quickly discover that after living in company-owned housing, earning company-issued currency, their salary is almost worthless anywhere else. It's an economic model once called the *company store,* and it was outlawed for a long time—until companies like ours started buying their own countries where they could enact their own laws. Our employees might lose their job after fifteen years and discover their life savings won't feed them for three months.

"The Foundation finds housing and work for Sonoma's corporate refugees," Lord Aaron adds, calmer, but sounding depressed now. I'm not sure it's an improvement. "A few dozen each month."

"So many?" asks Lady Mei.

"Sonoma Inc. is a very big company," Lord Aaron says with a bitter grimace.

"Replacing human workers is hardly new."

"But the jobs that currently still have to be performed by human hands—mechanics and technicians, mostly—can all be taken by these new bots, pretty much immediately. So that 'few dozen' will turn into *thousands.* The Foundation will be overwhelmed. And that's just the Sonoma employees that the Foundation deals with directly. Over the next few years, it'll happen worldwide. Millions upon millions of human beings, instantly obsolete. Jobless. Homeless. It's going to ravage society in a way we haven't seen since the Industrial Revolution."

"But the Industrial Revolution was a turning point in development of the world. A positive one," Lady Mei argues.

"Sure, decades after the fact," Lord Aaron snaps. "At the time, it happened so quickly that the rich got obscenely wealthy while the poor *died* in droves."

Lady Mei sits back, clearly affronted, and Duke Spencer murmurs something in Lord Aaron's ear. A long silence passes before Lord Aaron rubs a hand over his face and releases a noisy sigh. "I'm sorry, Lady Mei. You didn't deserve that."

"Already forgiven," Lady Mei says, leaning forward and patting his hand. "You're overwrought—it happens to us all."

"Thank you," Lord Aaron whispers. "I've been thinking of leaving Sonoman-Versailles for years. I adore our culture, our formality, but I wanted a chance to find someone in a . . . broader population. But also, I frequently felt . . . *wrong,* living the decadence that we take so for granted." He smiles sadly, his eyes turning to me. "I love it—you know I do. But it started to weigh on me, living so finely when I know there are so many in the world who are suffering. It's not that I thought I could save everyone—I know I can't—but I didn't want to sit up in a literally gilded palace and remain apart from the very real concerns of the rest of the world."

"But you stayed," I say.

"I stayed," he agrees, his hand sliding onto Duke Spencer's knee. "For love. I found someone I loved more than I worried about the rest of the world. In the end, I guess I'm just another spoiled, selfish noble."

I don't say anything. Aren't I doing exactly the same thing?

"I thought maybe I could make a difference from inside the company, and I've tried. But this? This is catastrophic."

"I think you're making too much of this," says Lady Mei. "It's one company making bots. You said it yourself—automation has been destroying jobs for centuries, and people always find something else to do. It's a time-honored tradition: if you're replaced by a machine, learn how to build the machine."

Lord Aaron shakes his head. "Not when they're good enough to build themselves. Most bots are purpose-built and can perform only a narrow range of tasks. Because of their versatility, the bots we have in the palace are far and away more advanced than anything anyone else in the world can get for less than a price tag in the millions. *Each*. Danica, how many years do you think it took for programmers to make a bot that could fasten all the little closures on your gowns?"

I remember the way my mother used to threaten to buy more stock in Amalgamated every time a human staff member made her angry. It doesn't seem amusing at all anymore.

"It looks like they're advanced enough now to mass-produce. They're ready to start raking in the profits and displacing workers by the millions." Lord Aaron looks so disgusted I start to feel ashamed that I can't work up the energy to care.

But I'm where Lord Aaron was two years ago: giving up my standards for the one I love. I suppose I should embrace the irony.

Lord Aaron grumbles under his breath and rustles around in one of the picnic baskets, bringing out a bottle of champagne. "I'm not feeling particularly festive, but I am suddenly very thirsty." We're all silent as he pops the cork with no formality or fanfare. Rather than the delicate flutes, he pulls out the tumblers that were intended for water and, with uncharacteristic disregard for fashion, empties the bottle into the four of them.

We sip silently, the air around us charged with negative energy.

"But . . . ," Lady Mei ventures. "I mean, that all sounds quite dire, of course, but that's not what we came out here to see, is it? I thought we were—" Fingers spread, palm in, she waves one hand in a circle in front of her face, and I realize she's indicating the Glitter adorning her cheeks. "Looking into this."

I laugh.

I can't help it. My little cabal watches with surprise and concern as the mirthless, raucous noise, halfway between a giggle and a sob, fills the spacious cab, and I can't seem to stop. It's not funny—it's terrible, but I can't stop the awful sound coming out of me.

"Danica?" Lady Mei says, concerned. She hands me a handkerchief, and I push it against my mouth, muffling the noise.

"You said you and Aaron weren't talking about the same thing," Duke Spencer says. I should have expected that he'd be the one who noticed and remembered my words. "What had *you* so concerned?"

"The fields," I manage.

"The fields?" Lord Aaron asks.

The hysteria finally melts away, and I take a few deep breaths. "The woman said they're growing *papaveris atropa*. It's the main ingredient in Sonoma's new wonder drug . . . and Glitter."

Lady Mei blinks.

Duke Spencer pales.

Lord Aaron curses and turns to look out the window.

"So Reginald is . . . *working* for Sonoma?" Lady Mei asks.

I shake my head. "Stealing from Sonoma. This isn't Sonoma's

fault, for once. Putting a few pieces together, it sounds like Justin has a team gengineering a new prescription painkiller or something. Reginald is smuggling out plants for his Glitter empire, and if Justin finds out I'm involved, he'll—" Another sharp-edged laugh escapes my lips. "Arresting me is the least of what he'll do."

"It's quite a security breach," says Duke Spencer. "But if we can determine who's selling the plants to Reginald, surely that would give us the upper hand?"

"I'd prefer to know precisely when those bots are scheduled to roll out," Lord Aaron grumbles.

"Either way, it sounds like we need more information." Lady Mei smiles. "Knowledge is power. Why do you think I enjoy gossip so much?"

"You're absolutely right," I say. "But how are we going to get it?"

TWENTY

"GRÂCE À DIEU." I sigh and discard my stiff posture the instant I'm through the door to the King's office, Saber close behind
me. The Wednesday masses seem even worse than usual with the
King away, leaving only one monarch to ogle. I whirl and push
the door closed, leaning my head against it. "If your arms aren't
around my waist in five seconds, I might literally go insane."

But instead of the feel of Saber's warm, strong arms, I hear
someone clear their throat. *Damnation.* I don't lift my forehead
from the cool wood—not yet ready to face my husband's slimy
assistant. My eyes fall closed and I count to ten, slowly, reminding
myself with each numeral that I'm far more highly ranked than
even this elevated employee.

Finally, with my fingers itching to clench, I straighten and
turn, my face passive.

Mateus has risen from his seat—an appropriate gesture, given
my station—but he manages to work a hint of sarcasm into it anyway. "How may I be of service?"

"You can get out of my office while I get some respite from the
crowds."

"Your office?" he asks, blinking as if he has no idea what I'm talking about. "Deepest apologies, Highness, I was under the impression I was in—"

"The King's office? It's my office too, and you know it." I slowly begin pulling off my gloves, one finger at a time. Not that I can blame Mateus for making liberal use of it in His Majesty's absence; it really is an impressive space, with an enormous desk and silk wall hangings and gilded molding along the perimeter of the ceiling, framing a fresco featuring cherubs and embracing lovers. Despite its elegance, it reeks of masculinity and expense, which is precisely how I would describe the King.

Mateus doesn't leave, merely glares as I make my way behind a small white desk—almost child-sized—that Justin had moved in here when I demanded unmonitored office space.

Saber catches my eye and raises his eyebrows minutely—his way of asking what I want to do now. I didn't really have any particular aim in coming here except getting away from the crowds— and, perhaps more importantly, the courtiers clawing for Glitter. Even with the ratty assistant here, returned to his seat and scribbling away at his tablet, it's the most convenient escape with limited access to others. I'll stay for a few minutes. Perhaps I can com Lord Aaron and go hide in Duke Spencer's new rooms instead. Better than nothing.

"Oh, for the love of—" Mateus bites off a curse, then blinks swiftly, clearly responding to some sort of urgent com on his Lens.

"Everything all right?" I say, my tone dripping with sugary sweetness.

"Tourists," Mateus grumbles. "Hardly better than animals. I need—I must—" He sweeps up his tablet, makes for the door, then pauses. "Damnable Wednesdays." He pats at his coat distractedly, and I don't understand what he's looking for until he tosses his tablet computer onto his own desk—larger than mine—and heads through the door with a growl.

Ah. No screens allowed in sight on Wednesdays, and Mateus had no pockets big enough to hide it.

The door clicks shut and every muscle in my body freezes.

Mateus's tablet.

Information.

I've been racking my brains for some way to disrupt Reginald's supply line. But my coconspirators, Lord Aaron especially, have maintained laser focus on our joint venture with Amalgamated.

But didn't our trip to the farm prove one simple concept? All roads ultimately lead to Justin.

And whatever secrets the King is keeping, there's probably something about them on that tablet.

"Saber, watch the door," I say, my hands trembling as I throw myself at the desk and sweep up the leather-encased tablet computer—which, in his haste to depart, Mateus failed to lock down. As long as I keep it active, I should have as much access to Mateus's files as he would. Cradling the device in one arm, I shake my own computer out of my reticule and realize I'm completely unprepared.

"I need a fiber-optic cable," I whisper. "I can't download over the network—there'll be a record." I look up at Saber with desperation, knowing such an opportunity will likely never come again. "Do you have a cable? In your bag?" I feel my eyes tear at the colossal waste this moment could be. "Please, *please* tell me you do."

In two strides Saber is beside my desk, dumping his messenger bag out onto the glossy top. Canisters of Glitter clatter across the clean surface alongside a host of miscellany: a leather wallet, gum wrappers, a comb, a few bits of black ribbon, Saber's own tablet.

And one Amalgamated-brand string of light-conducting silica sheathed in braided Kevlar and black polyethylene.

Blessing the gods of technical standardization, I snatch up the fiber cable and place Mateus's tablet next to mine on his desk. My fingers tremble, but I manage to plug both ends into the computers and initiate a backup of Mateus's personal files onto my own tablet's local storage. No time to go sifting through them, especially without M.A.R.I.E.'s assistance—but later, when I have more time, Lord Aaron and I can write an independent program to parse the contents.

"It'll take seven minutes," I say when the progress bar pops up. "Please stand by the door. Don't let Mateus back in."

"What do I do if he tries?"

I shake my head, my eyes glued to the screen. "I don't know. I can't think. Just . . . just don't let him in."

The minutes pass like hours, adrenaline surging through me, making my breath short and fast. As the time left to copy Mateus's drive drops to thirty seconds, each *moment* feels like an eternity. My eyes dart back and forth between the computer and the door as the bar comes so close to being filled. It pauses and flashes twenty seconds several times without changing. I'm feeling sick to my stomach when it finally moves on to nineteen seconds. Eighteen. Seventeen.

A beep of a code being entered on a keypad sounds from the door and the bolt unlocks with a loud click.

Swiftly, Saber turns the manual bolt from the inside, locking it again, his foot braced against the jamb. Another beep, then several in rapid succession, as Saber keeps throwing the bolt back into place.

Ten, nine, eight. A thud as someone kicks at the bottom of the door.

Three, two, one. I take the barest moment to confirm that the transfer is complete before yanking the cord out of both computers and stuffing mine into my reticule. Insofar as my gown allows it, I leap away from Mateus's desk, and the door flies open.

"Lady Cyn!" I say, surprise sadly transparent in my tone.

She's frozen, one hand on the knob, something clenched in the other, the door open and a handful of courtiers craning their necks to peer through the disturbingly wide-open doorway.

It takes every ounce of control to conceal the fact that I nearly jumped out of my skin, and even now dozens of questions are whirring through my head. Beginning, of course, with why the hell Lady Cyn is standing in the King's private—emphasis on *private*—office. "You startled me. Please do close the door."

Lady Cyn either isn't as good at concealment as I am, or simply doesn't find me worth the effort. Her eyes are wide and burning with anger and something that looks suspiciously like jealousy. Is she truly so deluded about her actual worth to the King? Or perhaps it's me the King is fooling? But no—I don't think so. His comment weeks ago about Lady Cyn reminding him of a yapping dog was made at a stress-filled and vulnerable moment, and I think he meant it.

I think.

But it's hard to be firm in that belief when my husband's mistress is standing in a room I thought marginally more . . . secure. Still, after another moment or two, she finds no benefit to herself in revealing the unfortunate scenario, so she turns and pushes the door shut.

"Did you need something, Cynthea?" I ask, as though meeting in the King's office while he's not within a thousand miles of the palace were entirely normal and expected. "Is that why you were looking for me?"

"Why would I be looking for you?" she snaps, her mouth twisted into an ugly sneer I know she would never dare let anyone else in the court see.

"I'm certain I don't know," I say calmly, my hands folded gracefully in front of me, clinging to the strings of my reticule, where my tablet feels like it weighs twenty kilos. "But considering this is my shared office space with my husband, and he's out of the country for the next several days, I can't imagine what else you might have hoped to find here."

Her face is white except for the spots of red high on her cheeks. "You're sharing an office with him?" she asks softly, and for the first time, I realize she looks very tired. It must be difficult being in her position. Not that I'm feeling any sympathy for her whatsoever. She's never had any for me.

"Of course we share," I say with a gentle, happy-sounding

laugh, realizing exactly how I need to play this. "Justin's parents did too. Why in the world would we *not* share?"

She clearly wants to lash back with the honest answer that we hate each other, but my words—my very presence here—has introduced just enough doubt that she can't. As she stands there, searching for something to say, I scrutinize her face, looking for any sign of shimmer, but there is none. I've still no real idea what withdrawal will be like for those using less than the megadoses Reginald doled out to hook my father. Am I learning something, even now? Is her inability to hold her tongue—or her temper— Glitter withdrawal, or just her usual winning personality?

Regardless, this battle of wills is one I've got to win. I hold my tongue, my eyebrows raised slightly, as though I'm listening most anxiously for her to speak, and I wait.

And I wait.

"Are you done in here?" she finally bursts out.

"Oh, certainly. But I'm not leaving you alone in my private office."

"It's not only yours."

"It is while my husband is away."

She hesitates, then seems to remember that I'm not someone to whom she should be showing any weakness.

"It's not important; I just wanted to leave him a little note." She smiles coyly, holding up a small, folded piece of parchment. "I'll give it to him in person instead."

"That sounds like an excellent idea," I say smoothly. I'm as cold as ice as she about-faces and leaves the office, closing the door behind her a little too hard.

I almost crumple in relief, and Saber rushes to place his hands around my waist.

"That was too close," I whisper against his shoulder.

"At least it wasn't Mateus," Saber murmurs back.

"I can't believe he gave *her* access—he's such a bastard."

"He doesn't think you care."

"I don't care. Not about them—not as long as she stays out of my way. But this is *my* office, too, and—" I snap my mouth closed. I sound like a jealous wife.

Saber's face may as well be a mask, for all the emotion it reveals. His hands continue to lend the support my corset doesn't.

"I can't stand to be here any longer," I say, pulling away from him and opening the door. I stalk out into the *Arrière Cabinet* and find one of our security guards—the human kind that the Society brings in only on Wednesdays; the ones who obey without concern for digital access protocols. Five minutes later, one such guard is posted at the door to the King's office with orders to allow no one inside except me, Mateus, and Saber, and Saber and I are headed to Lord Aaron's office with the contents of Mateus's profile downloaded onto my tablet.

Sometimes it's good to be Queen.

TWENTY-ONE

LORD AARON'S OFFICE feels surprisingly small with five of us crowded in it—though instead of gathering behind the desk with the rest of us, Saber leans against the wall, studying *me* rather than the technology.

"It's a lot of info," I say, handing my tablet to Lord Aaron. "I didn't have time to be choosy about what got copied. I expect much of it is encrypted, and most of it is probably useless, but if we whip up a multivariate crawler to filter through it all, there— there's got to be something we can use."

My hands are shaking from nerves and excitement as Lord Aaron digs through desk drawers, extracting cables and an offline storage drive. The sooner I've wiped my cloud-connected tablet clean, the less I have to worry about what some other hacker could find if they were looking in the right place at the right time.

"You're brilliant," Lady Mei says as I initiate the transfer. "It's moments like this that make me wish I'd paid a little more attention in my tech classes."

I shrug off the compliment, but it's nice to be working with tech again. I was near the top of my career coding classes when my mother bumped me onto the princess track. Plus, I can't help but smile at Lady Mei's amusement at my devilry. Since bringing her into my inner circle, I'm discovering that beneath her playful mischief-making runs a streak of genuine deviousness. Is that the Glitter working on her personality? Or did I simply not notice because I didn't have my own yet?

"I'm just lucky Saber had a cable," I say. "I'd have downloaded it over the network if I had to, but it would have left the most frightful trace. There's no way Mateus wouldn't have noticed."

"And thus, the King," Lord Aaron says.

"Sometimes I think they share a brain."

"If they don't already, I'm sure Amalgamated is working on it," he mutters.

I shut my mouth over a laugh when I realize Lord Aaron isn't joking. He's been wallowing in melancholy since we went to the Glitter farm and found the bots. I'm not certain I believe things are as dire as he says, but admittedly, my priorities are very much elsewhere.

"A lot of this isn't encrypted at all," Duke Spencer says, pointing. "Look, this one here is a calendar database—it opens right up."

"Here's something," I say, scanning the most recent entries as Lord Aaron's tech continues to siphon data from my tablet. "M.A.R.I.E. only tells me that the King is abroad. Mateus's calendar says where he'll be."

"Tokyo, at the moment," Lord Aaron says. "Berlin yesterday, São Paulo day after tomorrow, Los Angeles, finishing up in London." He whistles between his teeth. "He's really making the rounds. But why keep the locations a secret? If he were doing some sort of publicity stunt, he'd use . . . publicity. This is something else."

"He's got little files attached to each location," Lady Mei says, pointing at a small icon in the lower right corner of each calendar square. "I do that with my calendar all the time—scans of invitations so I don't forget the themes and hosts and such."

"Who wishes they paid more attention in their tech classes?" I drawl.

"It has its uses," she says with a shrug, though I can tell she's pleased. "But why so many? There are three or four files attached to each entry."

"Probably travel documents," Lord Aaron says, opening one. "That's the sort of thing a secretary would be expected to—oh!"

It's a one-hundred-and-fifty-eight-page, single-spaced document.

"That's no airline ticket," I say hollowly, meeting Lord Aaron's eyes.

"But what *is* it?" Duke Spencer says, scanning. "Something with Amalgamated. See their logo, there?"

Lord Aaron looks back to his screen and his eyes widen as he goes oddly pale.

"What?" I whisper, and my quiet words make him startle.

"What if . . . oh. Oh no." Lord Aaron pushes his hair off his face and ties it back with an elastic band from his pocket. Duke Spencer's eyes mirror my own alarm, and he moves behind Lord Aaron and leans low over his shoulder. The office is wrapped in tense silence for several minutes, save for an occasional indecipherable muttering from Lord Aaron. He opens another document. And another. Then he's flipping through files too fast for me to track what he's looking at. Finally he leans back; his forehead is misted with sweat despite the cool temperature.

"It's the bots," he says, and I hear the despair in his voice. "Contracts for the bots. That first one is a five-hundred-million-euro contract with the German government. Then a number of smaller contracts for private companies. It's the same in every location—contracts between Sonoma, Amalgamated, and local interests. Public and private sector."

"So . . . he's pitching the bots? We knew he was going to be doing that. Or," I amend, "we assumed that was the next step."

"These contracts are drafted and negotiated. They're final documents, ready for signatures. The pitch must have come ages ago. He's traveling around for the *signings*. That's why he's only staying a few hours in each city. Meet, sign, destroy the working class, and move on." Lord Aaron slams his fist down on his desk with a crack that makes us all jump.

I don't hear Saber come up behind me until I feel a supporting hand on my waist.

"This just goes on and on." Lord Aaron points at the calendar for next month. "See, there's the business trip he'll inform you he's taking in a few more weeks."

"Signing contracts with more countries." I don't need to look at the screen to know.

"Seven more." Lord Aaron props his forehead on his hands, elbows braced on the table. "He's out doing it right now. Impoverishing millions to line his pockets with a few extra billion."

"But there's nothing we can do about it," Lady Mei says tentatively.

Lord Aaron wheels his chair back, narrowly missing Duke Spencer's foot, a frantic gleam in his eyes. "I don't think any of you understand how drastic this is. This," he says, flinging his hand toward the computer screen, "is only the beginning. I could see that the Foundation was going to be overwhelmed—even with only serving the Sonoma employees—but I thought we'd have a couple of years at least before this turned into a truly global threat. Your husband," he says to me, almost accusingly, "has been working very hard behind the scenes."

"And that's my fault?" My voice is icy, and Lord Aaron gets the message.

"My apologies," he says, closing his eyes and rubbing at his temples. "I'm shooting the messenger, aren't I?"

"A bit." The sins on my own head weigh heavy enough.

Lord Aaron lets out a deep, rattling sigh. "Let me try to explain. At the moment, the wealthiest five percent of the world controls eighty-five percent of the world's money. Conversely, the poorest half—*half*—of the population do ninety-five percent of the manual labor. As those jobs are replaced, who benefits? The wealthy. That eighty-five percent of the wealth? It'll rise to ninety. That may not sound like a very big change, but in the bottom ninety-five percent that's like losing one job in every three." He spreads his hands wide. "Rough estimates, of course, but supported by centuries of precedence and economics. This is the beginning of a genuinely catastrophic change."

I let the numbers slide through my head, and it makes more

sense to me than his frenetic ramblings in the SUV. Numbers: that's a language I can understand.

Lord Aaron slumps back in his chair. "Bots don't stop to eat or sleep. Each one can replace three humans, minimum. Every human job supports about four people: spouses, children, elderly parents, you know. Every bot sold condemns about a dozen human beings to poverty, eviction, malnutrition. With money fleeing to corporate sovereignties like our own, national interests won't be able to bear the strain of so many unemployable poor. How long before they cast off responsibility? Leave people to starve in the streets?" Lord Aaron's eyes dart to Saber and he lowers his voice. "Hundreds of *millions* of people will be in the same straits that drove your friend's family to leave Mongolia a decade ago. But this time, there will be nowhere for them to flee."

My gaze whips around to Saber, but the stony look on his face tells me he already made that connection. My stomach hurts.

"The entire world will be in economic crisis," Lord Aaron finishes.

"Except the wealthy."

"Exactly."

"What are you going to do?" I whisper.

"I don't know," Lord Aaron replies just as quietly. He rises slowly from his chair and squeezes Duke Spencer's hand. "I need to walk. I'll not be decent company for a while. You'll excuse me, I hope."

Without waiting for an answer, he rises from his desk. Just before his hand turns the knob, Lord Aaron pauses. He doesn't look back at me as he whispers, "Justin Wyndham is nothing short of evil. *Evil.* You remember that. And don't you ever let him convince you he's anything less."

"I won't," I promise. My hands are shaking.

Duke Spencer starts to follow Lord Aaron, looking back at me and Lady Mei with apology in his eyes, but Lord Aaron lays a gentle hand on the duke's chest. "Stay," he says softly. Then gives a shallow, self-deprecating smile. "Let me sulk alone for a while."

Needing to do something once he's gone, I seat myself in Lord Aaron's soft, leather-upholstered office chair and begin assembling a data crawler from some of Lord Aaron's and my preexisting hacks. Lord Aaron has his mission—his passion, even—but I still have to find a way to personally get out from under the thumb of one of the richest and most powerful monsters in the world.

Preferably before he becomes even richer and more powerful.

The others in the office settle in as I code, occasionally pausing to consult Mateus's files—wiped clean from my tablet and residing offline on Lord Aaron's external hard drive. While I work, Lady Mei curls up in an armchair in the corner and pulls out her tablet—likely to play a game or read a book, but at least she stays. Duke Spencer paces, occasionally peering over my shoulder, but since I don't explain myself, it's more of a symbolic gesture of support than a helpful eye. Saber has resumed his post against the wall near the door, his eyes dark and unflinching as he watches me.

Soon enough I've cobbled together a search assistant to highlight potentially interesting tidbits, but other than the contracts, the unencrypted contents of Mateus's tablet prove mind-numbingly mundane. Manga—apparently Mateus particularly enjoys illustrated stories about the everyday trials of Neotokyo housewives. Reams of communication with a sister in Romania, a minor functionary in Sonoma's local sales force. The King's schedule in agonizingly minute detail, covering every waking moment, and some notations about his sleeping schedule as well. Surprisingly little actual information, which, in hindsight, makes sense: wouldn't want to carry around a tablet full of incriminating evidence.

"Oh, damn, look at this," I say, scanning through one rather simple document. "Mateus is writing a book."

"A book?" Lady Mei says, jumping up from her chair. "Is it any good?"

I snicker as I skim the first few pages. "Not really."

"It looks like a thinly veiled fantasy about a CEO who suddenly discovers an attraction to his stalwart administrative assistant," Duke Spencer says wryly.

I meet Lady Mei's eyes over Duke Spencer's head, and then we burst into undignified giggles. "I always suspected," I say, wiping at my eyes. The fit of laughter is just what we needed to break up the tension.

"How dreadfully *cliché* of him. But does His Majesty suspect?" Lady Mei asks dramatically.

"Surely he hasn't missed it," I say, closing the florid prose and moving on to the next weirdly titled document. "Oh! This one is marked *Trade Secret*. This should be good." I squint at the jumble of technical jargon, complete with equations that *might* be calculus but also bring to mind a chemistry assignment I once had, too many years ago. "What do you suppose this is?" I ask, scrolling down. "It's about seventy pages long."

"Oh, hey," Duke Spencer says, scooting closer. "That's a lab report. Looks like it's from the agricultural division."

"How can you tell?" asks Lady Mei.

"My parents headed up the ag division in the US," he explains. "They were reviewing documents like this all the time. Growing up in that environment, you pick up a few things whether you want to or not."

"Do you know what it means, then?" I ask.

"I picked up a *few* things," he says dryly. "Not all the things. I don't know what this is. But it's old."

"Old?"

"Early twenty-first century," he says. "Look at the time stamp there—2034."

"That's from before Sonoman-Versailles even existed. King Kevin's time. Well, CEO Kevin Wyndham's time."

"Might be his report," Duke Spencer says. "Before he was a King he was a scientific genius."

"And a bit mad," Lady Mei pipes up.

"Eccentric," I correct automatically, then chide myself. This is Lady Mei, who loves the finery of palace life even more than I do. Did? I certainly don't need to defend the founder of our country to her. "Why the hell would something like this be sitting on Mateus's tablet?"

Duke Spencer shrugs. "Could be related to a project His Highness is working on?"

"Do you think you could find out?" I ask. Despite having written the program that found this doc, I certainly can't make sense of it. I'll take code over bioscience any day.

"Maybe. I—still have friends, connections, back in the agro department," Duke Spencer says haltingly. "I might be able to consult with them. Lord Aaron can help me encrypt the document to send it along, right?"

I nod, then hesitate. "Can you trust them?" It might turn out to be nothing, but if it's *not* . . .

"To keep secrets? That's what scientists do."

I stare at the document for a long time before nodding. "You take it from here."

TWENTY-TWO

WE ALL WALK together back to Duke Spencer's new apartments, more because it's on the way to the main section of the palace than for any particularly friendly reason. Lord Aaron's absence seems to have made both Duke Spencer and me a little melancholy—Duke Spencer from empathy, I suspect, and me because I'm waiting for the consequences. If Lord Aaron wasn't already determined to leave as soon as possible, he is now.

Lady Mei, on the other hand, chats about what she's going to wear to the assembly tonight, and I hold tight to her arm, needing a connection to that memory of how carefree life used to be. We *all* ignore the tourists gawking on the other side of the velvet ropes that bifurcate the wide hallway. We're so accustomed; they're more like buzzing insects than people.

Duke Spencer enters a pass code on a concealed keypad before turning and fluttering his fingers in a rather pathetic wave.

"He'll be back," I say lamely. "These moods never last too long."

Duke Spencer nods, stoic as ever, and opens the ornate door to his opulent lodgings as I turn to continue on my way.

Lady Mei's scream brings me back around, and it takes several seconds before I realize what I'm seeing.

Julianna Tremain, hanging, swinging slightly, from the rafters.

"M.A.R.I.E.!" I shout. "Security! Now!" But of course—it's Wednesday. More shrieks and screams sound behind me, and with a sinking heart I realize all the tourists who happened to be strolling in the general vicinity have now seen a dead body in the Palace of Versailles. Despite the screen rule, I retrieve my tablet from my reticule and send an alert over the wireless. Even as I push the buttons that will summon security to me, I hear the artificial clicks of a dozen handheld devices snapping pictures and probably—God save us—recording video.

Justin is not going to be pleased.

"Inside," Saber says quietly, interposing himself between Lady Mei and the crowd, pushing her into the apartment and past the hanging form. "Spencer—Duke, whatever, come on!" He pulls on Duke Spencer's cuffs, and finally the duke staggers into the foyer.

"Cut her down," Duke Spencer chokes, tears streaming down his face. "Please."

"One thing at a time," Saber says in that same gentle, comforting voice he's used on me so many times. "Danica, the door. Crack it and tell me if security is coming."

He shuffles both Lady Mei and Duke Spencer farther into the apartment, and though Lady Mei stays on her feet, Duke Spencer slides down the wall into a heap. Saber assists the duke in tucking his head between his knees even as he sobs—awful, painful sounds coming from his throat.

I'm supposed to be keeping an eye out for security, but I'm still staring at the body, my hand clenched on the doorknob. Her face is contorted and white, cocked slightly to the side. Her eyes are not only open but bulging and bloodshot. The tip of a purple tongue peeks out from between Glitter-rouged lips, and briefly I wonder where she got it. I've never sold it directly to her, but many of the higher nobility share among themselves.

I stare up at her and feel nothing. No, not nothing. Nauseated. But emotionally? Nothing. I should. Maybe it'll come later. Maybe your third dead body is when you grow used to the sight.

Saber slips past me, righting a fallen chair—doubtless the one Lady Julianna used to do the deed—and climbing up on it. There's a box cutter in his hand, and he's sawing through the cord she used.

"Saber?" Should he be doing that? Interfering with a dead body? It feels wrong. Like desecration.

But before I can say anything more, he's lowering the limp, dully attired body to the floor, touching her wrist, her neck. I can't remember having *ever* seen Lady Julianna in such plain, unremarkable clothing, and in my puzzlement I almost don't see the moment Saber wipes the Glitter from her lips with a handkerchief, an instant before pressing his mouth to hers.

What? Oh. CPR.

There's no way it will work, of course. But Saber's quiet efficiency never fails to astound. He's just doing what any calm, reasonable bystander would do upon finding someone hanging from the ceiling. And in the process, making sure the inevitable autopsy fails to find Glitter on her lips.

This is a different Saber. Crime lord Saber. The person he so rarely lets me see, because I know what sort of experience would be required to make him this way. And even though he hates Glitter, hates Reginald, still he protects me. I don't feel guilty so much as relieved.

It's a particularly loud sob from Duke Spencer that turns me away from the *charade*. "She didn't deserve this," he says, his voice shaking. "She was the best of that whole family. I hated that she got dragged into everything. This—this is my fault."

He needs Lord Aaron. I blink, activating my Lens. "Summon Lord Aaron Williamson," I say quietly, knowing that within the walls of the Tremain-Harrisford apartments, M.A.R.I.E. will hear me.

My Lens flashes that he's set his status to unavailable.

"Emergency override, on the authority of the Queen," I snap, suddenly angry at M.A.R.I.E., of all things, for denying me what I need. "Contact Lord Aaron Williamson *immediately*."

Lord Aaron answers the new emergency call in moments. "Spence?" His voice is tinny in the speaker on my pearl earring, but the desperation is as loud as a shout in a silent room.

"No. He's fine. But he needs you. We're at his home." The call ends before I can utter another word.

Saber is still playing at CPR when the head of security bursts through the door, speaking into a screen on his wrist, presumably summoning extra officers. I catch Saber shoving the handkerchief into his pocket as he stands, looking bereft and hopeless.

It's surprisingly convincing.

I look away and peek through the crack in the door out into the hallway. The frenetic chatter of the bystanders—not to mention the irresistible pull of drama—has gathered a crowd of both residents and tourists that swells as each minute goes by, and I'm bracing myself for the inevitable, which can't be long in coming.

Sure enough, within minutes a frantic form comes bursting through the door in a cacophony of shrieks and wails.

Julianna's mother, Duchess Tremain. Now simply Madame Tremain, I suppose.

The former duke follows behind his wife, stone-faced and sober at the edge of the foyer, but Madame Tremain throws herself toward her daughter's body, only to be caught by Saber and a security guard in a simple blue uniform. They hold her back. One of the security officers has draped a thin satin tablecloth from a nearby console table over Julianna. It doesn't cover her wholly, but at least her face is shielded from view. I rush back to the double doors, which the Tremains unhelpfully left standing open, and slam them shut in my hurry. Everyone turns at the noise, but I don't apologize.

"Julianna!" her mother wails, and I can't help wishing that her husband would take her in hand. Keep her from making such a scene. They've lost a daughter; must they lose their dignity as well?

Apparently so.

Madame Tremain crumples to the floor, fully prostrate, and lets out more of those high-pitched squeals and even kicks her feet a few times, like a child throwing a tantrum, and I remember the reports of her behavior when they were evicted. I thought the stories overblown at the time, but the potential is there. The spectacle is so diverting I almost don't notice Lord Aaron's arrival. He slips quietly through the doors and crouches beside Duke Spencer, embracing him. I can't help but feel that the misused ex-husband's display of quiet grief is far more soul-wrenching than the performance Madame Tremain is airing.

"You!"

A deep voice cuts the air and Duke Spencer's head shoots up, fear laced through his expression.

"This is your fault," Monsieur Tremain says, pointing a red sausage finger straight at Duke Spencer's face. His voice rises with every syllable, until each forms an earsplitting blow. "Everything, all of this, your fault! You betrayed us!"

I expect Duke Spencer to wither within Lord Aaron's arms, but he surprises me by rising to his feet—fists and jaw clenched and a fire suddenly kindled in his eyes. "My fault?" he says, and though his tone is cutting, it's very quiet. The handful of people around us hush to hear him. "You *dare* to suggest this is my fault? You? You are a predator, sir. You took advantage of me when I was weak; you took advantage of her!" he says, flinging an arm at the doors, where, still, the crowd cannot see the body. "You forced us into your dance, into our roles, and when everything failed, you had the audacity to blame her."

I almost gasp. I've not heard any of this. I look to Lord Aaron, but his eyes glimmer with pride as he watches his love stand up to the man who used him. Lord Aaron knew. But Duke Spencer never let on. I suppose even misplaced loyalty is deserving of admiration.

"I most certainly did not," Monsieur Tremain replies, bristling, but his voice is a little weaker.

"You think I couldn't hear you? A mere two walls away? You shouted at her for hours," Duke Spencer murmurs, that dangerous edge carrying his voice farther than I'd have imagined possible. He steps away from Lord Aaron, drawing near to his former father-in-law, who physically shrinks back from the much smaller man. "Denigrating her for *your* failure. You called her every name in the book, dragged out every insult you could imagine, and rested only when your wife was ready to take over!"

Everyone's eyes shoot down at the woman no longer wailing on the floor, her face streaked with tears, her eyes and mouth widened in surprise.

"There was nothing I could do then," Duke Spencer says, "but you have no power over me anymore, and I'll be damned if you'll blame her for one more thing."

"Now, see here—"

But Duke Spencer is having none of it. "You, the both of you, controlled and bullied us every day of our marriage." He looks over at the doors and his face grows sad again, as though he could see through the thick, solid oak. "If I bear any blame in this sad affair," he says softly, "it's that I left her with you."

Monsieur Tremain sputters and blusters and then turns to me. "You're allowing this to stand?"

"Is there any reason why I shouldn't?" I ask blandly, forcing myself to remain calm. Emotionless.

He shoves a finger in *my* face now, the turncoat. "There will be a lawsuit. How did she even get in there? This is a case of wrongful death, or neglect, and you and that husband of yours will be hearing from my lawyers."

I laugh. "Truly?" I stalk over to Monsieur Tremain, who's forced to drop his finger as I bring my nose close to his face, speaking loudly enough for everyone around us to hear. "Your daughter isn't even cold after having *hanged herself*, and you're already scheming with your lawyers? What a shame we didn't vote control of this kingdom into your grasping hands."

"You—"

"Guards, I feel threatened." Two guards, with guns at their hips, step forward, between Tremain and me. His face is a deep red and he's clamping his jaw closed over angry words I know he wishes he could spew at me.

"I suggest," I say calmly, "that you help your wife up and escort her back to your home. I'm certain security will want a statement from you. And don't even consider saying a single word to the tourists outside this door or you'll find yourself in even more unbearable circumstances than you currently do."

He deflates like a balloon and slowly does my bidding, reaching down for his wife and dragging her to her feet. The security officers part to allow them through to the doors, and no one meets their eyes as they retreat.

"Take Duke Spencer to your apartments, Lord Aaron," I say gently once they've left. "There's no reason for him to be here."

"She wanted me to find her," Duke Spencer says weakly. "Because I abandoned her."

"Hush," Lord Aaron says, smoothing down the duke's wispy blond hair.

But Duke Spencer shakes his head. "I knew what they were like—how awful they are—and I left her to them." He sniffles. "She loved me, in her way."

"Go," I whisper. "Both of you. I'll take care of her."

The two men leave the apartment, trying to appear normal, and with a tight smile, I shoo Lady Mei after them. As soon as the door closes behind them, my legs start to tremble, and I feel bile rise in my throat. Saber stands in front of me, blocking me from the security officers' view. I grasp for control and only barely grab hold of it. I remember when we found my mother's body, how calm Saber managed to stay. I can do that too. I hardly knew Julianna—she wasn't my mother, or even Molli.

"Do you think anyone saw this coming?" Saber asks quietly, his head close to mine so no one else can hear us.

I shake my head. "I'm not convinced even Lady Julianna thought it through, to be honest." Emotion sets my voice trembling, and I force myself to hold very still while it passes. "If she had, she would have dressed more nicely. Or perhaps her manner of dress *is* her statement. Regardless, clearly she was upset. Angry." I hesitate. "Sad."

Saber nods silently.

We look down on her body, lying so still. She doesn't look like she's sleeping. There's a stillness to death that looks nothing like sleeping, and I despise when people make that comparison. A man in a blue uniform rises from his crouch beside her and walks over with a tablet in his hands.

I sign a few documents with his stylus—red tape and formalities. "I'll summon medical up here to take her down to the morgue," he says when I'm done.

"No!"

His chin jerks up and even Saber stares at me quizzically.

My throat constricts, and I swallow hard. "We have guests

today," I whisper. "She doesn't deserve to be wheeled out in front of them for everyone to see. Covered or not." It's something. Preserve whatever shreds of her dignity remain. "Late tonight. After the tourists are gone. I'll talk to Duke Spencer; I'm certain he'll agree to let her stay here until then."

The tiny smile of approval on Saber's face is all the confirmation I need that, for once, I'm doing the right thing.

The man bows, then says, "Will you want to contact the King, Your Highness? Inform him of this?"

"The King?" I ask, realizing that I don't even know how to contact him directly. I've always gone through Mateus. I suppose I could send him a com, but I want to handle this on my own. To show him that I can. "I don't think that's necessary; they weren't friends. An official report sent to his email will suffice. I'll leave that in your capable hands," I say, pulling my gloves on one at a time, pushing my emotions back as I push my fingers into the kid leather. I have to be the Queen. "I've a public assembly to host tonight."

TWENTY-THREE

WHEN SABER ESCORTS me into the Hall of Mirrors a few hours later, the air is fairly crackling with tension. Which is only to be expected, with the news of Julianna's death coming so soon after her family's downfall; Lady Mei says Madame Tremain is cloistered and sedated in the clinic, with her husband glued to her side.

But as I walk down the line of *salons,* I get the distinct impression that there's more to the mood than a suicide scandal. If the talk were simply about Lady Julianna, I would expect a frenetic rotation of courtiers from one circle to the next, swapping theories and gossip, and the social crucifixion of at least one innocent bystander. Instead, the crowd is split into two definite clumps on either side of the Hall of Mirrors. Judging from the placement of my nearest allies, I can't help but feel that the choosing of sides has something to do with me and nothing to do with the Tremains at all.

Most disconcerting. Even the tourists seem unusually subdued, hanging back behind the velvet ropes that keep the plebeians, the peepers, and the *poseurs* in their place.

"What's happening?" I ask Lord Aaron quietly when Saber

and I join him. I stride along between them, a hand on each arm. I've been taking advantage of the King's absence to keep Saber at my side instead of behind me. Not flaunting, precisely—merely keeping him more equal. He'll never be even a servant in my eyes, much less a slave.

"Does it matter?" my melancholy friend asks, lifting his eyebrows and his glass.

"The tension in here is palpable. Yes, that matters to me."

"I can't bear a scene tonight," Lord Aaron says, letting the barest edge of his weariness show in the form of a slight slur. "Promise me you won't do anything."

"That sounds like a dangerous promise," I say, catching a flute of champagne from a passing servant.

"Please? For Spencer's sake?"

"I promise—as long as you'll tell me." I give him a tight smile. "To be quite honest, I'd rather be angry than sad."

"Then this is your lucky day," he says dryly, more into his tumbler than to me. "Lady Cyn is down at the other end of the hall sharing the love emails your husband has been sending her while he's away."

I snort and cough on my champagne. "Well, those are fake."

"I have no doubt," he says. "But she's getting quite a lot of mileage out of them."

"A twenty-three-year-old woman—a girl, practically, for all the years she had on me—is *dead*. Violently and by her own hand. And Lady Cyn cannot muster the respect to give up her juvenile campaign against me for *one evening*?"

"She's always been a cold fish who cares for little beyond herself," Lord Aaron says, then leans so close to my ear that his lips touch my skin. "The emails can fairly easily be proved to be false. Especially once the King gets home. I can't imagine what she's thinking."

I steal a glance at the other end of the hall, where Lady Cyn is sitting on a chair with her long taffeta skirts spread about her in a graceful semicircle, her tablet in her hands—jacketed like a hand-stitched book, but still a fairly brazen flouting of Wednesday protocol—reading aloud to a crowd of courtiers, mostly young ladies, who appear to be eating up every word. "For all her faults, she knows the King. He has no interest in court gossip unless it impacts his business plans. He'll never follow up on this, much less take the time to publicly deny it. He simply won't care."

"She's so petty," Lord Aaron says, tipping back the rest of his drink. "The only thing worse than a bad loser is a bad winner."

"She hasn't won," I mutter, finishing my champagne and reaching for another glass despite Saber's sending me a raised eyebrow just before turning to address a young courtier. Julianna's death has left me in a gray mood. I suspect it'll be a big champagne night for me. "I'm going to grind her into the pavement. But not tonight. I will keep my word, not to mention behave as a decent human being. How is Duke Spencer? Feeling any better?"

"Truthfully? No. He blames himself because he has that sort of heart. But he's over the shock and more in control, and that's almost the same thing, isn't it?"

"Some days," I say ruefully. "He's not coming tonight, is he? I was surprised to see you here."

"We decided it was more respectful if we didn't arrive together."

"Decent of you," I drawl, but a flurry of movement catches my eye. "Oh dear, I'd better go rescue Saber." He's been waylaid by three young courtiers who all seem certain that laying hands on his person will somehow get them what they want.

"Darling," Lord Aaron says, stopping me with a hand on my shoulder as I start to walk away. "Once Spence arrives, he and I have something to tell you."

He doesn't meet my eyes, and a flutter of fear makes my heart race. "Should we . . . meet in your office?" I ask. "Perhaps at midnight?"

"I thought the middle of the *Salon d'Apollon*. Midnight is fine."

"The *Salon d'Apollon*?" I echo. "It'll be full of people."

The smile he flashes is grim. "What better place to share a secret than the middle of a crowded room?" He tips the rest of his drink into his mouth, and I return to rescuing Saber.

I position myself directly behind the two ladies and one gentleman harassing my green-eyed *paramour* and clear my throat loudly. As they turn, one of them removes her hand from inside Saber's breast pocket, and I barely control my temper as I glare at her. She raises her chin for a few seconds before realizing there's no hiding the bright red flush across her cheeks, then looks over my shoulder and mutters an apology. To me, not to Saber. I'd like to make a bigger deal of it, but what I'd like more is to simply get them out of here.

"Saber, have you completed your business with these *people*?" I ask sharply, still staring at the red-faced girl with the wandering hands.

"Indeed," Saber says stiffly.

"Then they'd better be off," I say, my eyes taking in each of them in turn.

They drop into bows with matching murmurs of "Yes, Your Highness," before scurrying off like rodents.

"You're going to have to raise the price again," Saber says when I take his proffered arm and begin promenading down the line of *salons*.

I nod. It feels a touch disrespectful to discuss my illegal business in the wake of a violent death. Still, I can't help but be grateful that at least this death had nothing to do with Glitter. It had everything to do with *me*, but the voice that insists on reminding me will soon be drowned in champagne.

"My list is completely full and I'm still dealing with people pushing money at me," Saber says. "Obviously."

"Already? But we just got a fresh batch."

Saber nods. "They're trying to claim their canister as far ahead as they can."

"No double orders?"

"I've checked it twice."

I take a shuddering breath. "Okay. Double the price one more time, but that's as far as I'm going to take it. From here on out, it's first come, first served."

"Things are going to get ugly," Saber warns.

"Do you think I'm wrong?"

"You know my feelings."

"I meant about continuing to limit the quantities."

"No!" he says quickly. "At least it's something. Don't go back on *that*. I'm just not sure how much longer it'll be possible. You made a million and a half since last week."

"*After* paying Reginald?" I ask. Saber just nods silently. I suppose I could have done the math earlier and predicted it, but I've been so busy I just haven't bothered.

Haven't bothered to count a million and a half euros. This is my life now.

"Could you find Lady Mei for me, Saber?" I ask, consulting my Lens. "She's somewhere in the Hercules Drawing Room at the moment, but on the go." I grasp his arm and lean my head close to his ear. "I need a report. Tell her to circulate a bit, find out what people think of Lady Cyn's newest stunt—if they're buying it—and to come find me later. And don't tell Lord Aaron. Or Duke Spencer."

Saber pulls back and looks down at me, with a wrinkle between his brow and wearing an expression I can't quite read.

"I know," I say. "It's ridiculous to be dealing with this right now, and I feel awful. But I can't allow Lady Cyn's petty grudge to interfere with more important things, and I promised Lord Aaron I wouldn't make a scene." I look down at my shoes. "Help me keep that promise?"

A labored sigh is my only answer.

"Tell Lady Mei I'll be in the *Salon d'Apollon*."

"If you're sure that's what you want," he says, waiting a moment for me to—what? Take it back?

"I know you don't like the games people play here," I whisper, "but so long as I *am* here, I need to know these things."

He nods curtly, then drops a low bow and turns to work his way through the dense crowd.

I kill time for half an hour—drinking too much champagne and not eating enough food to soak it up—but when at last midnight approaches, I make my way to the center of the *Salon d'Apollon,* feeling queasy. Unlike in the days before my marriage to the King, people make way for me, and I reach my desired destination easily. Lord Aaron and Duke Spencer are waiting there, but neither is looking at me. They're having one of those silent conversations that only take place between true intimates.

Before I can let out a sigh of exasperation and ask them to please speak their thoughts *aloud,* Duke Spencer says, "Tell her. She deserves to know."

We're gathered into a close cluster, but though the courtiers around us crane their necks to spy, no one dares actually intrude on this *tête-à-tête.* Meeting here was a good idea—the din in the *salon* makes it surprisingly private, provided one keeps a fan to one's lips, and we truly have been spending too much time shut away in the privacy of Lord Aaron's office. Who knows what kind of spy network the King left in place in his absence? And in the wake of Julianna's death, perhaps even the *illusion* of secrecy should be avoided for a few days.

Lord Aaron takes a deep breath before speaking. "We can't stay. And it's not just Julianna's death, although . . ."

"That made the decision easier," Duke Spencer finishes, then shudders. "I can't sleep in that house again. Not ever."

"But even before that, I was halfway to this decision," Lord Aaron says. "Once we found those contracts, it was . . . I think even you knew it was inevitable."

I swallow hard and nod.

"I've been working with the Foundation for years with the sole intent of helping people whose lives have been negatively affected by Sonoma. Until today that really wasn't very many. A handful, but it gave me a sense of purpose. Some good I could do even as I lived my life of extreme privilege. Now? It's going to be so many more than just Sonoma employees. It'll be millions, Danica. *Hundreds* of millions."

He looks at Duke Spencer, who nods approvingly.

I suspected as much—can't pretend I'm at all surprised—but reality hurts far worse than suspicion. A single syllable is all I can manage. "When?"

"Before the King returns."

"He's coming back in less than a week!" I almost explode. "I can't let you go so soon." Tears are burning my eyes and I blink them back desperately.

"We'll wait until the night before he returns," Lord Aaron responds. "We'll call it a pleasure trip. Unlike you," he says apologetically, "we're both of age and can travel without permission." He pauses to smile and raise his glass to someone across the room. "We'll tell people we're going to visit Spence's cousins in America. Get away from the Tremains and let things simmer down and all that. Eventually it'll become obvious that we're not coming back."

"You said you'd help me. Help with Saber." I feel betrayed, even though I know I'm being selfish.

"I know, but this is bigger than any of us."

"We spent the afternoon hashing it out," Duke Spencer says quietly. He glances at Lord Aaron. "It's going to kill him to stay. Even a few weeks. You've got to see that."

At Duke Spencer's words I take a good look at Lord Aaron. It's easy to focus on Duke Spencer at this moment—the person in our group closest to Julianna, miserable marriage or not. But he's right. I see the weariness in Lord Aaron's eyes, the way his shoulders don't seem quite straight. Like he's been hollowed out and now threatens to collapse in on himself.

"Millions, Danica," Lord Aaron says hoarsely. "Millions upon millions. A *billion* over the next decade—at the very least! Languishing in poverty, homelessness, malnourishment. I can't stand by and do nothing."

"I'll never see you again," I choke out.

"You're the one who promised to disappear so thoroughly, even I wouldn't be able to find you," he says firmly. "And I accepted that."

"Oh, sure," I say with a wobbly smile. "Make me follow my own rules."

Lord Aaron forces a laugh, and I try to follow suit, remembering there are eyes on us.

"What do I need to do?" I ask, fluttering my fan.

"Make the most of the time we have left?" Duke Spencer says when Lord Aaron looks at his feet.

I nod, because I don't dare talk. I'm already breathing fast and shallow to hold back tears. "Of course."

Saying goodbye—that's the part that's going to kill me.

Somehow I smile and simper my way through another hour of the party before I plead weariness and bow my way out. I even manage to listen to Lady Mei's report that the court simply doesn't know what to think of their new Queen. That so many still feel loyal to the woman Justin was raised to marry. It's hard to care anymore. I walk into my bedroom and lean back on the closed doors, unable to bear the weight of my existence, much less my evening gown. My entire body feels weak with the knowledge that Lord Aaron is leaving.

And that I shouldn't resent him for it.

My white knight is running errant, off to save as much of the world's doomed and impoverished as he can. What am I doing? Hiding in a murk of my own making until I can find a way to exercise my vengeance on those who've wronged me. I've never felt so much the villain.

"Hold me?"

Ever ready, ever reliable, Saber kneels in front of me, wrapping his arms around my waist, squeezing. His face presses against the hard busk of my corset, but his wiry arms manage to squeeze harder than my boning. I grip handfuls of his hair and hold them trapped in tight fists as I wait for the spinning of my mind to slow. I don't know how long it takes for my brain to calm down, but by the time I grow aware of my body again, my ribs are aching. Saber isn't gentle. I don't want him to be. I need that pressure, that pain. If only for a few minutes.

"He's leaving me," I whisper when I find my voice again.

When my fingers release his hair, Saber rises from the floor, his face close to mine, his arms around me as choking sobs shake my body. It's better, this awful yawning agony. Better than the numbness I've used to mask it in the past. Harder. But better.

"Who?" Saber whispers.

"Aaron." I never refer to him without his title. But he's leaving that behind along with everything else. "He has to. I know that. And if he didn't leave me, it would only be because I left him first. But . . ." I don't finish my sentence. I don't have to. Saber is the epitome of empathy. Anything that could possibly have happened to me, has already been worse for him. He knows what it feels like to be left; his whole family left him. And not to a life of pampered privilege that he was on the verge of escaping anyway.

The thought makes me certain all over again that I've made the right choice, in spite of everything. How can anyone on earth deserve freedom more than Saber?

And he won't fight for it on his own.

No, that's unfair. He *can't* fight for it on his own.

In a few days Lord Aaron and Duke Spencer will be out of the King's reach, and I've already sent my father to relative safety. Lady Mei has no desire to leave Sonoman-Versailles behind; in fact, she seems to actually be *gaining* both influence and confidence by backing me. The only person left to save—for better or worse—is Saber.

I won't leave until he's safe. No matter who else has to suffer—especially if it's only me.

I let Saber help me undress, something we've both come to enjoy. It gives us a chance to talk quietly while Saber unties and releases dozens of buttons on all the intricate pieces of my gowns, and we put a king's ransom in jewels into little velvet cases on my dressing table, as though they're worth nothing at all. To us, I suppose they aren't.

"You were beautiful tonight," Saber says, leaning in to kiss my forehead. "Your *ensemble* looked nice too," he adds.

His compliment catches me off-guard, and I blush furiously.

"Come on, then," he says, stripping his shirt off over his own head. "Time to sweat."

For once I don't complain. The pain in my abdomen cleanses as I hold plank after plank, crunch after crunch, until I'm so exhausted even my spinning brain can't keep me awake.

TWENTY-FOUR

FIVE DAYS OF good memories. Enough to chase away the ghost of one desperate, dead ex-wife. Enough to last us all the rest of our lives. I keep that thought foremost in my mind as Lord Aaron begins casting his spell, telling the courtiers of his and Duke Spencer's upcoming trip, promising American souvenirs to his favorites. I can't help but be reminded of the lies he spun about my make-believe honeymoon when he was drumming up Glitter orders right before the wedding. The honeymoon was always a lie . . . but somehow no one seems to remember his previous deception, and they fall equally hard for this one.

Though this trip will actually happen. He just won't be coming back.

After a spontaneous champagne brunch, barefoot games on the front lawn, and a late-night sleepover in my chambers, Duke Spencer pulls me into Lord Aaron's private office to transfer entrance credentials to his apartments—ostensibly for "housesitting."

"With luck, the King won't realize we're not returning for at least five or six weeks," Duke Spencer says an hour before the going-away *soirée*. A privately chartered helicopter is coming for them at the end of the festivities, when everyone will be too tired or soused to notice them slipping out. "Until then, here's my key card, and my access codes, and if you do a quick face scan I can add that to the front-door security list as well. Feel free to make use of anything within."

"Very generous of you," I mumble, even though I'm pretty sure I'm never going to enter that apartment again. I'm fighting the irrational urge to resent this quiet person who's as much a victim of circumstance as anyone. I know he's not really *taking Lord Aaron away*—technically, he's the reason Lord Aaron has stayed this long. But the fact that they're running off together, directly after Julianna's suicide, marks Duke Spencer as the catalyst in my messed-up brain.

"He'll be happier," Duke Spencer says after his scanner captures my facial imprint.

"I know."

"I wish this could be easier on you."

I shrug halfheartedly. "I wish the last two years could have been easier on both of you, but we're not getting very many of our wishes these days, are we?"

"Perhaps not," he says softly.

"Have you heard anything about that document we found on Mateus's computer? From your contacts in America?" I ask, needing to change the subject lest I disgrace myself with tears.

"I—it hasn't been sent, actually. Aaron thought it would be safest to hand it off in person, since we're going to be there. We'll find a way to tell you what they say." He grins. "Watch for anonymous coms, I suppose."

I nod silently.

"Speaking of—here," Duke Spencer says, handing me a scrap of paper.

"What is this?" I ask, unfolding it.

He hesitates, then says, "My parents' mailbox in New York City. The lawyers who manage their business interests in the States initially kept it up because they were on so many people's contact lists. After six months, I asked them to continue paying for it indefinitely."

I blink back tears when I recognize what he's offering me.

"It wasn't safe for the two of you to try to maintain contact with your original plan, because Aaron was going to stay here in the palace when you left. Any communication could have put both of you in danger. But now, with all of us getting out, maybe once you're established . . ." He trails off and looks down at the floor. "I'm not going to tell him I gave you that. If you decide it's a bad idea, or if things go wrong when you leave . . . but it's an option. He'd be thrilled. I hope you know how much he adores you."

"I do." Duke Spencer is impossible to hate. Even as he takes away my best friend, he leaves me a little piece of hope. So why does it only make me despair? Make everything about this parting seem so much more real? "Where is he?"

"Dressing. I told him I'd just be taking care of the nuts and bolts with you. And I am," he says with a soft smile.

I want to say something possessive—about how he'd better take care of my friend or there will be hell to pay—but it doesn't feel proper. If anything, Duke Spencer is more invested in Lord Aaron's happiness than I am. I've been eclipsed.

In preparation for going back on the grid, I open a contact container and put my Lens back in so I can com Lady Mei. I pull out a handkerchief to dab at the drips of saline under my eye. "It's a good thing I wear waterproof eye makeup," I grumble. "I pop this thing in and out so frequently my eyelids are starting to get sore."

Duke Spencer is silent, graciously allowing me to fob my red eyes off on my Lens. When we exit the office Saber jumps to his feet from a small chair in the communal lobby, and when his eyes meet mine, I know he can tell there's something wrong. His concern only makes it harder to hold back tears, so when he starts to ask, I give him a minute shake of my head.

I turn to Duke Spencer, standing in the doorway. "I'll see you at the ball, then."

"One last party," he says with a grin, but I can't muster one in return.

And so it is that I am, perhaps, in a more terrible mood than usual when, as I depart the administrative wing, I nearly run straight into Lady Garcia.

"*Pardonnez*, Your Highness," she says, dropping into a deep bow. I stare at her, and all I can hear pounding through my head is Lady Mei's voice when she reported about Lady Cyn's friends. *She's also been much in company with Lady Annaleigh Garcia and Lady Breya Voroman-Wills.*

Without the presence of my lofty husband to either confirm or deny my words, I curl my lips into a grin and prepare to lay the groundwork for my vengeance against Lady Cyn. Indirectly, of course. "Lady Garcia." I step forward and take her arm, turning her away from wherever she had been heading, knowing she won't complain. "I've been hoping for a moment with you."

"Yes?" she says, clearly taken off-guard. Everyone's jumpy after Julianna's death. Maybe it'll get better after the funeral. It pains me to say it, but maybe it'll get better when the King comes back. Tyrant or not, the kingdom is used to him.

"I wanted to speak to you about your daughter. Lady Annaleigh," I add, as I have no idea whether there's another daughter. If I were staying, I'd need to start memorizing the noble family trees. "I'm concerned about her."

"Concerned?" Lady Garcia parrots, still baffled. Unlike the Duchess Sells, Lady Garcia married into her title and doesn't have the calm *façade* and backbone of steel that some of the other noble ladies were raised with.

"I think she's in trouble. Or, perhaps more accurately, if you don't take her in hand, she's going to be in trouble." I let go of Lady Garcia's arm and spin to face her, letting my skirts swirl out around me and looking down at the rather diminutive older woman from my at least ten-centimeter height advantage. My eyes are hard, and Lady Garcia stiffens, clearly seeing the threat. "She hasn't been choosing her friends wisely." I lower my eyelids. "It speaks of a family trying to play both sides."

Lady Garcia gasps. "No, of course not!"

I walk very slowly in a circle around Lady Garcia. "You and the marquis are in the intimate circle of trust of His Highness. That's why you were there"—I hesitate for effect—"*that* night. So you're fully aware of how I treat those who cross me. Who cross my husband."

"The King cannot doubt our loyalty," Lady Garcia interrupts to protest.

"The *King* doesn't." I stop moving and simply stare her down. "Things are going to . . . get messy soon," I say softly. "It would be a shame if Lady Annaleigh were caught in the cross fire because she held on to a friendship that's no longer to her credit." I take half a step nearer and whisper, "I trust you understand what needs to be done?"

Lady Garcia gulps and nods.

I step back and give her a gentle smile now. A confident, cajoling smile. "We only give you this warning because We're certain you'll make the right choice," I say, invoking the royal *We* for the first time.

"Thank you," she whispers, the sparkling blush on her cheeks standing out, a garish pink on her now-pale face.

"Saber?" I call, and without looking, I put out my hand and he guides it to his arm and escorts me away.

"What was that?" he whispers.

"Groundwork. Taking Lady Cyn's friends away from her. Making sure she's alone when I decide what to do to her."

"What to—" But he bites off his own question, leading me silently through the broad halls and milling courtiers. He remains quiet until the doors to my bedchamber close behind us, shutting everyone else out. "Why are you doing this?"

"Doing what?" I say, pretending to misunderstand as I reach for a pair of diamond earrings. I was mostly dressed before I went to Lord Aaron's office, but I hadn't yet donned my jewels.

"Moving against Lady Cyn. Why does she even matter? Especially tonight?"

"I'm not going to do anything *tonight*."

He doesn't dignify that with a response—only stands there, face stony, awaiting a real answer.

I sigh and put down the earrings, turning to face him. "Saber, there are aspects of the social and political hierarchy here that are difficult for anyone outside of it to understand. If you don't get it already, I don't know how better to explain. You're the one who got locked up as a result of her petty grudge-holding, but that's only since you've arrived. She's tortured me for years, and it's got to stop. Stripping away her influence is the only way I can ensure she doesn't accidentally *or* intentionally destroy *everything* I've been working toward."

Saber shakes his head. "It's more than that. Why is this so important to you?"

"Because she's terrible! She's a self-centered bully who hates me and cares nothing for anyone but herself," I say, stuffing some tissues and lip gloss into my reticule, and not gently. "She is the worst kind of person—the kind who uses her power to crush those who are defenseless!"

"Unlike you."

"I haven't always had power. I used to have none, and she was more than happy to take advantage of that."

"So you'll sink to her level?"

Searing anger boils through me, momentarily robbing me of my voice. When I find it, it emerges sharp and hot. "I'm *not* like her. And Lady Cyn is hardly defenseless. After tonight, the number of allies I have in court goes down by *two*, Saber. And I didn't have very many to begin with. Lady Cyn will steal others if she can." I lean toward him, placing my hands on the back of a velvet armchair. "If I do this right, I'll have an army behind me, and she'll have nothing. You would have me give up and stand alone? That's not fair, Saber."

"None of this is fair!" he snaps back. "If you bring fairness into this, you'd better be prepared to give an accounting of the damage you've already done."

"Don't," I say, pointing a warning finger at him and suddenly reminding myself of Monsieur Tremain. I let my arm drop before I can consider that comparison a moment longer.

"Why?" Saber says. "Why not let her go on her silly, spoiled way? Why *destroy* her?"

"Because despite all her efforts to prevent me from rising, I have. Because now I'm in a position to do everything she tried to prevent, and she can't stop me anymore. Because I *can*, Saber!" I swallow hard and raise my chin. "Because I *want* to."

TWENTY-FIVE

SABER FOLLOWS ME about, physically close but undeniably distant. Unsure how to bridge the gap, I tip glass after glass of champagne down my throat instead, pretending all the while that my best friend and greatest ally isn't leaving me in a matter of hours.

"Dance with me," I say when I find Lord Aaron momentarily without Duke Spencer at his side for once.

"You are beyond tipsy, Your Highness," Lord Aaron scolds.

"Can you blame me?" I ask, though at least I don't slur. I think.

"No," he hedges, "but I'm not certain you can afford to be anything less than vigilant at the moment."

Lord Aaron is an impeccable dance partner—and I watch the crowds around us, his leading so skillful I can let all thoughts of my feet go. "The split between her and me grows wider," I say softly, raising one eyebrow so Lord Aaron knows I'm not being dreary.

"Except for that group there, in the middle," he says, gesturing minutely with his chin, "who are still calculating the odds."

"Loyal to no one. I've no need of that sort," I say flippantly, though it does bother me that there are still so many uncertain who will win the battle. I should be able to claim these vacillators on position alone. I have the backing of the King! Lady Cyn has the backing of no one. "I don't have time for her tonight," I say, forcing a smile. "And certainly I don't have the clear thinking for her."

"No, no you don't," Lord Aaron says. Wryly, but at least he isn't scolding me anymore.

"Well," I say cheerily, facing Lord Aaron as the song comes to an end, "I think we should take this party somewhere a little more private. Spread the word, only to *our* people, that the Queen is moving the festivities to her quarters." I give him a sly smile and add, "I'll order twenty bottles of champagne and a full spread."

His eyes twinkle, and I can almost imagine we're back to our innocent old antics: Molli, Lady Mei, and our window-hacking patron, Lord Aaron, running wild about the palace, pleasing no one but ourselves, breaking curfew, sneaking cigarettes, playing pranks on the pensioners. How long ago that seems—someone else's life.

I leave the dance floor and head through the Peace Drawing Room, back toward my bedchamber, through the *Salon des Nobles* and the *Antechamber*. On the way I inform a small handful of people loitering there that I am about to host a rather exuberant party, invitation only. As they've chosen to spend their time in my personal—if generally accessible to the public—rooms, I assume some degree of loyalty and invite them to attend if they desire. Perhaps not the most calculated decision, but I've had too much champagne for calculation.

Lord Aaron and Duke Spencer enter at the head of a crowd that spills loudly into my rooms, and after Lady Mei brings up the rear, I close the doors and lock them. Fence-sitters need not apply.

The food and wine flow freely—my royal salary is shockingly generous—and voices rise all over the *salons,* toasting Lord Aaron and Duke Spencer. Slurred shouts of *"Bon voyage!"* and suggestive hoots of laughter fill the space.

No one remembers that the ex-wife of one of these men hanged herself this week. No one wants to. How fast they forget the death of one of their own; how quick to move on to the next pleasant endeavor, the next opportunity to smile and simper and be seen in fine clothes and jewels.

Lord Aaron is right that I've had entirely too much to drink, and perhaps a step beyond that. What I need is some regular old water. I turn to ask Saber if he can get me some, but he's nowhere to be found. Hazily I recall that he bade me good night with an indulgent smile . . . some time ago.

But I should be finished drinking. I drop onto a chair, put my half-full glass on my dressing table, and look over the crowd. Because they're all "my" people, the sparkle of Glitter is ubiquitous; even as I watch, a few canisters change hands and more shimmer is applied.

I asked Lord Aaron once what it felt like to be high on Glitter and he called it "an aware euphoria." Utterly blissful, without the sensory haze so often accompanying recreational highs. I can hear it in their loud voices, see it in the languorous way they lean on each other and in the slightly vacant cast to their eyes.

An entire room buzzed on Glitter, and one would never even suspect if one didn't already know the signs. I'm more visibly impaired by champagne than they are by their makeup; this drug is going to truly revolutionize the underworld. In light of what I've learned about Sonoma's pharmaceutical dealings, I imagine the prescription version will be equally revolutionary. The possibilities are staggering—though I can't forget what they got my father, in the end.

Someone takes me by the shoulders and shakes me gently—when did I fall asleep? I'm not the only one; every *chaise*, settee, and *divan* in my rooms is occupied by people who have drifted off, or people on their way to it—those who decided that finding their way back to the residential wing would simply be too onerous after such gaiety.

My eyes settle on Lord Aaron, who's smiling sadly; he pats my shoulder and lets me go. "I wanted to let you sleep," he whispers. "But I feared you'd never forgive me."

"Indeed, I would not," I say, dragging myself to my feet.

Duke Spencer gives me a stoic farewell, thanking me prettily for the send-off party, then goes on ahead to give Lord Aaron and me some privacy. I thought I was ready, but when Lord Aaron enfolds me in his big, warm arms, my chest aches and my eyes grow hot.

"You're going to follow soon," he says, addressing my dismay. "You have a bit more work to do, and then it'll be you up there, catching your own helicopter to freedom." His hand covers the back of my head, pressing me tight against his shoulder. "A little while longer," he whispers.

"I'm not sure I can bear it, Aaron." The tears spill then, and I hate that I can't be brave for him.

"You can," Lord Aaron says. "But you have to remember, you're the Queen, and everything that comes with it. *Be* the Queen. No one can defeat you."

It's so odd to hear advice from him that runs so completely opposite to what Saber would tell me. I clench my fingers on his arms. "I've never been Queen without you. I'm not sure I know how."

"I saw you with Monsieur Tremain. You were *incredible*. You were born for this role, Dani. If only you could see in yourself what I see in you."

I feel sick about the unfeeling way I acted to a father whose daughter wasn't even cold in death. To hear Lord Aaron praise me for it only makes me feel lower. "It feels heady at the time, but it's dragging me under. The lying, the deceit. How do I play the game without becoming just another player?"

"Don't lose yourself," Lord Aaron says, clasping my cheeks in both hands. "Despite everything you've been forced to do, I know you're still in there. Don't let go of your goodness. Don't lose sight of your goals."

My chin shakes and I can hardly choke the words out. "I'm afraid I'm already lost. What will I do if you're not here to find me?"

He holds me tight against his chest, and I tell myself—one more moment. And yet one more. At last Lord Aaron pushes me away and steadies me before giving me a determined nod. With one last wave and sad smile over his shoulder, he's gone.

Half my inner circle, gone.

I'm still here. Despite my scheming and my sins, despite every desperate decision, I'm still here.

And I've never felt more alone.

THANKS TO THE theft of the King's itinerary from Mateus's tablet, I know just when *his* helicopter is expected on the following night. I stand in the shadow of the small overhang at the top of the steps that lead to the helipad on the roof, watching the bright lights approach. What I wouldn't pay to have Lord Aaron returning in this helicopter—for my husband to be the man who's never coming back.

The King, crisply attired, ducks casually under the still-rotating blades of the bot-flown helicopter to jog toward me.

"Hello, wife?" he asks, more of a question than a greeting.

"Welcome home, my lord." He casually offers an arm as though he fully expected me to be waiting for him.

"What are you doing?" he asks in a whisper as he escorts me down the stairs and back into the palace.

"A wife can't await the arrival of her husband?"

"A wife can. Not you," he grumbles, and I can see that he's travel-weary. And grumpy.

"I thought to warn you," I say sweetly.

"Now, aren't those the words every husband wants to hear as he arrives back from a week of grueling business travel?"

"You have some ruffled feathers to soothe."

"The Tremains, I presume. I received word."

"Lady Cyn's."

He pauses on the landing and turns to me, and his eyes reflect genuine anger. "What did you do?"

I let out a bark of laughter. "You dare to imply that I'm the guilty party here? Rich."

"Just tell me what happened."

"Lady Cyn walked in on me while I was writing some business emails in our private office."

So many emotions flash across his face I can't even begin to keep up—and I don't trust my husband when he's feeling contemplative. "You were in my private office?"

I widen my eyes. "I'm quite certain the surprising part of this story shouldn't be that *I* was in that office."

He groans. "I gave her access ages ago; I forgot."

But I know him better than that. "You never forget anything."

He turns and clomps down the stairs, barely looking over his shoulder to address me. "You're the one telling me I'm perfect now? That's a pleasant change."

"You haven't answered why she has access to *my* private office—and don't argue that wording. As long as we're sharing, it's my space, too."

"It was months ago. She wanted to tryst on my desk. I gave her access and never revoked it."

"Justin," I say, my voice dripping feigned disappointment. "Why didn't you tell me?" That brings him up short. At his confused expression I add, "I've touched that desk; that's disgusting."

He just rolls his eyes and resumes his descent.

"It's more than that, though, and you know it. She's in my face all the time, flaunting your favor, trying to undermine my social influence. It's been worse while you were away. At the ball last week, she . . ." I trail off without actually saying anything about the fake emails she was reading to her ladies. I'll let him imagine what happened. With luck, he'll come up with something better than reality.

"This is somehow more important than the Tremains' daughter *hanging herself*?"

"Well, no, but I assumed you wouldn't care a whit about that. Thought you might even be pleased."

"How cold do you think I am?"

I don't answer, only raise an eyebrow.

He growls and turns away. "All I hear coming out of your mouth is adolescent drama," he says, as though he weren't an adolescent himself. "What is it you want me to do, Danica?"

"I want you to stand by me as your wife, *Justin*," I shoot back.

"Hard to do that when I'm away on business."

"Fine. I'll tell you precisely what I want. I want her gone."

He spreads his hands helplessly. "Can't throw ladies in jail for being bitches, my love, else your mother would never have been a problem for either of us."

I don't cringe at the insult; it's one I'd have happily given on my own. I glare, knowing the malice is glittering in my eyes. "I gave you Tremain. Handed you his punishment on a damned silver platter. A more poetic bit of justice than you ever would have thought up." I thump my finger right in the middle of his chest. "You owe me."

Contrary to my expectations, a smile crosses the King's face and he sweeps a curl off my forehead and behind my ear. "There she is," he whispers. "There's my wife."

I turn and resist wiping away the feel of his touch. "I insist you revoke her access to that office. At the very least."

"When last we spoke of it, you seemed somewhat less than interested in sharing space with me."

"I suppose you could give me my own private, unmonitored office and end this conversation entirely."

"Where would the fun be in that?"

"Fun?" I shout. I've lost too much the last few days to suffer his condescension. "This is your idea of *fun*, Justin?"

His smile doesn't so much as dim. "Has it occurred to you, Dani, that sometimes I do things for the sole purpose of making you angry? I rather like you when you're angry."

I clench my teeth so hard my jaw aches, and in my head I hear Lord Aaron's voice. *You're the Queen. Be the Queen.* It takes several deep breaths before I trust myself to speak without worrying that my voice will shake. "You take care of her," I finally say, "or I will."

TWENTY-SIX

I DON'T HAVE it in me to do more than go through the motions of my *lever*. Of course, that means this is the morning that Reginald decides to refill my Glitter box.

"He came while I was out there?" I ask as I remove a hat, elbow-length gloves, two brooches, three rings, a bracelet, and a set of diamond buckles from my shoes and still have enough bling to make me shimmer under the low lights.

Saber nods, his jaw tight.

I sigh. I'm so weary. "I'll change into better shoes while you fill your messenger bag," I say quietly. "Then let's fill my *pannier* cages and see if we can't get all the product dispensed today. Forget about it for another week."

As if either of us could really forget about it. But perhaps it will let us ignore the awful secret that we constantly carry around.

For the next hour there's a continual stream of courtiers retrieving their canisters of Glitter. Most of them take it from me with their eyes lowered, and I wonder if they've finally gotten wise—wonder if that's why they're coming to me cowed and ashamed. But ashamed of being addicted? If there was ever a group of people more utterly inured to shame, I've yet to meet them.

Still, they mumble and toe the carpet like children caught hacking treats from the commissary.

Lady Nuala is the first to meet my eyes, even though she already has her canister of Glitter as payment for being on my *lever* staff. But she comes up and grasps my gloved hands in hers and squeezes gently. "You have my support, you know," she says, leaning close as though to whisper in my ear. She's sufficiently shorter than me that her words mostly go into my shoulder.

"There's absolutely no question of your loyalty," I say softly, giving her a genuine smile. She smiles back, but it's an expression full of worry. I watch her go and, keeping my face carefully neutral, glance around at the residents gathered in the hall.

They won't meet my eyes. They turn away—even some who have nothing to do with my Glitter trade.

Odd.

"I wonder why no one will look at me," I whisper to Saber once we get a break from the streaming crowds. "I know Lord Aaron and Duke Spencer left, but surely no one suspects anything out of the ordinary after so short a time."

Saber hesitates, then says, "I haven't seen your husband yet this morning. Possibly connected?"

"I wish you wouldn't call him that."

"You do it all the time."

"It's worse when you do it."

He grins. "Sometimes I need to remind myself. Especially when we're together in public." A little rasp in his voice makes warmth spread down my abdomen to settle low in my stomach, and I let myself smile, just a little.

A red light blinks rapidly in my peripheral. Emergency com—from Lady Mei?

DO NOT DO ANYTHING. DO NOT GO SEE HIM.
MEET ME ON THE FRONT LAWN.

I don't let the confusion and dismay show on my face, but I hate being the only one out of the know. It reminds me of those early days after my debut, when Lady Cyn's wide circle of friends would gather about and whisper behind their fans every time I danced with the King, and I had no idea what I was doing wrong—that I was doing anything particularly noteworthy at all. It's an awful feeling. Worse than whatever the secret ends up being.

"We need to go meet Lady Mei," I whisper to Saber. "She knows something." Then, drawing on every lesson Giovanni ever taught me, I raise my chin, cast a coy smile at the residents and tourists alike looking on, and glide out of the room slowly, as though I have no true destination at all. It takes nearly a quarter of an hour to amble our way down the stairs and through the long hallways to the front lawn, but when I see Lady Mei, she's the picture of a young noblewoman at easy leisure. Her pastel-green gown is blowing gently in the breeze, and her hat has a small veil that she's positioned to block out her view of most of the tourists. Not coincidentally, also their cameras' view of her face.

When we draw near she perks up and greets us with a smile, as though she had no idea we were coming. Lady Mei's arsenal of talents continues to impress.

"There you are," she says softly, dropping into a low curtsy at my approach. "Your Highness," she adds.

In a rather theatrical display, I take her hands and pull her back upright and then buss her on both cheeks before linking my arm with hers and heading away from the ropes where the tourists are gathered, frantically snapping pictures.

"What was your message about?" I ask. "And what in the world is that?" Tucked under her left arm is an ornately carved wooden jewelry box, and I can't imagine why she might have sent a red com to call me out to see a new bit of finery—no matter how expensive it might be.

Lady Mei comes to an abrupt halt and turns to face me. "You don't know at all? I thought that was why we just had that fancy show for the plebs. Puffing up your PR."

"Don't know what?"

Her eyes roll heavenward. "I was afraid of that. Well, better you discover it from me than from someone who would delight in torturing you."

My blood feels icy in my veins at her words, and fear of a magnitude of possibilities makes my whole body tingle with nerves. Lady Mei angles us away from the crowds and lifts the top of the box to reveal her tablet computer. She taps a few buttons and a video begins to play. "The King's *lever* this morning."

With a casual smile pasted on my face, I look down at the screen and recognize the enormous bed with its gold-and-red paisley drapery in His Highness' public bedchamber. I can't imagine what could be so important about the King's rising ritual until one of his servingmen throws back the draperies and an auburn head pops up in apparent alarm.

An auburn head—and very bare breasts.

Well, that's one way to make sure everyone, in *and* out of the palace, watches this video.

The blood drains from my face as I watch Lady Cyn yank the sheet up to conceal her chest and flash a naughty smile at the audience. The King's staff does well covering the gaffe, bundling Lady Cyn out in a blanket as they circle the bed and begin their ritual with His Highness.

"That's essentially it," Lady Mei says, snapping the box closed. "Multiple videos were uploaded within minutes. Went viral worldwide in less than an hour. Do smile, darling."

Like a light switch flipping on, I beam at her. "Thank you for bringing this to my attention," I say, utterly genuine. "Lady Nuala informed me of her support just a few minutes before your com, but I had no idea what she was talking about. This day would have been a humiliating *charade* if you hadn't had the will to be forthright." She's just saved me hours and hours of stomach-churning anxiety.

"She's not pregnant, is she?"

I smile warmly at Lady Mei. "No," I say softly. "And I think you've more than passed your test."

"Thank you," she says, and there's a touch of emotion there that I didn't expect. Perhaps she took my two-truths-and-a-lie trial far more seriously even than I did.

I squeeze her hand in reply and we begin walking again, Lady Mei taking my arm on one side, and Saber on the other. I feel protected and loved at this moment, even though I know it's illusory at best, and temporary for certain.

"There's no possibility this was truly an accident, is there?"

"Not a chance."

"The King was in that bed as well," Lady Mei says, her words at odds with the placid expression on her face.

"Yes," I say slowly. "His Highness is far from innocent, but I'm inclined to think he had no part in this particular display." I shake my head. "It's not his style."

Though I'm speaking calmly, rage simmers within me. Purposeful or not, I warned him, and he *let* this happen. Not the affair itself; that has been common knowledge since before we were even engaged. He has Lady Cyn, I have Saber, and we both know it. It's Lady Cyn's *publicizing* things that wins my ire. I gave the King an ultimatum twelve hours ago. If this is his idea of taking care of her, it's clearly my turn to have a go.

"I'm left with no choice. I have to act."

"What will you do?"

I don't answer for a long time. "I'll need to meet with His Royal Highness," I finally say, "but I think I'll let him stew for a bit first."

I AVOID THE King all day: remaining outdoors most of the time, playing lawn games with the younger lords and ladies, posing for pictures—which I never do. I keep track of him via Lens, and if he ever heads even remotely near to where I am, I take myself off in another direction. Just before dinner, I decide he's probably ready.

With my formal gloves draped in one hand and the force of a thousand whispers at my back, I parade down my roped-off path.

The eyes of the gathered tourists follow me—every last one of them surely knows what happened in my husband's bedchamber this morning. Many likely witnessed it. I hold my head high, jaw clenched.

I don't even slow as Mateus scrambles to get the door all the way open without striking me. Positioning myself directly in the middle of the carpet laid before the King's desk, I wait for the door to click shut behind me.

The King is standing with his back to me. I say nothing.

"It wasn't my doing," he says, sounding weary, turning his head so I can see only his profile. Coward. But I expected no less. I remain silent, my face utterly neutral. The silence hangs, thick and stifling.

"She's supposed to leave before morning. She *knows* that. She's never stayed before. Not on a Tuesday night. I don't know—" He seems to realize he's blathering and turns at last, his jaw tight, doubtless holding back a stream of flimsy excuses. "I was exhausted. I fell right to sleep."

"It was dreadful PR" is all I say. "And the timing was particularly bad."

He groans. "I *know*. When I realized what was happening, I wanted to throttle her—" He stops himself there, and I have to hold back a cruel chuckle; I can see that he remembers I've seen him literally throttle someone. "Not actually—I wouldn't—oh, for the love of all that is holy," he says, throwing up his hands and then dropping into his chair. "This was not my doing."

"You do seem to have a lot of unintentional incidents in your love affairs, my liege. Perhaps if you spent more time thinking with the brain in your skull rather than the one in your breeches, you could avoid this pattern in the future."

He glares at me, his cheeks flushed. "So lay it out, Dani; what is to be my punishment?"

"Oh, I imagine the court—not to mention the press—will bring worse consequences down on your head than I could possibly think up. You still have a lot to prove, even after winning the vote. But I never for a moment thought it was your idea. I know who did this."

"What is to be her punishment, then? Will you ban her from my bed?"

I laugh gaily. "Why would I do that? As long as you're sleeping with her, you're not sleeping with me. One might say she's doing me a great favor."

"One might," he growls.

"No, I shall deal with Lady Cyn as I see fit. You had your chance, and now I get mine."

"What are—"

"No, no," I say, cutting him off. "This is women's business, and you need not concern yourself. I'm here for an entirely different purpose."

He looks at me in consternation. "You are?"

"My birthday's almost here. Are you throwing me a party, or should I get the staff going on that?"

The King is so taken off-guard he actually sits with his mouth a centimeter or two open for a long spell. "Throwing you a party?"

"Of course. What in the world did you think I wanted to discuss with you?"

The anger flashing in his eyes makes my little heart sing. "You—I can't—" He stops himself and points a finger at me. "I despise you."

I laugh my special Giovanni-coached laugh. "Of course, Justin. That's why this marriage works so well. A perfect symmetry of affection between us. So shall you take point on the party or shall I? We want to keep up appearances, but there's no need for us to be duplicating each other's efforts."

"Well, if you're offering," the King says, feeling his way carefully, obviously expecting a trap.

"I am. If I do the planning, everything will be exactly as I want it, *non*?" I pause, tapping one finger on my chin. "I don't think I'll go to the trouble of faking a surprise birthday party—so done to death—but I can certainly take charge of the food and *décor*."

"That would be lovely," His Royal Sleaziness says, still wary.

"I'll be charging it to your account."

"I would expect nothing less."

"Oh, and please get me a gift. Something expensive. I don't much care what. Ask Lady Mei if you need suggestions."

"Lady Mei?"

"Zhào. You know her. Her parents, at the very least: Marquis and Countess—not your inner circle, but an old and distinguished family. From Sonoma-Versailles' founding, I believe."

He coughs and then clears his throat. "Indeed."

"It's only a publicity gesture. It needn't take much of your time. I know you're busy catching up after your travels."

He nods without speaking and studies me, clearly waiting for me to begin shouting or demanding favors or restitution. I do neither.

"That was all I needed," I say after a long silence. "Shall we go in to dinner together? It *is* Wednesday."

He's untrusting, but he comes around the desk and offers his arm. I refuse to be what he expects anymore. Besides, I'll take great pleasure in seeing him squirm, watching me warily, waiting for the consequences of his foolish actions to arrive.

All the better when they finally do.

TWENTY-SEVEN

TWO DAYS, I GIVE IT. Two days during which the court chooses sides and I take notice. It's funny to see Lady Cyn parading around. She actually thinks she's won. For all her careful plotting and venomous cruelty, I confess, I find her less than clever. She's taken her jab—cuckqueaning me before the court and the outside world alike. But so soon after the King's crucial vote, days after Julianna's suicide, her actions have left our scandal-smeared court struggling with a bitter sense of buyer's remorse for their young, adulterous King.

She has punished *him*, not me.

I don't like the ways I've learned to constantly consider the secondary and tertiary consequences of my actions, but it's a good habit to be in. Lady Cyn thought only of humiliating me, of staking her claim. She sowed the wind and will reap the whirlwind. With my help, of course. I've been searching for a way to punish her since she turned Saber over to the King. How kind of her to lay the opportunity in my lap.

I stroll into the Drawing Room of Plenty on the King's arm, and we wait together while the crier quiets the crowd so everyone will hear our names announced. A pinch stings in my heart as I remember the night this whole nightmare started. The night my friends went ahead of me so this same crier could announce my name. The night the King moved me into the Queen's Bedchamber.

Tonight most of those friends are gone, and I am actually the Queen.

But in another few minutes, everyone in the palace will know it.

There's a general buzz of displeasure in the *salons* as the King and I step through the red velvet curtains. Those shareholders whose minds the King changed with his speech are clearly having second thoughts, and even those who agree with his policies and positions must be shaking their heads at the lack of maturity shown by their randy, impulsive young King.

Justin has a great deal of work in front of him, and I have no doubt he's already had a damage-control meeting with his PR team. I wonder if he's realized yet that his best shot at a reputational comeback is through his wife.

Bad news for the King. Good news for me.

As soon as we're in the drawing room, the King mutters something about a drink and abandons me. I smirk—he ought to know better.

I turn and beckon to Saber. "Will you escort me?"

He hesitates. "Will His Majesty like that?"

"I don't give a damn."

"You probably should."

He seems surprised when I just grin. "You're right. And tomorrow, I will. But right now I need you on my arm."

"Of course," he says instantly, and I love that. Though always ready to speak his mind, he'll be whatever I need him to be, consequences be damned. I find Lady Mei leaning against a wall, Lady Nuala hovering nearby, and I wave both of them over to *tête-à-tête*.

"Where is she?" I whisper.

"Hall of Mirrors," Lady Nuala answers. "Far end. What are you going to do?"

"Ruin her," I say softly. And I can't help but enjoy the fact that Lady Nuala—once a pawn in Lady Cyn's pathetic attempts to embarrass me—will now be instrumental in her former friend's downfall. "My dear ladies, I'm in need of a crowd of very influential people. As much high nobility as possible. Do you think you can arrange that?"

Lady Mei glances first to Lady Nuala at her side, and then to the far doorway of the Hall of Mirrors, where more residents than usual are mingling. Likely because of the recent scandal. I wonder if Lady Cyn thinks all those eyes will keep her safe. Well, she isn't the only person who knows how to use an audience as a tool—or a weapon. "It will be my pleasure," Lady Mei says, an eyebrow raised.

"We'll walk slowly," I say, and let a serene smile curve my lips as they hurry off. My hand rests on Saber's folded cuff, and we stroll casually toward the hall. Before I dressed this evening, I asked security to bring up the single set of diamonds in the palace proven to have belonged to Marie-Antoinette. The unmistakable piece is all the jewelry I need, aside from my huge wedding ring. The crowd parts to my right and left as the train of my sapphire gown flows like waves behind me, the diamonds at my neck glinting like sea spray on the figurehead of a mighty ship. Even unimpeded, at my stately pace it takes several minutes to make it through the line of *salons* and to the threshold of the Hall of Mirrors.

I hear Lady Cyn's loud laughter before I can see her. But I don't so much as incline my head in her direction. Not yet.

Lady Cyn seems oblivious to the looks of censure being cast in her direction by those who have remained loyal to me. She's surrounded by her own personal court of beautiful young ladies, who form a barrier of adoration between her and the displeasure of the court. Social nearsightedness: she sees only the opinions of those she's chosen to keep close. She doesn't understand how vulnerable that leaves her.

I narrow my eyes a fraction when I see Lady Annaleigh Garcia standing at Lady Cyn's right. Doesn't matter. She was warned—she had her chance.

"What do you know of Marie-Antoinette?" I ask Saber in a quiet voice, smoothing my expression back into passivity.

"The basics, I guess," he murmurs. "Queen, cake, lost her head."

I laugh at the simplicity of his explanation—doubtless representative of the views of most outside Versailles. "There's a story of when she was yet a princess, and her husband's grandfather was king: Louis XV. His own queen was dead, but his mistress lived in the Palace of Versailles, acknowledged as such, and with great influence at court. But Marie, at seventeen, was a prudish little thing." I turn my head enough to meet Saber's eyes, but not quite in Lady Cyn's direction. "She refused to acknowledge the mistress in public. In those days no one was permitted to so much as *speak* to royalty without being spoken to first. And Marie wouldn't. Not one word to the immoral woman. After months of intense conflict with the King, little Marie decided that for his sake she would condescend to speak one sentence to the woman and never acknowledge her presence again."

"One sentence?" Saber asks.

"One," I confirm. We're some ten meters from Lady Cyn, and in the roiling of the crowd around me I can see Lady Mei and Lady Nuala's work. We're not only drawing general attention, but several of the most powerful members of the court have gathered close, forming a circle around Lady Cyn and me.

Out of the corner of my eye I catch the short form of Lady Garcia as she pushes her way through the crowd ahead of me, then glances back at me with fear sparkling in her eyes as she reaches her daughter. Without a word, she grasps Lady Annaleigh's arm and begins pulling her away, despite her squawk of pain.

"I suppose it matters what that sentence was?" Saber whispers. His eyes take in everything, and a wrinkle forms between his brows.

"Oh, certainly." I almost laugh when Lady Annaleigh, even as she's being dragged off by her mother, swats at her friend Lady Breya Voroman-Wills's shoulder and looks meaningfully toward me. With wide eyes, Lady Breya takes two steps backward. Just enough to say to the entire crowd that she doesn't stand with Lady Cyn.

Not in the face of her Queen, at least.

"It wasn't the actual words that mattered," I whisper, continuing my story. "It was the delivery. Hundreds of years later it's a sentence every Sonoman-Versailles young lady knows by heart. A cautionary tale to remember your place."

I'm so near that no one could mistake my destination. But the stupid woman is drunk on what she's mistaken for triumph and pretends, viciously, not to notice my imminent approach. Saber's hand begins to drop beneath mine, but I clutch at his knuckles, and he reacts instantly by again supporting the weight of my arm.

I draw up before the impeccably dressed Lady Cyn and simply stand there, my hand on Saber's arm, waiting.

The crowd quiets until Lady Cyn has no choice but to turn and face me. Lady Giselle, the only friend who remains physically at her side, drops into an appropriately low curtsy and avoids my eyes. But Lady Cyn is still as a statue, her chin high, knees straight, a satisfied smile tugging at the corner of her mouth.

My face is stone, and I let a few silent seconds pass while all the whispering around us falls to utter silence. I raise one brow, and though I maintain eye contact, I turn my body so I address her dismissively, over my shoulder, repeating the words Marie-Antoinette once spoke, long ago, when she was just my age.

"There are a lot of people here at Versailles today."

The gasps of the nobles around me are so loud they buzz in my ears as I stride away from Lady Cyn on Saber's arm.

I want to turn. I want to see the result of the dire insult I've just struck her with. But I value the impact of giving her my back over the indulgence of seeing my revenge. I've publicly labeled her what she is—all she will ever be: the King's mistress.

And not the famous kind—the forgotten kind.

The kind with no friends.

The kind that could never, ever hold a candle to Marie-Antoinette.

As Saber and I walk away, the whispers break upon us like waves on the sand, bringing with them a strange clarity—an epiphany.

The King is right. We *are* alike.

The suffering I've caused in desperation harrows my soul, but desperation no longer forces my hand. I've punished Lady Cyn with utter ruination, I planted the seed of the Tremain family downfall, and even now I plot to destroy Reginald utterly, even if it hinders my own efforts to leave Sonoman-Versailles.

I've become as ruthless as my husband.

I understand now what Justin meant when he said we could be a power couple. You don't gain power by fighting the people greater than you; you gain power by joining them, taking it as your own, and making it bigger. Stepping on your enemies to make yourself taller. I've been trying to cross a great sea by walking around the beach, afraid of getting wet. I need to just wade in and cross it.

It's time I grew up.

I squeeze Saber's hand. "Thank you for your help," I whisper. "But I have to go the rest of the way on my own."

He looks at me in concern, but after a searching glance, he merely bows and gives me back my hand. I continue on, leaving the person I thought I was to drown in my wake.

Though I don't see my husband, I see the frenzy of the milling crowd that tells me he's at its center. I draw myself up and approach, knowing the crowd will part for me though I refrain from so much as clearing my throat. I walk slowly, regally. The King doesn't see me at first, but as the circle about him hushes, he finally looks up.

Our eyes meet, and when his widen very slightly, I don't drop my gaze. I tremble inside, not in fear of him, but in fear of myself, fear of this step. Can I keep the good part of me tucked away? In hiding until I can let it back out again? I suppose I'm about to find out.

When I reach his side, rather than formally setting my hand in the crook of his elbow, I slide it down his arm and entwine my fingers with his. Everyone's eyes are on us. The King's expression asks the question his lips can't: *Are you with me?*

I smile back—a practiced expression. Literally, in a mirror. The smile that tells someone, *You are the most important person in my world.*

Justin seems to understand that now is his time to make a choice, and he lifts our joined hands to his lips, making sure everyone sees that, despite everything, the King and Queen are in complete accord. I turn back to the crowd, snuggling close to his side. We are the picture of solidarity.

I don't look at Saber, who's been trailing along behind me. I can't. He'll have to understand this for the playacting it is. This is my price. And his. No one escapes payment.

The new wave of whispers starts, the two of us its epicenter, and I fancy I can feel the moment this wave of gossip meets the one that was coming the other way after my confrontation with Lady Cyn.

They crash. They multiply.

And suddenly the entire milling population of the palace is alive with the news: the Queen has forgiven the King, the King has chosen the Queen, and the mistress Lady Cyn is disgraced. The mood of the assembly turns jovial as the King and I put on a show so worthy we almost believe it ourselves.

Don't lose yourself, Lord Aaron told me. But I finally know exactly who I am. I am Danica Wyndham and I am the Queen of Sonoman-Versailles. I will protect my loyal subjects, I will avenge my loved ones, and I will take what's mine by any means necessary.

PART TWO

THE PRICE OF LOVE

TWENTY-EIGHT

THREE WEEKS LATER

"CAREFUL, THERE'S A STEP HERE."

I laugh as Justin guides me, his hands on my shoulders, a silk cravat tied over my eyes. I've been blindfolded, spun, and led about the palace for ten minutes at least, but I have the odd suspicion he's simply brought me back to my own chambers. The back rooms. But still *my* rooms.

"Ready?"

"More than."

He fusses with the knot for a few seconds, and then the silk falls. Sunlight pierces my eyes, and I hold up one hand and blink. I'm in a good-sized room with heavy white molding around the crown. A pastel fresco of a pastoral landscape on the ceiling, and pale green textured silk on the walls. Ivory curtains over two windows allow for plenty of natural sunlight, and a graceful crystal chandelier hangs from a dome in the middle of the fresco, ready to take over when the sun sets.

I've been in here a hundred times. More. The books are in here. "It's . . . my library," I say lamely, my eye settling on the only new sight—a white desk with intricately carved legs, with a velvet-upholstered office chair posed behind it.

"It's your office."

"It's my . . ." My eyes widen. "My office? Unmonitored?"

The King leans casually against the doorframe, looking un-ruffled. Honest, even. "Truly, I owe you an apology for the delay. I should have given you one the first time you asked. You proved you wouldn't betray me at the vote, and I should have responded in kind."

I can't keep the shock from registering on my face. I thought I was prepared for anything from this man I'm married to. Scorn, derision, lies, downright cruelty. Feigned romance for the public eye, certainly. But . . . an apology?

"Try not to look so surprised," he murmurs, and his eyes dance with amusement. "I do like to learn from my mistakes." He takes my hand and spins me under his arm before pulling me close. Not an embrace, exactly, but a moment of physical intimacy—something I've had to grow accustomed to the last few weeks. "I need you to be happy," he whispers in my ear. "And if I have to eat some crow to make that happen, I will. So happy belated birthday. You're of age, the world can stop muttering that I'm a pedophile, you can sign all your own contracts without a guardian, and yes, you get your own office space, as befitting a major shareholder."

"Thank you." I'm not sure I dare say another word lest I rock the rather precarious boat that is our marriage. The last three weeks have been an interesting case study. Despite everything that happened before, I've convinced the court that I adore my husband. I've begun to think I've convinced my husband. Some-times I worry that I'm living the lie so thoroughly that I'm starting to convince myself. "I've always liked this room," I say, untangling myself from his loose embrace. "The windows overlook the Queen's Courtyard." As if he didn't know that. But I'm rambling as the atmosphere settles into a companionable aura with which I'm still not comfortable.

"It was the private office of all the Queens who lived here during the original reign of the Kings Louis. My mother never used it as such, obviously, nor my grandmother, but I thought it fitting for you."

Fitting indeed. I grace him with one of my special beaming smiles. "Thank you, Justin."

He waves away my gratitude with a disdainful twist of his lips and in an instant he's the impatient, spoiled monarch again. Still, at least the impatient, spoiled monarch is giving me what I want for the moment. For many moments.

Lady Cyn's downfall has been a joy to behold. Some of it was slow and almost meaningless to most, but I saw it all. Ladies Annaleigh and Breya immediately joined my retinue, their parents looking on proudly. The night after I snubbed her, a group of older noble matrons turned their backs when Lady Cyn walked in—alone—to the ball. But my greatest pleasure came from watching the King himself engage in a public argument with her on the very morning of my birthday—one that eventually resulted in his bodyguards dragging her away. He had adjusted his mussed cravat, looking satisfyingly bored while she continued to screech like a harpy. The exquisite necklace and bracelet set he publicly bestowed upon me at the party that evening wasn't half so pleasurable.

Less happily, it's become impossible for me to go anywhere in public without an entourage. I'm the darling of the court, and much of the time it's the King himself beside me. We dance, we laugh, we exchange very public kisses over glasses of champagne, and together we create an entirely new public opinion, serving it up for the consumption of our observers—who devour it like a child with a *crème* pastry.

That's the *charade:* we're young, we're in love, and we're the rulers of a pocket sovereignty backed by one of the wealthiest global corporations in the world, and certainly one of us could not be secretly planning to undermine everything. It's a strange thing to discover that happiness is my best disguise.

When the King finally leaves me alone in my new office, I sink down onto the new chair behind the new desk, exhausted. It's satisfyingly soft, and I take just a moment of rest—a moment to close my eyes and massage my temples. This act, this *farce,* takes so much more energy and stamina than I ever could have imagined, especially considering the amount of time and focus I'm already pouring into my own personal projects on the side. Well, unmonitored office space in my own chambers will help with that. A little.

I should check on Saber. The King sent him away, and I hated the hollow look in his eyes before he bowed and turned from me. This spell of make-believe *amour* the King and I are casting for the court takes its toll on Saber as well as on me. It was tolerable at first, but even the pretense of affection for someone else has driven a wedge between us.

Things are … fragile. And it's far too easy to stumble into an argument. We both hate it, and the emotional cost is driving us into a devastating amount of psychological debt. And it's not just Saber—the acting makes my own mind blur what's real and what's false, and sometimes I need a reminder from him that I didn't make up what we have, the way I conjured my "relationship" with Justin from nothing. From less than nothing.

Oddly, it doesn't leave Justin untouched either, but in an entirely different way. The animal wanting I first witnessed that day in the Hall of Mirrors, months ago, has reignited. I don't know if he even realizes it. But his caresses and smoldering glances seem increasingly genuine, and his kisses will haunt my nightmares for years to come. Of course, I'm expected to return them with apparent appreciation.

I'm not even certain His Highness realizes that *all* my pleasure is an act. Which is perhaps just as well—I want him pliable and thinking highly of me. If my plan is to work, the cooperation of the King is essential.

But playacting a romance makes me long for Saber all the more, and watching me hang all over someone else can't please him, either. Worse, instead of the mutual-infidelity compromise my spouse and I used to have, now I have to conceal my affection for Saber. I hate hiding—as though we're doing something wrong.

As if summoned by my thoughts, Saber appears in the doorway of my office, his eyebrow lifted in silent question.

"There you are," I say, jumping up and flinging myself into his arms. His fingers dig almost painfully into my back, and I wish I didn't have to put him through this.

"What did the King want?" Saber asks. He hides the brittleness in his tone adequately, but I know him too well.

Still, his question brings a genuine grin. "My office," I say, arms spread wide. "Private and unmonitored."

He smiles back—soft and unfeigned—and I warm from the inside out. "Congratulations. And right here within your personal rooms. Convenient," he adds wryly.

"Indeed." I slump against his chest. "He has no idea how much easier he's made everything for me."

"Seems fair, considering he's the one who made them difficult in the first place."

I merely give a quiet hum of agreement. We stand that way for a long time, and I'm just starting to relax when Saber clears his throat and his fingertips stiffen on my back.

"It looks like we've finally reached a decent balance," he says.

"What do you mean?"

He kisses my forehead and leans his cheek against my hair, breathing in my scent. I don't know what it is that he likes—my conditioner, maybe, or perhaps my pomade—but he often smells my hair, and I love it.

"With the Glitter," he says, not meeting my eyes. "I didn't feel like I was a leaf blown around in a storm today. There was something akin to organization and, dare I say it, *manners* in the way people gave me their orders. Their desperation isn't gone," he adds after a moment of thought, "but it simmered instead of boiling madly."

"That's good, right?" I say, stepping back to him and twining my arms around his neck. I don't want this moment to get away from us. I don't want to talk about Glitter. That never ends well.

He laughs as he tries to untangle himself from his messenger bag without ending our embrace. "I'm not going anywhere," he says with a laugh when the strap of his bag twists around my bicep.

"Better not," I say into his chest, then reluctantly let him go, if for no other reason than so that he can shrug out of his jacket and waistcoat.

"We have work to do," he says, pointing toward my room.

I groan. "Now? Can't we do it later?"

"That's what you said yesterday and we . . . never got around to it," he says with mock-severity.

"I was rather pleased with how yesterday turned out," I say coyly as he leads me into my bedchamber by the hand. "Weren't you?"

"Indeed," he says, touching the tip of my nose. "But your core only gets one day of rest."

I fall to my knees and sprawl melodramatically on the carpet. "If I must, I must," I say, a gloved hand to my brow. "I am your—" I snap my mouth closed on the word *slave*. "Yours to command," I finish lamely.

Saber just raises an eyebrow at me, a grin tugging at the edges of his mouth. I hate that he's so cavalier about his life, and I hate even more that I've grown so accustomed that I almost made a joke about it. It makes me a little sick to my stomach, truly.

"Roll over," Saber says, bursting through the tension with the grace of a stampeding bull. "I'll loosen your laces."

He puts me through my abdominal workout, and I'm soaked in sweat when we're finished, but for the first time, I hold my plank for sixty seconds and collapse with a whoop of elation.

"Splendid," Saber says, with a faux-snobbish accent. It's what he thinks we sound like, but I'm long past actually feeling insulted. "You deserve a reward." He scoots his lithe, shirtless form next to me—sweat and all—and pulls my face gently to his, kissing me soft and long, his lips playing with mine. No one else has ever kissed me like that: like my mouth is a fascinating subject worthy of languid exploration.

I roll on my back, enjoying a rather perverse sense of satisfaction at getting sweat on the ludicrously expensive carpet, as Saber props his head up on one elbow, looking down at me.

"I think you're even more beautiful like this," he whispers.

"Sweaty and disgusting?"

"Free," he says with a shake of his head. "Hair down, corset off, lying on the ground with no thought about what's all proper or anything." He kisses me again, a feather-light touch this time, waiting for me to lift up to press harder against his mouth. He knows I will, and by the time I relax again, he's smiling.

I stare at that smile. I'm not the only one who seems freer this evening. "I want a life with you," I whisper, reaching up one finger to touch his skin.

His face shuts like a book and he sits up to reach for his shirt.

"Saber!"

He pauses, then turns, his face like stone.

"You won't let me *imagine* a future for us?"

"Imagine away, but I can't talk about it," he says without looking at me, sounding sad rather than angry. "When the illusion shatters, *you're* left in a frustrating situation. I'm left in . . . in my life. It's . . . it's too hard. I just can't." He hesitates and then adds, "I am sorry. I wish I could imagine." I don't think he realizes that he's rubbing his chest like his heart actually hurts. He stops and drops both arms, then turns back to me and smiles sadly. "I'm proud of you, though. You've worked hard, and you're doing amazing."

"Thank you," I say, but when he heads to the bathroom to splash off, I let him go. I roll back and flop my arms over my head, and my hand meets Saber's messenger bag. "Can I look at the list?" I call out.

At his muffled acquiescence, I dig into his bag and extract his tablet, already open to the list when I touch the screen. It's not a short list—several hundred names—but I seem to be satisfying everyone.

My lips tighten as I continue to read. Saber has the list pre-numbered, but there are a few blanks at the bottom. Spots left over. Left over? That seems too good to be true.

I push to my feet with a groan at my aching muscles, but note with satisfaction that I'm walking upright with a steadiness and confidence that don't come from the corset crumpled on the floor behind me.

As I come around the corner into my bathroom, Saber flips back his damp, chin-length hair, dark strands tumbling about his face in such perfection it makes my mouth go dry.

"What's up?" he asks as he runs the towel over his damp shoulders one more time before reaching for his linen shirt.

"Um," I say with exceptional grace and wit.

Finally he pauses and looks at me in question, his shirt half unbuttoned. Whatever he sees in my face makes him grin, and he stands a little straighter as he finishes dressing. "Did you need something?" he asks, meeting my eye in the mirror.

It takes a few seconds, but I finally find my voice, not to mention the snippet of an idea I'd completely lost track of at the sight of his bare chest. "Do you think we have a canister of Glitter from . . . maybe three or four weeks ago?"

He snorts and shakes his head. "Where would you keep it that it might have gotten missed in the frenzy? Especially last week. Some of the courtiers nearly came to blows over my last dozen canisters." Managing Glitter sales has fallen increasingly on Saber's shoulders, and in some cases he has even returned to me mildly bruised, or with a crushed toe, from the ministrations of our . . . enthusiastic *clientèle*.

"True." But there's got to be one somewhere. Surely.

Saber turns away from the mirror. "Even if you found some, how would you know it was older?"

"I'm not certain." I pause, considering. "Do you think there's any in Duke Spencer's apartment?"

"Maybe. They were both cutting down."

"Theirs would be at least four weeks old. That would work. Assuming I can . . ." I shake my head. One step at a time. "I should be able to slip up there before the assembly if I rush my *toilette* a bit."

"Sixteenth-century hair would be faster than a *pompadour*," Saber suggests, and I kind of adore that even he knows the difference now. He certainly didn't when he first arrived at the palace.

"Perfect. I can slip up there on the excuse that I think I left a trinket. Assuming anyone asks, which I doubt." Part of my new influence at court—no one questions me.

Except the King, but he's his own problem.

"Why do you want old Glitter?" Saber is clearly trying to keep the judgment out of his voice, but I hear it. I always hear it.

"I'm just . . . curious. I—" I hesitate. "I want to check it before I get either of us too paranoid."

Saber looks at me hard but doesn't argue. I suspect he really would rather not know, but that's not a choice he's ever been allowed to make. "I'll come with you," he says after a moment.

"I'd love that," I say, pleased. Maybe I *am* being paranoid. On the other hand, is it still paranoia if someone really is plotting against you?

TWENTY-NINE

BY CHOOSING A velvet gown with a plain skirt and stiff bodice, then catching up my hair in a jeweled net before it's even quite dry, I'm able to finish early while still looking Queenly. I add a little extra shimmer to my makeup to offset the less intricate hairstyle; then Saber and I are off to Duke Spencer's apartments to "find" the ruby-and-pearl brooch I want to wear to tonight's festivities.

Lord Aaron and Duke Spencer have been gone for a month; their secret can't last much longer. Even the King asked me the other day—in passing, luckily—if I'd heard from them. I answered, honestly, that I hadn't, and suggested I missed them and hoped they were enjoying themselves. When His Majesty claimed to feel the same, I was surprised, but on reflection concluded that my husband has ample reason to miss influential young shareholders on whom he can lean for favors.

I've been to the Tremain-Harrisford residence only once since my friends departed—strictly to ensure that everything was as it had been left—but Julianna's specter haunts every darkened corner. I can only imagine how bad it would have been for Duke Spencer. Why would she do that to him? He says she was his only ally in the Tremain family, but her choice of places to hang herself leaves me wondering.

"Bedside tables," I say to Saber—if I let myself dwell too long on ghosts, Lady Julianna's is sure to recruit others I'm less able to exorcise from my thoughts. "Bathrooms next."

We split up and check drawers and cupboards throughout the dwelling. The near-absence of personal effects makes for easy looking. Saber finds a Glitter canister in a bathroom medicine cabinet, and I pull one from the back corner of Duke Spencer's office desk.

"This one's just about gone," Saber says, showing me little more than a shiny residue of a colorless gloss.

I give a soft sniff of amusement as I take it. "This is from back when you and I were making it." I proffer my own canister—almost full. "This is Reginald's stuff, but old enough for comparison."

"What are you thinking, Danica?" Saber asks.

"I can't say," I whisper, my eyes darting to the ceiling.

He opens his mouth, then closes it, taking my meaning. *The walls have ears.*

I drop the canister into my reticule and palm the ornate brooch, giving us our reason for searching the Harrisford apartments in the unlikely event that someone should question it. "I'll com Lady Mei and Lady Nuala and see if they can bring canisters to the revels tonight. I'm completely out."

I pause in the doorway of Duke Spencer's abandoned home. "It feels like leaving a little bubble of freedom that isn't really part of this world," I say very quietly.

Saber comes up behind me and kisses the nape of my neck. "I know."

"My rooms represent who I've become in the public eye. Here? I could be no one. *We* could be no one."

"Did you ever think you'd sacrifice so much to be no one?" Saber asks, close to my ear.

The search took less time than I'd feared it might, so we arrive at the Hall of Mirrors almost unfashionably early. His Highness swoops down like a brocade-clad bird of prey, carrying me off into a dance. "You look different tonight," he says.

I don't even glance down at my *ensemble*. "I do vary my style sometimes."

"I'm a fan of this one on all the ladies," he says with a lascivious glance toward my bodice—which, in keeping with the style, serves my pushed-up cleavage for public display atop a square neckline.

Old Danica would probably have snapped, "You're disgusting." New Danica is amenable and always looking for the advantage, so I take a deep breath instead, further enhancing the King's view.

"I'm leaving again in a few days," he says, pulling me closer, our cheeks almost touching as we dance.

"I saw that on my calendar," I say smoothly, "though like your last trip, you've left out the details and made no public pronouncements."

I let my sentence hang, question unasked.

He lets it go unanswered.

He's not getting off that easy. I need answers, and this is the best opening I've gotten in three weeks. "Something to do with all those charts from the shareholders' meeting?" I press.

A half-smile. "Perhaps."

"So mysterious," I tease. I'm going to have to give something to get something. What can I give? "Your profit projections for our robotics division involve Amalgamated. Rumor among the courtiers is that it has something to do with our bots."

"And that interests you?"

Does it ever. "I inherited a rather substantial number of Amalgamated shares from my mother when she passed," I say, lowering my eyelashes.

He hums in agreement. "That's right. I'd forgotten."

"Sonoma has always specialized in agriculture. You have a great number of people here at court wondering why we'd try to break into robotics at all."

He lifts an eyebrow and says, "I can neither confirm nor deny—"

I cut him off. "What those people don't see is that we're already *in* robotics. We've got M.A.R.I.E., the most sophisticated distributed robotic intelligence network in the world, humming away in our basement. We've got purpose-built bots crawling all over the palace, cleaning, repairing—but they're old news, of course. People have been building those for ages. What good is a bot that makes *macarons* when I want *crème brûlée*?" I hesitate. Can I make this jump without him knowing I've found out what he's up to? "The true innovation would be general-purpose bots—ones that can fasten corsets as easily as they can serve drinks."

"Purpose-built bots are far more economical," Justin says, not taking the bait. "Fortunately, we needn't concern ourselves over-much with economy, here."

"Fortunate indeed," I say. "Still, a bot with strong arms must still be shown how to lift. A bot with nimble fingers must still be taught how to sew. And a bot that can sew a *chemise à la reine* can apply almost none of that ability to sewing a *jabot*."

"You see the challenge, then."

I shrug demurely. "Challenges are easy to see. Overcoming them is where we prove our worth. *Hypothetically,* if it were my job to develop a general-purpose bot, I'd want to deploy a huge number of networked test units inside a closed, heavily monitored proving ground. Oh, rather like this palace." The King doesn't so much as glance around the room as I gesture; he only has eyes for me.

"That approach would take longer than you might think," he says. "The testing. It's endless. You know, our pharmaceutical division has a product in testing now, and it seems a task with no end."

"Oh?" I say, hoping I sound unaffected. Ignorant.

He grins, an expression I don't understand. "Finding willing volunteers for the early rounds of testing proved most difficult, but thankfully we're past that stage now."

"Still, robots aren't pharmaceuticals," I say, trying to yank the conversation back on track. "Information technology doesn't de-velop on a linear scale. It progresses exponentially. The smarter machines get, the easier it becomes to make smarter machines. They're tools that make better tools."

"My father would have liked you, I think," Justin says, and

there's an odd mixture of pride and sadness in his voice. He misses his father—an emotion I truly don't understand. I suppose I miss who my father used to be, but he was retreating into himself even before Reginald found him. And my mother? The less said of her, the better.

"Why?" I ask. "Because I figured out that the reason we buy bots from Amalgamated is only to sell them back the testing data they need for a successful global launch? Which we then also gain profits from?"

"No, no," Justin says. "Everyone knows Google ruled the twenty-first century because their business model was doing just that thing. And if they can't see those parallels today, that's hardly my fault. No, it's because you're *interested*." He sweeps me into a low dip. "Because no matter how much you loathe me, you loathe ignorance more."

"I *am* interested. My mother's bullish outlook on Amalgamated isn't the only thing you forget about me." I raise an eyebrow. "Before I had my coming out, I was training to work with M.A.R.I.E., down in the basement. Machine intelligence happens to be my specialty."

"Why, Dani," the King breathes, close to my ear, and it takes all the willpower I can muster to not flinch away from him. "Are you asking me for a job?"

I laugh—carefully, delightedly, so it's very clear I'm not laughing at him, or even at his proposal, but at myself. "Of course not—I'm nowhere near qualified for the life of an executive. But I enjoy my little hobbies." I hesitate, and then dive in. "And I have to say that if there were—hypothetically, of course—if there were someplace I could get a sneak preview of a production-model, general-purpose Amalgamated bot before the public even knew such a thing existed . . . Well, that," I say with a coy smile, "would be very, *very* exciting."

"If I did know of such a place, I certainly couldn't say anything about it," the King muses. "But my assistant has a knack for ferreting out interesting locales. Shall I have him make a few inquiries on your behalf?"

"Could it be done before you leave on your trip?"

He pauses, as if he's forgotten what started this conversation to begin with. "If you like." He pulls me closer. "I would love a night out with you."

"A night out?"

"In Paris. Dinner. The theater." He shrugs. "Might be fun."

I smile, hoping the expression reaches my eyes. "I'd be delighted."

As the dance comes to an end, he bows low, and I curtsy in return—and then we're beset by the inevitable tide of nobles whose petitions simply *cannot* wait until their scheduled meeting. His Majesty, clearly feeling indulgent, allows me to slip away as he undertakes the arduous diplomatic task of refusing to speak with any of them without actually telling them so.

"He looks pleased," Saber says when I reach his side again, my arm sliding onto his. It's a formal escort, but it's as much as we're allowed to touch in public.

"Terrifying, isn't it?" I say, my placid smile clashing with my words. "Apparently my husband and I are now to begin dating."

"Dating?"

I hum a vague response and Saber maneuvers me around a raucous group, somewhat worse for drink.

"He's looked happy with you often of late." There's the tiniest note of censure in Saber's words.

I can't look at him. "I'm trying a new method of catching flies."

"Honey instead of vinegar?" he says ruefully.

"Exactly."

We walk silently for a long while before he asks, "Why do you need to catch the fly? Why can't you go on avoiding the fly and then leave the fly behind? You never thought you needed the co-operation of the fly before."

I can't help but smile at the transparency, the bluntness of Saber's allusion. "It's more than me now. There's another fly, and I need what one fly has to swat the other."

Saber lets out a noisy sigh.

"You asked," I say wryly.

"I guess I should just stop asking."

"Actually, I think that's a fairly good idea. For your sake," I add, turning to look at him. "Because if you really asked, I would tell you everything. But you don't want to know. You're safer this way. But it means you have to trust me to go on as I see fit." I pause and then add, "In this case, he has something I need, and I suspect a night on the town is the best trade I'm going to get."

"I worry for you," he whispers.

"I know. But I'll be safer if the fly thinks I'm an ally. This is exactly what I've been working toward," I add in a whisper.

He grimaces. "I wish I were the recipient of all your honey."

"Believe me, all the honey that means anything belongs to you."

"Then I'm honored," he whispers, and bows low over my hand and kisses my glove.

I'm feeling quite warm and pleasant when Lady Mei appears at my side, linking our arms. "I brought my Glitter; what's the matter?"

"Retiring room," I say to Saber. Then, feeling suddenly desperate, I add, "I'll be back soon." He merely nods as Lady Mei sweeps me off.

"Lud, the two of you," Lady Mei says. "I don't know how His Highness convinces himself you care for him a whit when the glances you share with your secretary are so fiery."

Fiery? I like that.

"Now, what's the emergency?" Lady Mei asks as soon as we've stepped into the retiring room—mercifully empty, at least for the moment.

"Let me see your canister," I whisper, digging into my own reticule. "I just want to compare. You'll have it back momentarily."

Lady Mei hands hers over, and I place both on the brightly lit makeup counter, careful not to mix them up. Then I remove a white handkerchief from my bodice, and using opposite corners, I rub a bit of pink rouge from each of the canisters onto the fabric.

I hold them both up to the light and call Lady Mei closer even as my heart falls. "Do you see a difference?" I ask, my fingers trembling at the hope that my eyes are deceiving me.

Lady Mei looks and then sets her face closer, her nose almost brushing the soft linen. "That one is more sparkly," she says, pointing at the smudge from her own pot of rouge. "Significantly more."

"I knew it. Bastard!" I snap, wadding up the handkerchief and throwing it at the wall in a pointless show of *pique*. Reginald has been raising the concentration of Glitter in the makeup, *without* telling me. "That's why everyone's been so much happier. I'm going to *kill* him."

THIRTY

"I CAN'T BELIEVE HE DID THIS," I say, pacing back and forth in front of my enormous bed, where Saber sits, cross-legged. He looks weary, but I'm too keyed up to sleep. "*I'm* the one who decides how much Glitter everyone gets, not him!"

"What, you expected him to act with honor?" Saber scoffs.

But I hardly hear him. "The next time you speak with anyone connected to him, send a message that I need to meet with him. In Paris."

"No!" Saber says. "It's too dangerous."

"It can't be here," I say softly. "If you have a better idea—"

"My better idea is that you let that damned Foundation take you away with the money you already have, and you don't look back." His voice is a whispered hiss, but I know he's barely keeping himself from shouting at me.

"I . . . I can't, Saber. Don't you understand? *You* are my life. My motivation for waking up every day. None of this—*none* of it—is worth anything if I can't take you with me." I hold his clenched hands in both of mine, rubbing them gently, but his fingers don't relax. "It's more than Reginald's . . . power over you." I can't even bring myself to talk about his enslavement. Not in those words. "I love you so much. You want me to escape? It's not an escape without you. Merely jumping from one hell into another."

"Nothing has changed for me, Danica! This is my life, it's all my life will ever be, and I accept that. But you have a chance for something better." He pauses and then adds, "I think my life would be better, too, if I knew you were safe. Safe and away from this life. This drug. You may not be using, but it's making you crazy all the same. Maybe you can think about it that way."

I hate that this makes me angry at him. The last person I want to have any sort of negative feelings toward is Saber. But for him to truly believe that I could bear to be in my own company if I left him to Reginald makes me wonder whether he knows me at all. I tried to leave him once and it almost killed me. Despite everything that's happened since Reginald dumped me back on the palace steps, I'm glad—yes, glad!—that he did. Leaving Saber would have been the greatest mistake of my life. And considering the last six months, that's really saying something.

I sigh and let my head fall against his chest. "I'm in so deep," I say, my face muffled in his linen shirt. "But it's the whole sunk-costs thing. I've invested so much. When you're halfway into the woods, it's easier to go forward than back, right? I know I've got to be close to breaking through the murk. Just a little while longer. But every time I say that, I go a little further and I'm still not there. Where is the end, Saber?"

He lets out a sigh and holds me closer, knowing I'm not actually looking for an answer. That there simply isn't an answer. I run my hands down the sides of his face and pull him forward. Kissing him never gets old. His mouth is warm and soft, a tentative exploration that grows quickly bold until we're both making little sounds of want and his hands are pulling at the laces at the back of my dress.

A muffled thump sounds on my door, like someone's body slamming into it, and I tear my mouth away from Saber's, gasping for breath. I recognize the voice cursing on the other side of the rattling locked door, and I practically shove Saber away from me as the King enacts his royal privilege to override my locks. Something he's been doing frequently of late, having convinced himself—admittedly, with my help—that I actually want to see him at any given hour of the day.

From the corner of my eye I see Saber melt into the shadows along the wall, and I flop on my stomach across the bed and grab my tablet just in time to make it look like I'm simply reading in my room. Nothing to see here.

"Danica," the King says, bursting into my chamber as though he had any right at all.

I look at him wide-eyed. "You could have simply knocked, my lord."

He shrugs. "I'm the King."

My left eyelid twitches.

"Join me," the King says, loosening his cravat and utterly oblivious to my displeasure. "We're drinking."

I suppress an eye roll. He looks as though he's already had a few too many. After a long assembly, *with* dancing, he thinks I'd like to go drink with his friends at two in the morning? "I'm a bit weary, Your Highness," I say stiffly.

"Justin. Come on!" He grins. A true, beaming smile. It's odd how it lights up his whole face. He could be handsome if he weren't such an asshole. "There's been so much formality of late. This is just going to be fun."

Fun? I have grave doubts.

He jogs over and wraps his hands around my thighs and drags me to the edge of my bed, where he pulls me up and sets me on my feet. I have to bite down on an alarmed squeal at his manhandling.

"Let's go," he says, twining his fingers through mine and yanking me forward. "Almost everyone in the palace has forgotten that you and I are still teenagers. And you're the worst of them. Tonight I'm going to remind you."

I open my mouth to protest again, but then I remember: he's taking me to see the bots. This week. Before he leaves on his trip. I need that. *Damnation.*

I'll go.

I look back at Saber, but His Impatience is dragging me along so rapidly I almost get flung against the doorframe. Tipsy Justin. My favorite. "Slower, Justin," I say between clenched teeth. "I cannot run in these heels."

"Kick them off," he says, scarcely glancing back at me.

I'm beyond annoyed at this point, but I go ahead and ditch my five-thousand-euro custom-made jeweled slippers in the chamber outside my bedroom. M.A.R.I.E. will see them back to their rightful place.

Justin leads me through the darkened and empty Hall of Mirrors, then through the grand *salons* to his private dining room, but surprisingly, the entrance is barred and we're subjected to retina scans before M.A.R.I.E. opens the door.

"Exclusive guest list," Justin says at my questioning glance.

Inside is exactly the kind of party Lord Aaron and Lady Mei and I would have loved a year ago. No one over the age of twenty-five, food that doesn't require a silk napkin, and liquor in every color and variety the Palace of Versailles has to offer. My allies are there—Ladies Nuala, Breya, Annaleigh, and Mei, and Mademoiselles Tamae and Simone—as well as almost a dozen younger guys who must be the ones His Royal Highness considers *his* friends. Exclusive? To some, I suppose.

I feel a sharp pang at the remembrance that Lord Aaron and Duke Spencer aren't here, but have an equal and opposite reaction to Lady Cyn's absence. Then I wonder how often this sort of gathering has been held previously, with the single variant of me not being invited and Lady Cyn on the King's arm instead.

I let myself smile at that.

There are fewer than a score of us, and no dress code seems to be in force. No shoes for me or cravat for Justin, but others have slipped into nightwear and I even see a few T-shirts. Bots—only bots, no human servers—bring in food and drink. Bots don't gossip belowstairs. Glasses are refilled so quickly one can hardly take a sip without being topped off, and the group swiftly becomes languid and jovial.

I take a moment to notice the sparkle of Glitter everywhere, and worry that with Reginald's higher concentration, several of these young nobles could be on the brink of overdose. How much does it take? It's so very irresponsible of me not to know . . . but surely that's the least of my many sins.

The sun is rising and I'm completely exhausted before the

drunken young nobles finally call it a night and begin walking—weaving—back to their rooms. Several head off together, though I happen to know that their residences are not actually in the same direction. What happens in the palace . . .

Without waiting for the room to clear, Justin bids his remaining comrades *adieu* and holds out an arm. "Walk with me," he requests. But with the King, nothing is truly a request, only a nicely worded demand. It's a habit I utterly despise and wish I could emulate.

"*Bien sûr,*" I murmur, wishing for nothing but my bed with its downy-soft comforter. My head aches and I feel like I left things with Saber in a bad place. That seems to be happening more and more of late, and I've got to do something about it. I just don't know what.

I'm so close. More than halfway through the woods, surely.

Justin heads, not toward my rooms, but toward his own, and a prickle of intuition makes the hairs on the back of my neck rise. The King is vivacious with drink, and I don't trust that. I'm not even fuzzy, having realized on that pivotal night three weeks ago that, brainless courtier *façade* or not, I could no longer afford to be anything but clear-minded. Tonight, with the liquor flowing so freely, I suspect Justin is hoping I'm a little tipsy. A little more malleable. But I faked most of my sips, only letting the liquid wet my closed lips. Whatever my husband has in mind, there's no reason for me to make it easier.

His only slightly unsteady path leads us into his private bed-chamber. I work hard not to meet his gaze, standing less than a meter from his huge royal bed, but I fail to see his arm move until it snakes around me, pulling me close. Not roughly, *sensually*. Which is worse.

"I want you," he whispers in my ear, one arm twined about my waist and the other lowering to clasp my backside. Thank goodness for *panniers* and petticoats; I can hardly feel a thing and I imagine he can't either. "I'm certain you know that. But perhaps you don't realize how much."

"My lord—Justin—I—"

"No, no," he says, cutting me off. "Not tonight. You're tired and I'm drunk. But think about it," he says, rubbing his cheek along mine. "The more you say yes to me, the more I'm inclined to say yes to you."

"Justin, I don't—"

"Not like that," he says, his hand along the back of my neck, tilting my face up. "Not a transaction. Just the both of us working together. Being nice to each other. Mutual."

My jaw shakes with the desire to scream at him that nothing could ever induce me to come to him willingly.

Then I think of Saber. If Saber's freedom were on this sacrificial altar, would I let myself be more pliable? And with a sinking heart, I realize, I would. So Danica 2.0 files away the suggestion for potential use.

Even though I hate myself for doing it, I lift my gloved hands to frame the sides of the King's face and I kiss him, slow and deep, until his fingers dig desperately into my waist. I bring him right to the edge. Make him want me. Make him *want* to please me.

Then I turn away, sweeping my shawl from the floor where it fell when His Highness pulled me close.

"I need sleep," I say, taking a large step backward.

"You could stay here."

"Don't push it," I whisper, though my eyes must betray my levity, because he backs off.

"Until tomorrow."

"Don't even think about comming me until after noon," I say as a parting shot over my shoulder.

His chuckle echoes down the hallway after me.

THIRTY-ONE

HIS HIGHNESS SENDS me a com about our "date" at 12:01, complete with a cheeky comment about it being after noon. It's happening *today*. Tonight. I have no idea how drunk King Justin put this all together so quickly. The itinerary suggests that in addition to inspecting a company warehouse, we'll be dining in Paris, visiting the theater, and taking a moonlight boat ride on the Seine.

"Dating," I mutter to myself. "We're *dating*." Though truly, it's more about PR than romance. Such a public outing means being seen, and being seen means the King is image-crafting—something he's been doing more or less nonstop since Lady Cyn's full-frontal *faux pas*.

He's using me. Which will hopefully distract him from the fact that I'm using him. I find myself pleased; this is what I've been working toward since the night I threw down Lady Cyn. I'll be the King's most reliable weapon in whatever battle he cares to fight, but for every victory I bring him, I'll set my own price.

Saber and I sneak up to Lord Aaron's office in the early afternoon, ostensibly to borrow some tech equipment—which I actually do need—but also to carefully transport the almost five million euros I've been storing there. Thank goodness for my new office—I was out of truly believable excuses to be seen in the business wing of the palace at all, much less in an absent voting shareholder's office. Not to mention good disguises for the large bundles of cash.

The CFO, Duke Florentine, raised the credit/euro exchange rate for the second time just last week. The king was in a mood at dinner that night and ranted about the sudden recent instability of the Sonoman-Versailles economy. For months I've been pulling millions of euros from the kingdom. Which wouldn't be so significant if that didn't represent over a billion in Sonoman credits. In my mind it serves them right for running such an unequal system of currency.

It can't go on much longer. It's like a tower of blocks that I keep stacking higher and higher. It's going to topple. Almost certainly sooner rather than later. I suspect I'm down to weeks. I've got to get away.

Saber had the idea of loading up a cart with various tech and office supplies disguising the bricks of cash in the middle. We even summoned a bot to come push the cart. Everything appeared remarkably aboveboard. I almost wished we would run into the King. He'd never suspect a thing.

We didn't, of course. He's never around when I'd actually like him to be. Instead, I'm greeted by three rather small boxes on my bed with a note to "be ready for photographs."

"Photographs?" I say to Saber as he closes the doors to my bedchamber.

He rolls his eyes. It makes Saber uneasy, I think, that the King has been putting actual effort into our marriage, perhaps because

Saber wasn't raised to see such separation between personal and professional relationships. The King desires me, true, makes use of me, but he doesn't love me, and I could certainly never love him.

I lay the boxes on the bed. None is large enough to hold a gown, but all are too large for jewelry. So what—

I'm not sure what to think of the *chic* Parisian evening dress that slithers from the first box. It weighs almost nothing in my hands and is hardly more than a satin shift with chiffon overlay as light as spider silk. The deep blue dress is sleeveless, and the hem and neckline are edged with hundreds of tiny, glittering beads; a thin band just higher than the waist is a braid of metallic silver threads that wink with the sparkle of what must be true sapphires. It's pretty, and the fabric is clearly very fine, but compared to the clothing I'm accustomed to wearing, it's . . . *ephemeral.*

In the second box I find a beautiful matching shawl—which anyone wearing so little clothing would surely need—and in the third, stunning, formal heeled sandals.

"High fashion?" Saber asks, eyeing the dress suspiciously.

"It's branding," I say, scrutinizing the strappy sandals, wondering how long I could possibly walk upright in them. "To the world, we're the privileged elite in permanent cosplay. But the King is expanding his business. Suddenly he cares what the world thinks of us, and—"

"And that means being a nice, fashionable Parisian. So he dresses you. Like a doll."

"No, *you* get to dress me like a doll," I say to Saber, before the tension can take root. It works. He grins and unfastens my bodice when I turn my back. I shed my gown in pieces, allowing

M.A.R.I.E.'s little helpers to carry each layer back to its proper place.

"I don't think this will fit over your corset," Saber says, frowning at the tiny blue dress.

"It might," I say, but realize that over such thin fabric, the boning and the hooks on the busk will show—at minimum.

Saber smiles with more than a touch of smugness. "Then I think it's a good thing you've been doing so many planks."

The realization of what he's suggesting gives me a rush of nerves sufficient to induce nausea. Saber must see the emotion sketched across my face, because he moves a few steps closer and grasps both my hands, rubbing my fingers gently.

"You're ready. It's one evening without a corset. You've been sleeping without it anyway; think of it as simply a few hours more."

I shake my head. "Sleeping is one thing. Standing and walking and sitting? And with him! I'm not ready."

"You *are* ready. You can do it."

Tears well at the corners of my eyes and I can't blink them away before they're falling on my cheeks. Not crying so much as simply leaking. "I'm so nervous," I confess in a whisper. "It seemed a better idea in theory."

"Think of it this way," Saber says, picking up the dress. "This, with no corset on underneath? It's going to be sexy as hell."

"I don't want to have to be sexy for him."

"Then be sexy for me."

I meet his eyes and what I see there gives me courage. While I find a guy in a formfitting set of breeches and a well-cut jacket incredibly appealing, this dress is surely the kind of outfit Saber most prefers. Considering their different backgrounds, in this dress I'll likely be *more* appealing to Saber than to His Majesty. I grasp tightly on to that concept.

"I'll try it," I say, blinking my damp lashes and trying to draw more than a shallow breath. My Lens shows me that it's almost time to go. My husband certainly didn't give me much prep time.

For Saber, I remind myself as he loosens my laces and my corset falls away. Without my usual many layers of underclothes, I find myself feeling oddly shy, and I quickly shimmy into the dress. The satin whispers over my skin, sliding into place with the perfection of a simple cut.

I turn at Saber's intake of breath. "It's not that I ever didn't think you were beautiful," Saber says, looking me over like a parched man at a cool stream. "From the first moment I met you, you've . . . sparkled. But this—" He gestures at me. "You look absolutely amazing."

"Wish I could stay in with you tonight."

"Oh, me too," he says with a smirk.

All too soon, there's a familiar pounding at the door, and I'm as ready as I'm going to be.

At Saber's suggestion, I've forgone my ordinarily elaborate hairstyles, opting instead to let my wavy tresses cascade down my back, tied at the nape of my neck with a blue velvet ribbon. The girl in the mirror is a stranger to me, dressed not in the dramatic excess of the Baroque court, but in the understated elegance of the outside world.

"Oh, good, you're ready," the King says, closing my bedroom

door behind him. "I'd hoped the modern mode of dress wouldn't be too difficult for you; you seem to have managed."

I see Saber's silent scoff in the dressing table mirror and raise my eyebrow a fraction of a centimeter in response. *Managed indeed.*

The King is also dressed modernly, in a sharply cut tuxedo, though his bow tie still dangles down either side of his neck. I hope he doesn't expect *me* to know how to tie such a thing. He's carrying another small box, and as he approaches he waves for me to remain sitting. "I have something special for you."

"You don't want to bring in an audience to witness you bestowing it on me?" I ask sweetly.

He waves away my suggestion as though it weren't a mockery. "No need. This necklace will speak for itself."

He's not wrong. I can't stop a gasp from escaping my mouth as he pulls from the box the largest piece of jewelry I've ever seen— and my collection in the vaults includes pieces from the crown jewels of France. Multiple strands of diamonds, falling in layers of scallops, meet in the center of the piece, where three square-cut diamonds the size of my thumb are mounted in a vaguely heart-shaped setting of white gold.

"This isn't from the vault," I say.

"No. I commissioned it for you. It's over five hundred carats of flawless diamonds. Some taken from outdated pieces, and some new. Two of the three in the middle," he says, pointing excitedly, "were bought by my grandfather almost fifty years ago. He always intended to commission a necklace that would challenge the

Mouawad L'Incomparable." He scoffs at the name of the famous necklace. "No one on earth is ever going to find a center diamond that big again, but the three in the middle of this one are over a hundred carats by themselves."

He lifts the ornate chain from the box and lays it across my collarbones. The weight is almost choking.

"Had a devil of a time purchasing them. Smithsonian, of course, refused all my offers for the Hope, so I did have to settle a bit on the biggest stone, but I'm pleased enough with the finished piece."

"Sapphires?" I ask, raising my fingertips to the center trio, but stopping before touching the gems when I remember I'm not wearing gloves.

"Sapphires? Please. Blue diamonds." His fingertips settle on my collarbones, right next to the necklace. "Perfect blue diamonds."

My eyes widen in the mirror, and I try to calculate the worth of the bauble he's just fastened around my neck. But he beats me to it.

"Priceless," he whispers. "Approximately. But it's easily in the top three most expensive pieces of jewelry in the world. The Danica Wyndham Blues, what do you think?"

I can't speak. He's going to name it for me. One more tie binding me to Sonoman-Versailles, even once I'm free. I can't appreciate its beauty anymore. It feels like a collar.

He mistakes my horrified silence for awe and preens like a peacock. I wish for nothing more than the security of my corset as

I rise and turn under the weight of that ghastly necklace. I think it weighs more than my dress.

Saber drapes my new shawl over my shoulders, and I bid him an unemotional farewell, telling him he may as well take the night off, in an aloof tone meant to set His Highness at ease. Saber takes it in stride, sweeping me a low bow and giving me a secretive smile as the King escorts me out the door.

I see the worry in his eyes. The last expensive gift the King gave me was at my request, and before an audience of hundreds at the birthday party I planned for myself. This was a private gift with my name attached.

The King is very much acting as though he'd like to keep me near.

THIRTY-TWO

I DON'T OFFER up the slightest argument when the King insists on replacing the necklace in its box before we enter the warehouse district. "Security and all," he says. I've barely managed to smile through the publicity pictures on the steps of the palace with the precious anaconda around my neck, squeezing, choking, threatening to drag me to the ground. I want to fling it back at him instead of graciously turning so he can remove the beautiful, terrible thing with careful, gloved fingers.

He hands the boxed necklace to an armed guard, who joins us right in the cab of the vehicle for the sole purpose of casting his body in front of the jewelry should anyone threaten it. Our car is both fronted and followed by two others, also transporting armed guards, and I'm jealous that I don't have my own retinue of soldiers to call on without the knowledge or consent of the King. I can't help but fantasize about how much easier life could be if I had some honest-to-goodness thugs working for me.

"I apologize that you're here in such formal attire," His Majesty says as he pivots to help me from the backseat of the car, "but I can't imagine you'd turn out very well if I asked you to dress in the car."

"Certainly not," I murmur in agreement, ignoring the insinuation that I'd agree to undress in front of him.

While the warehouse is hardly what I'd call clean, it isn't particularly dirty, either, and though I lift my hem and hold it close to my body so it doesn't rub against walls or crates, it's not the dusty, neglected building I envisioned when I heard we were visiting a *warehouse*. Perhaps I shouldn't be surprised; there are millions upon millions of dollars of inventory in these crates.

Crates. I should have also expected that. It's not a warehouse full of bots standing at attention, their faces inclined toward the front doors, awaiting orders. Steel shipping containers line the interior, stacked fifteen meters high; some on the ground level are open, revealing wrapped pallets full of wooden cubes, about a meter to a side.

"This is amazing," I say, affecting a hushed whisper, as though I were viewing a rare display in a museum. "A bot in every crate?"

"Each and every one."

"Can we"—I pause and bite my lower lip in a show of innocence—"open one? Can I see?"

The King snaps at one of his men and points. Doesn't even say a word; I'm deeply envious of how naturally he wears his authority. The guard retrieves a crowbar that he must have brought along for this very purpose while two others drag a crate toward us. Soon they've pried off the front and a man with a box cutter strips away layers of plastic packaging.

The reveal is anticlimactic. Released from its casing, the bot activates, straightening and unfolding its limbs. It looks more or less like the bots at the palace, but ... naked. We dress our bots in livery, with blank-faced masks and powdered wigs. I'd never thought before just how much it humanizes them.

This bot is tastefully generic, a blank white torso on articulated treads, as suitable for climbing stairs as for level ground. The harsh angles of its frame are concealed by a friendly curve of decorative ceramic panels, giving its arms a more humanoid profile—though its agile, three-fingered hands barely resemble their biological counterparts. Atop its broad "shoulders" rests a cylindrical collection of sensors and scanners that I suppose would look like a head from afar.

I walk around the bot, examining it from all sides. When I reach out to touch the machine, the King doesn't stop me, and soon I've located an access panel high on its back—though I suppose, to a machine with three hundred sixty degrees of spatial awareness, *back* is a pretty meaningless designation.

"It's very nice," I say to the King, making a mental note of what I find beneath the bot's exterior. While I have relatively little understanding of the materials and mechanical engineering that must have gone into its construction, its innards tell me a very interesting story about its development. "And it operates without a central server? No need for M.A.R.I.E., I mean."

"Not once it has a role assigned. If it's given a task it doesn't understand, it checks with a central server for new programming—which will be provided for a modest subscription fee. We'll be building our servers here in Europe and expanding south and east. Amalgamated will cover Asia and the Americas."

"So right now it's . . . blank?"

"More or less," the King says, nodding.

"And each bot has to be programmed individually?"

"Exactly. We'll have multiple templates for easier programming. And some larger companies will have bots that program the other bots. It's beautiful, really."

"Indeed," I say softly, my head already spinning.

By the time we step back into our motorcade, bound for the glitzy center of Paris, my brain is buzzing with possibilities. All through a gourmet dinner at a high-rise restaurant overlooking the City of Light, all through a musical production that must surely be exceptionally well performed, my mind fills in the details of what, until tonight, had only been an outline—a framework of what might be possible.

I know that I speak, I converse, I pretend to pay attention. Luckily, even if His Highness wanted to have an intimate discussion, we're surrounded by security everywhere we go. People whose names I don't recognize, but who must be important, are continually permitted into our presence; I smile and shake hands. I endure compliments—and leers, sometimes, that I'm expected to take as compliments—but two minutes later I couldn't have picked out one face in a lineup or regurgitated a single name.

An hour or so after a final round of edge-smoothing champagne along with a bit of fresh air on my face, I'm once again sufficiently present to worry about what's happening around me. Just in time for my husband's head of security to assist me into a wide-bottomed boat, where Justin waits, reclining in a pile of blankets. I'm clearly supposed to join him there, to snuggle close against the cool breeze that rolls off the river.

It's the first time all evening we've been essentially alone.

Instead of a Nav system, there's a man steering the boat—an amusing anachronism—but he's sequestered from us in a little boxlike shelter at the bow, and Justin's security detail have stationed themselves on the shore, rather than with us in the boat. As we float out onto the water, Justin strokes the skin along the bottom of the necklace—not coincidentally, I'm sure, just barely above the line of my *décolletage*—and I shiver.

"Poor thing," the King coos. "Your dress really is far thinner than you're used to. You must be freezing." He gathers a thick blanket around us both, but the soft fabric is no match for the ice in my spine.

I say nothing and we float along silently for a long time. I wonder if he's as weary from the whirl of social gaiety as I am. Maybe we won't have to talk at all.

"So I'm off tomorrow," he finally says. There goes that hope.

"Where are you going?" I ask, even though I already found the answer to my question in the itinerary I pilfered from Mateus's tablet. But I want to know what he'll say. If he'll lie.

"It hardly matters. But I'll be gone for about a week, just like last time."

It's now or never. "I think I should have more power while you're away from the palace," I say, as though it were truly a casual topic.

But I feel him stiffen at my back. "What do you mean?" he asks, not sounding like he's even paying attention. I'm not fooled.

"The incident with the Tremain girl was a PR nightmare," I say, keeping my voice low. Without accusation. "In part because security followed cut-and-dried procedure instead of exercising actual judgment and discretion. If you'd been around, they'd have consulted you, and you'd have crafted a narrative before word got out, and everything would have gone much more smoothly. Instead, the death was all over the news so quickly one could almost think we had a reporter there in the palace. I know I told you I didn't want to be an executive, but I think I've changed my mind."

He stretches and leans back a little, still holding me close, but no longer pushing his attentions on me.

"Hear me out," I say to his silence. "I'd like a position in security. So it's clear to everyone who they answer to while you're gone. I *suspect*," I say, heavy emphasis on the word, "that you'll be traveling frequently the next few years in support of your latest project. And things happen. You can't micromanage the palace while you're out globetrotting."

He doesn't answer, but shifts and brushes his lips along the skin at my neck. I tilt my face away, giving him better access. The better to keep him distracted. He moves his hand a little higher as his lips kiss their way up to the curve behind my ear. "I did return to a bit of a public relations disaster," he admits.

I suppose that's as close to groveling as I'm going to get from someone as lofty as him. "You've got to learn to trust me," I whisper, letting my lips brush his earlobe.

"How about this?" he says, sitting up so quickly I have to brace myself against his thigh. Maybe that was his goal. "Senior vice president of palace security."

That seems promising. A position like that should give me all the access I need. It's the last piece of my puzzle. "That sounds a bit intense," I say demurely, knowing my reluctance will prod him on far better than an eager willingness.

"It's a job often assigned to the crown prince or princess of the royal family, to bolster their *résumé* and justify paying them a salary while they wait their turn to take the throne. It was my position for a year before my parents . . . before I became King." He laughs softly. "Technically, it's still my position, I suppose."

"And since we certainly don't have a crown prince or princess . . ." I trail my fingers up his leg.

"Giving it to you instead would establish a clear chain of command in the court while I'm away."

For a moment, I completely forget how to breathe. This is it. It's perfect. Now I have to act like I don't really want it that badly.

"You've been an amazing Queen these last few weeks. Truly grown into the role," he says, settling against the back of his seat, his fingertips brushing the sides of my neck. I hope he can't feel my racing heartbeat. "But this is a big step. Especially for a woman who was fighting against marriage to me a mere few months ago. Such a position—so much control—requires a great deal of trust."

I turn around so I can face him. "Do you?"

"Trust you?" He smiles. Only at the very corners of his mouth. "Let's say . . . I'd *like* to trust you," he whispers, a jagged dissonance to the way he's nuzzling my neck. "We could be good together, and I think you're finally beginning to see that. You're like a bird in a golden cage, Danica. If I want to see how high you can fly, I suppose I must eventually open the door and stop clipping your wings, mustn't I?" He runs his finger down my neck, and along the *décolletage* of my thin dress, pausing in the center to dip two fingers into my cleavage and pull me forward by the delicate edge.

"Then—"

"What's your game, Danica?" he whispers, barely a breath away from my mouth.

I cradle his face in my hands. "Does it have to be a game, Justin?"

"With you? Yes. With me? Yes. So with *us*? Absolutely."

"Then maybe I should be asking what your game is," I say, keeping a firm grip on my rising fear.

His nose strokes up my chin, drawing out a shiver, and he sets his lips close to my ear and says, "Wouldn't you like to know?"

I certainly would.

"What do you want, Danica? Be honest for once." And then his mouth is on my neck, his tongue lathing. I close my eyes. This is a price I already decided I'm willing to pay.

"I want to be able to handle a crisis while you—"

"No, no," he says, waving a hand. "That's the plausible explanation you had to concoct—the bait, as it were. And I'm tempted to take it—I've seen enough of your discretion and your technical acumen to know you can handle such work as may arise. But I'm uncertain of your true motivation." He leans forward, his face a breath away from mine. "What is it that you really want?"

How good an actress am I? I lower my eyelids. "Isn't it enough that I want *you*?"

Justin's ego is utterly blinding; in his mind, how could any woman not want him? He shoves my light skirts out of his way and his hands slide up my thighs. "Do you?"

I grab the front of his bow tie and shift so our hips meet snugly. "I want you to be happy." And it's so very true. I want him to be happy so I can work right under his nose.

Justin sucks in a loud breath and lets it out in a low moan; I give him another deep, long kiss and end by pulling his bottom lip between my teeth. Without releasing him from between my teeth, I demand, "Are you happy?"

Justin makes a noise of primal wanting; he pulls away and I taste blood against my teeth. Then he yanks me toward him—hard, violent. In that moment I gain an intimate understanding of what Sierra Jamison might have been feeling the night she died in the arms of the King. She chose to be with the King that night—I believe that now. But she paid a terrible price.

"Are you?" I repeat as he rocks against me, because I can only get those two tiny words out without letting my agony pour out with it.

"God's teeth, yes," he groans. "Let it never be said you're not as conniving as the rest of us." And his lips devour mine, rough and punishing.

I close my eyes and kiss him back. Because I don't just need him to be happy tonight. I need him happy tomorrow and the next day and every day until I leave. I need him to *adore* me.

And maybe I've been lying to myself for weeks. When I took the first step on this road of seducing the King, did I really not know where it was going to end? Perhaps there's part of me that simply wanted to conquer him.

But the answers to those questions don't change this moment. This is my choice. My decision. And I make it.

I close my eyes and pretend I'm somewhere else.

THIRTY-THREE

I WALK BACK into my rooms at three in the morning, hoping Saber is asleep. I don't want him to see me, at least not until I've changed my clothing. I feel empty and bereft—a somewhat faded version of myself.

But I'm to have a new position in court, and Justin assured me he would make the arrangements before his helicopter takes off in surprisingly few hours. By the time *I* awake, I should have near-total control of palace security. More than enough to accomplish what I must before Justin's return.

"Dani?" Saber asks from the darkness, and I'm not fast enough to stifle a yip of surprise. "Sorry," he says with a wry grin. In my defense, he did pop up from a corner of the bed I couldn't see at all. "Everything okay?"

"Everything's fine," I say, lacing my hands together in front of me.

Saber looks at me oddly. "Did you have a good time with the King?"

Adrenaline drowns me from the inside out, and I turn to set my small purse on my dressing table. My hands are trembling;

I've got to get control over myself. "It was Paris," I grumble. "Fine food, good theater, too much alcohol."

Saber makes a sound of amusement in his throat. "You were out quite late." His question is utterly innocent—idle, even—but my nerves are clanging like cymbals and everything makes me feel guilty.

"Big boat ride after the show. You know the King," I say non-committally. "Has to make an event out of everything."

"Think he'll let you sleep late?" Saber asks, scooting to the edge of the bed and pulling me close. "Or is that too much to ask?"

Tears well up beneath my closed lids and I breathe slowly, forcing them back. I can't let him know that anything is amiss. I'd never stand up under his close scrutiny. Someone else's, certainly, but never his. I carefully set down my valise and unwind the shawl, trying to buy myself some time. "Maybe? I thought I'd shower before I retire."

Saber studies me intently and I can hardly bear to hold eye contact. "Are you sure you're okay?"

"Groggy. I fell asleep in the car on the way home," I lie. I lie like I breathe these days, but I hate lying to him. I keep secrets—but not lies. Though sometimes I wonder if they're ultimately the same thing. "I probably had too much wine."

After retreating to the privacy of my bathroom, I splash water on my face and stare into the mirror. I expect to look different—but no. Same face, same mouth, same eyes. Maybe my eyes are a little different. Maybe.

I open the door and start to bustle out, but I run right into Saber. It's not unlike running into a brick wall. I'm not small, and when I run into people I'm used to them giving way—not me. But I practically bounce off Saber and he doesn't move even a centimeter. He was braced here. He was waiting.

"Is this about *him*?"

Him? I feel the blood drain from my face.

"Is this about Reginald? Is that why you won't tell me?"

Finally, something I can be honest about, if only tangentially. "Yes," I say, gluing my eyes to my feet so he doesn't catch the half-lie. It is about him. Sort of.

"Then just *say* that," Saber says, frustration in his voice. "You think I can't tell when you're trying to hide something?" He rubs his hands up and down my arms and when I chance a peek up at him, he's smiling, albeit tightly. "You do a marvelous job for everybody out there," he says, gesturing vaguely. "But I *know* you. I can tell. And when you're hiding things and won't tell me what, I'm forced to use my imagination. And trust me, neither of us wants that."

I squeeze my eyes shut, disgusted with my dissembling. I'll fob this secret off on Reginald, because I suspect that even Saber's imagination won't come close to the awfulness of the truth. "I'm sorry," I whisper, and I've never spoken truer words.

Not sorry enough to have made a different choice, but so very, very sorry that it was necessary.

Saber releases a long sigh and wraps his arms around me. "I've been thinking about this all day. I'll tell him you want to meet, if that's what you want. Because at the moment—even if it's at Reginald's orders—I work for you. But, Danica, please reconsider."

I swallow hard, hating that he's been agonizing over this.

"Please don't fight him," Saber says, his voice cracking on the word *fight*. "If you do, he'll win, and we'll both lose."

"You don't know that."

"I've been working for him for more than a decade, Danica. I *do* know that."

"So I should just leave you with him? Leave him to terrorize the streets of Paris?" It feels good to direct my self-loathing at someone else, even if only for a moment. "If his dealings with me are any indication, he's a despicable human being who deserves to be so utterly destroyed he'll never recover enough to cheat and manipulate anyone ever again." My voice is shaking with anger. Emotions I didn't realize I had pent up.

"You're right," Saber says, and I look sharply up at him. "And I agree with you. But it's going to take more than one girl with loads of righteous anger. It's . . . it's going to take an army."

"Maybe I have an army," I whisper.

"Where would you get an army?" he snaps, and my mouth goes wide with indignation. "No, I mean it. Everyone here reports to the King—if you took palace security on a field trip, you know he'd wonder why, and this is definitely not something you want him looking into. Paris is worse—anyone you could hire who doesn't already work for Reginald probably works for the government. He's unbeatable, Danica, and I pray I can convince you of that before your stubbornness gets you killed."

I scoff. "He won't hurt me. Pathetically enough, I'm too valuable."

Saber is quiet for a long time until I look up at him. My insides clench at the look on his face. Not anger, but anguish. When he speaks, his words are so quiet I scarcely hear them, even mere centimeters away. "Your passion, the thing I love best about you, is dragging you away from me." He hesitates, then the words seem to burst from him, as though he has no power to hold them back. "You're becoming like him."

"Because I want to save you!" I lash back, stung by his words.

He shakes his head. "You can't. You think you can, but it isn't possible."

"Why won't you let me try? If I were in your shoes I would let you try to save me."

"I *am* trying to save you." His hands are tight, but not painful, on my upper arms. "Someone's got to save you from your*self*. Your life; your choices!"

"I can't ever live a life without regrets knowing that I left you in his hands." I don't know when I started shouting. But I can't stop. "I'd rather regret what I've become, because *I can fix that*."

He laughs quietly, a harsh sound, like ice shattering on the surface of a frozen pond. "You think that now, but you don't understand how overwhelming it is. The blackness of this life. It might leave you breathing, but trust me, you'll be dead. No one fixes that, Danica."

I hear him. I understand him. But I can't accept it. I've sacrificed too much already not to see this through to the end.

Everything between us is going to change tonight. In one minute. I'm going to make him do what he doesn't want to, and the only way everything is ever going to be right between us again is if I emerge victorious.

I've learned the hard way not to count on victory. But I've also learned the hard way that everything carries a risk.

This is the first step.

I close the distance between us and kiss Saber with every ounce of emotion and longing and wishing that has existed between us since that first day at Giovanni's, when I figured out he wasn't Reginald. The first time I saw that fire in his eyes and knew he wasn't satisfied with his lot in life—perhaps, the moment I saw myself reflected in those eyes. I tell him how much I love him and how I have to try to save him even if he doesn't believe he's worth it. That I believe in him enough for both of us. I tell him all that and more with my kiss.

And then I step back. "Tell Reginald," I say, keeping my voice steady, "I want a meeting. In private. In *Paris*."

Saber hesitates, then nods before turning away. Nothing has ever shattered my soul more than the disappointment in his eyes.

WHEN THE CAT is away, the mice will play: that's the refrain I want on everyone's lips as I leave the palace for a day at the spa with my dear, dear friends Lady Mei and Lady Nuala. Saber comes along for security, per the instructions of the new senior vice president in charge of such things. A small crowd has gathered to see us off—several courtiers who doubtless hope to be invited along at the last moment. We slip into our vehicles and wave and smile: elbow, elbow, wrist, wrist, wrist.

If any of them wonder why we're taking two cars when we could easily fit into one, well, they don't question the excesses

of their Queen any more than they did in the days of Marie-
Antoinette. *Thank you, Lord Aaron.*

It's striking, really, how often I find myself contemplating the
young Queen I never had any desire to emulate. It makes me wonder if she was hiding as much beneath her *façade* as I keep beneath
mine. I suppose we'll never know.

Today's *mascarade* includes shoulder bags, with towels con-
cealing all sorts of fun supplies beneath, and the largest picnic
basket I could locate—no food required. Lady Nuala has one small
bag with a few toiletries for herself and Lady Mei, but truly, how
stupid are the courtiers? When you go to a five-star spa, you don't
bring *luggage*. You could show up on the doorstep with nothing
but your bank account number and they would happily provide
everything you could possibly require—so long as the funds
cleared in advance.

Which is precisely what Ladies Mei and Nuala are going to do.

Saber and me? We have other plans.

THE COM IS waiting when we return from Paris in the late
afternoon. It's from Duke Spencer's Sonoma address—a slight
risk, that, but at worst they can track where it's been sent from,
and everyone already knows he and Lord Aaron went to New York
City. The document itself is encrypted, but with Lord Aaron's key,
which I've had for years, it's a simple task to decrypt it.

I set the message to move offline before decrypting and take
a moment to put my packages away. Saber has been conveniently
uncurious all day. When we split from the other ladies, when he

helped me with some minor breaking and entering without comment or argument. Even now, he hands me my purloined bubble-wrapped parcels without meeting my eyes. He seems to have decided not to fight me.

I'm not sure what to think of that. I like it when he fights me. It helps me gauge when I've gone too far. This silence makes me worry that I passed that line long ago.

"Thank you," I murmur, stowing the precious packages in the largest drawer of my desk. "Oh, I have a com from Duke Spencer," I say brightly, wanting to clear the air of the tension that secrets always bring.

Saber smiles genuinely at that. I rarely saw them together, but I think he and Duke Spencer bonded in much the same way Lord Aaron and I did. Both are quiet and steady, while both Lord Aaron and I are . . . not. "How is he? They, I guess."

"Let's find out," I say, opening the message—now decrypted for display on my tablet, but scrubbed from the network.

The note is surprisingly short.

> *Your Royal Majesty,*
>
> *My apologies for the delay, but I consulted several sources to be certain, as I'm afraid you're going to be disappointed. The document we found contains detail and analysis on a series of clustered regularly interspaced short palindromic repeats (CRISPR) for the Norwegian Blight and the resistant GMO, the Sonoman Rally.*
>
> *In layman's terms, these are nothing more than*

the lab recipes for the Blight and the Rally seeds.
Everyone here is familiar with both reports as part
of the company's history and because the Rally
seeds continue to be one of their largest exports. I've
no idea why the file was marked as a trade secret;
though the time stamp was pre-Sonoman-Versailles,
so perhaps it's an eAntique of sorts. The data is
today quite public and, I'm afraid, not useful to
your particular aims.

We are well. Aaron sends love.

Spencer Harrisford

I'm weak with disappointment. I expected something from this document, but weeks of waiting have yielded absolutely nothing. Why was the doc even on Mateus's tablet? It doesn't make sense. But thinking about it just makes my head hurt. I don't realize how hopeful I truly was until that hope is extinguished, a single candle being snuffed in a dark room. I fight back tears and slap my tablet down on the top of my desk a little too hard.

Saber raises his head. "You okay?"

Even his concern doesn't calm me. I crumple a blank piece of parchment from my desktop and throw it against the wall. "That document, the one I hoped was *anything* I could use?" I glare up at him.

"Wasn't?" Saber guesses.

"Worse." I crumple another sheet of parchment and throw it, too, tempted to throw something heavier, more expensive, more breakable. "It's just technical data on the day Sonoma saved the world. The day they were the bloody superhero of mankind. What the hell good does that do me?"

Saber hesitates, then steps into the office and picks up the two wads of parchment.

I sigh and rub at my eyes. "My apologies—I'm too old to throw tantrums."

"Are you ever really too old?" Saber asks playfully, tossing the pages into the wastebin.

"Aren't I supposed to be?"

"In this palace, does anyone ever grow up?"

I snort my amusement, but it's sadly true. What are we all but overgrown children, still playing dress-up? Pretending the world around us isn't so vastly different from the lives we lead. Pretending we know what we're doing. Certainly that's all I do every day—and, more often than not, well into the night.

"Come," Saber says, offering his hand. "You have a party to prepare for."

THIRTY-FOUR

IT'S LADY NUALA'S first chance to keep a secret for me, pre-paid with her decadent day at the spa. So far she's passing with flying colors, but I keep a wary eye on her. At least she got to remain with Lady Mei. I, on the other hand, got roped into a conversation with a cluster of high nobility, and I'm trying to pretend to pay attention but rather failing as I continue to glance in envy at Lady Nuala, laughing with Lady Mei and Tamae on the other side of the room.

I'm drowning in uncertainty, my confidence in my decisions utterly fled. My victory over Lady Cyn, which is proving more total than I'd have thought possible, feels shallow compared with the daunting tasks I've set myself on other fronts. I'd hoped by now to have some leverage for that final exit. I find myself lashing out too often, especially at Saber, who's been my lighthouse in turbulent seas. Leaning on him for access to Reginald, even for Saber's own benefit, makes me feel petty and small.

"Anxious to have your husband back?" Duke Florentine's jovial inquiry is, I realize, directed at me.

"He's never far from my thoughts," I say, smiling. "Five more days."

"Counting every one of them, aren't you?" he teases.

Days? I'm counting the hours, truly—my remaining hours of freedom. Despite how assiduously I wear my *charade,* I can't help but be surprised at how fully they've fallen for it. Aren't they supposed to be the best and brightest of Sonoman-Versailles?

"Can't wait to hear about his business trip. Don't suppose you'd drop a hint in an old friend's ear?"

I stare at the duke, unable to hide my surprise at his request. Old friend? This man didn't know I existed as recently as a year ago. I force a demure smile and flutter my fan just below my nose. "Oh, Your Grace, I couldn't."

"Ha! I knew you knew," he says, gesturing with a very full martini that I'm afraid he's going to splash all over the front of my silk gown. "Of course he'd tell you early. He's going to brief the rest of us when he returns. Beginning of a new era. Profits like this company hasn't seen since the days of the Blight," he adds, referencing the discovery that earned Sonoma Inc. its first billion. Its first ten billion.

My disappointment over what turned out to be the formula for that very thing threatens to spill over, and I have to clench my teeth against it. "Indeed."

"I do think we were right to keep him."

The Duke prattles on, speculating about business of which he assumes I'm fully informed; he's right, but only because I stole information from Mateus's tablet.

I find the company of high nobility incredibly tiresome. It's probably a generational thing—the youngest among them is in her forties, and some have grandchildren older than me. They seem to reminisce constantly while I obsess over future plans. And when they've run out of memories, they resort to reciting history to one another—which is where Duke Florentine has now meandered.

"I'm sorry," I say when—against all expectations—his recitation manages to catch my interest. "What was that you just said about the Rally?"

"That the King's present plans might even eclipse it," he says, beaming. "Wouldn't that be amazing? It'll be like the golden year of thirty-eight all over again."

"Wasn't the Rally released in 2034?" I ask, puzzled. I learned the story as a child, of course—all children of Sonoman-Versailles do—but I was always more interested in math than history.

"Oh no, Your Highness," Duke Sells says, inclining his head respectfully. "It was certainly thirty-eight. A momentous year, indeed; my grandfather told me about it in detail. It was thirty-six when the Blight raged so badly, and thirty-eight when Sonoma's great discovery was unveiled."

"Oh," I say lamely. "I must have forgotten." Heat rushes to my cheeks because I'm quite certain I *haven't* forgotten—but the thing I haven't forgotten I only learned quite recently. A terrible, horrible idea enters my mind, and I feel my knees weaken at the thought. "I'm afraid I must return to my rooms, if you will all excuse me."

"You look quite flushed, dear," Countess Poe says, laying a gentle hand on my arm. "Are you well?"

"I had a heat wrap today. At the spa," I add. "It must have . . ." My words trail into a meaningless mumble.

"Oh, certainly," the countess says. "I've had the same reaction myself. As lovely as a spa day can be, one does come home quite exhausted. Where is that man of yours?" The Countesses Poe offer their arms for support, and Countess Maria looks around and then signals to Saber.

"To her rooms," she commands when Saber bows low. "Try not to let it appear as though she is unwell."

As though that matters. The damned heat wrap excuse certainly worked well enough.

"What's wrong?" Saber asks, bending close to my ear.

"I have something to confirm, immediately," I say hoarsely.

On arriving at my rooms, I gracelessly kick away my heels and strip off my gloves, letting them fall to the floor behind me. Saber follows, my silent shadow. Unlocking my private office seems to take forever—I keep moving just as the face scanner is about to finish. I don't close the door, but Saber seems unwilling to cross the threshold, instead lingering in the doorway.

"What year did Sonoma Agriculture discover the cure for the Norwegian Blight?" I ask my Lens daemon. *Cure* isn't precisely the right word, but the search engine will understand what I mean.

Sure enough, a date scrolls across my peripheral: *November 2038.*

"When did the Norwegian Blight first appear?"

A moment. *March 2036.*

Just as the Duke said.

The type blurs, and I feel dizzy as I reach for the drive where Lord Aaron stored my copy of Mateus's tablet. It takes a few minutes to hook it up, and my fingers tremble as I access the document

Duke Spencer took to America for me. I check the time stamp of the file's creation.

February 8, 2034.

This, *this* is what I was missing.

Two years before the Blight appeared, wiping out crops around the world, spreading famine, collapsing economies, and eventually putting Sonoma Inc. in a position to occupy the Palace of Versailles as its corporate headquarters, our biotech division already had the full formula both for the Blight *and for Blight-resistant crop strains.* The damned Sonoman Rally.

Kevin Wyndham didn't save the world from the greatest agricultural disaster in the history of mankind.

He *invented* it.

He could have stopped it at any moment. But he didn't. Not until a billion—*a billion*—people had died.

This young, ambitious CEO wanted so badly to put his company on the map, to immortalize himself and his work, to make more money than most companies could ever dream of, that he allowed more than a billion men, women, and children to starve to death.

And the current King, the one I'm married to, knows it.

My throne is built on the lives of a *billion* innocents. More, depending on secondary effects. The Norwegian Blight led to a complete collapse of the third world. Whole nations languished in anarchy for decades. Wars were fought over the economic fallout. Sonoma shone a beacon of hope into that darkness—hope for the salvation of humankind.

It's a lie.

It's worse than a lie. It's an act of such inhuman depravity I can scarcely comprehend it. I'm not certain there's any single person in history responsible for more destroyed human lives than my husband's great-grandfather. I feel sick.

Who else knows? Surely it's a closely held secret; I doubt even the highest of the high nobility is aware.

It's surely the greatest of all Sonoma's secrets.

With the hot burn of tears in my eyes, I realize that this terrible, devastating discovery is exactly what I'd hoped for.

Blackmail.

And the thrill that sends through me says, more plainly than anything else possibly could, that the good part of me I thought I could tuck away, the last remnant of conscience I thought I could lay claim to, is gone.

THIRTY-FIVE

I AWAIT MY husband's helicopter in paralyzing fear. Not of him—not really. Not anymore. It's me I fear now. This is the hardest I've ever had to work to hide my disgust for the man. My disgust for myself. How many people suffered and died so I could wear this pretty dress? It'll take every ounce of self-control, every trick Giovanni ever taught me, to disguise what I feel for Justin. I even asked Saber to stay in my chambers tonight. I can't face Justin with a smile when I know Saber is watching me. Maybe tomorrow, but not tonight. Not this first time, when my pretending will be put to the ultimate test.

I can't rationally blame Justin for the actions of his great-grandfather—money and power may be heritable, but guilt isn't something any child should be expected to bear for their ancestors. No, not even if they're descended from the most prolific mass murderer in history. But grave damage was done, and even though Justin knows it, he's preparing a move that will enrich his company in similar ways by causing similar damage, through his robotic revolution. Not only does he not care, he *revels* in it. Guilt isn't passed from parent to child, but that doesn't mean the apple falls far from the tree.

Last time—the Norwegian Blight—we *saved* the world. No one will think us so heroic this time.

Or will they? In five hundred years, will anyone care about the people who will suffer, perhaps die, as a result of the poverty triggered by Sonoma and Amalgamated's robots? Or will they only speak of the pioneers who invented a new way of life? Visionaries who paved a broad and bloody path?

If I've learned anything in the last year, it's that everything has a cost. All the awful things I've done, desperately or deliberately, were the price tags on what I desired. But I would never, never, sacrifice a billion—*a billion!*—lives for something as hollow as *profits.*

For all my loathing, it's impossible to miss the fact that His Highness looks both stunning and extraordinarily pleased to see me. He sweeps me against him, then smiles broadly at the small crowd that has gathered to greet him.

"You're looking ravishing," he growls in my ear, and I pretend to preen. His fingers burn like fire on my arm, and I swallow hard as I simper up at him. I'm pleased he thinks I look well—I've been up until the blush hours of dawn, coding and programming, for days, and the foundation hiding the circles beneath my eyes is probably thicker than my skin. But I'm only going to get one chance, and when it arrives, I'd better be ready.

"Did you miss me?" I whisper.

"Miss you? I burned for you."

Evil, Lord Aaron said. Lord Aaron is always right. My hands quiver and I grip the lapels of the King's velvet jacket to still them, hoping he doesn't notice. I play my role as devoted Queen to the hilt, as much to hide from Justin as anything. The King waves at the assembled crowd, then reaches around my back to pull me closer.

Oh dear. I'm going to have to kiss him, aren't I?

And then his lips are pressed to mine, his tongue snaking past my teeth, making it quite apparent that this is a kiss I'm meant to very fully participate in. I close my eyes and think of England. Or Canada. Or Spain. Any place except the square of marble on which I'm standing.

When at last he pulls away, my face is flushed, and I'm certain the audience thinks I'm pleasantly blushing rather than surging with fury.

"Did you have a nice week?" Justin asks, smooth and quiet.

"I did, yes," I answer, wondering if I'm supposed to object that any week in which we're separated cannot possibly hold much enjoyment. But such a lie is so gaping I can't force it out of my throat.

"Good, good. Enjoying your new assignment, Lady Senior Vice President?"

"Luckily, I had little cause to consider it." If I were wearing pants, they would be aflame. I've lurked in so many high-security rooms this week that I could never have had access to before.

It's only when the welcoming crowd begins to thin that I realize a bot is trailing after Justin. Catching my glance, the King grins and leans close to my ear. "One of the new-wave ones. A little personal testing. All dressed up, I doubt anyone will notice the difference."

I steal another glance at what looks like an utterly harmless bit of machinery. Even a few weeks ago I'd have simply seen it as the tool Sonoma and Amalgamated will use to enrich themselves and impoverish others.

Now? After discovering how ruthless Justin's great-grandfather was—knowing a hundred years later how devastating and far-reaching the consequences of his greed would prove—I feel this new threat as keenly as Lord Aaron. It seems so urgent suddenly, in a way Lord Aaron never could quite convey, much as he tried. How ignorant he must have thought me. Unfeeling.

I understand now.

"I was in Washington, DC, three days ago," the King says, oblivious to my dismay. "The United States government has signed a contract with Sonoma and Amalgamated for one *million* of these, to be delivered in batches over the next five years."

"Congratulations," I say, my heart sinking at the thought of how many human jobs those bots will replace. "That's wonderful." Government work remains one of the few stable industries in many nations around the world. If the United States replaces their federal workers with bots, the rest of the world will be eager to follow.

"It's more than wonderful," he says. "It's . . . revolutionary!"

I successfully keep myself from cringing at his choice of words. Sometimes one must be content with the small victories.

"Consider the implications, Danica," he crows. "Manufacturing, retail, law enforcement—even military operations, if we can get a few of the peskier treaties amended. Ridiculous, isn't it, to insist that countries defend themselves by shedding human blood? Think of the lives we'll save selling these little mechanical surrogates. It takes twenty years to grow a soldier—but we can manufacture a new bot in less than a week."

That's what he'll emphasize, of course—to put it in Justin's own terms, that's his plausible explanation, his *bait*. What he won't emphasize is that we'll be selling bots to both sides. Meanwhile the hundreds of soldiers these bots might spare—thousands, even— will be unemployed. How many children will go hungry? How grateful can a soldier be to escape the front lines when he and his family are starving to death?

To say nothing of what a despot could do with an army of unfailingly loyal robotic servants. Even history's greatest tyrants had to have *some* way to ensure the loyalty of the men and women who supported their rule. The unfaltering devotion of Justin's new bots can be had for, what? A monthly subscription fee? It's terrifying.

My brain tells me this is a slippery slope, a situation hardly likely to happen within my lifetime—to be banned by some new treaty or other intervention—but in light of the fact that this man's great-grandfather personally engineered the most traumatic agricultural disaster in recorded history, nothing seems far-fetched.

"IT'S HARD TO even look at him," I confess to Saber after a long and sweaty core workout. I'm exhausted, but the ache makes me feel good. Strong. "Harder than before I knew about the Blight. Knowing what I know, I couldn't stay, even if nothing else had happened. I can't even passively condone such a thing. I can't. All those people," I finish in a whisper.

"I don't blame you," Saber says. "Just don't get yourself killed in the process, okay?"

I wrap my arms around his neck and pull him close without saying a word. It's not a promise I can make with a clear conscience.

He's not stupid. He knows I didn't say the words and he sighs long and loud and then shakes me theatrically. "You're impossible."

"You think I'm hard to deal with? You won't even let me dream."

But my joking words sober us both. "I'm sorry about that," he says.

"I know."

"I saw Reginald this morning," Saber says.

I look up sharply, eyes wide. "Reginald himself?" I shake off a shiver when I realize Saber's countdown must have been low. Still—it's been hours and he didn't tell me. "You didn't say anything. Did you give him my message?"

He shrugs with one shoulder. "He says no."

"What do you mean, 'he says no'?"

"He says no, Danica," Saber snaps. I'm not sure he's ever raised his voice to me. Not like this. "You can't just demand his presence. He's not a courtier. Despite everything I've told you, and shown you, *and* that you've found out on your own, you have no idea who you're actually dealing with. He doesn't come when you call. And if he doesn't want to see you, he's not going to see you."

"He's seen me before," I say weakly. I need this meeting. And I need it soon. I can't live with Justin. Not with what I know. What I've *done*.

"Yeah, when there was something he wanted from you," Saber yells, flinging a hand out toward me. "He has no reason to meet with you anymore. It gains him nothing. You think he's doing you a favor? You think you're really *business partners*? He respects no one. He's an insane, hate-filled, power-hungry—"

I see the moment Saber realizes he's shouting and watch him shut down entirely. He closes his mouth, slumps his shoulders forward, shoves his fists in his pockets as though he wishes he could turn invisible. It makes my heart cry out in agony to watch him close down everything that makes him my Saber, and to transform into a lowly slave instead.

I can't let this stand. I have to get him out, whatever it takes. I never want to see this side of Saber again—but that's a goal I can't reach without making use of the very subservience I hope to banish. With guilt stabbing at my heart, I say sharply, "Well, then, I guess I need to do something to make it worth his while."

Before he can stop me I'm tearing down the hallway and into my private office. After yanking supplies out of drawers, I scribble on a piece of parchment, then fold it up small and retrieve a stick of sealing wax.

"What are you doing?" Saber asks, sounding scared as he lingers just outside my doorway.

I hate that shiver of fear in his voice, but I have to do this with or without his approval. As soon as I press my royal seal into the warm wax I rise from my desk and approach my damsel—so to speak—in distress.

Someday, I'll stop being a source of that distress.

"Danica, don't," Saber pleads, spreading his arms across the doorway to block my way. "Leave this alone. Don't antagonize him. I've never, ever seen anyone rebel against Reginald and live to tell about it." He implores me with haunted eyes. "I'd rather see you live than have both of us die."

I pause at that. But only for a second. "And I would rather die than see you remain in slavery to that man for one more day, so I guess we're both going to be disappointed."

His eyes widen in surprise, but he takes a step back and drops his arms in surrender. I step through beside him and close the door. Not even Saber can be allowed to stand in my way. Not anymore. "M.A.R.I.E., change of access to my private office. Accessible to no one but the Queen, Danica Wyndham: fingerprint and facial scan required."

"You're barring me from your office?" Saber whispers.

"I'm barring you from the room where the *money* is," I say softly, choosing my words with care. "So when his man comes and asks where the payment is, you can honestly tell him you have no access to it. Instead, you will give him this note: it says that he gets paid when he agrees to meet me, and not sooner. He can grant me a face-to-face or stop selling in Versailles altogether. *Now* he has something to gain."

I hold out the note, but when Saber doesn't take it, I shove it into the top of his waistcoat and push past him on my way back to my bedchamber.

"Danica, wait—"

"No!" I shout, turning back around to face him. Now I'm the one yelling. "I'm doing this with or without your permission, and you're going to have to trust me."

Saber is quiet for a long time. When he looks up at me, there isn't sadness blazing in his eyes, but anger. I take a step backward. I've never seen him angry with me. Not like this. "I am a slave," he says, the words cutting like a blade to my heart. "But don't you ever make the mistake of thinking that I'm *your* slave."

THIRTY-SIX

SABER DOESN'T COME BACK.

For three days.

Every single night, I sit on the edge of my bed, unable to sleep, watching until sunrise is a blush on the horizon and my eyes drop closed without my permission.

Reginald has never not sent him back.

The money, I tell myself. This must be about the money. I *made* it about the money. In the end, Reginald is a businessman, and his dealings with me have always been about his greed. He's holding Saber as collateral. He's sending me a message.

I'm so weary I scarcely have the energy to put one foot in front of the other as I walk through the door, into my bedchamber, alone, dreading yet another night of fear-driven insomnia. I slide through the door before it opens fully, then push it closed, leaning against it and throwing the bolt.

"Danica."

Startled, I open my eyes to see a tall, slim figure emerge from the shadowed doorway of my wardrobe.

"Saber." His name escapes my lips in a whisper. My heart leaps and drops at the same time and I cling to the golden doorknob, trying to stay upright as fear and relief war for space in my heart.

He's here. He's *alive!* At the moment that's all that can possibly matter.

But he approaches me with eyes so dark I have to suppress a shiver. Then my head snaps to the side, face burning with pain, the force of Saber's blow sending me reeling. With a strangled cry, he dives to cushion my fall as I collapse to the floor. His hands are on the sides of my face, and his lips cover my stinging skin with soft, gentle kisses. I hiss and pull away when he kisses the side of my mouth; when his face comes back into view, there's blood on his bottom lip.

My blood.

I touch my face, and my fingers come away bloody. I look between my hand and his mouth. "You hit me."

His chest spasms, and a horrible sound bursts from his throat for a moment before he stifles it. "I'm so sorry. I had to. It's like he told you: if I don't do as he says, he'll do it himself—and worse." Saber's arms are shaking, his teeth chattering, horror darkening his eyes. "T-t-tonight. He said he'll meet you tonight, at midnight, but don't you ever threaten him again. He—I left a mark. I *had* to leave a mark. Dani, you've got to *run*. I know you don't want to leave me behind, but I don't know what he'll do—"

"Reginald told you to make sure I got the message," I say flatly.

"He said if you showed up unharmed, he'd—he said he'd make sure I'd wish I'd just killed you. I had to do something. You need a mark, and you need to look defeated. If you show up with a split lip and that look in your eyes, he'll believe I did my whole job, but you shouldn't show up *at all*, he's so angry—"

"Your whole job . . . ?" So he was supposed to do more. Reginald believed he *would* do more. It's nearly killed him to do this much—and honestly, I'll be fine.

"I'm sorry," he says, on hands and knees, shaking so hard he can barely hold himself up. "I'm so, so sorry."

"I'm fine," I say, though my heart is pounding. "It'll heal."

Saber shakes his head.

"Saber." I'm the one with my hands on either side of his face now, comforting him. "I'm fine; *we're* fine. It'll all be over after tonight." But I can't say more than that. For a few more hours, I still have to keep it a secret from him—he'll only try to stop me.

Gingerly he sits back on his haunches, looking utterly defeated. When I put a hand on his back, he flinches, and I don't think it's only from guilt.

"Saber, what did he do to you?" I ask, fury building in my chest. I reach for the untucked tail of his shirt, but he swats my hand away.

"No," he says. "It'll only make you angry. And if you go there angry, I don't think you'll make it back." He smiles sadly. "You've never been good at hiding anger. But if you don't go there looking at least a little afraid, he won't talk to you until he's *made* you afraid."

I look up at him, letting myself feel the throbbing ache deep in my jaw. Let it show in my eyes.

"Yes," he says, his voice a mumble of shame, "that's how you need to look."

I nod stoically, running my tongue along my teeth, making sure none of them feel loose or damaged. Saber hits hard, and I have no doubt he was holding back. But my lip is definitely split, and I dab a handkerchief gingerly against it.

"He said come alone," Saber mumbles, delivering the last of his vile taskmaster's message.

I stop trying to convince him that I don't blame him; it won't make any difference. But I don't. He has no choice, just as he's always said.

That changes tonight.

MY CAR PULLS into the deserted parking lot of a decrepit warehouse—just the kind of setting I'd hoped for. With trembling hands I toss a collection of duffel bags out the door before exiting the vehicle, more nervous than afraid.

Luggage unloaded, I slip out and rise to my full height, heels included. I wonder what Reginald's minions will make of me, decked out in my finery. No jewels; I'm not a glutton for punishment—or robbery. But my *panniers* are wide, my hair high, and flounces abound; it's quite a departure from our first encounter. Do they know who I am, or has Reginald been keeping the royal nature of this business deal a personal secret?

I guess I'll know soon enough.

A slew of thugs in dark leather jackets materializes from the shadows, stalking toward me with the predatory confidence of pack hunters that vastly outnumber their prey. The biggest of the lot shoves me away from the car as a thin one slides a set of thermal-imaging goggles over his eyes. He pokes his head through the open door of my vehicle and glances around.

"She's alone," he says in French, pulling off the goggles.

"Check the bags," a fair-haired woman instructs, also in French. Four more goons unzip my bags, rifling through bound stacks of euros, waving bug detectors over every surface. I wonder briefly if this is standard procedure for Reginald's organization or if I'm just getting the royal treatment—so to speak.

"Pat her down," the woman orders, and the ruffians begin mussing my dress most unceremoniously—checking every seam and ruffle, turning out my *pannier* pockets, and in general handling me with completely unnecessary roughness. But the ordeal is over soon enough, and I don't move so much as a muscle.

"I fear I can't carry these all myself," I say, addressing them in French, gesturing to the duffel bags once they're zipped up again. I sling one over my shoulder, but they're all essentially identical. "I'll need your assistance." The man in the lead—only my height, though he seems twice as broad—grunts and flicks his head toward the door of a warehouse, now propped open, a beam of cheap fluorescence pouring out into the night. I raise my chin and turn toward it, my gloved hands clasped tightly around the strap of the bag draped over my shoulder.

Reginald waits within, standing beneath the single buzzing light source, flanked by two men whose impressively large guns are pointed directly at me. I don't let myself flinch. I walk to a space about two meters in front of Reginald and stand very still. Steady. I don't even try to hide the split on my lip, though I did put makeup over the developing bruise on my cheek. He'd have expected no less.

"Put them there, please," I say to the guards carrying the duffels, indicating the bare concrete to my left. "They're not his yet. We haven't made a deal." This last sentence I direct at Reginald, who's glaring at me as though I've done something very naughty rather than request a simple meeting between business partners. But he nods to his goons, who deposit the bags where I asked.

"Some of it is mine," Reginald says in heavily accented English. "You owe me."

"You're right," I say calmly. "I'd almost forgotten. Here, this one's yours." I lift the bag off my shoulder and toss it onto the ground between us, ignoring the cloud of dirt that puffs into the air when it lands. "Payment in full. And that's all the payment you're going to get, because I'm done. No more selling Glitter. I won't do it."

"And why not?" He manages to sound like a coiled snake, poised to strike.

All the more reason to remain calm. Utterly controlled. "You undermined me. You raised the concentration of Glitter in the cosmetics. I was trying to lower the doses my *clientèle* received—which is my right—and you sabotaged my efforts."

"Which is *my* right," he says with a grin.

"No, it isn't. We had two deals. Two. And you've cheated me on both of them."

"Cheated? Do you have any idea who I am?" Reginald bellows, his arms spread wide, the sudden volume taking me off-guard.

"You are the demi-Queen of a false court, but I, *I* am the king of the streets of Paris." He pauses, then takes a step closer. "I don't think Saber's lesson on manners went very far. Perhaps you need a refresher."

I say nothing, though every nerve within me itches to argue, and I can almost hear Saber insisting that I run.

"You've become more trouble than you're worth," Reginald says, giving me his back. Coward. "The time has come to give you what you paid for. You're leaving. Tonight."

"Not without Saber."

Reginald spins back to face me, his face reddening as he shouts, "Saber has nothing to do with you!" Then, straightening his leather coat, he continues, almost conversationally. "I need him to continue working in Versailles. Now that Glitter is so popular, I have no doubt he can help me find a new seller. There's probably a dozen who would sell their souls to take your place in my business."

"One in particular."

"Excuse me?" I've finally caught him off-guard.

I look up with one eyebrow arched, as though I had not a care in the world. "There's one lady in particular who would do anything to redeem her place at court. And she'd be especially eager if she heard she was replacing *me*. You don't need Saber. Let me have him, and I'll tell you everything you need to know."

He places a hand on his hip and slouches. "I feel as though we've had this conversation before. And it was boring the first time, too."

"Then let me make it interesting. Five million euros, cash. You told me last time I could have him if I paid for him. I'll pay you a Queen's ransom—the same price I paid you for my own freedom, not that you've ever delivered. That's got to be quite a return on your initial investment."

Reginald's eyes narrow. He hasn't made a decision, but I've caught his interest.

"Five million euros," I say, nodding to the bags resting on the ground near me. "On top of the two in that bag that I already owed. That's you and me square, plus a combined ten million euros for one Queen and one nobody. I think that's more than fair."

"Or," Reginald says, and guns click to life all around me, "I could kill you for being an underhanded bitch and just take the ten million euros. I think that's an even better deal."

"If that's how you want to play it," I say, shrugging. I blink carefully to activate my Lens, then close my eyes and take a deep breath as the air around me explodes with gunfire.

THIRTY-SEVEN

I HOLD VERY STILL. Bots are exceptionally accurate, and if I remain completely motionless, I should be fine. It's hard to convince myself of that when I *feel* the rush of air from a bullet that zips past my nose. But when the noise dies down, nothing hurts. That's likely a good sign.

I open my eyes to see the mass-produced profiles of my press-ganged bots rolling into the room, having shot their way through the flimsy aluminum walls with guns from the palace armory gripped in their three-fingered hands. I had a plan B programmed just in case the walls were more solid, but this was the least risky option. For me. The position of senior vice president of palace security at Versailles comes with some fabulous perks—and truly, it's hardly any work at all. No wonder they reserve it for princelings.

All of Reginald's guards are down, though there are groans coming from at least two of them. Reginald himself is crouched on one knee in the center of the carnage, looking satisfyingly surprised to find himself alive. Not *safe*—my bots have their guns trained on him—but alive.

"Duchess?" I say, and one of the bots turns and rolls toward me. A compartment on her back opens, and I retrieve the handgun within. "Thank you," I say. Even in a life-and-death situation, one ought still observe social niceties, if possible.

As Duchess returns to her post, I add my firearm to the dozen already pointing at Reginald. He flinches—perhaps sensing that with my human frailty I'm likely more dangerous than the bots. Smart man.

"You're insane," he spits.

Well, perhaps not *that* smart.

"Did you really do this? Bring military hardware onto foreign soil to assault French citizens?" Reginald laughs. "I wonder, how many treaties do your little friends violate just by *existing*?"

Truly? "I didn't come here to talk politics."

"No? Then let's talk commerce. I'm impressed by your demonstration. I'm sure I can find buyers for every murderbot you can deliver." He grins, holding his hand out in excitement. "If you think slinging Glitter has been profitable, the international arms trade is going to blow your mind."

I'm almost impressed at how quickly he's shifted from threatening me to pitching me a new deal—talking fast, looking for a way to regain control of the situation. But this is my show. "Did you bring Saber's slaveminder, as instructed in my note?"

Reginald rolls his eyes and reaches for a messenger bag that looks disturbingly like the one Saber always carries.

"Stop!" I order, and his fingers halt centimeters from the satchel. "I haven't gotten to where I am now by getting myself dead," I say; I'm sure he'll remember speaking those words to me, back in the catacombs, a lifetime ago. "One hand only, and move very, very slowly. And just so you know," I add as he uses one finger to prop open the lip of the bag, showing me exactly what he's reaching for, "the bots are monitoring my heart rate. If I die, you die."

"Message received," Reginald grumbles.

"You know," I say, unable to resist the urge to brag just a little, "in this age of technology—on the very cusp of the robotic revolution, in fact—I would have thought you'd do more than simply scan my vehicle for warm bodies. Luckily, I wagered on you underestimating me. Most people do. Something about a pretty dress makes people think there's no brain atop it. More fools they."

Reginald glares up at me with a ferocity that makes me very glad to have more than just my own gun pointing at him. In his hand is a surprisingly small device—a black cube about the size of my fist. He holds it up wordlessly.

"I had no intention of doing anything but making a deal here tonight, Reg," I say, enjoying the narrowing of his eyes at the diminutive. "You're the one who tried to cheat me. Again. Clearly there's no honor among thieves. And we both know you're a thief. You have no one to blame but yourself."

I give him a chance to speak, but he continues to glower in silence.

"I made the offer—I have no intention of reneging. I'm still willing to pay you the five million for Saber. And I fully intend to use your services to spirit the two of us away. In addition," I say, raising one gloved finger, "I'll also tell you the best person to replace me as your contact in Sonoman-Versailles. Because I'm a woman of my word, even when those I deal with are not. Now, do we have a deal?"

"A deal at gunpoint?" Reginald scoffs.

"We both know the gun isn't to convince you—it's very rightly to protect *me*. I'll ask you one more time, and one more time only: Do we have a deal?"

He waves his hand, almost dismissively. "Yes, yes, of course we have a deal. What kind of moron do you think I am? I'll take your damned deal."

"Good. Before we begin let's get specific about *the fine print*, as you once called it. *When* will you take us away?"

"Can you leave tonight? It's not all that hard on my end."

"You bring me Saber and I can leave, yes."

"Then tonight."

"Together?"

"Together," he says as though I've tortured the word out of him.

"I want the transfer of Saber's ownership made right now. I don't want you pulling anything between now and when we're reunited on the basis that you *own* him." I straighten the arm holding the gun a little more as I speak, and Reginald definitely notices.

"Fine," he says, looking down at the little device. "It's simple— I enter my code, I indicate a change of ownership, and then you choose your own new code."

"Do it."

He messes with the device for a moment, then holds it up

where a blinking cursor is visible. "Your turn," he says, and starts to rise from his knee.

"Oh no," I say, taking half a step forward. "You stay where you are. That bot nearest you? Give it to her. Countess," I say, "bring that device to me."

A flicker of rage crosses Reginald's face, confirming my suspicions. He really is a nasty piece of work. The bot brings me the slaveminder—so small and simple a device for such a monstrous purpose.

"Enter your own code," he says, sounding bored.

"Any rules about the code?" I ask skeptically.

"Nope. It's quite user-friendly."

I choose a nine-digit code, making very sure to type it correctly, and store it firmly in my memory. When I enter it, a line of type flashes across the screen:

TRANSFER COMPLETE

I have trouble breathing for a moment. It's done. I lift both eyebrows haughtily. "Very well, he's mine now. It's no mystery what I intend to do with him." I hold out the device. "How do I set him free?"

Reginald gives a low, vicious chuckle. "You're too soft, Danica. But whatever; he's your business now. Freeing him is simple enough. Put in your code and scan his mark. It'll give you an option to deactivate the collar. You won't have to worry about a countdown ever again."

Collar. Of course that's what the device implanted in Saber's brain is called. I suppress a shudder at the wickedness of some people's ingenuity. "I just push the deactivation button?"

"And all your problems go away," Reginald says with a hint of a smile.

"None of this is funny," I say, straightening my arm with my finger on the trigger.

"No, of course not," he says, sobering.

I shoot him in the leg.

He screams, high and clear, then bites it off with a string of French invectives. "Why the hell did you do that?" he bellows, hands clamped hard on his right thigh. "You might have hit an artery! I could bleed out!"

"Because you lied," I say, very calmly. "Again. Just as I knew you would. Now that we both know I'm not buying your bullshit, care to tell me what the deactivation button does?"

He glares at me with hate-filled eyes, but I point my gun at his other thigh, and he raises one bloody hand to stay me. "All right, all right. Deactivate the collar, deactivate the slave. Forever. Dead. Okay?"

"Ah," I say. "So you would not only have cheated me out of the slave I just bought—for an exorbitant price, mind you—but killed a completely innocent man just to prevent me from getting what I want?"

"I don't like you," he spits, his face blanching from the pain.

"The feeling is mutual, but you'd better find it in your heart to answer my questions honestly if you want some medical aid, hadn't you?" I gesture at my robotic security retinue. "My bots are fully programmed for first aid. I imagine they could have you all patched up in five minutes—*if* you'd give me the information I need."

"Fine!" Reginald says, breathing hard. "But you won't like the answer. You can't free a slave. Why would anyone dealing in slaves leave security holes for do-gooders to exploit? It's a one-way trip. There is no freedom for a slave." He manages a pain-filled grin. "Only a prettier master."

That I didn't expect, and bile rises in my throat at the realization that my intention to "own" Saber only until our next meeting has become, quite possibly, a lifelong commitment. But I swallow my panic—it's a knot I'll have to untangle later.

"So tell me how to reset his countdown."

"When you get back to that little worm, you enter your code again, and use the scanner on the back to read the mark on his arm. It'll ask how much time to add, but you can't go higher than fourteen days. That's the final step." His voice is ragged and sweat has broken out on his forehead. "Same process every time the clock gets low. Don't suppose these bots of yours have any morphine, eh?"

"No more lies?" I ask sternly.

"None," Reginald grunts through gritted teeth, looking like he's about to lose consciousness. "Now get these bots to work on me!"

I point my gun at his manhood. "Should I shoot off your bollocks just to ensure you're not lying?"

"Damned female, I'm telling you the truth." His face is white, and a growing puddle of maroon has formed beneath his leg. His arms are shaking and desperation shines in his eyes.

"I rather think you are," I say softly.

"Are we done, then?" he rasps.

I hesitate, as though mulling it over. Then I raise the gun a few centimeters and pull the trigger, splattering his brains all over the concrete floor.

"Yes, Reginald, I do believe we are."

THIRTY-EIGHT

I EXPECT TO feel victorious on my way back to the palace. Instead, I feel numb. Perhaps I'll never feel again. If I do, then I'll have to feel what must certainly be the proper emotions associated with killing a man in cold blood.

There's no one waiting to sign my car back into the motor pool, and a sense of wariness creeps over me. It's very late, but there should always be a parking attendant on duty. Still, not one to look a gift horse too closely in the mouth, I call out to my new bots and load them up with the black duffels I brought back from the warehouse.

They follow me like automaton ducklings trailing behind their mother. I spent the drive dressing them in palace livery—no one will think twice when they see multiple bots trailing after the Queen, and because their guns are still locked in my car, security should receive no alerts at all. Especially since the bots don't answer to M.A.R.I.E. It's almost a shame I'm leaving; clandestine personal bots could come in quite handy.

I hold the slaveminder in my hands—within the confines of my reticule, yes, but I'll not allow the awful device out of my grasp until I can put it into Saber's. If Reginald was telling the truth—and this time I do believe he was—at least Saber can own *himself.*

It's well past two in the morning—revelries in the palace often continue until dawn, but there's nothing particularly special scheduled tonight, so most have found their way to their rooms, if not their beds. There are a few groups from the younger set, mostly tipsy and giggling. Some going so far as to snort most indecorously.

I nod politely to those who see me, but no one tries to start a conversation. I must have that look in my eye. "M.A.R.I.E., my door," I say, passing into my rooms.

Saber sits straight up from my bed when the doors open, and his eyes are as haunted as I've ever seen them. Relief makes his entire body sag when he sees that I'm in one piece—not bleeding, not missing so much as the tip of my little finger.

Suddenly giddy at the thought of the gift I'm about to give him, I can't help but laugh when his eyes widen at the bevy of bots trailing me. Those eyebrows lower in suspicion a few seconds later—he's counted the bags, and I've returned with every single one he helped me pack up before I left.

"Bar the door, M.A.R.I.E.," I order. "Duchess, put down your burdens and take your ladies to the corner. Power down, please." The lead bot and her five followers place the duffels carefully on the floor before rolling off in an orderly line and positioning themselves in a tight group; then they fold themselves into compact cubes, less than a meter to a side.

Saber studies them. "Are those the bots I helped you *borrow* the day everyone thought you went to the spa?"

"They are indeed." Sparks of pride erupt in my chest and I can't help but smile. "I've been working on programming their motherboards for weeks—though finally getting a look at their full specs advanced the project nicely. They all performed their tasks admirably tonight, if I do say so myself."

I see Saber's throat convulse as he swallows. "Dare I ask what their tasks were?"

"I told you I would destroy Reginald, and I have," I say with a level of confidence I'm not sure I really feel. But I don't want to think too hard about the details just now. "Here," I say, as much to distract myself as him, holding out the reticule. "I've brought you a gift."

Saber reaches out to take my offering as his eyes bore into mine, full of questions. I hand him my reticule, the purse strings pulled together at the top—like a bow on a reticule-wrapped present. His eyes don't leave mine as he unties the ribbons and loosens the puckered folds.

But the instant he peers into the bag, he cries out in alarm, dropping the reticule like a hot potato, leaping away from it, falling onto the ground and crab-crawling backward as though the pouch were about to explode.

The silken purse tumbles through the air—I don't know how fragile the little device is, but I definitely don't want it damaged. Pain lances through my ankle as I dive at the floor, burning my elbow against the flooring as I catch my reticule. Belatedly I realize that practically nothing could break on this thick, plushy carpet.

But I can't take even the slightest chance. This tiny piece of tech means my Saber's very life.

"Are you trying to kill me?" Saber yells, and the blood drains from my face at the fear and anger in his eyes.

The anger wins. "I'm trying to *free* you!" I shout back, all the pent-up emotions of the last few hours coming to a boil and leaking out my eyes. "You have no idea what I did to get this," I say, wrenching the slaveminder out of my reticule and holding it out to him. "No idea how much *more* I would have been willing to do." An angry sob wells up in my throat, but I swipe at my tears with my forearm—cursing every single one of them—and get to my feet, ignoring the twinge in my ankle.

"You can't—I can't—" He stops talking and clenches his fists against the floor and I can see him breathing deeply, trying to get control of himself. "I can't touch it."

All the fight drains out of me, and I feel limp and boneless. I almost sink back onto the floor—but after the swing of emotions I've endured tonight, I'm not sure I could rise again. And my work is not yet done. "What do you mean?" I know what he means. But I need to hear him say it. Like needing to be told twice when someone you love is dead. You know it's true, but you need to *know*.

"I can't touch it." He looks up at me, despair pouring through the shattered walls of his practiced stoicism. I wonder—having given up all hope, had Saber also given up despair? If so, it would appear I've given him the wonderful, terrible gift of hope. "A slave can never touch their slaveminder. That's a death sentence—no chance of tampering themselves free. Slaves have been accidentally killed while resetting their timer, if someone gets too close."

"That's despicable," I say, my mouth dry, my tongue clumsy.

"Is there any part of slavery that isn't?" Saber says, agitated.

I can't argue with that. "He could have told me," I mutter, a bit of the guilt over killing Reginald chipping away.

"He's a bastard."

"He was."

Saber's chin jerks up sharply.

"He's dead."

Saber's fingers tremble. "My countdown," he whispers.

"He sold you to me." They're the most abhorrent words I've ever said. "I meant for it to only last until I could get back and set you free. I would never—I didn't want this to—" I shove my knuckles against my mouth to hold back the dreadful wail that wants to burst forth. I never, ever thought I would be in the position of owning a slave. Regardless of what the technicalities might be. "I don't own you," I whisper, as though saying the words could make them true.

"Better you than him."

But I shake my head spasmodically. "I don't. I won't. I'll care for the device that keeps you alive. That's all. And if—" My shoulders are shaking so violently I have trouble making my voice work. "If you ever want someone else to have it, I'll hand it over. You have only to ask."

Saber stares at me, silent and no longer trembling. "Put that down," he says.

I look at the little device in my hand. "What?"

"Put it down." He inclines his head to the side. "Over there."

I set the slaveminder down on my nightstand, then step away

slowly, toward my bed. Once I'm sitting again, Saber crawls forward and brings a hand to my face, cradling my cheek. His lips touch mine like they're asking for permission before deepening, trying to tell me something I don't understand.

"Why would I ever, ever want anyone but you?" he whispers.

Tears stream down my cheeks and I inwardly curse that I've become such a watering can. "Why?" I choke out. "Why *would* you want me? I'm not a good person. I've done terrible things. I wanted to give you your freedom and I even failed at that. Everything I touch turns to ashes."

He scoots forward a little more, his knees on either side of mine, both hands framing my face. "I've done some pretty awful things myself."

"It's not the same," I argue. Truly, it isn't.

"I know. I do. But we have a chance to go forward now, together. To be the kind of people I know we both want to be." He kisses my eyelids as I close them in surrender, wanting his sweet words to be true with every piece of my shattered heart. "If I've been able to fall in love with you, despite wanting desperately to *not*—"

I laugh brokenly at that.

"—and to stay in love with you in spite of everything that's happened, don't you think we can make it with a fresh start?"

"Is there such a thing as a fresh start? A real one?"

He hesitates. "Three hours ago, I reached what might have been the lowest point in my entire life. I hit the woman I loved and then sent her off, alone, to be tortured, mutilated, killed— who knows. If you didn't come back, I was fully prepared to sneak away and hide from Reginald until my clock ran down. I knew that if you were harmed—if you were killed—I didn't want to live with what I'd done." He kisses me again, a gentle brush, like the tickle of a feather. "Now? It feels like a brand-new *world*. I'm expecting things I never let myself even dream about before tonight. If that's not a fresh start, Dani, I don't know what is."

I clutch at his arms, needing to feel his heart beating in his veins, just beneath my fingertips. "And you're sure you want me in this new life of yours? I'll always be a reminder of your old life."

"There is no new life without you."

His whispered words are an arrow to my heart, and I shake my head. "You deserve this, but I don't. I'm not who I thought I was. I haven't earned any kind of happily ever after."

"Then isn't it wonderful," Saber says, his breath warm on my earlobe, "that you are an integral part of mine?"

He holds me so tight I almost fear I'll break, but he seems to understand that's what I need to hold me together. I scrunch my face into his shoulder, and though it seems like this is the right time to weep, my eyes are dry.

"I was like this the first time I killed someone," Saber says. "I told myself I had no choice—that it was them or me, and even if I gave up my life, someone else would kill them anyway. I decided that at least I'd been as humane as possible. But it didn't make me *feel* any better." His fingers are stroking my hair, decimating what was left of my elaborate updo. "Time makes it easier. It doesn't heal all wounds; I hate that saying, actually. But it has a way of smoothing edges, like the ocean smooths a stone."

It feels like nothing will ever dull this knife's edge pressing into my heart, but I understand that I don't have to say it. He knows.

He holds both my shoulders until finally I look up and meet his eyes. He's smiling sadly, and that edge of sadness somehow makes me feel a little better. He's not lying to himself, so maybe he's not lying to me.

"Reginald was my dragon," he says. "And isn't that what heroes do? Slay dragons?"

I say nothing. He's not going to convince me I was right, even if it did save him. Because I don't tell him the sale was already made. That Reginald was unarmed and bleeding on the floor. I certainly don't tell him that I killed Reginald because I wanted to. I just didn't know it would kill a part of my soul, too.

I force myself to get hold of my emotions and rise from the floor. "It's time."

"Time for what?"

"What we've been training for," I say coyly. "You made me a promise several weeks ago."

"I did?"

Saber continues to look baffled, but I let him wait a bit longer. "Help me with my laces?" I ask, turning to give him my back. He unlaces my bodice and starts to push the sleeves off my shoulders, but I stop him. "No, just the corset."

Soon the familiar polyethylene stripes are loosening their hold on my middle. Habit makes me brace for the rush to my head, the sick feeling in my stomach, but neither of them has manifested for at least a fortnight. I wrangle the garment out from beneath my dress and let it drop to the floor.

"Lace my gown again?" Once I'm done up, I retrieve a warm cloak from my wardrobe and throw it around my shoulders—though I forgo a hat. I emerge from the back room and my eyes sting with an entirely different kind of tears.

"You promised if I worked hard, I could walk out of here completely under my own strength. You just didn't think you'd be coming with me."

I hold my hand out and he stares at it for a long time, as though he can't believe it's real. Finally he grasps it tightly in his and smiles up at me, his own eyes shining.

"I've never been so happy to be wrong."

THIRTY-NINE

THE KING IS waiting for me. Truthfully, I was shocked he didn't confront me as soon as I returned to the palace. But my Lens tells me he's in his office, so that's where I must go. I knock on his door, trailed by Saber and my six bots—each bearing a black duffel bag.

Saber has the most important bag: the one with all my documentation, his slaveminder—carefully wrapped for both its and Saber's protection—my tablet, and as much money as we could fit inside and still close the zipper.

We're ready.

I knock on the door, a little surprised Mateus isn't there guarding it. We wait for a good half minute in the Clock Cabinet, the lights dimmed to emulate low-burning candles, and I'm raising my fingers to knock a second time when the door is opened by my husband's rat-faced assistant.

"Just her," Mateus says, narrowed eyes fixed on Saber.

"No, no. I'll be setting the terms tonight," I say quietly. It's not a threat, merely a statement of fact.

Mateus hesitates, and I peer over his shoulder at my husband, sitting at his desk, leaning over papers as though he hasn't even noticed that I'm here.

"His Majesty speaks with both of us or he speaks with no one," I say. Loudly.

"Oh, there you are, Danica," Justin says, rising from his seat to greet me, sounding jovial. "And alive, too. Thank goodness. You took those guns hours ago. What the hell have you been doing with them?"

"Cleaning up some rubbish," I say evasively.

"Well, I suppose we have much to discuss, don't we? Oh, Mateus, it hardly matters. Let the boy in."

I hate the way he uses the word *boy* even though they're the same age.

"She's going to run back and tell him every word anyway, and I'd prefer he hears the nonedited version."

My mouth drops in indignation, but I realize he's trying to unbalance me. I snap my jaw closed again, refusing to be riled.

"Would you like the bots as well, Your Highness?" Mateus says nasally, addressing me.

"Certainly not. Duchess, remain outside with your ladies."

"Duchess?" the King asks, his face a blank slate.

I meet his eyes directly. "You're surrounded by nobility who may as well be robots. I thought I'd dispense with the pretense."

"Amusing," he says, his tone suggesting it's anything but.

"I don't want your man in here, though," I say, tilting my head toward Mateus. "And by the time our conversation is through, you won't either."

"Really?" His Highness says, barely holding back a smirk that I can't wait to wipe off his face. "Well, you've frequently given me good advice, wife. Off with you, Mateus. You'll have to settle for the edited version. In the morning, I suppose."

"You may not want to send him that far."

His eyes dart back to me. "Oh no?"

"You might need him. Soon."

The King is already standing, using his slightly superior height combined with heels to look down on me, but I don't have to hide feeling cowed, because I'm not. I hold the trump card now; he simply doesn't know it. "As the lady says," he murmurs, addressing Mateus but looking straight at me.

As soon as the door clicks shut, I sit on the arm of the embroidered armchair without waiting to be invited. The King looks like he wants to call me out, then decides this isn't the night for petty jabs, and instead flips out his tails with a bit of extra *panache*, reclaiming his own seat behind his massive desk. "What is this little meeting about, Danica?"

"The time has come for me to leave, Justin."

"Leave?"

"And never come back."

He smirks and I feel irrationally angry that he can't have one conversation without playing the arrogant snot. "Why would you leave? You have everything you could possibly desire."

"Oh, do I? Pray, enlighten me."

"Well, for starters, you must have the thing you went seeking tonight, else you wouldn't be here."

"You're not going to ask what it was?" I ask, though I've no intention of telling him.

He surprises me by shrugging. "If I'm ever asked to testify against you, we'll both prefer that I don't know the details."

I grant him the point.

"So, as far as I can tell, you've wrapped up your problems, you've gained the affection of the court, we've reached an . . . accord, between us, that has been to our mutual benefit, and I'm about to cement our kingdom's prosperity for generations to come."

I glare up at him, hating the emphasis he puts on the word *accord*, but I can't call him out on it and risk him telling Saber exactly what he means.

"Why leave now? You've washed the linens, prepared the *hors d'oeuvres*, set the tables, and made yourself presentable. The work is done! Won't you enjoy the *soirée*?"

"The whole point was to avoid the *soirée*."

He stands up again, but rather than come around the desk and circle me like a vulture, he crosses his arms over his chest and leans his hip against the desktop. "I don't understand you, Danica. You've never wanted the things I wanted. Even when I thought you did. Even when it seemed impossible to want anything else."

"Well, here's what I want now: a divorce."

He sniggers. "Of course you do."

"Moreover, I want helicopter transport out of Sonoman-Versailles for both Saber and me, to a location I'll program into the Nav after we've taken off."

"Anything else?" His Highness asks, his laughter barely held in check.

"You will take over my father's residence fees at Languedoc-Roussillon and continue to pay them for the rest of his life. Although that's a bit of a draw, as he's so biddable that even without my say-so, he'll vote however you desire in the future."

"And what about you, my love? An astronomical annuity, perhaps?"

"Certainly not." At his raised eyebrow, I continue. "I want nothing to do with your dirty, humanity-crippling money." I slide a glance over to where Saber has positioned himself, unobtrusively, in the corner. "Trust me, my own money is dirty enough."

"Is that everything?"

"Have I covered it all?" I ask Saber.

He considers, then gives me a tiny nod.

"Oh no, one more thing." I lean forward, my hands tightly gripping the armrests. "Don't look for me. Ever. Make up some Banbury tale for the court and the reporters, but don't you ever come looking for me."

He drums his fingers on his desk. "*Now* is that all?"

"Yes," I say, confidently this time.

"Good. The answer is no. Who the hell do you think you are? Go to bed." With that he resumes his seat and starts shuffling the scattered papers into one stack.

I grin. I was hoping he'd choose to do this the hard way. "I know about the Blight."

"Pardon?" He looks far less amused now.

"The Norwegian Blight. I know your great-grandfather was able to create a resistant strain only because he developed the Blight to begin with."

"That's a very bold accusation."

"I have proof."

He shuts up, studies me. "And what do you intend to do with it?"

"Use it to get what I want and then hold it over your head, of course. For the rest of my life, if that's what it takes to keep you from trying to drag me back—or do away with me."

"Damnation, Danica. You've always thought me the villain. Will you lay this at my feet too? I didn't do it! What do you want me to do, apologize for my great-grandfather?"

"I don't want an apology; I'm sick to death of listening to lies."

He studies me with glittering eyes. "What sort of proof do you think you have?"

"A document with both the Blight and Rally CRISPRs, time-stamped 2034."

He smiles. "Time stamps can be tampered with—I'm not sure a judge would buy it."

"Who said anything about the legal system? I'd take it to the press." It's my turn to stare him down, to lean over his desk with my hands flat on its surface. "They'd eviscerate you and you know it. And wouldn't that be a shame, just as you're trying to roll out Sonoma's newest economic apocalypse. Your promised profits might suffer. And then where would you be?"

His face is flushed. At last—at *last*—I have him.

"I'm not asking much. You never wanted me anyway; we both know that." I swallow hard and let him see one shred of my humanity. Like he did a few weeks before we were married, when he made me the offer I should probably have taken, given what I knew at the time. "Let me go, Justin."

"What the hell am I supposed to tell people?" he asks in a

whisper. The whisper of a man who's had one too many PR crises in the last year.

"That I was young. And foolish. And not ready. That I broke and ran away. I don't care about my shares. I'll sign papers reverting them. I don't care about my public image." I spread my arms wide. "Make me your villainess; I don't give a damn."

He's silent for a long time, his finger drawing an invisible shape on the top of his desk. I've never seen Justin uncertain. Even when he was violent and brutal, he was always calculating. I haven't seen him so truly at a loss . . . since the night he killed Sierra Jamison. "And if I refuse?" he asks, so quietly I wouldn't have heard him if the office weren't so very, very silent.

"Don't refuse," I plead.

"But if I did?"

I shake my head. "I'll go to the press. You can't watch me forever. Not with a company—a kingdom—to run. I'm the senior vice-bloody-president of palace security; I'll slip out eventually, and then you'll be ruined."

"Do you feel nothing for me?" He looks up and meets my eyes, searching.

It catches me off-guard and for a moment I don't know what to say. "I feel many things for you, Justin. It's just that none of them are positive."

"These last months. No, mostly the last few weeks, when we truly worked together. A *tour de force*. I loved it; I thought maybe you did too." He leans forward on his elbows. "Was it all false?"

I suppose this once he deserves my honesty. "No, Justin, not all of it. To my everlasting shame, no."

"It's heady, isn't it?" he says, a hint of a smile tugging at the corners of his mouth.

"It is. And that's why I have to leave." I take a deep, shuddering breath. "There are many ways to become an addict. This path would assuredly be mine."

Our eyes meet and somehow, in spite of everything else that has passed between us, we share an entire conversation in a look. I blink slowly and break away, as if afraid to be ensorcelled.

"Mateus!"

The King's barked command cracks through the silence, making both Saber and me startle. Mateus's head pops in so quickly I know he's been listening at the door.

"Summon the helicopter."

My legs start to tremble, threatening to dump me unceremoniously on the floor.

I won.

"Now, my liege?" Mateus squeaks.

"Now!" barks the King.

A soft noise of distress and then the assistant is gone—the door closed again. "It will take me a few minutes," he says, waking up his tablet. "There are some documents to compile."

"As long as you're not stalling."

His hand stills over the tablet. "I haven't much of a choice, do I, lady wife?" A growl edges his voice and I know I've pushed as far as I ought. I resume my seat, and there's no sound but the rubbing of the King's feathered stylus on his tablet and the ticking of a clock on the wall.

"I'm not going to find crown jewels in that bag of yours, am I?"

I laugh, then stop myself, lest I expose the depth of my relief that he's cooperating. "No. Even I can't nick jewels out of the royal vault. At least I don't think so—last time I tried, I wasn't in charge of security." At that, he looks up and raises an eyebrow, but I merely stare back, my gaze utterly unwavering.

He looks away first.

Only then do I say, "I'm taking only those things that are inarguably mine."

The King grunts and taps at his screen a few more times, a bit more firmly than necessary. "There, done," he says, turning his tablet around and sliding it closer to me. "Drawing up papers is made a bit easier by the fact that I recently ordered the divorce of another couple. I hope it isn't habit-forming."

"Indeed," I say ruefully.

"They're not coming back, by the bye, are they?"

I flick my eyelids up, peering over at him, unsure of what the proper response should be. Does it matter now if he knows Lord Aaron and Duke Spencer aren't returning? "No," I finally say. Just the one word.

"I thought not," he says, handing me the quill.

But when I reach for it, he doesn't let go right away, holding the two of us there for a moment. "Be very certain about this, Danica," he whispers. "If you sign, it's over. You can still turn around and walk away. A girl only gets one chance to be Queen."

I look up at him and see that he's serious. He would let me go back to my bedchamber, forget this conversation ever happened, and wake up tomorrow continuing my role as the Queen of Sonoman-Versailles.

All the more reason that I shouldn't. I tug on the stylus and he relinquishes it. "I only ever wanted to be a programmer," I say softly. "You're the one who made me a Queen."

I put the stylus's tip to the first page and sign my name.

"You there," the King says to Saber. "Danica's lover, come witness this."

"That's rich," Saber says.

"The irony is hardly lost on me," the King grumbles back.

"Do you even need extra signatures?" I ask, handing the stylus to Saber. "You simply ordered the Harrisford divorce."

"Because Spencer Harrisford was there to back me up. You'll be gone. An ordered divorce with an absent *divorcée* simply looks like I'm trying to cover up a death. To be quite frank, I've had more than my fill of that, this past year."

I sign several documents detailing stock ownership and voting rights that simply don't concern me in the least. I don't care about anything I'm leaving behind. Only what's in store.

"Are we done, then?" I ask as I sign the final page of the document.

"Indeed." The King rises, awkwardly expectant.

"Don't," I say, holding up a hand. "Just don't. Sit back down and we'll walk out the door. I know where the helipad is."

The King rolls his eyes, reminding me again of how childish he can be when he doesn't get his way.

Though I had no intention of spilling this particular secret, his immaturity pricks at me, and I impulsively say, "And I didn't vote for you."

"Pardon?"

"At the big vote. My father and I—we didn't vote for you. Everything you did—your cruelty and machinations. In the end, it was pointless. You didn't win because of me; you won in spite of me."

The blood drains from his face in a purely physical reaction he couldn't possibly have faked. If nothing else, in this I've surprised him. No, *shocked* him.

And it feels amazing.

"Let's be off," I say to Saber, shouldering my duffel and tucking my arm in the crook of his elbow. "I'm certain the King has many things to consider before he faces the world again tomorrow."

Saber, who has always been better at self-control than me, does nothing more than glance back at my now-ex-husband before leading me out the door. As it swings closed, I hear a low chuckle, and I can't help but smile at the surety that it's the laugh of a man who can do naught but that, lest he cry.

FORTY

JUSTIN AIDAN PHILIP KEVIN WYNDHAM, King of Sovereign Versailles, chief executive officer and chairman of the board of Sonoma Inc., president of the Haroldson Historical Society, meditated on the wisdom of murder.

There were any number of ways to lose the company helicopter now speeding its way toward whatever destination his ex-wife had chosen. It didn't seem entirely prudent to detonate its fuel tanks remotely, though that option would best ensure the deaths of its occupants. A botched landing attributable to manual overrides would be easiest to cover up, but sometimes people survived those. He could just ditch it in the ocean and hope for the best, but the length of that trip would likely alert the passengers to their peril and give them time to formulate an escape plan.

"Sir?"

A raised index finger was all it took to silence Mateus. It wasn't hard to guess what the man was thinking—that every passing moment brought them closer to losing their quarry. That every second of silence was a new opportunity for escape. Danica was a loose end, no denying it, and Justin wasn't the kind to leave loose ends.

So why was he reluctant to pull the proverbial trigger?

It wasn't as though murder made him squeamish. He hadn't intended for Sierra Jamison to die on that fateful night, but he couldn't deny it had been thrilling to watch. Would have been more so if he'd known in advance it was going to happen. Killing Angela Grayson had been less thrilling, but deeply cathartic. She'd been satisfyingly distraught when he told her he'd located and destroyed every copy of the video she was using to blackmail him. The heavy dose of *papaveris atropa* he'd forced on her had been just what the doctor ordered. It was almost a shame Danica would never know the favor he'd bestowed on her that day. Likely she'd be grateful; hatred of Angela Grayson was just one of many things they had in common. But, pity, it was more important for Danica to believe him ignorant of the drug.

In the years since his coronation, Justin had often capitalized on ignorance. People tended to believe what they wanted to believe. If they *hoped* something was true, they were much more likely to believe you when you told them it was so. Foolishly, blatantly ridiculous things. The high nobility, who hoped their endless plotting was clandestine, believed him when he said their offices were unmonitored. The Frenchman who called himself Reginald, who hoped he could revenge himself on Sonoma for indignities so ancient as to be irrelevant, believed Sonoma would actually have such lax security that its most important new product could be smuggled onto the black market with predictable regularity. Danica herself, who hoped she was smart enough to manipulate the King, believed that getting what she wanted meant she'd succeeded.

Though, on reflection, she *had* surprised him on more than one occasion. Was that why he hesitated to end her life? Some gentlemanly scruple, that a worthy opponent ought not be done in so underhandedly? Or was it the things she'd done for him that he'd been unable to do for himself? That tryst between Aaron and Spencer—they'd been careful enough that neither M.A.R.I.E. nor his private monitoring network had caught on. Without Danica, the damned activist might *still* be running his society of vandals and thieves from right here inside the kingdom they despised. And she'd killed the Frenchman too, with so much style Justin was tempted to watch the replay from the video feeds of her stolen bots again, this very instant. She'd turned out to be something of a prodigy in that regard; the program she'd loaded into those bots was amazing work, already being tweaked for inclusion in the next palace security update. For all she'd sought to undermine him, she'd proven invaluable time and again.

Had she actually voted against him? Or had she only said that to make him squirm? The idea that he might have actually won over the court in spite of the Queen's shares—was that success or failure?

It was hard to muse on murdering someone so delightful. So ruthless, so *competent.* There simply weren't enough competent people in the world. That was why the new line of bots would succeed, never mind what soft hearts and soft heads feared. The only humans who would suffer were already deadweight on humanity's highest aspirations, anyway. The strong would survive.

Well, most of them.

"Mateus, tell me honestly—am I getting sentimental in my old age?"

"I . . . beg pardon, Your Highness?"

Justin Aidan Philip Kevin Wyndham, King of Sovereign Versailles, chief executive officer and chairman of the board of Sonoma Inc., president of the Haroldson Historical Society, did not want to kill Danica Maeve Grayson Wyndham. What he felt for her might be the closest thing to respect he'd felt for another person since his parents died. What he felt for her might, he thought, have even been something approaching love.

"Blow it up," he said, decision made. Best be sure—no sense leaving a potential rival alive to interfere later. No sense leaving loose ends. "Then let the detox people know we're ready to move on to phase two of the *papaveris* trials. The more indulgent courtiers should begin feeling the effects of withdrawal quite soon."

"Very good, sir."

The King of Sonoman-Versailles retrieved two tumblers and a crystal decanter of his finest cognac. Splashing the exquisite liquor into each glass, he sighed.

"To my Queen," he said, toasting her one last time.

"Ah . . . Your Highness?"

Justin glared darkly at his manservant. Mateus usually knew better than to interrupt his King.

"She's—" Mateus swallowed, clearly nervous. Ridiculous man; if Justin was the kind to kill servants for their incompetence, he'd have no servants left. "She's locked me out of the controls, sir. Some kind of virus. She's—"

"Give me that!" Justin snapped, closing the distance between them in three long strides, snatching Mateus's tablet, glancing over the remote interface to get some idea how Danica had managed to hack the helicopter controls so quickly.

The tablet screen went dark.

The room went dark.

And then, softly at first, but with increasing volume, Justin Wyndham heard singing.

It took him a moment to place the words.

Que veut cette horde d'esclaves,
De traîtres, de rois conjurés?
Pour qui ces ignobles entraves,
Ces fers dès longtemps préparés?
Français! Pour nous, ah! quel outrage!
Quels transports il doit exciter!
C'est nous qu'on ose méditer
De rendre à l'antique esclavage!

It was the national anthem of France, playing through the palace loudspeakers.

All of them.

Danica hadn't hacked the helicopter. She'd hacked *M.A.R.I.E.*— who was now blaring a seldom-sung verse, the one about conspiratorial kings and breaking the chains of slavery, to everyone in Sonoman-Versailles, in the middle of the night.

And as Justin Aidan Philip Kevin Wyndham, King of Sovereign Versailles, chief executive officer and chairman of the board of Sonoma Inc., president of the Haroldson Historical Society, stared at the glass of cognac remaining on his counter—the one he'd intended to pour out in memory of his departed ex-wife—Mateus's tablet came back on, displaying just four words, a calling card in elegant Baroque script.

Let Them Eat Cake!

EPILOGUE

TWO YEARS LATER

I STAND VERY still in my office, my face shadowed by the sweep of my bangs, scanning the map covered in pins and flags. I'm *chic* and stylish in my tailored pantsuit but still feel too modern and plain. I wear no corset; my core is strong. But Saber knew the truth—what I most needed was a stronger mind.

I pause in the glow of the setting sun streaming through my window and look at the most recent blue mark on the map. We've just confirmed whispers of a slaving ring in Sweden. Sweden! Who could have believed that would be the right place?

Just one more thing to do. I take three steps forward and place a red square over a small spot in China. I shiver—from excitement, from horror—and stand staring at the mark. A slaving ring, smudged. Slaves rescued. Slavers . . . dealt with. A few seconds later—though I thought I was alone—warm arms snake around me, and I close my eyes in appreciation.

"You're home."

"I'm always home when you're with me."

I turn for a long kiss, running my fingers through Saber's hair. "Where did you go?"

"Pickup. Got another collar from the medical examiner."

I straighten, eyes wide. "Did you? Where is it?"

He lifts a box from my desk and holds it out to me. I don't ever let him touch the retrieved collars, just in case. Everything I know about the slaveminders tells me that touching wrecked collars shouldn't have any effect on him, but I learned long ago that I'm not very good at thinking like a street criminal.

I take the box and open the top. The collar is in surprisingly good condition. They often aren't, due to the very nature of . . . blowing up. The capacitor that destroys the brain usually warps the device, but this one is barely singed. I'm glad to have a new one, and sad at the same time. These only fall into the medical examiner's hands when someone in slavery dies.

I lift the device and its trailing wires from its container, holding it up to the light. "It's the third one this year," I say soberly.

"Things are getting pretty desperate. Jobs disappearing left and right. People turn on each other."

"I heard on GNN that the suicide load has doubled in the last twelve months."

"Dark times," Saber says.

"Damn bots," I whisper. "I feel responsible."

"You're not," Saber says firmly. "You can't save everyone. We're doing what we can in our own little corner of the world."

I nod but don't tell him I agree. Because I don't. Two years ago I had so much power in my hands; I wish I'd found something better to do with it. But if there's one thing I've had to come to terms with, it's that you can't defeat evil by *being* evil. It's been a long, hard lesson.

I'm itching to take the defunct collar back to the lab, but considering how little I've accomplished since embarking on this project, a few minutes won't change anything. Two years and I've done hardly more than identify all of the *parts*. I sigh. "I've made so little headway. Sometimes it feels impossible."

Saber kisses my forehead. "You're the one who taught me to believe in the impossible." A shadow passes over his eyes, a sadness I rarely see these days. And when I do, it's almost always on someone else's behalf. He has a mission now.

With the money I made from Glitter, a little philanthropy from Aaron and Spencer, and a lot of work, Saber and I started up a slave refuge—which Saber mostly runs. I'm . . . tech support.

We started with one child we found on the streets of Los Angeles when we were still midbuild. I'd never seen Saber quite so angry as that night when we stumbled upon her—and the man who was beating her bloody. Saber pulled the man off as I checked her wounds, but when Saber saw the slave mark freshly tattooed on her forearm, her assailant only lived long enough to point us toward her owner.

It was a race against the girl's unknowable countdown to locate the slaver's den, where we found three slaveminders— including the girl's—and two more slaves. I didn't ask how Saber got their pass codes, but he certainly didn't buy them. These days, I'm the one who doesn't ask questions.

Saber has been like a machine ever since, working tirelessly at finding slaves, rescuing them, and bringing them back to the small but cozy compound of our shelter. Sometimes we find their families. Sometimes we don't.

Sometimes they don't want to go back to their families. Regardless, there's always a home here for a former slave.

And if those who run the rings—who install the collars and locate buyers of human chattel—occasionally meet less-than-clean endings at the hands of Saber's employees, well, I'm in no position to judge. I broke the law—as well as my own standards—for myself. Saber is a vigilante for the oppressed. And I love him for that.

It's amazing to see him. The hollowed-out shell that two minutes in Reginald's presence could reduce him to is gone forever. Now he's alive with purpose and passion. I'm not sure even he understood at the time how much of his will he was forced to give up to Reginald.

Ah, Reginald. Pulling that trigger may be the only choice I never second-guess.

At present our site is home to eighteen residents. I know the exact number because I keep all their little slaveminders on a shelf in my office, countdowns synchronized so no one has to be reminded of their continued bondage more than once every fourteen days. And even then, they all come in together—supporting one another.

Saber comes with them. I hate that. I hate it even more than I hated Reginald. But our residents find comfort in the fact that they're not alone.

The official and very strict policy is that every resident here owns him- or herself. I'm merely the steward of their scanners. Our refugees can't touch their little boxes, but I can, and each one bears their name and picture. A *smiling* picture. Once I get to know them, I decorate the boxes with their favorite things and colors. My wards can't escape the tether of their collars—not yet.

But I can remind them that I always—*always*—see them as individual, free human beings.

And I remind them, every fourteen days, that I'm working hard to find a way to make them free in truth.

Saber clears his throat, and I know he must have something to say that I won't like hearing. I roll my eyes over to him. "Tell me."

"Sonoma Inc. officially unveiled their new antidepressant today."

I freeze and have to consciously unclench my fingers from around the box, lest I damage the best collar I've gotten my hands on thus far. "So that's what he made from the Glitter."

"The media is heralding it as a timely breakthrough, with so many people losing their jobs and falling into depression."

"Imagine that. The Wyndhams finding a way to capitalize on a crisis *they* created. I'm shocked." Once I would have said that with the vile burn of bitterness on my tongue. Now it simply fills me with pity. I don't run on anger anymore.

Saber is silent, so I know there's more.

"Out with it," I say, smiling sadly.

"You know me too well." He sighs. "Lady Mei was in the newscast. She's been made a countess in her own right and is running public relations for the pharmaceutical arm."

Oddly, I smile at his news. "I see Justin's hand there. I imagine she's thrilled. Is it awful to say I'm happy for her?" Worried too, but after helping me she can have no illusions as to what she's getting into. We wanted very different lives, in the end, and I owe her better than to judge.

"No, it's not. She always loved her life at the palace." Saber twines his arms around my waist. "You did too. Admit it."

"I will. I miss it. Not everything that went with it, but I miss the elegance. The beautiful clothes. The food," I add after a pause. "But I don't regret leaving. This is more than I deserve."

"Dani—"

"By rights I should be behind bars, and you know it."

He's silent, which means he doesn't have a good argument.

I take a deep breath. "If I can beat these collars, it'll be a start. If I can really help people for a change, instead of hurting them, maybe I can put Molli behind me. Put away the terrible person I became."

"You never became anyone else," Saber says, soothingly. I don't argue, because then I'd have to reveal all the things he doesn't know. Betraying him with Justin, the fact that Reginald was unarmed and helpless when I shot him, my immediate satisfaction when I realized that the death of a billion innocents could be used to blackmail my ex-husband. That's who I was, who I let myself become. Saber has always thought me better than I am.

But I want to be the person he sees when he looks at me. And I'm taking small steps in that direction. I'm making progress. It's something.

Saber goes to call our boarders in for dinner, and I take the package into my lab. I have two tables covered with defunct slaveminders, laid out in carefully sorted and labeled pieces. Saber's raids bring back not only rescued slaves, but also pieces of tech.

His work is rescuing the slaves. Mine is freeing them.

With the help of my employees at a little tech firm I run in San

Francisco, I've been developing swarms of server-controlled nano-bots, infinitesimal versions of the appliances that once dressed me and cleaned my rooms. With them I hope to unlock the secrets of the slaveminders and—especially—the collars. But I can't stop myself from tinkering with the pieces we have now, particularly with a new addition to the collection.

Two hours pass unheeded as I work on the tiny pieces of the new chip. I only notice the time at all because that's when Saber brings me a plate of food.

"I thought you were just going to have a quick peek," he says, nudging me teasingly with his hip.

"Saber, look," I say, not taking my eyes off what I've done. Not entirely sure I can replicate it.

Saber crouches beside me and peers at the collar and slave-minder sitting on the table. The black box is half destroyed, acid-etched where the tamper seal blew, but the core still functions.

"Okay," I say. "Keep your eye on the collar."

I tap out a sequence of numbers on the keyboard I patched into the slaveminder, press Enter, and hold my breath.

The collar lights up, glowing blue for almost a whole second before going dark.

"Wow!" Saber says. Then more quietly, "What just happened?"

My heart races with excitement. "I synced the collar with this slaveminder. They communicated with each other, just for an instant."

"And that's . . . good?"

I can't stop a smile from curling my lips. "Progress," I say. "It's progress."

ACKNOWLEDGMENTS

This book was hard. *Hard.* It's funny how the books we love the most are the ones that are the toughest to write; and I love this book like whoa. And I wrote it the way I wanted to. So, for better or for worse, thank you to my publishing team, who let me stretch a lot of boundaries. My editor, Caroline Abbey; my agent, Mandy Hubbard; my publicist, Josh Redlich; and the myriad wonderful people at Random House Children's Books who had their expert fingers in the production of *Shatter:* thank you for dealing with me.

No one besides myself worked as hard on this book as my husband, Kenny, who read it almost as many times as I did. And no one had to survive my mental absence quite so starkly as my children: Aud, Bren, Gid, and Gwen. How they all live with me, I do not know. What I do know is that I couldn't live without them.

During the writing of this book, I found myself very much drawing away from the world and into myself. Thank you to the friends who reminded me that there is a world outside of my head. Melissa Marr and Sandy Black, thank you for making sure I got out of my house once in a while. And thanks to Lauren de Stefano, for reminding me that it's okay to stay home too. Also, cheese.

The Glendale Public Library in Arizona was generous enough to make me its writer in residence while I was editing this book, and that's basically the reason I made my deadlines. In particular, thank you to Kearsten LaBrozzi and Ray Ceo, who watched over me . . . but mostly made sure I was left alone when I needed to work.

Special thanks to Emily Ruth Morris, who did a final, very fast beta read for me and didn't spare my feelings when it came to making my characters stronger.

While revising this manuscript, I literally spent over 200 hours watching the BBC's *And Then There Were None* on my Kindle, right beside my laptop as I worked. I'm quite sure I have every line memorized. ("I just open my mouth, and it comes out.") The characters of Philip Lombard and Vera Claythorne—brilliantly portrayed by Aidan Turner and Maeve Dermody—had precisely the *feel* I was going for with Justin and Danica, and I found their performances so very inspiring. I watched *ATTWN* so many times while editing that the characters started to feel like friends, especially those two. So much so that when I realized I needed middle names for Dani and Justin, the characters were christened after these two, in homage. So thank you, Aidan. Thank you, Maeve. Even though chances are neither of you will ever read this paragraph. You are both absolutely sparkling, and even now—long after the book is finished—when my writing on my other projects feels dull, I still find myself pressing Play.

APRILYNNE PIKE

is the critically acclaimed, internationally and #1 *New York Times* bestselling author of the Wings series. She has been spinning stories since she was a child with a hyperactive imagination. She received a BA in Creative Writing from Lewis-Clark State College in Lewiston, Idaho. She lives in Arizona with her family. Visit her online at aprilynnepike.com and follow her on Twitter at @AprilynnePike.